HER

Xóchitl García Guillén

Editor: Indie Proofreading

Cover Design: 3Crows Author Services LLC

Formatting and Interior Design: Indie Proofreading

Keeper of my Mental Faculties: Carlos David Guillén

CONTENTS

Author's Note

H E R is a dark, contemporary romance. It is sexually explicit, contains mature content, profanity, and topics that may be sensitive or triggering to some readers.

Reader discretion is advised.

I would hate to reveal details of related content in case readers do not want spoilers, but if you would like more detailed information regarding triggers, please visit my website xggbooks.com

This book is dedicated to Flor Florecita.

You *may* forever live with imposter syndrome, but we did it!

PLAYLIST

Camila Cabello - Never be the Same
Lady Gaga - LoveGame
Ariana Grande - Into You
Matchbox Twenty - Push
Muse - Undisclosed Desires
Jaymes Young - Infinity
Rihanna - Love on the Brain
Carla Morrison - Disfruto
Radiohead - All I Need
Red Hot Chili Peppers - Hard to Concentrate

Noah to Justice

Shawn Mendes - Stitches
Everclear - Santa Monica
Calvin Harris ft. Florence Welch - Sweet Nothing
Banda el Recodo - Pena Tras Pena
Marca MP - Ya Acabo

1
Justice

The rain outside pours mercilessly. Thankfully, I've always loved a good thunderstorm.

It wasn't the noisy banging of the water droplets against the black railing near the open window, or even the cold rain covering my face and now-drenched tank top, that woke me. This, I understand immediately, whether from instinct or fear. I throw the thick cover, now peppered with a layer of tiny droplets, off of me. I dozed off fully clothed with my boots on. I didn't pay for a night at this dump to sleep. I came here on business—a stakeout, not a vacation.

The putrid stench of the soiled carpet reeks and the mugginess clings to my neck. I peel strands of my thick brown locks off my face and neck and gather them into a loose braid.

"I heard it too," my younger brother Jule whispers. He sits straight up on the twin-sized bed. I realize now he never even covered himself and that he, too, is fully dressed.

I creep low toward the wall across from me as a ray of lightning illuminates the small room. I reach for my equipped backpack and throw a baggy, hooded sweatshirt over my drenched tee. "Stay low, don't close the window."

Jule nods. The grown look on his face reminds me of the fright that used to cover his big brown eyes. Now at fourteen, he thinks of himself as a man—someone to protect me and not cower away. But I need him safe, and this isn't a job for a young teen trying to prove himself.

"Here," he whispers in Spanish. "You never know."

I roll my eyes, but take the pointed, travel-size blade by the ornate hilt. I never carry weapons, but he insists the dangers I face during these outings require it. I guess, somewhere within, I agree. I open the door to our double-bed rented room as gently as I can manage and wriggle my way out. The hotel corridor feels damp and overheated, and I instantly feel sticky under my sweater.

"Nikoletta!" I turn, alerted by the harsh whisper of my brother's voice.

I'm momentarily taken aback by his towering stance. It seems just yesterday he was at waist level, and now he's a foot over my five-foot-three-inch stance.

"If you come to face a danger beyond your kung fu karate knowledge, look in the bag for your birthday gift from me." He winks and closes the door before I can properly roll my eyes at him. I only manage to snort out loud at the door.

I'm smiling as I run toward the exit that leads to the roof, and I welcome the icy water falling hard. I pull up the hood and fasten my pack.

My birthday. I wince at the thought.

This is, thankfully, the end of my birth date. My best friend Jasmin and my brother Jule forced me to celebrate. They even managed to save up for a damn cake. They both know I dread this day, and although I understand they only mean to cheer me up, all it does is remind me of my parent's murder.

Seven years ago, days before my *big day*, my mom and dad were gunned down by two men, led by a gang leader named Vork.

So, when midnight rolled around, and I'd officially turned twenty-two, I ran off to avoid Jasmin and Jule. I was sure to be rid of them but only found a fucking cake, with twenty-two burning candles, and their gift wrapped in newspaper.

After force-feeding a slice of the too-sweet frosting-filled, cotton candy-flavored cake, Jule and I hurried to the motel in the heart of this fucked up city. An anonymous follower had reached out, letting me know that Vork would be here, only they didn't give a time, just a date. Sleep took us as we waited for something, *anything,* to happen.

Shriek-filled cries alert me to the southeastern corner of the block, just two buildings down. I shake my head to clear any thoughts of birthday shenanigans, thankful that this day has finally come to an end, and run onto the puddle-covered roof to get a better view.

Most, if not all, of the beatings, drug trafficking, forced prostitution, and rapes lead to Vork. Shadows pulse in the collected puddles near the dark alleyway behind the butchers. No one in their right mind buys their meat at this location unless they're desperate, which seems to be just about everyone in my neighborhood. Once again I hear the cry I'm sure woke me, the one my brother Jule heard—the yells of women. Out on the roof and in closer range, I hear more than one victim and surely about three assailants.

I run to the fire escape, almost forgetting to grip the railing tight, the black metal extra slick in the rain. Once my feet hit the ground, I reach into my backpack, dig inside, and smile when I finally find the object I need.

I was grateful, but now I'm over the moon that Jasmin got it for me. The need for a good camera wasn't lost on me. One that could withstand drops, bear some load, resist water submersion, and still snap decent photos while I was on the run; which was right now.

My hunched shoulders lean even further when I crouch forward. I'm rushing in this awkward posture until a large man comes into view. I slam my back against the brick wall, my breaths come out in dramatic force and rain is furiously drenching my face. The attempt to wipe it dry is useless. Fucking rain is making my work tonight a whole lot more complicated, and I truly have hardcore evidence this time around.

Usually, I get glimpses, long shots, distant and hazy photos. When I'm lucky, I might get a recording of a muffled conversation without truly being able to identify who the people on the other end are. Nothing that could stand in court, not a sliver of evidence deemed competent enough to put away the fucking criminals that rule these streets.

I've grown tired of the corrupt system that's supposed to offer us protection. Just the mere thought of the sorry excuse of a police force could send me into full hysteria. Either that or I'd sit there and wish I could set the station on fire. I would even extend an invitation to the fire department so they could stand behind me, and together we'd watch them die before our eyes. Better them than us. They're useless.

I flip the switch to my Pentax and hang it around my neck. Then, focusing on the screen, I zoom in and turn the corner. The large man has his back to me with a girl dangling from a chokehold. I push the button to record the images before me, thankful for the streetlamp highlighting their corruption in the way tungsten lighting illuminates a studio set. It's like my personal beacon of hope, and I'll take whatever the universe hands me.

"Come on, just get it over with!" someone barks and a young woman squeals. They're all still hidden from my direct view.

"No! I own these fucking streets; I want to leave our evidence here." I recognize the voice but can't quite place it.

A woman writhes in her attacker's arms and her shouts grow louder, begging for both her life and the other woman's.

There's so much going on, but what's clear is that the two women need help. Another man comes into view; his blonde hair, slick with water, glints with help from the street-lamp. He's even taller than the one before me, a mammothly huge, Hulk Hogan-looking fucker. Something else catches my eye, and I zoom in to get a closer look at him.

The man with his back to me speaks under his breath, just loud enough for me, and hopefully, my camera, to hear. "This fucking slut thinks we're going to let her go." He spits his guttural laugh on her face.

The image on my camera is far better than the one my eyes have, so I focus on it and gasp. I not only recognize the blonde mammoth, but I fucking know him.

Vork–subordinate to only one other.

No one knows who reigns above him and leads the ever-expanding crew that threatens civilians. Vork is good at keeping ordinary citizens cowed, using blackmail and the promise of a slow death, unless they comply with his demands.

He and his invisible boss have the police force eating out of their hands, keeping their pockets full of cash, their noses stuffed with coke, and their dicks slick with whatever pussy they demand. He owns every infamous gang banger, each hustler, drug dealer, and pimp.

He's exactly who I *wanted* to catch on surveillance.

I send a silent *thank you* to my anonymous tipper and zoom back out to emphasize what his surroundings are. Perhaps this will be good enough to put him away. Vork is finally going to be part of the documents I record and publish to the public.

My blog is a source for the people–it's what they rely on for *real* news broadcasts. My reporting offers them a sense of comfort. They know just what to expect, who not to trust, and places to stay away from. While the media projects what they want the public to believe, it's my posts that they turn to.

What I share has never been enough to put anyone behind bars for good. I guess, in this city, criminals are offered the best lawyers for their defense. Maybe, aside from owning the cops, these fuckers keep the best lawyers money can buy. The people have been fucked long enough. It's like living in Gotham City, only Batman isn't coming to rescue us.

A noise behind Vork rattles him, and he turns around to yell at his other comrade. "Hey, didn't you hear me? Finish her already so that we can get the fuck out of here."

A nervous jolt makes my camera quake in my now freezing hands. Vork and his men are going to kill these women and leave their bodies as evidence. He's trying to show how impervious he is; that he, and not the police, own the streets. He has no fear.

I have to do something. I can't let Vork take these women's lives. I don't give a shit if prostitution is illegal; it's no reason for him to brutally rape and slaughter them.

I dig in the front pocket of my sweatshirt and grab hold of the knife, then drop the camera. It hovers over my chest, and I make sure it has a clear view of what is happening in front of me before I step into view.

"Hey!"

Both men turn around. The half-naked girl in the guy's arm struggles to stay on her feet, yet squints in my direction. Vork looks amused by my knife and small stature. I know what he sees–I'm short and appear to be fifteen years old. To him, I'm a nobody. I'm sure he thinks this is some kind of joke.

The guy who hasn't shown himself comes into view; he has the frail body of the other female bent over and dangling in front of him, his arms gripping her limp torso.

The one who has his back to me, with the girl in a stranglehold, scopes me up. "Is she for real?"

"As real as the one this fucker's got," Vork barks.

"Want me to take care of her, boss?"

Vork puts a hand up. "Johnny, *please*. What are you going to take care of? This little girl and her butterknife don't scare me."

"I called the cops and they're on their way." I'm not sure what governed me to say it, but it's out before I take another step.

Vork laughs. "I'm sure you did, sweetie."

No one calls the cops anymore. For what? Maybe out of fear, but I think people have gotten used to turning the other way.

The man gripping his victim shoves her to the ground, then zips his pants. "We haven't even done the other one. What're we going to do now, boss?"

Vork smiles. "That's easy. Fetch me the *butterknife girl,* and we'll simply add her to the list."

Obeying Vork's command, he walks my way with a smile on his face. I freeze, unwilling to disappoint the people who check my blog by showing them how much of a coward I am when approached by danger. But this isn't some grocery store robbery with an assailant and his crowbar. This is fucking real.

Suddenly, I recall my brother's words and flip my bag, then desperately dig inside. The man is in no hurry to get to me. In fact, he seems to rather enjoy his leisurely retrieval. I'm his prey and he gets off on the hunt.

My hand fists an unfamiliar and heavy object, which makes me figure it's Jule's birthday gift. I pull it out without looking and pose it in front of me. The guy gasps, frozen in place. Curious, I look down and almost drop the weapon from my grip.

Where the hell did my brother get this, and why would he give it to me?

"Boss?" The fright in his voice is unexpected, and I hold on to the firearm with much more confidence, although my hands are practically sputtering in front of me.

"She's got a tec9." Johnny stutters while pointing at me. Vork lets go of the girl in his arms and gives me his undivided attention.

"Well, hell, seems like I've underestimated you, kid."

Sirens ring out in the distance. It surprises up, but I cock an eyebrow and smile at Vork. "Seems about right," I say, my grin stretching.

Vork signals for his men to stand down and retreat. They follow his orders instantly, rubbing their noses angrily while jogging toward their getaway car.

Vork lingers and points at me from his short distance. "You and I got unfinished business, *Butterknife*." He walks backward toward his car.

"Schedule a time with my secretary," I call out to him. I hear him laugh, then they speed away.

I stand there frozen for a minute until one of the girls moves. The sirens are closer now, and the realization that we have to get the hell out of here hits me. "Hey, are you alright?"

The redhead who'd been in a chokehold grunts and moves to stand. She looks to be in her twenties, super slender–she's pure skin and bones.

"Are you out of your mind, kid? What the hell were you thinking? Do you have any idea who that was?"

"A quick thanks would suffice." I ignore her calling me a kid. I'm used to it.

No one in town knows my age, and they all think my brother is older, which has led me to think I appear to be around his age instead of my own.

The redhead shakes her head while trying to cradle her friend who'd been beaten so badly she can barely stand, let alone walk.

I reach for the other side of her and straddled a limp arm around my shoulder. "Where to?"

"Who are you?" she hisses.

"I'm the one who just saved your fucking lives. Now, where to? We got seconds before the cops get here."

We drag her friend to the inside of the butcher's joint. The smell makes me want to gag, but I'm glad to be out of sight, away from the cops who are now outside scoping the area. The blue and red lights dance on the walls around us and the siren wails uncontrollably. It's been forever since I last heard one and my eardrums seemed to panic at the deafening vibrations.

"To the back," she whispers.

We lower her friend gently to a cot lying on the ground. Her short blue dress is torn, and she's missing a shoe. Her dirty blonde hair is splattered all over her face, and when the redhead soothingly pushes it back, I gasp under my breath.

"We don't need your judgment," the redhead sneers.

I shake my head and my hood falls back, making the dark strands of my braid fall to my face and over my brown eyes. "She's so young."

The redhead looks back at her friend. "Yea, she's just fifteen."

I quickly retrieve a thick wool blanket from nearby and cover her. Then I collapse against the wall, twirling my fingers around anxiously.

"I'm Piper, this is my sister Macy."

"She's your *sister*?" My voice comes out harsh and accusing.

Piper leans back, her eyes huge. "What's your problem?"

My *problem* is that my brother Jule is just months shy of that age. I can't bear the thought of him beaten and unconscious, let alone allowing him to be used this way. I shake my head at Piper, who's still waiting for an explanation for my outburst. "I... er... have a brother."

"Yea? Welcome to the club."

Piper hugs her knees to her chest, giving me an unwanted glimpse up her torn dress. She isn't wearing any shoes and she must be freezing, yet she sits near her sister's head without showing any sign that she would want to share the small blanket and therefore offer her sister Macy less warmth.

I notice no other blankets are around. "You live here?"

"If you call this living."

The lump in my throat threatens to come out as a whimper, so I swallow it back and nod. I have to distract my wandering thoughts, so I walk to a blackened window. Two detectives are across the street scouting the area, and I snort.

"What's the matter?"

"The force sent two fucking cops, like that would've been enough."

"Yea? Well, *you* were enough," Piper chuckles quietly and joins me. "Hey, I don't recognize that one."

I'm instantly distracted. I rarely see cops and have no idea who they are. But the one she cocks her chin toward is young, maybe thirty, give or take a couple of years. The other one looks to be twice his age and size in circumference.

"Must be a rookie," she says, more to herself than to me.

I watch, amused by the older one's awkward movements. Not only does he slosh around, but he looks too terrified, like they aren't supposed to be here. It makes the younger officer's movements stand out.

The rookie walks around with his gun in hand, truly searching, looking for clues and probing the area. Out of curiosity, I reach for my camera, still hanging around my neck, and flip it to picture mode. I zoom in and catch the cop's swift moves up close.

His body, slightly angled with strong legs ready to sprint, seems trained and fully capable of taking someone in a fight. He holds his visibly strong arms out in front with a pistol in hand. His face, etched in sharp edges, with a piercing, deadly glow in his dark eyes, glowers. His lips pucker tightly in concentration, and his unshaven jawline matches that of his rough appearance. His black hair falls in short waves, covering his ears and grazing his jawline. He's tall and his muscled shoulders stretch and tug at the now soaked material of his black blazer. I watch in awe as his veined hand grips the Glock, and notice black lines on his skin, *tattoos*.

"What's that for?"

Piper's voice brings me back and I turn to her. She's pointing at my camera and my shoulders go up. "I'm a reporter, more or less."

I face the window again and snap a picture of the rookie. Somewhere in my mind, hidden from the world, a warm glow spreads like liquid gel. I get this giddy feeling, desperate even. I don't know why. I want to investigate it, but Piper's hissing evaporates my thoughts.

"What the hell does that mean?"

I whip around and glare at her. My insides churn and black irises appear whenever I blink. "I'm the one that runs the Justice Hotline blog."

"So *you're* Justice? *Oh my god*, you're going to get us fucking killed! I swear, if you post any of this, I'll kill you myself!"

"I don't get it–I can help you. This will put Vork away for sure, Piper."

She starts pacing back and forth, whispering harshly at me, and flailing her arms around herself. "No, what this is going to do is put me and my sister in a grave. And you, too, *and* your brother."

"Not another word about my brother, Piper. I'm fucking warning you." I run my finger over the air separating us for emphasis.

But Piper merely points an accusing finger at my chest, my stare fixed on her dirt-caked fingernail. "There are bigger things at stake here that you don't understand, kid. You're wrong if you think Vork is at the top of the food chain, and if you let this little video of yours leak, you're only going to send the real *mafiosos... on all of us.*" She expands her hands dramatically to signify that she means the entire city and not just us three.

"Well, what am I supposed to do? Stand back with my hands crossed behind my back?"

"All I know is I got rights, and I forbid you from showing this video. That and my sister is underage. You'll need my signature if you don't want to end up in jail."

I roll my eyes. "*Please.*"

"I mean it, kid. I'm thankful you saved our lives, but I can't allow you to let this out." She grills closer. "We'll be killed for sure, and then where will you be? In front of your computer screen, checking up on your Facebook?"

Facebook? What the hell? I don't even own a computer. I have to pull a thousand strings in order to get online and upload my videos. I shake my head. "What if I obscure your faces?" It's merely a suggestion; I never alter what I post.

"No. Everyone will know it was us." Piper's face looks glum, and she turns to look at her sister. "This is our turf."

There's gotta be room for negotiation. The point is to send a message. People will see the footage and know that somebody is willing to stand up to Vork. It will give the people hope. "Who's your pimp—"

The words barely leave my lips when Piper nearly leaps on top of me. She pins me against the wall and holds her forearm to my neck. "There is no pimp. Get that through your thick head, kid. *I'm* my own boss, okay?"

I know how to escape from her weak grip and frail arms, but I don't want to hurt her. A deep breath enters my lungs and I allow it to clear my head. Piper and Macy are victims, and I won't allow myself to lose my shit here. "I'm sorry if I offended you. It wasn't my intention. I just really want to help."

"If you *really* want to help," her arms fall to her sides and she takes a step back, "*don't* help. The cops are gone now. You should go, too."

I jog to the window and peer out. My lips dip at the corners, but I don't understand my frown. Sure, the young cop is cute and all, but what was I going to do? Go out with my tec9 in hand and say hello? I almost scoff under my breath. What good will knowing a cop do, anyway?

They're all the same, a bunch of corrupt law pushers that cower under their donut-filled desks instead of putting the bad guys behind bars where they belong. And although this guy seems different, like he *needed* to do good, I know better.

They're all the same.

"Okay, Piper. I'll leave. Just remember, the hell you're going through is the same pit we're *all* in. Vork owns you, he owns us all. And I, for one, am sick of it. You know where to find me if you change your mind. Or when he comes back, because he will."

2

Redemption

"**I** fucking told you it was nothing."

I roll my eyes. My new *temporary* partner, Detective Peter Lloyd, is a lazy son of a bitch who looks closer to death than retirement. He heaves dramatically after slamming the door to my black 1975 Chevrolet Camaro.

"Watch it! She's a fucking classic."

He shrinks at my glare. "Just drive," he mumbles.

The inside is sleek and modern, the dash glints, and I want to fucking launch his face into it, but he isn't worth the damage to the console. It's my first week on the job, and already I want to shoot my gun up someone's ass, only it isn't a deserving criminal but *this* fucking idiot.

Lloyd is a sad excuse for law enforcement and definitely one of the many reasons this city has gone to shit. The entire fucking police force is a band of idiots. But I still don't miss my home city. I needed more. Not sure what exactly, maybe something *meaningful?* I'm still searching, but at least I feel useful now.

I was beginning to doubt my career choices until Mike found me and took me under his wing. Since then, I've endured one shithole to another, cleaning out the trash. I accepted this allocation, a metropolis with five counties and one ruler, because of its extremely corrupt status. New assignment: find the source of the chaos and retire it. More or less.

I grip the leather steering wheel, trying to gain a smidge of control. I'd rather work alone, but apparently, I'm forced to *train* with the asthmatic beer gut.

"I thought we were supposed to show up when someone rang."

The asshole actually rolls his eyes and I want to fucking punch him. "Yeah, whatever. You'll learn how we do it around here soon enough."

Like hell I will. I know exactly how shit is done around here, which is precisely why I was sent down—to fix their fucking mess. I turn and almost smile at how his enormous torso bobs sideways, like Humpty Dumpty about to tip over. The fifteen minute drive to the station is torture with him in my car and I almost shove his ass out.

"I have to make a call. I'll be right in."

Lloyd struggles and I grind my teeth as he throws the door behind him. I'll make him pay for that soon enough. My phone is in my hands and I'm dialing up my boss like a petulant child, but I don't give a fuck. I didn't sign up to be babysat by a Ghostbuster looking fucker.

"Well, that was quick." Mike holds back his laughter.

"You didn't tell me I'd be paired up with Detective Dumpty."

This time he laughs. "It's just a formality. You'll be working alone in a couple of days. I'll talk to Ron."

I nod, even though he can't see me. "Fine, but if I have to give that fucker any more rides, I can't promise I won't uppercut him."

Mike swears under his breath, and a muffled tapping tells me he's texting someone.

"A girl with a gun–what the fuck is going on down there?"

I sigh and tap the steering wheel, the tight leather bumpy under my fingertips. "It's a decoy. Whoever made the call was desperate for someone to show."

"I'll talk to Ron about your partnership and I want a report in a week."

"A fucking week? Who do you think I am, Bruce Wayne?"

Mike ignores my witticism. "Focus it on any preliminary findings."

I sigh again and push the phone deeper into my temple. *Fuck.*

"And, Dylan..."

I glance at the device as if it's a video call. "Yea, boss?"

"Don't forget what you're *really* there for. Track the filth and dispose of it."

Mike rented a month-to-month apartment. It's small, but I don't care. All I need is a shower and a toilet. The industrial space consists of an open layout, with the living room and kitchen in one space. There's a bedroom with an attached bathroom, and I'm grateful for the high ceilings because I'm sick of always having to duck. My height forces me to bend through doorways and squeeze into elevators. At least while I make this my temporary home, I can walk without constantly hunching down.

Max lounges on the smoky gray wood floor right outside the bathroom, and his clipped ears twitch as I drag the electric razor over my locks. It's time for a haircut.

The nostalgia of seeing my military clean and cut look drags memories, usually kept tucked away, to the surface, and I suddenly want to scratch at my skin. It's a chameleon effect that pulls me closer to who I was forced to become during that time of my life. It's who I need to be now in order to deal with the sick fucks barricading the city, forcing those who were already low to dig their own graves and crawl six feet deeper into the earth for shelter. All the more close to hell.

The desire to live larger than they are capable of, an impulse to want to be above everyone else, is a hunger that comes naturally to these criminals. It resulted in them tying up whoever they could scramble and suspend them by their necks. The crew uses civilians as leverage, assaulting their bodies, a fuel to indulge their fantasies of control.

I'm not sure yet who is in control—the police force or the criminals. Maybe both, an alliance. I'll take this town just as I did the rest and hand the power back to the people. As if warning me, an invisible touch grazes the tiny hairs on the back of my neck, telling me to be cautious of something that awaits in the darkness.

I shake my shoulders roughly like Max would, brushing off the adrenaline coursing through me. The hair I've buzzed off occupies the space around me, falling slowly to the white tile. I don't give a fuck which side rots away in the crevices of this forsaken town. I'll kill each and every dumb ass who gets in my way. I'm already eager to get to the next town to do the same.

My cellphone buzzes–it's Lloyd. "Give me something good," I murmur.

"Looks like the girl exists, after all. We have a location for her. Want to tag along while I interrogate?"

What the fuck is he eating? I pull the cell away and grimace at the sound of his chewing. Sometime soon he'll follow my lead, and I can't wait to leave his ass behind. I'm not sure which law enforcement personnel to watch out for, but everyone is guilty until proven innocent. I'm not a fucking lawyer, just the executioner.

"I'll meet you there. Text me the address and details of the girl."

I'm not letting this fucker ride in my car again. I hang up and jump in the shower. I can be ready in less than ten minutes and make it there before him.

I'm sure that whatever he was consuming is more important than interrogating a ghost and that he'll take his sweet time.

I take one last look in the full-length mirror near the apartment entrance. I barely recognize who reflects back. The buzzed cut reveals the tattoos on the back of my scalp that connect with those on my neck. I don't care about covering them up anymore.

I'm dressed comfortably. What the fuck is this sick joke of a police force going to say? Lloyd can barely fit into his cheap suit.

I bend down and ruffle the spot between Max's ears. "Be good while I'm gone."

I make it there before Lloyd and scope out the restaurant. It's an upscale place, Vincent Tavern. They even have valet, like hell if I'm going to trust them with my baby.

I pull around and park it around the corner. Humpty Dumpty isn't here yet, and I flash my badge at the front to slip inside without needing to be on some stupid list or reservation.

The place smells of butterfly bushes, and I looked up to find them hanging from the ceiling throughout the dark and luxurious interior. There are smooth black leather lounge chairs, brushed metal fixtures, and rosewood candle-lit tables. I think it's supposed to be romantic, but I'm not sure. I don't really give a fuck about things like that.

"Something to drink?" The exotic bartender looks me over, and I'm not sure if she's intrigued or afraid.

"Whiskey neat."

I want to scope the area before the clumsy duck arrives, and after shooting back my drink, I walk to where a server discreetly divulges where I can find the young girl Lloyd claims is the source of some chaotic events that continue to ravage the city.

He sent me a picture of the file. I'm looking for a fifteen-year-old girl, five-three, dark mid-back length waves with brown eyes. She's got a twenty-two-year-old brother, five-ten, who shares the same hair and eye color. According to the file, *she's* the troublemaker.

Before I make my way around to the left, a woman's bright laugh tugs my muscles to a table lining the back wall. The bar lines the entire floor, and I select a barstool with just enough distance to watch them without being spotted.

There are four people, two women and two men. I don't see a fifteen-year-old girl, so neither woman can be *her*. Four people, but I can only focus on one.

My gaze is transfixed, directed toward a woman with her dark locks trapped in a bun, and I subdue the sudden urge to walk over and let them cascade over her milky skin. Her strapless black dress clings to her feminine curves and my mouth waters, suddenly jealous of the fabric.

She laughs and her head tips back, exposing her long neck, and the desire to wrap my hand around the delicate skin while bringing her face closer to me, so I can nibble on her full lips, hardens my dick.

She sips on a dark bubbly drink, coke I assume, and her cheeks hollow as she sucks through a straw. *Fuck*, I'd plunge my cock so far into her tiny throat and gladly watch her gasp for air while she chokes on me.

I barely notice the man possessively close to her, his hand draped over the back of her chair. She doesn't seem to notice him, though. Not how I'm sure she would melt if I pressed against her like that. She would succumb to my heat, molding to my flesh like it's just one body.

My phone vibrates, and I have to force my eyes on the screen.

Shit, Lloyd is here.

I take one last look at *her,* then saunter to the front.

The shoddy excuse of a man looks angry that I made it all the way inside without him. Not my fault he's so fucking slow. He looks me up and down, as if he's finally seeing me for the first time, and I smile devilishly as he cowards back.

He glances at a clipboard instead of me. "They're in the back. Come on."

I nod and let him lead, *for now.*

My heart drops to my stomach and stays there. I swear it pulses in my fucking gut and is ready to pass through all the channels of my digestive tract. *No fucking way.*

Lloyd clears his throat as he approaches the table with four people. The one with my woman. "Nikoletta Justice Fox."

And the black rose of a woman I was salivating for turns around and gapes at us.

My throat tightens, and I want to fucking hurl. *She's fifteen?*

My thoughts spiral and I'm shouting in my head. An angry man growls at me and thrashes on the ground. She doesn't look like a child. Everything about her is sensual, and my senses are permanently fucked because I still don't see how she can be younger than twenty.

Fuck.

3

Justice

I expected Jasmin and Jule to be waiting for me, but I hadn't anticipated them to be dressed up like gangsters about to dash the streets in some poetic justice rampage.

"There were sirens," Jule explains. "*Sirens.*"

Jasmin crosses the room and hugs me. "I didn't even know they would still respond to a call." She lets me go and takes a seat on one of the beds. The window is still open and the rain trickles in.

"Word on the street is they saw a gun in the hands of Justice." Noah's voice rings through the rain as he drops his feet to the ground with a loud thump. He'd climbed in through the window and is soaking, his gray t-shirt drenched.

Fuck, gossip in this city spreads faster than a forest fire. I grimace and my brother smiles unrepentantly. I cross my hands over my chest and Noah comes toward me.

My eyes are still shooting daggers at Jule from across the room when Noah pulls me into his arms. "I heard a lady say she didn't see a gun, she saw hope, and called the cops."

My brother chortles. "There, you see? You owe me, Nik."

"You shut up, Julius. Do you have any idea how dangerous that thing is? I don't kill people... I *report*."

Noah takes hold of my shoulders, which are trembling with pent-up rage. More than anything, I wonder how Jule got his hands on a weapon at all. Oh, God, I hope he didn't steal it!

"That gun saved your life, Justice."

"No," I scoff. "The siren did."

"Actually," Jule pipes in. "It was the gun that caused the sirens to be called."

"Whatever." Jasmin raises her hands, exasperated, then glances out the window. She squeezes Jule's shoulder, a sisterly warning to shut up already. "The point is, she's alive. Now, what happened out there?"

Noah kisses my temple lightly as he lets go and moves to hug my back against his chest. He holds on to my waist, one hand on my hip, and crushes me tighter to him. I feel the heat of his breath near my ear and can't help but wonder if this is how it would feel if that rookie cop were holding on to me.

Noah is three years older than me; he's tall, strong, quick on his feet, and even quicker with a weapon at hand. He keeps his chestnut-colored hair at chin's length, and I rarely ever see him without facial hair. I know he shaves though, like today his beard is more or less a shadow across his cheeks, upper lip, and chin.

I hadn't seen Noah in over a week, which is why he holds me so closely. I wonder if anyone else notices how tight he's holding me, or how he grazes my temple gently with his lips. I shudder in his grip. I don't want his hands on me; the proximity is suffocating. On instinct, I reach for my mother's charm bracelet. I twirl and count each charm quickly and then ignore my insides screaming at me and clear my throat. "I saw Vork."

A collection of gasps from the three people surrounding me makes my skin crawl. In fact, the reason it'd taken me so long to get back was because I was obsessed over the images I'd recorded. I slowed the film and froze it on Vork's face, wishing I could have shot him. But my parents taught me better, and I wanted him to rot in prison. He'd make a dashing girlfriend for the inmates.

I wriggle in Noah's arms, unable to hold back the feeling of suffocation. I walk to the dresser for my camera and take off my drenched sweater, then throw it over the hissing radiator. I sigh. "I got him on camera, Jule. I finally got this son of a bitch."

Jule's eyes focus on my hands, and he approaches me slowly. His lips quiver. "We got him, Nik."

Across from my brother and me, Noah tenses, and I know what he's thinking. So many times he'd already told me what Piper had an hour ago: that it was too dangerous to hope to land Vork, and that he most likely was working for someone higher. That I should stick to reporting the news and not risk my life by uploading any dirt on Vork and his bandits. I guess he hoped I wouldn't get the opportunity to find the evidence I needed. Yet here it was, already in my hands.

But it wasn't like me to break promises, and I intended to further press Piper and convince her that we should leak this new footage. Now I just had to break the news to Jule. His gaze is locked on my camera as I plug it into the nearest outlet and signal him to sit next to me on the floor.

Jule's back collapses against the wall and he slides down next to me, our shoulders touching, and he leans into me.

"Show me."

"Justice, I don't really think that's the best thing for you—"

I silence Noah's protest with a glare. "Jule has the right to see the man who killed our parents."

Jasmin sits at the edge of my bed, watching us closely. I know from the look in her sad, tired, and bloodshot brown eyes that she agrees. Noah scoffs under his breath and resigns by crossing his arms across his chest. I turn on the camera and play the footage for my brother.

The sound is as bad as I dreaded with my harsh breaths, thunder, and loud rainfall—the distant voices are muffled. Still, it's way better than anything else I've managed to get in the past with my cheap cameras, yet it would've been better if there'd been no rain. When Vork comes into view, my brother goes rigid beside me. He holds his breath and grips my fingers. He squeezes so hard I think he might break them.

Once the footage is done, he lets go of the camera. So much unlike me. If I were in his place, I wouldn't be able to let go. I'm relieved, though, because I don't want him to flip forward and see the picture I took of my rookie cop.

Whoa. *My* rookie cop? Get a fucking grip.

"When can this go live on the blog?"

I inhale a deep breath and keep it in my lungs for a long while before breathing out. "I can't do that just yet, Jule."

My eyes stare at the camera in disbelief. I can't believe I managed to sputter the words out loud. My brother stands up frantically, his hands balled into fists. "Why the hell not?"

From under my lashes, I peer up at Noah. He's smiling and looks relieved. I roll my eyes at him; he's never seen eye-to-eye with me regarding Vork. Whatever, fuck Noah. I'm desperate to explain things to Jule before he storms out of the room and does something stupid. So I stand, leave the camera on the floor, and grip my brother's arms, giant in comparison to mine.

"Try to understand. You didn't witness what Piper and I discussed because I shut off the camera—"

"Who the fuck is Piper?"

I ignore my little brother's outburst and inhale sharply before I lose it. I have to be the calm one, the responsible one. He shakes me off of him and angrily slides his hands over his stubble-filled face, then through his short hair.

Did he actually think I would let this man go so easily? Jule wasn't there to witness how my parents were taken from us; he didn't have this enclosed and restricted rage ready to explode on just about anyone who tried to stop me. I wanted to kill Vork with my bare hands. He has no idea how much it took for me not to empty my birthday present into him. Mom and Dad wouldn't have wanted that.

"Piper is the redhead from the footage, the other one is Macy: they're sisters. Piper won't let me expose Vork, says he isn't the source. Getting rid of him will pry open Pandora's box."

Jule snorts. "So you're gonna let this tramp decide how we expose this ... *monster*!"

It wasn't a question. Jule is enraged, and he flails his arms, drawing attention to his anger directed at me. He feels betrayed.

Jasmin's calm voice sighs behind him. "This girl, Piper... she's right, though. Assuming that Vork is the mastermind of the pack is giving him way too much credit."

"I don't give a damn. I'm not looking to enlighten anyone: I'm looking to settle a score. Even if it brings on more shit, at least we'll be rid of *one* problem."

I have to admit that what Jule says makes sense. If, in fact, there is someone higher in ranks than Vork, then we have more than just one issue. But in getting rid of Vork, we would have less to worry about, right? And after the footage leaks, we would be presented with that *other* issue and therefore given a chance to resolve what's exposed.

"My plan isn't to just delete this and forget about it. I want to convince Piper to let me show it. Her sister is underage, and if I expose her circumstances, Piper threatened to have me arrested."

"Slut has a brain. How convenient."

"Watch your mouth, Julius! Ask yourself what Mom was doing before she met our father and see how comfortable you feel with the name-calling."

I'm the angry one now. My control is lost to the abyss of seeing Vork after so many years. That and the reality of my mother having once been in Piper's shoes. She'd proven to be the best wife and mother to us. My father never wanted her to regret her choices because she'd done what she needed to do in order to survive in her hell. Jule knew better than to judge the sex workers in the video and he responded by lowering his head.

Jule nods suddenly. "You're right, Nik. I'm sorry." His hands go to a simple silver cross around his neck. It belonged to my mother, and he grips it, squeezing his eyes shut.

I approach him and gently pat his muscled bicep. "I understand your anger, trust me, little brother. Piper is just afraid."

My hand falls to my side, and he opens his eyes, then gives me one solemn nod. I look at Noah, who's leaning against a wall, his arms still crossed. Jasmin sits on the edge of one of the small beds. She rolls her eyes at Noah and hugs herself.

"Piper works alone, with no procurer to manage her actions or money. This tells me she *is* smart. She also genuinely cares for her younger sister. I think if I use the right words, and perhaps offer some sort of protection, I can convince her to help me trap Vork."

"I want to help," Jule stresses, his voice cracking.

Jasmin nods. "I'll do whatever you need, you know that."

I smile at my best friend, who is more like a sister. She'd lost her mom when she was eight, and my mother took her in and we grew up like siblings. We lived in one of the neediest counties, but we were lucky to have had such great parents who worked their asses off to buy a small trailer. We still resided there now, and it's our home. Many of our neighbors struggle to keep up with plot rent, maintenance, and all other utilities, but we're lucky. Jas and I had been working since we lost my parents and we were surviving this hell just fine.

Noah cocks his head. "You know I got your back, Justice. Always have, always will."

I smile at him. I've known him since we were two kids running around in our underwear while our moms washed our clothes in the river five miles into the woods. His father left when he was twelve, and he started working right away to help his mother come up with the money to pay off loan sharks.

We'd been dating for a couple of months now, mostly because I grew tired of constantly turning him down. Noah is handsome, strong, and adventurous, and he knows me. He loves me and I love him. Although our love is wildly disparate, I decided to give him a chance.

I'm not sure if it helps, but it feels nice when he holds me, kisses me, and whispers seductive suggestions in my ear regularly. I admit that I somewhat enjoy his company and expect his arms around me. It's easy to be in his arms, familiar. Sometimes he presses his hard cock against me and I'm positive I will let him fuck me soon. Suddenly, an unbidden rookie cop materializes in my daydream and he takes Noah's place.

Fuck.

Thankfully, my brother's voice interrupts the dream. "Alright, so let's do this. Let's go."

I laugh. "We can't go *now*, Jule."

"But we may lose them!"

"Settle down." I place my hand on his chest–his heart beats crazily against his ribcage. "I know where they're staying. We need to do this right if it's going to work. We need to give them some time to recover."

Jule nods. He'd cringed throughout the entire footage, surely at the sight of Macy's beaten body. I'm glad he agrees, and even more so, that he seems to understand. I sigh in relief and the release causes my stomach to growl.

"*So*, breakfast, anyone?" Noah laughs quietly.

Breakfast.

My eyes snap to the alarm clock on the broken-down bedside table across from me–it's five in the morning. The tense knots in my stomach loosen some at the thought of food. For days now, Jule, Jasmin, and I had been living on scraps and water. We could always count on water. But the trailer was empty of food. Crumbs had been licked off wrappers and the foot-long countertop.

I look at my brother, growing taller each day–his eyes glisten at the mention of breakfast, which is his favorite meal of the day. Jasmin swallows and stares at nothing.

"I'm sorry, Noah. We're out of food."

"Well, what kind of boyfriend would I be if I didn't take my girlfriend, her sister, *and* brother out to a birthday feast?"

I try to grin past the annoyance I don't want to feel and throw my arms around him. I look up and his chin grazes my forehead due to his height. "My birthday was yesterday."

Jule ignores me. "Where to?"

"How about we eat breakfast at the corner diner and what do we say...Vincent Tavern for dinner?"

I hear Jasmin rise from the bed and my brother's heavy footsteps approach us.

Jule gapes at Noah. "*Vincent Tavern*... no one goes to VT's."

"That's because no one here can afford it. I've been putting in extra hours, which is why you haven't seen much of me," Noah explains.

He lets me go to hold my hand and now stands beside me. The last time I enjoyed a birthday dinner that was somewhat fancy was when my parents lived. They always saved up for birthdays. I, on the other hand, could do with fewer celebrations. Jas and Jule understood. There were other more important expenses, and we were disciplined enough to not break our budget.

Jule had been risking his ass by hauling water from the river, and that was forbidden. I cautioned him to only take amounts he could carry alone and not force himself to bring larger loads.

I'm a penny counter. Precisely why I forbade Jasmin from buying me such an expensive camera, but she, *of course,* does what she wants.

"I suggest we wear our best clothes."

Both Jasmin and Jule brighten and begin to gather our things. They're out the door before I can retract the charger from the power outlet. I leave the camera on the counter to put my sweater back on and don't notice Noah flipping through the images.

"Why'd you snap a photo of a cop?"

"Oh, I don't know." I tug the sweater over my face and shrug. "I actually used it to zoom in. I found it strange to see cops respond to a call, and I was curious."

Noah nods and sets the camera back down. His expression is serious. "He's new–Detective Dylan Montreal. Transferred about a month ago."

I'm not surprised Noah knows who the rookie is–he's been arrested various times for petty law-breaking habits, fighting with the men who abuse the sex workers' time, and disgruntled arguments with loan sharks.

A somber guilt I've never felt before travels up my starving gut and squeezes my chest to where it becomes difficult and even painful to breathe. Noah isn't only my boyfriend, but my best friend. He knows me so well, and I can't help feeling he understands *exactly* why I took the photo–because I fancy the handsome rookie enough to have his image among my stash.

Noah deserves better than my half-assed attempts to be his girlfriend, so I reach for the camera and erase the image. I barely even allow myself to stare at it again.

"It isn't important." I raise the camera and quickly snap a photo of Noah smiling at me.

He blinks away the blinding flash and I giggle, then tuck the Pentax into my bag. I rush to him, wrap my arms around his neck to bring him lower, and kiss him in a way I never have before.

4
Justice

The young host at the fancy restaurant hesitates upon our entrance. Noah is, after all, infamous, and I... the reporter who constantly attempts to put thugs and corrupt shit on the map. I expose the information everyone prefers to keep hidden, yet just as desperately, they seek it out due to fear of not knowing what is happening in their own town.

I recognize the boy, he's Jule's age. His family lives four trailers away from us. I know his family struggles; his mom is the sweetest. She often invites us over for dinner. I send a silent thank you to my parents. If they hadn't paid off the trailer and property in advance, my siblings and I would have been forced onto the streets.

After Noah explains why we're here, the kid finds us a booth in the farthest and darkest corner of the restaurant. The waitress mumbles the specials and takes our orders quickly, barely looking at us.

"I guess our nice clothes aren't as nice as we thought," Jas says while looking at her deep blue, knee-length, silky dress.

As usual, she wears her dark, tight curls down. Tonight, she's combed it all to one side, exposing a long silvery earring. Her chocolate complexion glows, and she looks so elegant but simple compared to the outrageous outfits on some of the women here.

My brother shifts uncomfortably and he stares down at the suit he wears. It belonged to my father, but Jule is already taller and beefier than he was.

Jule wiggles the tie up and down while pretending to not be able to breathe in it. "I don't understand why I couldn't wear a T-shirt with a jacket. I look like an idiot."

Noah laughs. "We all look great. Especially you, Justice." He winks at me and nestles me close before kissing my temple.

Jule rolls his eyes while he tugs at the wrist of the jacket. Jasmin gives us a weak smile and shifts in her seat. I know she's comfortable in her dress. Jasmin is one of the girliest girls I know. I suspect being here with Noah is what's making her uncomfortable.

I, on the other hand, feel noticeably uncomfortable in the tight, black, strapless dress. My mother's tube-like dress reaches just below my knees and it hugs my curves, leaving nothing to the imagination. My dark hair is pulled back in a side braid and then into a low bun close to my left ear. My mother's silver charm bracelet rolls up my wrist, tugging on the tiny arm hair, and I smile. Every time it does that, I pretend it's my mother pinching sense into me. She was wearing the bracelet the day she was killed. I put it on that night and never took it off.

I close my eyes and turn to breathe in Noah's scent. Underneath his black, military-style jacket, he's wearing a light blue, buttoned down, cotton blouse. He has his best black trousers and combat boots. I smile at the sound of his deep voice carrying on a conversation with my brother, evidently trying to ease him.

"Just take off the tie and unbutton the shirt. It's a modern thing." He signals discreetly to a few young men nearby, all tieless.

"Now you tell me?" Jule undoes the tie and tosses it to Jasmin, who folds it neatly into her clutch. He opens the first three buttons on his shirt and gives out an exaggerated sigh.

We stay silent when the quiet server comes back with our meal. Steam rises off our plates and we control the urge to not devour the food like starving animals. Noah pulls his arm away, and I frown when my body relaxes once his arms leave me, the suffocation replaced by a warm ease.

I concentrate on my food and carefully cut into my sirloin bavette steak. My fork digs into the lusciously plump mountain of mashed potatoes and then I pick up a tender green bean with my fingers and bite into it. A pleased moan escapes me and I know I'm smiling like an idiot.

We're all humming softly in delight until a deep, scratchy voice belonging to an older gentleman steals my attention. "Nikoletta Justice Fox?"

I turn slowly at the mention of my complete given name, food in my mouth and all. Everyone turns with me. I mean, who the hell knows my *entire* name? Besides, the only person who calls me by my first name is my brother.

Noah tenses and grows ten inches beside me. He's the first to speak for the table and we all sit up straight. "Well, if it isn't Officer Lloyd and his *shiny* new sidekick. What do you want with Justice?"

Two cops stand near our table, already attracting some unwanted attention from the rich fuckers surrounding us. One of the two is the rookie I snapped a picture of, and instead of his detective uniform, he embodies another tonight.

The rookie appears as though he just clocked in for his shift as a grim reaper. Black from head to toe, black jeans, a black t-shirt, and a leather jacket. *Fuck,* he looks good. I'd lay down and let him carry me to hell if he showed up to deliver my death.

He shaved. The rookie's hair is gone and in its place is a buzzed cut that makes his thick, dark brows stand out. His black eyes pierce me and my meal stays stuck somewhere in my food pipe. He frowns and his full lips part just a fraction, enough to make me squeeze my thighs together.

The older one, with what looks like a large pregnant beer gut, grinds his teeth. "It's *Detective*, and this doesn't concern you, Noah."

"Like hell it doesn't. What do you want with my girlfriend?"

Lloyd smirks and doesn't seem at all taken aback by Noah's declaration, but the rookie named Dylan furrows his brows further and leans in. Across from me, I see my brother sit straight up and square his shoulders.

"Aren't you too old for her, Noah? Besides, all we want is to ask the little lady some questions."

From my peripheral, I catch Noah's jaw tightening and he's about to speak, no doubt to correct the assumption of me being too young for him, when my brother blurts out, "Can't you wait until we're done eating? Have some respect."

Lloyd takes a nonchalant glance at a clipboard he has in hand and then stares at my brother. "You must be Julius Fox *Junior*. Defending your little sister, are we?"

Jule suddenly grins. "Sure am." He looks my way and winks. "What have you done now, *little sister*?"

Oh, for fuck's sake. By this time, I manage to swallow, reach for my glass of Coke, and chug some of it down. Dylan leans toward me. "We heard you held a Tec9 in hand. Care to explain what that was about?"

"Big gun for such a small girl," Lloyd adds.

I tense and look straight into Dylan's big, dark eyes. They truly are something–large and expressive with gray, almost silvery slivers on the inner area of the darkest brown I've ever seen. I planned on joining them outside and my intentions were to fully cooperate until he smiles at his partner's stupid joke and stands to stare me down with a superior look about him.

Jule points accusingly. "Who the fuck is this?"

"I'm Detective Montreal."

I face my empty plate and reach for my drink again. "I have nothing to say to either of you."

Officer Lloyd snorts. "Happy fifteenth, Justice."

Jule laughs when they turn to leave and Dylan halts to stare at me with a befuddled look. Dumbasses messed up and twisted our ages. I just smile. Let them think what they want. I face Jasmin. Her shoulders are hunched like she wants to crawl underneath the table but recovers once the officers are out of sight.

"Do I really look fifteen?"

Jule chortles, almost spitting his drink out in front of him, but Jasmin shakes her head. "Not in *that* outfit you don't. I think it's your youthful face... it looks so..." she thinks, fingers groping her chin, "clean and refreshed?"

They all laugh. Her face looks fine, it isn't filled with wrinkles. Were twenty-year-olds supposed to have any? Noah's face is flawless, and no one takes *him* for a teen.

"You're just so tiny, Nik. You're barely five feet and you're all," Jule looks like he's getting ready to squeeze into a cramped space, "itty-bitty."

I look down at my body. I don't consider myself thin. I barely fit into my mother's dress due to my curvy figure. I have wide hips and a full chest. Noah suddenly loops an arm around my waist and brings me closer. His lips graze my cheek and then my earlobe, making my body tremble beneath his expert touch.

"You're perfect."

On instinct, I turn to meet his lips with mine. The sudden kiss intensifies into one of hunger. His hand, which he'd placed at the back of my neck, brings me closer and my fingers grip his jacket near his throat, pulling his face deeper into mine.

Jasmin clears her throat. "I guess they're ready for dessert," she whispers, and Jule pretends to gag.

Then suddenly I hear someone else clear their throat. A deep voice that sounds irritated and infuriated. A chair screeches against the floor as it's dragged back and then forcefully pushed forward. It hits our table with a loud shake.

Surprisingly enough, I recognize who it is and turn slowly to meet Dylan's penetrating gaze. Fuck, he looks like a damn robot cop; patrolling, examining his surroundings, ready to lift up his machine-gun-made arm and blow us to bits. His eyes hold mine, exploring my insides, and I cower away from Noah.

"I thought perhaps I would leave my card, in case you decide you want to talk."

Noah takes the small rectangular business card. I touch my lips and wipe away the extra moisture.

"And *this*?" Noah's brow is arched as he waits for the rookie to respond. I take the card from his hand and notice Dylan's hand-written a number on the back.

"My cell phone. I'm hardly ever at my desk, too much to do out here."

My face burns, and my voice gets lost somewhere between my lungs and throat. Noah's arm around my waist tightens, most likely trying to control his impulse to attack the cop, and I'm brought back to the reality of being his girlfriend. Of how fucked up it would be for me to make an inappropriate and perhaps flirtatious comment. It reminds me of the fact that I had promised to try harder, and as difficult as it may be, I grit my teeth and toss the card across the table.

"That's not necessary. I won't be calling since there's nothing for me to recollect."

Dylan seems torn as his eyes sweep over me and then to Noah's arm around my waist. His glare stays where Noah's hand possessively grips my hip. He freezes and then looks at his business card. His lips twist in agitation. "Whatever," he grunts and then stalks off.

"What a strange guy," Jasmin suddenly says, a straw between her lips. She takes a long sip from her coke. "Hot as hell, but *strange*."

"Kind of young to be a detective, ain't he?"

Noah shrugs at my brother's inquiry, then he takes his hand from my waist and rolls his shoulders. I glance at him—his tight jaw, furrowed brows, elbows firmly on the table, with angry, balled fists under his chin.

Noah never halts his advances or backs away from me. On the contrary, he enjoys and takes advantage of every instant he's by my side, and he never takes for granted my acceptance or responses. The distance unsettles me.

"What's wrong?"

Like he hadn't realized he'd backed away, he turns slowly, his temple rests over his fists, and smiles. "Nothing," Noah scoots closer, then wraps his arm around my shoulders, bringing me closer. "Are you having fun?"

I quickly glance at my brother and best friend, both giggling and truly enjoying our time in this fancy place. I nod, then give Noah a small kiss. "I am."

It's been too long since I last saw my brother this happy. Usually, his eyes are glazed with sorrow.

"And this is just part of your gift."

"What are you talking about, Noie?"

Noah's wide smile quickly morphed into laughter. "I love it when you call me that."

I usually called him Noie to poke fun at him, but lately, I voiced it more as a term of endearment. Ever since we were kids, it was my nickname for him, and I'd enjoy watching him writhe, but now it only caused him to laugh and then kiss me. He didn't disappoint. Noah brings me close, embracing me. I mumble under my breath about him not answering my question when the server comes back with the dessert menu. Our faces light up.

A hard pounding at the door startles me out of my half-twin-sized bed. I fall to the floor and stir Jasmin to unearth from her cocoon. We share a tiny mattress and we worked late last night. She worked at a club and I scrapped for metal. I worked whatever odd jobs the agency supplied me with.

Her eyes are rimmed with dark make-up and she opens them to slits. "Did someone knock?"

I'm on the floor and crawling to the door. "Who the fuck would even think to wake us up? Whoever it is knows better." I'm mumbling nonsense under my breath when the trailer's door creaks open and lets in the eye-stinging sunlight.

I shield my eyes. "What!" I growl at the person who I still can't manage to see through the brightness and temporary blindness the sun caused me.

"Is this a bad time?"

My legs straighten from my awkward position on the floor, and I rub my eyes. I can't believe who it is and I'm unable to speak his name for fear of being wrong. But after taking in his ordinary, casual clothes and the steel hard body clearly underneath, and then briefly allowing myself to gaze up to those large dark eyes, I question instead whether I'm hallucinating or dreaming.

"Who told you where I lived?"

Dylan chuckles and sweeps his hand over his scalp as if forgetting he chopped off his short, tousled hair. He then digs his hands into his jean pockets. My eyes trail over his heavily tattooed arms, the black swirls slipping away from my view under his gray t-shirt, and I desperately look elsewhere to distract my already wandering thoughts. Why does this rookie cause such twisted feelings inside me? I don't want to like him, let alone be attracted to him. Besides, I'm Noah's girlfriend and I *love* Noah.

"Can we talk?"

My answer is automatic. "No." And like he didn't expect that to be my response, Dylan leans his weight on one leg and frowns. *Fuck.* He's even sexier when he seems vulnerable.

I look behind him and around, my skeptical neighbors watching us closely. It's obvious, even out of his uniform, that he's a cop. Damn it, if people around here begin to think I'm cooperating with law enforcement, I'm dead! It's an unspoken oath of mine—I share my information with the people and the people alone. My credibility would be shot. Cops never help us, so why help them?

"Listen, I just want to help you. I understand you don't trust me. Are your parents around? Perhaps I can speak with them instead, and seeing as to how you're a minor—"

I cut him off right there. Any attraction is sliced off by the blade of his ignorance. "You *obviously* haven't done your research. Have your partner tell you all about Case 97-081E. And don't you *ever* come knocking at my door so damn early in the fucking morning again."

I slam the door in his face and crawl back to the bed.

Or at least I think I do because when I finally wake up, I'm on the floor and *still* a few feet from the bed. Jule is home from work and the smell of the strongest coffee hits me like a train.

Jule chuckles under his breath. "Hi, Nik."

I roll to face the ceiling of our two-hundred-twenty square footage living quarters. I'm not an expert in measurements, but if I were to lie down with my hands raised above my head and my feet touching the wall, my hands would need to only reach a few more inches in order to graze the wall. That's how big it is in width. Regardless of its size, it's home.

I bend my knees, plant my feet on the ground, and stare at the ceiling until another scent reaches me. "Where did you get bacon?"

"Noah sent it over." He chews a mouthful of a thin, crispy strip.

"It's *so* good, Justice, seriously. You've got to try it." Jasmin sits in the tiny bed with a plate filled with bacon and a steamy mug between her knees.

My mouth waters. I hadn't had bacon since my parents cooked in this kitchen. Jule tosses me a strip and smiles, reading my mind. When I sit up, he extends an arm, a mug in hand. "Black, just how you like it."

"The bacon or the coffee?"

"Both," he laughs.

I take a bite at the same time I reach for my coffee and sigh, a warm buzz in my belly that reminds me of home takes over. Well, it's more like a moan. I sit on the floor, with my back to whatever wall holds me there, and travel to a much simpler time. A time when working like a slave through the night until five in the morning wasn't on my agenda. I close my eyes while I chew and sip. I wanted to go to college, be a journalist. I had dreams.

It's all I can do to hold on to the past until Jasmin brings me back. "Hey, didn't that cute cop come by earlier, or was I dreaming?"

I groan. Dylan isn't cute, he's fucking hot.

"Ugh, I sent him off. *Who* in their right mind would wake me up?"

Even my roommates, who are my family, know better than to wake me. Hell, even if I was on the ground they wouldn't, hence them savoring breakfast while I snored on the floor.

Jule leans toward me. "A cop?"

I nod, unable to respond. I'd stuffed like three hot and crispy slices of bacon into my mouth.

Jasmin speaks for me. "I didn't hear much, since I was really more asleep than awake, but he said he wanted to help. Then I think he asked to speak to your parents and Justice slammed the door in his face."

"Now that's my Nikoletta!" Jule chortles.

I shake my head, still unable to understand why Dylan insists on playing the role of 'good cop'. It doesn't suit him. He looks more like a well-groomed biker about to bash someone's head in with a crowbar. Besides, he gives off this eagerness to be part of something and acts like wearing a badge is an honor. It doesn't suit him.

I can't stand the thought of a cop near my home after all they haven't done for us. He wanted to help? Help with what? And that reminded me, how had he known I was there that night? I doubted that someone would actually fully cooperate regardless of recognizing me in that terrible storm. Did this mean Piper spoke about me?

"Justice, are you alright?" The concern in Jasmin's voice unfreezes me.

I blink and set my coffee on the ground beside me. "I was just wondering how that cop heard I had a gun, how he found out where I lived, *and* why he's pretending to care so much."

Jule straightens. "We gonna go talk to those two girls now?"

I nod. "I think we should."

5

Justice

Jule fidgets impatiently while Piper serves us tea. I watch her, enthralled by how she expertly pours the hot water from the metal pot into four fragile, tiny cups. I'm not a tea drinker, and neither is my brother, yet our hostess politely declined our inability to act like guests.

This meeting had turned into an evening chit-chat and not the aggressive scheme I had in mind. I had come here, pounded on her door with my overly grown teenage brother at my side, and then barked at her. It wasn't until I realized she was dressed differently, in sweats and a hoodie, with a warm smile on her face while inviting us in, that I quieted and relaxed.

Her sister Macy sits in front of me, perched quietly with her hands folded over her lap, her tired and puffy eyes scrutinizing our every move. She is prettier than I remembered; her dark blonde, straight hair is combed ordinarily, and she wears simple, tight black sweatpants with a red t-shirt that says *Volleyball* in white bold lettering on the front.

"Sugar in your tea?" Piper calls to us.

It's all so fucking strange. Having tea in a meat shop. Sure, the place has been renovated, although its basic structure is still the same. The backside is turned into a rather small yet cozy living area, complete with one loveseat, two recliners, a coffee table, and a cot lying near the far wall with puffy, warm blankets folded neatly near the edge. A basic plastic table, I hope has never held raw or cooked meat on it, has a few basic pots, pans, two plates, two plastic cups, as well as a handful of spoons. I have no idea where Piper materialized these four tea cups from, and I don't care to find out.

Jule nods to a question I'm not paying attention to—I'm much too engrossed with how this space has transformed in just one day.

"Thank you."

My brother's voice is husky, and it quakes slightly. Nothing too obvious for our two hostesses to spot, but I know my kin.

"Why don't we cut to the chase, Piper? I'm not here to drink tea, so might as well get to it."

Macy's eyes grow wide with my outburst, yet she smiles politely at her sister while carefully cupping her tea as if it were flammable. She dares a look at me, and her cheeks burn red when she notices me looking at her. Her eyes drop to her tea as if she wants to shrink, dive into it, and drown instead of listening to me speak.

Piper sits next to her sister and plants my cup on the coffee table directly within my reach. I roll my eyes at her and she smiles when my brother takes a small sip. Something about the taste makes him grin like a fool, and I look away, ignoring the traitor.

"I know why you're here, kid," she says calmly.

I grit my teeth. "Did you tell those cops about me?"

"*What*? No! Why, did someone witness what happened?" Piper's voice cracks, and something about the way she moves tells me she isn't lying; she has no idea the cops are on to me. She sets her tea down, her eyes glued to my face. Next to her, Macy reaches for her hand, the blood drained from her cheeks.

"Apparently someone did," I stutter, taken aback by their reactions. "Those two cops tracked me down, said they were told about the gun and everything."

The cup in Macy's trembling hand rocks. She picks her feet up and folds them up and underneath her.

"I thought you were here to persuade me to show the images on your blog," Piper whispers.

"Well, that's partly why I came, but only because I was confused. First, you didn't want me to share the info, and then you tell the cops? It didn't make sense."

Piper throws an arm around her sister's shoulders. "Yeah, well, it didn't make sense 'cause I'm no snitch."

It's as if she's trying to control herself, but her voice increases in volume and the veins on her forehead pulse. This was the Piper I had met the other night, and it dawns on me that the only reason she was trying to control herself was for the sake of her sister. Who, unlike the previous day, is wide awake and attentive to our conversation.

I draw a deep breath. "Right, I get that now. Well, it must have been the person that called the sirens to begin with, I guess."

"What is it that you're not telling us?" I almost jolt out of my seat upon hearing Jule's thunder-like voice. I forgot he was here.

"*That's* none of your business. I'm going to ask that you please leave... now." Piper's voice morphs into a menacing, low growl. Macy buries her face into her sister's chest, obviously terrified by our conversation.

I understand Piper's eagerness to protect her sister, but Jule is right. There's something she isn't telling us, and if it puts my family in danger, I have the right to know. I stand and signal Jule to do the same.

"Remember what I told you before–we're on the same side here. You can trust me."

Piper's eyes glisten, and she buries her chin in her sister's hair. "I'm sorry, kid. But I don't trust my own shadow. What makes you think you're an exception?"

I nod and turn to leave.

Forget her. If she doesn't want my help, then her problems will no longer interest me. I have far too much to worry about to be concerned with helping out a pair of skinners that don't want my help to begin with.

I'm mumbling exactly those words under my breath and reaching for the doorknob to the back door when I realize Jule isn't by my side. I turn, panic-stricken, and see him place a small piece of paper on the coffee table.

"We truly do want to help. Believe me, there's a lot we may not seem to understand, but we do. Nik's just hard-headed." Jule is looking at them, his back facing me as he points in my direction. He turns, still smiling one of the most charming grins I've ever seen on him, and joins me.

Piper's brows furrow in confusion, but it's her sister's gleaming green eyes that strike me the most.

"Thank you," Macy says, staring at Jule.

It's the first time I hear her speak. Maybe even the first time she's *ever* spoken by the way Piper stares at her, shocked. I'm not about to stick around to unearth the secrets of their vocabulary, so I stalk off. Jule waves like an idiot and repeats the words *you're welcome*, like eight times before finally closing the door.

"What did you write on the paper?"

Jule has this stupid grin on his face, one I can only recognize as a 'star-struck smirk'.

"Our home address."

I stop walking. "Why the *hell* did you do that?"

"That *could've* been our mother, Nik. I'm sorry, but what else was I supposed to do? They look terrified, and if we don't help them, who the hell will?"

I look away, rolling my eyes in the process. I hate it when he's right. When did my little brother grow up, when did he begin to understand the complexities of life, when did he mature enough to outwit me? Wasn't I chastising him to respect these two women just the other day?

Fuck. "Alright fine, just wipe that stupid smirk off your face."

We walk and then jog through the sharp bends and curves of the maze-like quadrants, stopping against dark alley walls only when we come close to being spotted. We can't afford to be detected. On our way, we notice various police vehicles, as well as a few officers, walking the streets.

Jule says nothing, but we share the same expression and most likely our thoughts coincide. Either these cops are seriously looking to find the girl with the Tec9 or Vork has finally attacked prime skin. Who the hell are these two girls, and what do they know? I can't risk going back. The evening is rolling by quickly, and I have to get ready for work.

My hungry stomach rumbles as I squeeze into some black pleather tights. I curse under my breath and wriggle into an equally tight, dark blue corset, which makes my already abundant chest stick out. I sit on the small, squeaky bed and feel the bodice wrap around my torso like an anaconda about to feast on its prey. I can barely breathe.

"I'm not going to last the night with this ridiculous outfit, Jasmin."

"Well, that's what you get for not owning your own."

She sounds like my mother, but she's right, though. I have to wear one of her many skimpy work outfits tonight since my regular attire—jeans, sneakers, and a t-shirt—are unacceptable dress code.

I stare at my best friend. The differences between Jasmin and me go beyond height. Aside from being five inches taller than me, Jasmin is thin with smooth, dark skin, bright caramel eyes, and luscious, tight curls. She's a Dominican goddess.

"Whatever, toss me my shoes."

"Are you insane? You'll ruin the look with your Chuck's. Wear Mom's heels."

"Now you're the one who's insane."

What did it matter what shoes I was wearing? All I was going to do all night was usher partygoers of a much higher class into a busy nightclub on the outskirts of this fucked up city. I would not sit for the rest of the night, let alone lean on a wall, so why would I want to parade around in heels? Only a crazy person would put their feet through such torment. But Jasmin reaches for my shoes and shoves them inside a drawer, then digs around until she finds a pair of insanely high-heeled pumps she seems satisfied with.

"Damn it, Jas. Curse the day I said I'd fill in for your friend."

"You need the money, Justice... *That's* why you agreed, so just keep your mind on that and not your clothes. Besides, everyone there will be dressed in much less, *trust* me."

I'd been dodging Jasmin's attempts to get me to work with her at the nightclub. The thought of being surrounded by people, loud music, sweat, and booze I can't drink? No thanks. But she's right, we could use the extra income. I nod dismissively and reach for my camera. I sit on the floor and skim through the footage.

"It's gone," I gasp.

Jasmin spins around. "*What*?"

"The images, the video... it's all fucking gone." I press the buttons frantically and scroll left and then right.

Jasmin drops to the floor next to me and resists the urge to yank the device away to search for it herself. Our gazes lock.

"Has this ever happened before?"

I look around, my eyes bouncing from one surface to another. "Yea, but ... I always thought it was due to my weak ass equipment. It's the first time with the Pentax."

I drop the camera and lean into the wall. My eyes burn. For the first time, I had concrete evidence. My first initial thought rushes to Piper, but she's never even held my camera. I don't know of anyone else close enough to erase the data, who would want to jeopardize my work.

"Fuck," Jasmin and I both blurt in unison.

6

Justice

I'm all business, or so I think, as I stand around, ignoring the throbbing ache of my sore feet. Really, it's like being a poster girl or something. As if my stance alone will lure people inside. *Ribbons* is a massive brick building with tinted black, door-sized windows. It's a warehouse of booze and frivolity and dancing; a mixture between alley and dark class inside, and somehow, it's packed with more people I think exist in my district alone.

It's unnerving.

My hands feel all clammy and fidgety, *so unlike me.* My job is to stand near the three security guards as they pretend to assess IDs and maintain a somewhat civil conduct of the long line rimmed around the building's exterior. A blackened, thin, and poorly set up tent hovers above us, not nearly protecting us from the light droplets of the rain.

I've been out here for three hours, and my shift requires me to stay four more. It's excruciating and fucking boring. Mainly, I walk the line and glimpse IDs with a tiny blue flashlight, smiling like a complete fool. If they're over twenty-one, I provide their willing left wrists with a bright, canary-colored bracelet. I've strapped them on quite snugly, motivated to prevent underage drinking on my clock.

But since the rain started, Howard, the eldest of the guards, ushered me to the dry area of the tent and asked me, in his commanding yet polite voice, to simply stand around as if I were the club's muse or something.

I never got a chance to explore inside. We arrived right on time and I entered through the back door and went downstairs to report. Then I went out back and was guided to the front with Howard and the rest.

"What's your name, kid?"

I look up and smile. Howard's black leather jacket has collected rain over his shoulders, and his drenched hair cascades over his bright gray eyes. I realize then that none of them have engaged me in conversation, just orders. In fact, I only know his name because I heard the others calling him. Seems he's the one in charge of the security bunch.

"Justice."

The smile he gives me doesn't reach his eyes. "Are you cold?"

I shake my head, aware that my arms are covered with tiny goosebumps and that I've wrapped my arms around myself. This is strange weather for us, where it hardly rains. And I get cold easily. Always have.

"Sure? You can go inside… help your friend. I believe she's filling in for a server today."

I smile big. I would like nothing more than to go home, but meeting Jasmin in the somewhat comfort of the warmth inside is enticing. Better than this, at least. I nod.

"Be careful in there, kid."

I frown but head in, puzzled by his warning. Those thoughts quickly scatter once I'm inside. A kaleidoscope of waving lights assaults me and I immediately look down. Besides the pulsing of the lasers, it's dark, and the loudness of the music vibrates off every surface of the hall. The lights flash in sync with the music, a song I recognize, and it's a relief it isn't some bad techno beat that no one can move to, anyway. *Closer* by *Nine Inch Nails* reverberates through the air.

Strange, I thought it would be filled with songs by pop artists. I shrug my music thoughts aside and approach the young and stunningly pretty girl in a booth to my right.

"Do you know where Jasmin is?"

She scrunches her face, managing to look as striking as a model, and pivots her head. She brings her hand to her ear. "What?"

"Jasmin! Where is she?" I shout back.

"Oh! Not sure, but she's in there somewhere."

I nod back, mouthing a simple *thanks*. Why couldn't I get *her* job? She gets to sit down!

With as much grace as I can manage in these killer heels, I waltz in and stand near the entrance between the end of the corridor and the beginning of the colossal dance room before me. On each side of me, a porch-like balcony circles around the club's interior. Every fifty feet or so, four steps lead to another balcony and then fifteen steps toward the main floor.

The main floor is alive with bodies moving to the beat of the obscene, non-censored lyrics. On the second level, near each staircase, a pole dancer moves in synchronized, calculated staccatos. I swallow and brace myself. I've stayed away from clubs, too many people. I mentally thank Jasmin for urging me to stay outside.

The dancers are clearly in their element. I watch them, envying their sexy glares and pouting lips. It's as if they were born to dance and entertain. I can't imagine Jasmin taking their place—public nudity isn't really her scene. She's got a seductively thin body with siren-like looks. I writhe uncomfortably. Would I fit in? No, I'm short, petite, but thick, with a condescending attitude and a face that says I-can-care-less and I'm-too-young. I know this, Jule tells me all the time. My personality is shit and clearly, you need people skills in order to work in a place like this. Which is why I work with metal scrap... it doesn't talk back. I've never been the loquacious type.

"Looking for Jas?"

Startled, I spin to my left, hands coming out as if I'm the new *Karate Kid* and this is my movie.

"Easy, I took your timecard, remember?"

Giving him what I know is an uneasy smile, I try to relax. My cheeks burn. Thank God it's dark. He smiles back, and I notice a tray in his hands. It has three glasses filled to the brim with a dark brew.

"She's over there. Here, take this to her. She'll teach you what to do."

I swallow hard and take the tray and he leaves almost immediately. I take the steps down to the swarming bodies and edge closer to my best friend, who's leaning near a table with four men our age.

They're all taken by her, grinning like fools and showering her with large, gratifying tips. As I get closer, I realize they're playing a drinking game and she's acting as their referee. I stand nearby, tray in hand, and gawk.

This is not my best friend/sister, Jasmin. This is Aphrodite working a well-stowed magic I've never before, until this day, seen. She giggles, only it doesn't sound like the silly laugh she exhorts at home. Not even the frantic ones when she's being tickled by Jule and me.

It's as if she has an alter ego, a vixen hidden away for work, and suddenly I feel like I'm intruding. Here I thought I'd be able to find comfort in someone who would be equally loathing their time here—she always complains about how much she hates her job.

"Hey, who's your friend?"

Jasmin turns and her face drops. Hastily, she grabs her tips and shoves them in the tiny apron hanging on her hip. "Excuse me, boys. Don't go far now!"

Her sexy smile drizzles away once we're out of earshot and she tugs at my arm toward the long bar against the opposite wall. "What are you doing here?"

I shrug. *Why am I in trouble? You're the one with the secrets!* "Working."

She sighs heavily, then takes the platter from me and places it on the bar. "Melanie, we're taking ten."

Melanie is short and curvy like me, but *unlike* me, she's in her element. She nods at Jasmin and then snaps her fingers. We don't hear the sound but two girls pop out from the back, both wearing black brassiere tops and boy shorts with long, knee-length, high-heeled boots. Jasmin tugs at my arm and pulls me through the swarming bodies and out to the back alley.

Two security guards nod their greetings and resume their breaks. Four usher boys, one smoking, two drinking out of water bottles, and one leaning on the wall like he's about to crumble from exhaustion, ignore us. Jasmin leads me to the edge where no one can hear us, but they can still see us.

Her eyes are wide with—what? Shame, guilt, fear? I don't know, it's hard to tell, but what *is* obvious is that my best friend is back, her vixen stowed.

"I can explain."

"No, you don't have to. You're working... I get it."

She sighs and leans against the brick wall, letting the light rain cover her face. I notice just then that she's changed. She's wearing the same red corset, but her pants are gone, replaced by tight, black spandex-like boy shorts and her red pumps. "I hate my job."

"Doesn't seem like it," I retort and regret my words instantly. She's looking at me, her big honey eyes tearful, and that heavy shame-filled expression is back. "I'm sorry. I didn't mean to hurt your feelings or anything, but it's the truth. You know I don't do the sympathy thing very well."

"No, you don't. Listen, I hate this shit, don't doubt that. Most of us do."

I grimace and begin to roll my eyes when she snaps her lips.

"Yes, even the dancers. You think this is some childhood dream that has come true for me? Growing up, I wanted to be a fucking nurse, for fuck's sake. A nurse!"

She's angry, an emotion I hardly see evoked from my best friend. It's such a shock that a small, palliative smile pulls at my lips.

"You don't look even a bit threatening, especially in underwear."

She gasps, realizing that she's in her actual uniform in front of me.

"Oh, shit." She takes a deep breath, calming herself, I think. "I knew this was a mistake."

Mistake… bringing me to her job was a mistake? Suddenly, I want to convince her otherwise. "I'm not upset." Am I? Well, yes, I am. But not for the reason she thinks. "Why didn't you tell me?"

She turns and gapes at me. "I don't know. It's not something I'm proud of."

"Well, it isn't like I'm proud of being a garbage picker, Jasmin. Shit, you make way more money than I do. No wonder you bought me that expensive ass camera!"

We laugh suddenly, the atmosphere instantly changing between us. "I guess it's the reason I haven't left. Besides, I'm good at it. I don't know why… I just am."

She looks lost, contemplative, and guilty again. It tugs at a bond sewn by years and years of loving her as if we shared the same womb once, and I pull her into a tight hug. "I'm not ashamed, Jas, just upset you felt you had to lie to me."

She nods and my eyes hold her. "Just because I thought you worked at a regular dance club," meaning no nudity, "doesn't mean shit, Jas. I don't care."

"In that case, maybe next time you should come work at the other club. I'm a supervisor there and the money is—" she sucks in air and smiles wide. "*Phenomenal.*"

"Hey! Lesbian Night is on Wednesdays. Back to work!"

We both turn to face the manager, a tall man in his mid-forties, all business-like and erratic about keeping his employees busy. We giggle to ourselves. "This is my sister, Mr. Carver, not my lesbian partner."

"I don't care about your relationship, Jasmin. Back to work, all of you! Break's over, we have some very important clients inside. I need all hands on deck."

Jasmin and I nod, then make our way in through the kitchen. "Speaking of lesbian partners, does Sara know?"

The look on her face gives me the answer, and my heart sinks. I stop walking and she turns when she realizes I'm no longer at her side.

"Jasmin, no more fucking secrets." My voice is serious and husky.

She nods sheepishly and takes my hand.

The men who were out back taking their break, scuttle through anxiously. One of them gives Jasmin a knowing look. "You won't guess whose car just pulled up."

Jasmin gives him a quizzical nod. "Who?"

"Justice, you *cannot* be caught with this, or my boss will have us both gagged and thrown in crates until we suffocate on our own fucking bile."

We're behind the bar area and she's holding my camera and has this if-you-get-me-fired-I-will-be-the-one-to-kill-you look. It's very amusing.

"Relax, I do this for a living, remember? Besides, do you think I'm going to pass up sharing this? The mayor is here—*Ribbons*! He's out there, occupying a private section. He's ordered expensive booze and entertainment. *The mayor*!"

Jasmin rolls her eyes at me. "I know, I know. Very juicy gossip—"

"I don't gossip, I'm a journalist. It's very different."

"Well, there's a fine line between those two. Look, Mayor Carlton has paid for our private deck. No one is supposed to know he's here. He's *paying* for privacy and *discretion*."

"What he's paying for is young girls, like you and I, to dance around naked at arm's length. He's spending our tax money on booze and girls, and you're worried about the cerro's *privacy*?"

Jasmin sighs, fully exasperated, and it's quite unsettling. Usually, she's very supportive of me. What's the deal? It's not like I'll get caught. I'm a pro at what I do.

"I can care less about the pig. What I do care for, in very high dosages, are our asses."

"No one here recognizes me. Your boss will never know it was me who filmed him. Please, Jasmin, *please*."

"Fine," she sighs and I hug her, a squeak escaping my lips.

I stuff the camera into my apron and head on out. Melanie's swamped with drink orders, and I decide to help her catch up before resuming my duties. It's half-past two in the morning, the peak hour of the night. *Ribbons* stays open until five, yet half the people here are drunk already. I silently wish they either have half a brain to order an Uber or had arranged to have a designated driver among them.

"Melanie, I need Bridget to attend to our guest in the left wing. A very important visitor has specifically asked for her."

I'm filling five glasses with fruity drinks, my back to Jas's boss and Melanie, but I catch her reaction in the mirror in front of me. Her face pales and her lips press into a hard, grim line.

"She's only fifteen, Robert, you know this. It's the reason she *only* works the coats."

The boss, Robert, approaches her. He's inches from her face, a head taller than her. "It's the mayor, Melanie. What am I supposed to tell him?"

"Well, her age, of course."

"I did. The bastard said he already knew that. He asked her himself on the way in. He likes 'em young, Mels. What am I supposed to do?"

My body freezes; I've heard too much. Mayor Carlton has pedophilic desires and pays a great deal to keep it a secret. Here I thought him sick to enjoy girls half his age strip. No, it's way younger that hits his sickening funny bone. And I get to catch the perv—it's my lucky day. I watch Melanie's face fall and she reaches for the bar as if to stabilize herself.

Robert looks to the ground and then recovers. "Don't make him wait."

I serve the already drunk guys their fruity requests, shove the tips into my apron, and sneak underneath the bar. If I'm to do this, I mustn't be seen heading in that direction.

The left-wing is a fairly large chamber with a burgundy red, plush rug, deep purple walls with gold piping, and there's a single white and very long U-shaped couch with round cherry wood end tables on each side. An extraordinary chandelier hangs from the center of the room, its light a dim, omniscient shade that makes the room look more like a womb. Directly across from the couch is a small stage with two dance poles. Behind that are layers of wine-colored satin curtains separating a hidden corridor from the entire room.

I find refuge behind the curtains and crouch near the edge, my camera in position. Bridget isn't here yet, and Mayor Carlton is angrier than a rattled bee. The bastard positioned himself right in the center of the couch, a glass in hand with what seems to be brandy served with a few cubes of ice. Three security guards, no doubt his, linger behind him, each standing with their hands folded in front of them.

"I've been waiting for half an hour! What's fucking taking so long?"

The guard to his left, my right, moves, and seconds later returns with a very timid, beet-red Bridget. She's wearing red panties, a sheer and sparkly red tutu, along with a simple black bra. She's barefoot.

Mayor Carlton licks his lips and extends his hand to her. "Oh, so sweet, come here, baby. Come."

She's frozen in place, staring at her hands and fidgeting uncomfortably.

"I won't ask you again, baby."

Bridget looks up, startled, and it takes all my strength to not run out there and insult him and then run away with her. My first instinct is to throw an oversized raincoat on her, put her in some slippers, then serve her something warm while she sits comfortably and safe. My hands are trembling, and I realize I've been holding my breath. So I sit on my ass and rest the camera on my knees to steady it.

Bridget moves cautiously toward Carlton, but doesn't take his hand. Instead, she readjusts her tutu and squares her tiny shoulders, her chin up high. "You've requested a dance, yes?" Her voice is small, but surprisingly strong, in a way.

El cerro smiles wickedly and signals to the pole. He nods at one of his guards, who steadily walks toward one of the end tables and starts the music. It's a fancy Bluetooth speaker–I think it's the first time I've been in the presence of one, but I remain still, not once eyeing it, and keep my eyes on Bridget and *el cerro*.

Bridget's face is full of fear, and her eyes are glistening. My camera catches this, he does not, because when she turns back toward him, she's morphed before us. I'm reminded of Jasmin, how she, too, transforms drastically before my eyes. Bridget takes hold of the pole and slowly slides down and begins a rather awkward dance.

I'm thrown back, unable to keep watching. So instead, I focus on the camera, making sure it stays on cue, and I go numb. Such corruption and sickness, I can't bear it. Bridget turns suddenly and faces my direction and bends, then grasps her ankles. Carlton's breath hitches and he moves to stand. It's really the first time I'm seeing him; I've only ever heard of him but have never had the pleasure, or disgust, of seeing him in the flesh.

Oddly, something about him makes me think of Piper and her sister Macy. Mayor Carlton has the same reddish hair and light green eyes. His square jaw matches that of Piper's, his nose exactly like Macy's, the way his mouth sets in a thin and pleased way. And now that he's smiling like a fool, I realize his smile is a copy to Macy's.

No! Didn't Mayor *cerro* have two daughters and one son? Yes... what were their names?

My thoughts are quickly scattered when *el cerro* approaches much too close for both Bridget's, and my, comfort. He suddenly reaches out and grasps her hips, pulling her toward him. He leans down and stuffs his face into her neck.

"You smell so good, baby."

"Please, I'm only here to dance. No touching allowed."

Her voice trembles and her next breath catches in her throat as he lowers one hand to cup her ass. He squeezes, then slips his hand inside her panties. She screams and he shoves his hand deeper. I can't bear it. I shut off the camera, toss it into my apron, and I'm about to attack him with all I've got when Howard appears out of nowhere. He's standing behind Mayor Carlton, all tall and beefy and menacing.

"Enough! This isn't that kind of place and she isn't that kind of girl. Let her go!"

Shocked, Mayor *cerro* lets her go and Bridget runs out of the room. As quickly and as quietly as I can, I walk backward and sneak out to the main floor like a fucking fox.

Jasmin pushes me into the maintenance closet and shuts the door. "Fuck, Justice, you look like you've seen a ghost. What the hell happened in there? I was so worried! I sent Howard to check things out, just in case you'd been caught and were slowly getting killed or something. Did he see you?"

Her voice is panicked, and I want to reassure her that no one saw me, but I can't. The words can't find their escape; they're stuck somewhere between my lungs, throat, esophagus, pharynx, *whatever*.

Jasmin shakes me. "Say something, Justice. Did they catch you? Oh, God, they caught you!"

"No," I manage to croak out. I shake my head, trying to clear it. "No, I wasn't caught. But if you didn't send Howard over, I would have been."

"What are you talking about?"

"Mayor Carlton requested a private dance from Bridget." I nod as my best friend's eyes go wide and she gasps, her hand clutching her chest and then her mouth. "She was doing her thing, and the next thing you know, that fucking pig gets up and starts fondling her goods. Right before I could kill the fucker, Howard came in and stopped him."

"Shit, that asshole!"

"Not so concerned about his privacy now, are you, Jas?"

She ignores my snide comment, her bewildered expression haunting. "What happened next?"

"I don't know. I ran out of there, just as Bridget did. But I did get enough data on my camera. This pedo is going down, Jas."

She breathes a sigh of relief. "I don't know what I would've done if something happened to you. Let's go find Bridget."

I nod, and she takes my hand. We emerge from the smelly closet and warily look around.

"Hey, Melanie, where's Bridget?"

Melanie calls us over like she wants to tell us a secret. "Where have you two been?" she hisses.

"We were with Drunk Guys Fifty-Two."

Melanie nods and accepts Jasmin's explanation. I have no idea what she just said, but I nod like I do.

"Bridget's gone home. She wasn't feeling good. Gerald took her, and I'm not sure she'll be coming in tomorrow."

"*Oh*, okay. If you see her, tell her I have her money." Melanie arches a brow in question and Jasmin sighs. "We take part in money pools, and her number came up. I'm sure she needs her cash. Just tell her to sweep by my place anytime."

This, I know, is true. A few people enter a pool of savings. Each person gives fifty dollars every week for three months. At the beginning of the draw, every person has a number which refers to the order in which you get your money. It's sort of like a savings—money that you're stowing and aren't touching until your number comes up. I never knew Bridget entered them, because usually, only the person in charge of the drawing knows the details.

Melanie nods but looks deep in thought, far away, and I'm sure I know what she's thinking. She's wishing the rag her hands are wringing was the *cerro's* neck. Hell, I wish that!

Jasmin pulls me toward the table upstairs with a bunch of drunken men our age. "This group is Drunk Guys Fifty-Two. We usually name our repeated guests."

Right when she's explaining, one of the guys throws a deck of cards in the air and they fly around, making them all laugh hysterically, and they signal us over. Jasmin smiles at them, then turns to me and rolls her eyes. "Hence fifty-two. They throw a deck of cards in the air and have us pick them up so they can stare at our asses. God, I hate my job. Come."

I follow her and she's all goddess, Aphrodite, vixen, and siren, all in one.

"We're back," she says in a sing-song voice I definitely do not recognize. "Shall we pick these up again?"

Oh, me? She's talking to me. I smile awkwardly and drop to my hands and knees with her. The guys are all roaring and hooting and somehow I get it. Her words connect to the explanation she gave Melanie. Drunk Guys Fifty-Two are all so wasted, they'll confuse the time frame and become my alibi. Oh, my best friend is so smart.

"They're going to lavish your waistband with wads of cash. Do *not* swat their hands away, Justice."

As she whispers this to me, I feel three rough hands on my ass. My first urge is to turn around and kick them off their stools, but Jas's warning halts me. It takes all my muscles to coil and retreat. I breathe out as I pick up the last two cards. We stack them on the table neatly and discreetly stow the cash into our aprons before it falls.

We spend the rest of the night with them and even walk them to their cab. I'm relieved to know none of them will crash due to their intoxicated states, and we wave them off. In my backpack is a gallon-sized bag fat with money.

"We'll catch a ride with Howard. He lives in the lot following ours."

We turn and freeze. Leaning against the exterior brick wall of *Ribbons* is Dylan. He shoots us a glare and saunters toward us, and my eyes scan for a way out. Fuck, these damn heels, I know once I make to run off, I'll fall flat on my fucking face.

Jasmin reaches for my hand and squeezes and we watch Howard's pickup truck drive away slowly behind Dylan.

Fuck, fuck, fuck!

7

Justice

Dylan's towering stance reaches us and fills my space with his leathery scent. It activates my senses, and suddenly I'm fully aware of the beast of the man before me. He's over six feet, covered in tattoos, and I don't doubt that if he took off his shirt, they'd invade his entire torso. He's angry, but I don't know why. *Do I even want to know?*

"Stalking is illegal," I blurt out. And Jasmin almost breaks my fingers in her grip.

He angles his head toward the noisy structure behind us. A dark, alternative rock song with explicit lyrics is playing, and the music swirls around us as someone opens the door to exit. My fucking cheeks fume a bright Elmo red, but I act like nothing fazes me. Hopefully, my act will steel my spine. Either that or the ground will miraculously open up and swallow me whole.

"Underage club employment is illegal. Your friend's kinda young, Jasmin. Why'd you bring her to *Ribbons*?"

Jasmin stifles a laugh, and I roll my eyes. Surprisingly, her grip loosens.

I'm so fucking annoyed that people assume I'm eight years younger than I really am. It may be great when you're *old, old,* but when you're already young and people think you're *younger...* it's not a good thing. Young blood is discriminated against quite enough for there to be more hostility. And the night has been so shitty my nerves are all over the place, and my anger doesn't care what aroused it; it's just looking for someone to blame.

"You know, I normally let people assume whatever the fuck they want, but I've had quite enough of it. I'm twenty-two years old, rookie. A consenting, legal adult. Now you can go and fix the fuck-up that your buddies placed in that file of yours."

Jasmin's breath hitches and she's back to squeezing my fingers flat and purple.

The rookie's eyes blanch, the black in them expanding somehow. They pulse and threaten to pop out of his perfect face. His features smooth just as suddenly. "You're far from home. I'll give you two a ride."

He isn't asking, and I ponder this while I'm sure my face turns eleven shades of red. His fists are in his pockets, and I have to look away because I know how much I love to watch his muscles flex when he stretches his arms into his pants.

Noah, Noah, Noah. I chant his name like a fucking mantra to remind me that I'm taken.

"Actually, that would be great. Our ride left us."

I snap my head and gawk at Jasmin. *The fucking traitor!* I want to speak up and tell them both I'd rather walk, but as if reminding me that I most definitely cannot walk thirty something miles back home, my knees buckle with a throbbing pain at the ball of my feet, my poor ankles threaten to give out and put me on my ass.

I give a reluctant nod and Dylan's eyes glimmer in the darkness. His eyes pull enough light from the buzzing lightbulb above the door, illuminating the silver specks that dance in their midnight bliss at something unknown. It's like he's delighted to drive us home, and instantly I'm suspicious. But not enough to say no.

Dylan's car is as sexy as he is. It's all black, leather, and steel and fucking seductive. The engine purrs as he accelerates and grips the steering wheel with one hand while the other adjusts some dials to perfect the air and radio station. I barely hear the music playing softly in the background, my heart is beating in my head.

"You could have sat up front, you know. No one is being arrested tonight."

Jasmin nudges me and I want to fucking smack her thigh away. She wiggles her eyebrows at me and smirks. *He's talking to you,* she mouths. Yes, I know he's fucking talking to me, but I don't know why. I have a boyfriend. I look up and find him staring at me through the rearview mirror.

"We're fine back here," I mumble.

"So, you two work at *Ribbons*?"

Jasmin gives me an angry glare. She wants *me* to talk to the rookie, and I shake my head at her. She relents to pinching my arm and I hold the spot dramatically.

"Um, *I do*. Justice picked up the hours for the extra cash."

The rookie nods and lets out a breath. The small interior allows me to breathe in that same puff of air, and I hold on to it, expanding my chest to feel the mintiness of him inside my lungs, mingling with my own. Jasmin watches me and I exhale in shame, caught up, and I want to sink into the leather seat. Dylan shifts suddenly and his shoulders tense up. I watch his hand grip the steering wheel as if he's falling, and it's the only thing keeping him in this car.

"Where do you normally work?"

He's still talking to me, and Jasmin stabs one finger into my thigh. "She does odd jobs here and there, whatever the agency throws her way. Mostly physical work."

I glare at her and my lips move slowly to mouth, *what the actual fuck?*

He's a cop, damn it. Shut up!

"Physical work?" His words come out slow and husky, and I have the sudden urge to tell him to keep his mind out of the gutter. "And what does Julius do?"

"Are you interrogating me, Detective? Because you haven't read me my rights."

He lets out a chuckle, and the sound literally pulls me toward him. One hand grips the seat directly in front of me, while the other touches the armrest between the two front seats. I want to lean my face into the leather so that I can get a better look at him. His profile view is all sharp-edged, and I can see his neck tattoo dip down past his shoulder. My arm trembles with the need to graze my finger and follow the intricate black ink.

"Relax, Niki. I'm not interrogating you. Just curious."

I bristle at the nickname. "Well, curiosity killed the cat."

"Are you threatening me?" He catches my glare in the mirror, and his eyes swallow up the shadows in the car.

I shrug, feigning a cockiness I don't possess. Not with him, and not about this, but I can't back down. "Maybe."

Jasmin almost clamps her hand over my mouth. "She most definitely is not. I'm sorry, Detective. Justice's mouth gets her in trouble, but she's harmless."

Dylan's knuckles go white from his strong grip on the wheel. I'm afraid it'll crumble to ash from the pressure. "Is your friend right? That mouth of yours get you in trouble?"

I roll my eyes and stare out the window while pushing back into my seat. What the fuck am I supposed to say to that? I cross my arms and glare at Jasmin.

Her eyes are wide as she mouths *Ohmygod,* and she's fanning herself, trying to shrink behind Dylan's seat. I want to strangle her; this is her fault.

"My brother is a minor, and I don't need to tell you what he does unless this relates to an official line of questioning. So, I'll ask again, are you interrogating me, Detective?"

"I already told you I wasn't."

I throw up my hands in frustration. "So why the twenty questions? Can't you just drive in silence?"

Jasmin buries her face into her hands. I shrug, *what*?

She clears her throat. "We aren't used to law enforcement being nice for no reason, Detective. It's... unnerving."

He nods, as if accepting Jasmin's excuse for my shitty attitude. She isn't wrong, but mostly I'm just terrified of how Dylan makes me feel. I should be weak at the knees for Noah. I should be craving Noah. I should be eager for him to return and envelop me in his arms and cherish me the way he does.

Yet all I want to do is run my tongue all over Dylan's skin and taste him. I want his scent permanently seared into my receptors. I want to trace my mouth over the inked lines etched all over his body. I want his full lips between my legs, lapping up the desire he owns in me.

I need to get the fuck out of this damn car.

It takes us forty-five agonizing minutes to get to our county, and it dawns on me that we're in a cop's car. We're a five-minute drive away from where our trailer is, and if anyone spots Jasmin and I getting out of a detective's vehicle, we're fucked. It isn't a police car by any means. In fact, I don't know any officer who owns a car like this one, but still.

"You can drop us off here. We can walk the rest of the way."

"Why would I do that?"

Fucking hell, this man is impossible. "Because you're a cop," I spit through a tight jaw and even tighter lips.

I think I hear Dylan growl, but he pulls over and steps out. His seat folds forward, and Jasmin graciously steps out. I shuffle eagerly and plant one black pump on the ground when my other foot gets caught on the seatbelt. I'm going to fall flat on my fucking face, but Dylan reaches out and firmly grips my waist, and my hands press against his rock-hard chest.

Our eyes lock, and we both hold our breaths, as though we are united by the same life thread—if one seizes to breathe, then so does the other. An innate link that relies on the other for survival. The suppression lasts seconds and then we're breathing again, and we both blink as we inhale one another. His pupils dilate, reminding me that his irises are barely a shade lighter. It's beyond a mere attraction; something about this moment magnetizes itself to my core memories, superseding above all other encounters, practically obliterating any other hold on me.

I don't know if it's because we're afraid to breathe the air between us, or if the jolt of electricity shocked us into immobility, but our next breaths are slow and uneven. I feel his heart beating and the heat of him permeates through his t-shirt and brands my skin. I want to mold into him and press myself against his body and allow the current of my desire to push me past the inevitable fall that tugs at me like a force of fucking nature. His hands move to hold me steady by my elbows, and he stretches behind me to free my trapped ankle. My heel clicks on the cement.

One hand stays cupping my elbow, while his other moves to my face. The familiarity of his hold renders me to this moment, halting me from reacting the way I normally would to anyone else's touch, even Noah's. His thumb grazes my bottom lip, and he tugs it down and dips the tip to touch my teeth. He tastes of salted mint, and I fight the urge to bite the tip of his finger.

As though he heard my thoughts, he inhales a sharp breath and leans into my ear, his lips dangerously close to my pierced lobe, and I imagine his breath collecting on the gold-plated metal. I can feel his stubble scrape by cheek and liquid heat pools at my center.

"I don't believe you're harmless, and I can think of the perfect punishment for this mouth." He squeezes my lip, then lets go.

Fuck, I should've bitten him. I stumble back a step, a cold breeze sweeps up and around me, my skin already feeling the void of his heat.

"Careful, a heel like that can kill a man."

I glare at him. "Here's hoping."

Jasmin rolls her eyes. I'm stumbling toward her when she loops her hand through mine and calls. "Thanks for the ride, Detective."

8
Justice

I'm not sure if she's the greatest best friend/sister in the entire fucking world, but Jasmin has yet to say shit about what she witnessed the night Dylan dropped us off. Aside from looking at me as if she was trying to decipher what was going on in my head, nothing. Not a peep. I was glad because what am I supposed to say? I have the hots for a fucking detective, but I'm dating my childhood friend? No. I can't say that out loud.

I haven't seen either men in four days, and honestly, it feels amazing to not have those thoughts lingering over my head and suffocating the air out of my lungs. The guilt has surprisingly subsided, and I won't question why or what the fuck is going on.

I haven't slept, but at least neither Jule nor Jasmin are talking about my perfect boyfriend or the annoying detective. I'm staring at the ceiling right above my half-twin bed, where I taped a photograph of my parents from before we were born. The picture is of horrible quality, but it reminds me of them, nonetheless. Jule and I have my father's milk chocolate brown eyes and my mother's auburn waves. Jule looks so much like my mother, but in the best way. Not like slapping a wig on Jule would make him her twin or anything like that. I have my father's big toothy smile, and the hole in my chest aches to see it in real life versus the picture. Jule smiles with his mouth closed, like my mom.

It's almost ten in the morning, and the smell of coffee, eggs, and bacon fills the trailer. I only slept about six hours, but I'm too anxious to force it.

"I fixed you girls some breakfast, compliments of Noah."

I frown. *Noah*. The thought of him materializes my guilt, and it sits on my stomach, its steel grip chokes me. "Where is he?"

Jule's mouth is full of scrambled eggs and bacon. Oh, how I love bacon. "Said he would come around later before he went to work." He hands me a foam plate full of eggs, bacon, a slice of toast, and my black coffee.

Jasmin kicks off her shoes and is stuffing her mouth greedily. Her feet look impeccable, although I know she's been strutting her stuff all night in six-inch pumps.

"I'm starving," she attempts to say, her mouth full.

"Noah dropped the meals off about an hour ago and said he would let you rest. I think it was wise of him. You look like hell, Nik."

I roll my eyes and frown at the thought of Noah being incredibly sweet with someone who doesn't deserve it. He knows me well, though, which is why he didn't stick around. What can I say? I cherish my space. But right now, for some inexplicable reason, I want to see him. Maybe it's the guilt. At times, he shares his earnings with us, and why shouldn't he enjoy breakfast with his girlfriend? *Because you're a grouch and have repeatedly growled at him to not be around when you're deprived of energy and food, and right now... you're depleted.*

My frown deepens at my subconscious, but she's so right.

"Hey, where're you going?" Jasmin's got her face buried in her plate but manages to speak through the mouthful of food again.

I grimace while slipping into my Chucks. "I'm gonna go see Noah. You two eat up." I go to my brother and kiss him gently on his forehead, which he wipes away instantly. "Safe trip to work, Jule. Chin up."

With my plate in hand, I walk to Noah's trailer. It takes me fifteen minutes, but once there, I nibble on some bacon while I knock on his door. His mom works the morning shift, so I freely stand before his door with my hair all puffed up, some of the shortest shorts I own, and a tank top. Fuck, I should've thrown something else on.

He opens the door, and his brows shoot up, his eyes sweep down and back up. I think I wear the same expression. He's wearing his PJ bottoms, and they sit low at his hips. He's shirtless and my mouth goes dry. He recovers quicker than me and smiles wide. I stay locked.

"Good morning, beautiful."

I still can't find my voice. I just stare at him with my plate in one hand and my coffee in the other.

"Want to come in?" He moves to the side and I squeeze in past him.

The need to reciprocate his desire for me washes over me like a cold shower.

He's been gone for about a week, and I watch him as he fixes himself something. I'm not sure if it's coffee, tea, or a glass of water. I'm distracted by my obsessive thoughts–why can't I muster a fraction of the enthusiasm he exhibits for whatever it is we have between us?

Noah is attractive, tall enough that if he were to raise his hands, he wouldn't be able to extend them in the trailer. His elbows would probably touch the low ceiling. His body, all V-shaped and toned, moves with grace about his kitchen. I can actually see the muscles of his back flex as he moves about. He turns, rock-hard and rippled abs a mere foot from my reach, and takes a seat in front of me.

Yes, he's beautiful, but I don't want him. *Fuck.*

I notice now that he's fixed himself a plate and a cup of coffee. I take a sip from mine and smile. "Is everything alright?" he asks, eyes hooded, and I have to look away.

He's damn sexy... so why can't I reciprocate his feelings? I love him, that's a fact, but just not in the same way he does me. I wish I could change that, perhaps, if I stop focusing on the guilt that consumes me, I'd be able to just hone in on all the good he does.

"I... just... I–" I sigh. Why am I stuttering?

His brows furrow. "What is it, Justice?"

"I wanted to say thank you—for breakfast."

He looks relieved but also caught off guard. But he smiles wide, my favorite smile, and my chest tightens. Yes, perhaps my feelings for him can deepen. And suddenly, I relax, consoled by the idea that I won't hurt him by not countering his feelings toward me.

"Would you like to stay? I was actually going to catch some Zs before work. You can... lay with me... if you'd like." My cheeks burn. "To sleep, Justice. Not to have sex or anything."

His reassurance makes me redden further. A pang of... what? Disappointment? I'm not sure what the hell I'm feeling. But he fills the silence with his worry. "Or you can just join me for breakfast. Whatever you want is fine with me."

The sleep pattern in our group is a fucking mess. I think Jule is the only one that sleeps during the night. I tend to work two, sometimes three jobs, in one day. If I sleep four hours, that's amazing. I tried to lie down when I got home at two in the morning, but just managed to toss and turn while Jule snored. My shift won't start until one today. My shoulders are up to my ears, and I lean back a bit in an attempt to stretch out the tight muscles.

"I want to stay, if that's okay." I don't look at him.

I think I'm nervous because I *can't* have sex. Or rather, I took a celibacy oath. For months, Jasmin begged me to see a therapist about my promiscuity until I finally relented. According to her, it'd gone too far. I should've never told her I let a random guy at work fuck me on the ground near a pile of scrap metal at the junkyard.

I only agreed because she put her foot down and threatened to tell Helena, the only woman I'd be too embarrassed to admit how far I'd gone to feel something, anything that would hopefully fill some gaping hole inside my chest. The therapist prescribed celibacy for a year. I failed over and over until finally something in me snapped.

Three months in, and I ceded to Noah's pleas to be his girlfriend. But we hadn't had sex, or any other delicious treats.

"Okay. I'm sure you're hungry, though. After we eat, we can sleep, alright?"

I nod, staring at my eggs like an idiot. Noah's hand reaches for mine and he brings it to his lips. "Just let things flow, Justice. There's no pressure here. Just go with your gut."

And his words are like a mantra. He knows me so well. See? This is what I love. It's easier to talk to someone that has an instant hot wire to your thoughts. I'm not much of a talker, and knowing that he understands even though I haven't said a word is a relief. Suddenly, my shoulders relax and I slump down in the chair. Fuck, I didn't even realize I'd been holding in all the tension and finally releasing it feels so good.

"Better?" he asks, his voice soft as he grazes my knuckles against his lips.

"Yea."

"Eat up, Justice. You look like hell."

We eat in silence. Noah reads his paper, sharing with me what the *real* press has to say about my news blog and comments on what he believes has been clearly omitted. It's nice, peaceful, and it settles me in a way I never thought, to be sharing my morning with him. He takes our empty plates and washes them.

"Ready for bed?"

I love Noah's trailer. It's bigger than ours and actually has rooms. Two rooms, to be exact. His mom keeps it tidy and fresh. Being in his home makes me feel like I'm fifteen again... like when my parents were around. The feeling is welcoming, and it almost seeps into my chest. *Almost.*

I nod, my lids heavy. And I'm suddenly thankful for the offer to get some sleep.

We're on his bed, and I twist around and nuzzle into his chest, then unexpectedly run my lips over his skin. Noah presses his body against mine and reaches under my shirt. Thoughts of blackened irises flash before my closed lids and I spring back suddenly.

Son of a bitch. Dylan.

I shuffle away from Noah and move to stand.

"Hey, wait. Don't leave, Justice. I'm sorry."

I stand up and turn. I don't understand why Dylan continues to make an appearance in my head. I don't get it. But Noah thinks he's done something wrong, and he moves hastily off the bed and hugs me close, forcing me to wrap my arms around his torso. He lifts my chin and kisses my cheeks.

"I love you, Justice. I want us to have a future together. I want to marry you someday and maybe kids–the whole enchilada. But you don't want all that... *yet*. I get it, I always have. I'll be as patient as you need me to be."

I can't tell him why I pulled back. It has nothing to do with him. He didn't do anything wrong except the one thing we cannot avoid. He isn't Dylan.

"Come on, let's go to bed." He grabs my hand and then gently coaxes me under the covers.

In an instant, I'm in his arms, my back to his front. I'm suddenly filled with petulant anger. Why the fuck does the rookie get to command my body even when he isn't around? I want to tell it who's boss and force another man into my mind so that the rookie can disappear into nothing.

That being said, I reach for Noah's hand and place it under my top and he caresses my belly gently. My skin tingles and goosebumps cover me. Noah has never touched me like this before, and my body tenses at the intrusion, but I force it to flex and relax. I'm going to force the cop out one way or another.

He opens his palm and pushes me closer to him. His nose is at my neck and he growls. I close my eyes and force myself to melt into his sheets. I have to do this; fuck the celibacy pact that I made for a reason I can't recall.

I can't keep allowing this fucking cop to command jurisdiction over me and govern my every breath. I focus on nothing and enter that empty space in my mind, the one that always waits for me whenever I'd give myself to strangers.

A soft moan escapes my lips as Noah's hand travels up to cup my large breasts. He pinches one nipple and then opens his palm and grips. It barely fits in his hand, and he hisses into my ear. I'm slick and hot between my legs, and I push my ass into his hard dick and wiggle my hips. Not having sex for over six months has me quivering with need like a bitch in heat.

Inked skin coats my inner lids, and I grind my teeth. Time to take it up a notch. I take off my top and press my naked back to his blazing front. He gasps, clearly not expecting this, but recovers by turning me around and in one swift move, he's on top of me.

I keep my eyes shut, afraid that if I open them, reality will stomp out this fire that I lit a match to.

He kneads my breast and bites my neck, and my body involuntarily arches at his touch. His lips are at my jaw and I tremble when my hands glide over his abs and I hook my fingers into his waistband. He groans, the vibrations of his desire firing a need I had locked away.

My lips are at his shoulder, tasting him, and I revel under his rigid yearn for me as he parts my legs with his knee. Suddenly, an ear-shattering pounding at his door rips us apart.

"Who the fuck is that?" Noah hisses.

He's pissed, and I have half a mind to tell him to ignore it, when the person on the other side speaks. "I need a word with Miss Fox. I know she's in there."

Shit, it's Dylan. It's as if the force I projected on shoving him out of my mind caused the universe to summon him.

Noah's eyes go black. "Let the bastard wait in vain."

Dylan pounds on the door again. "I need to talk about your parent's case, Niki. It's important."

He sounds as pissed off as Noah. *Fuck!* But his words tame the sexual deviant in me. I watch as she slips away to the darkest part of my mind. I squeeze Noah's shoulder, and his eyes lock with mine. He trembles past his fury as he hands me my top and stalks to the door and creaks it open.

"This better be good. Justice isn't too keen on having her sleep interrupted after she's worked all night."

Dylan's voice is like hot metal and dry ice. "I can assure you it is. May I come in?"

"Like hell you can. We'll be right out. Just thought I'd let you know before you pounded my damn door down." And with that, Noah shuts the door in Dylan's face.

I'm sitting on his bed when he returns, all jittery and nervous. "What do you think he's gonna tell me about the case?"

Noah combs his hands roughly through his hair. He does this when he's trying to calm himself... it's very cute. But right now, I'm focused on what Dylan could quite possibly have to say. *And not the man I was working out of my thoughts.*

"I don't know... Hey, you better put this on." He tosses me his hooded sweatshirt.

I look at him quizzically and his eyes sweep over my chest, my hard nipples visible through the white material. My face flushes as my shoulders hunch. He wants me to cover my goods since I'm commando under my top. I put the sweatshirt on, thankful he doesn't say anything out loud, and head on out.

Noah shadows me, all bare-chested and grouchy. It's actually in the mid-seventies outside, but I didn't have the strength to argue. He holds my hand and leads me around the trailer where the rookie cop is waiting next to his car.

Involuntarily, I wriggle out of Noah's hand. One of the charms on my mother's bracelet digs into my palm and I focus on the sharp pain. He glances down in question but doesn't say anything.

I hold my breath. It's all I can do to hold back my gaze. Dylan's wearing denim jeans and a black t-shirt. I don't think I've allowed myself to truly see him in daylight. Clearly, he works out. His dark eyes bore at me with an unknown emotion. He glares at Noah, and I think his lips twist slightly, but I'm not sure. He straightens his shoulders and peers at his notepad, then shoves it into his back pocket.

"Think I can have a word with you in private, Niki?"

My response is quicker than my thoughts. "No. Whatever you have to say to me, you can say it to Noah." Beside me, Noah grows ten feet.

Dylan's full lips twist in agitation, and my insides go all nervy, like I'm in third grade and about to get quizzed on shit I've got zero knowledge in. The cocky asshole looks confident, in his element, and all business-like—he's *so* attractive. But I'm soon reminded of Noah, my *boyfriend*.

My emotions begin to feel all twisted and murky again. Fuck, why couldn't the beer belly cop named Lloyd come and deliver this news? I seriously need to put my feelings in check. But for now, I decide to pay attention to the rookie that brings out all these unexpected, and quite frankly, unpleasant, feelings in me.

"Fine, have it your way." Dylan shifts his weight, like a panther who's forced to back away from a kill.

It's very unlike his usual demeanor, and he leans against the hood of his car. I bite my lip and start nibbling at the skin. What if Dylan mentions the night he gave Jasmin and me a ride? I suddenly wish I would've mentioned it to Noah beforehand, but who knew this fucking cop would show up *again*?

He crosses his hands and suddenly appears uncomfortable. "I'm sorry for bringing up your parents when I last came. I looked into the case you mentioned. It's gone cold and kept in a classified, *restricted* section."

He pauses, his brows furrow, and his mouth is set in a tense line. I get the sudden urge to reach out and smooth my thumb over his lips and instantly slap my inner conscious at the ridiculousness of this persistent and nagging craving for this fucking cop. Can't this inappropriate feeling even try to keep itself locked away for the sake of Noah standing here beside me? Fucking hell!

"That's when I realized I needed to get my hands on it," Dylan's voice drops to a low whisper as if he were talking to himself.

"That doesn't surprise me," Noah suddenly says.

"Does it surprise you, Niki?"

I lower my gaze to the dried dirt road. "No."

"Why not?" He's asking the both of us, but his eyes stay on mine.

Noah crosses his arms over his chest. "I guess you missed the orientation session, then. All cases that lead to Vork go cold and end up never being touched again. Regardless of the mounting evidence."

Dylan cocks his head to the side. "Vork?"

Years of calculated undercover work and training, the time I have committed to my blog and reports, pour out of me in an involuntary throng. "Vork, street name for Kennedy Miller: the thug that comes second in command, a henchman, leads an impressive number of corrupt men in the surrounding counties. He owns the fucking streets... all crimes committed begin and end with him, I assure you."

Dylan's big dark eyes lock with mine and they soften, peeling back a sliver of his composure, but all too suddenly, it snaps back, the smooth and cool look of control and professionalism on full blast again.

"There's a lot I'm not aware of... I apologize. It's going to be handled very differently from now on. The point of my visit, however, relates to the increasing amount of data that's been entered into the file... nothing's been sent to the lab *yet*."

"What kind of evidence?" I step forward. I'm practically two feet away from Dylan.

He stands, startled by my approach, but regards me thoughtfully. "Data, not evidence."

"What the fuck is the difference between the two?"

I hear, rather than feel, as Noah puts his hands on my shoulders tenderly, in a gesture to calm my coiling nerves. Without thinking, I shake him off. I don't want to calm down.

"Many, in fact. The data hasn't been looked through, no one's been questioned, and it hasn't been screened. Like I said, nothing's been sent to the lab. Evidence, however, would be concrete, a confirmation. None of the data on your parent's murder has been confirmed. Nonetheless, the information verifies that something isn't right." He strokes the five o'clock shadowy stubble with the back of his hand and scans the dry grass suddenly. His eyes dart back to mine, and I let out a sigh, realizing that I'd been holding my breath, watching his every move. "I'm taking the case."

"Why?"

"It's obvious something is wrong, Niki. Now that I'm aware of this, I can't just stand back like every other damn detective. I'm not the type that can be bought."

His voice is low, threatening. It chills me to know this man has a gun permit.

"Well, I appreciate it, I guess."

"You'll let your brother know for me? He'd already left for work when I stopped by your house."

Which means Jasmin sent him to Noah's trailer. What the fuck.

"Of course. He'll be... pleased."

"I know it isn't much, especially since the case will remain sealed, but it may offer some closure."

I look away then, to the blinding light of the deep blue sky and white puffy clouds. "Not sure that's possible, Detective. You see, I *witnessed* the murder of my parents. I know exactly who took them from me." I turn and meet his unwavering gaze. "The fucker responsible is protected by your force."

Dylan inhales sharply, as if it's the first time he's heard this information. "The file says there were witnesses. It even says they were killed in front of one of their kids... I thought it'd been Julius."

"No, Jule was..." I don't want to get into this. It's early, but a couple of my nosy neighbors are beginning to sprout. Noah is trusted blindly, but I still feel wary about talking to a cop where people can see. I shake my head and Noah turns me around and holds me against his rock-hard chest. I let him hold me.

"If you're finished now, we'd like to go to sleep. We both work long hours and *my Justice* here worked the entire night—"

"Right." Dylan's eyes stay on Noah. "You have my card, Niki. Call me anytime and I'll update you with any new information."

"Update me with any and *all* information, Detective."

His black eyes finally land on mine. "Dylan. You can drop the title."

I nod, my mouth all dry as if I just swallowed a handful of cotton balls. I want to say goodnight, but I know it's more like good morning to him, and my face turns red to think of what Dylan may conjure–Noah and I are going to bed together.

"What's wrong?" We're back in Noah's trailer, and as soon as the door is closed, his stance changes. He's no longer holding me and he seems upset for some reason.

"He calls you Niki."

I shrug. "It's my first name."

"It's a *nickname*," he snaps. "Besides, you don't let *anyone* call you by your first name. Only your parents and Jule. You practically tore my head off the *one time* I uttered it."

I realize just then that he's right. But hearing Dylan's voice speak my name sincerely didn't affect me. Usually, my skin crawls. It irks me even when coming from my brother Jule, but I've learned to tolerate it over the years. It wouldn't have been correct to yell at him for it. After all, he too lost his parents.

My dad loved my first name. *Victor of the people, a champion, mija. That's what you are. A heroine.*

I squeeze my eyes to the point of pain. "I'm sorry, Noah. I hadn't even realized..."

I understand just then how dangerous it is that Noah and I have known each other since we were kids, that he knows me better than most people. I mentally kick myself. He doesn't deserve a half-assed attempt.

I take a deep breath to steady my next words. "I was desperate to know what he had to tell me. All I could focus on was my parents—"

Noah's arms embrace me suddenly. "You're right. It's stupid of me to bring up my jealousy now."

"You're... *jealous*?"

Noah eyes me. "He's conjured his own little nickname for you. Of course, I'm fucking jealous."

I sigh a frustrating breath. I don't want to deal with a jealous bout. Noah is the first boyfriend I've had, and perhaps this is how they all act, but I irk at the idea of having him prey over me with ownership and contemptuousness. I am not *his*.

"I'm gonna go home now."

"Yea, you have to go to work in exactly seven hours. I guess I'll see you."

My head drops as he leads me out. He leans into me, to kiss me maybe, but I turn and exit his temperature-controlled trailer and head back home alone. So much for coming over and smoothing things out.

I focus my thoughts on what the night will bring instead of Noah. He's leaving on a work trip and I won't see him for almost three weeks. But I can't be near him right now.

9

Justice

Tonight I'm working with Jas at *Nym-Pho*, a club sixty miles west.

Not just any place, but a nightclub reserved for those with dark tastes, and although the money is going to be fucking amazing, I'll be wearing very little clothing. On the positive side, my face will be hidden. *Nym-Pho* is a private club and discretion is key. It's excellent bank, and although Jasmin has lectured me constantly about how I'm expected to act and how she wants me to handle touchy clients, I can't shake the nerves off.

"No sex?"

"We snuggled." I shrug and watch from the corner of my eye as Jasmin's face screws up and she shakes her head.

"I'm just wondering, with your past and all."

I avoid looking at her. I don't want to discuss my very recent past riddled with indiscretions and promiscuity.

We're busy readying ourselves for a night shift. I have Jasmin, and her supervisor promotion, to thank for the gig.

I can't keep scraping by with all the other jobs I get from the agency. And the couple of nights I worked at *Ribbons,* I was able to gather enough money to register Jule back into the prominent school program he deserves to attend. I was *also* going to be able to see our little *cerro* friend in action. He wasn't going to return to *Ribbons,* but he was becoming a regular at *Nym-Pho.*

I had a feeling it wasn't his first time fondling an underage girl. If the fucker wouldn't come out of his cage, I had to find a way to him. My readers were already anxious to find out what else I'd reveal about him.

"We can do our makeup and hair here, but we'll have to get dressed at the club."

The attire at *Nym-Pho* is... no attire. Jasmin's outfit consists of a black thong with fake diamonds in the front, nipple covers, and six-inch heels. Her mask is what will cover the most skin, only her eyes, mouth and chin will be visible. Once she convinced me to pick up some shifts, she purchased me an outfit.

Jasmin's thin and petite. I'm curvy, with thick hips, a small waist, and huge tits. I suffered the night I wore her corset and pants to *Ribbons*. I couldn't breathe, and the girdle left me with bruises. I open the bag and look around to make sure Jule is still in the shower. I want to tell him not to waste water and hurry the fuck up, but I take this time to look at my uniform for tonight.

Fuck. It's just stretchy belts. A small triangle will cover my nipples and pussy.

"What the fuck, Jasmin!" I lift up the bands. "How am I even supposed to wear this shit?"

She laughs and holds it up. "This part is for the top—it's more or less a bra." She shrugs.

"More like a *piece* of a bra." It's more material than she'll be wearing, but shit, I'll be walking around with bandages and harness bands that connect to my thong. *Fuck.* I swallow.

"You'll look hot. Stop whining. You'll come home with over a thousand tonight."

I nod, allowing the idea of working a few nights while earning this amount to flow through me and hopefully ease the butterflies in my stomach. It'll be our fucking salvation. Jule can return to school, and I know it will help our cause and we'll be able to slip away, hopefully unnoticed, to the farm my parents left us. Unbeknownst to the police force, apparently. And we want to keep it that way. I never could get rid of the trailer, but my parents would want us to leave.

I try to keep my mouth closed as the click of my heels on the black marble floor is drowned by the music blaring through unseen speakers. The blue strobe lights blind me and I straighten my spine. *Don't fucking fall, don't trip, keep walking. Back straight, shoulders stiff.*

I'm on the second floor and I look up through the mask's holes. I'm wearing a black mask with pointy ears, a fox.

The third floor is visible, and I can see a man leaning on the black metal banister. The lights pierce through the crystal chandelier and twist and bend past it. I turn and place the empty silver platter on the bar, and the masked man behind it produces a new one with shot glasses brimmed to the top with vodka. I can smell it and I wrinkle my nose. I'm a tequila girl through and through. Vodka fucks me up–I can't hang.

I'm wearing black pleather gloves that go up to my elbows and they pull at my forearms painfully. Everyone is wearing a mask to conceal their identity. Men in suits hold leashes that lead to naked womens' necks. Some of them walk and others crawl. I keep my eyes on empty hands, supplying them with shots if they desire. Another server walks around with a glowing tray carrying three bottles with shooters, and I twist away from the sparks. The move causes me to trip over a crouched Sub. The tray clatters to the floor and the glass shards fly like fucking bullets.

"Shit, I'm sorry."

She ignores me, doesn't even look up or acknowledge me. A security guard dressed like a *Men in Black* character approaches me and helps me up, squeezing my arm in the process. He materializes a broom with an attached dustpan and hands it to me. I catch Jasmin's wide eyes from across the room and she quickly sashays toward me.

She looks like a fucking mermaid dancing her way to me, her thin frame moves coquettishly, and I'm a fucking clutz gathering the broken pieces of my soul scattered on the pristine hollow marble. The Dom who's mate I tripped over turns to glare at me, like I touched what belonged to him without his permission, and my face burns beneath the mask.

"Allow me to offer you a bottle of our finest, on the house. Please excuse my friend. She's new." Jasmin bows her head and then snaps her fingers to the bartender, who produces a bottle of red.

He takes it and then hands it to his mistress, who finally stands. Aside from sky high stilettos, she's completely naked, only wearing a diamond encrusted collar with a chain linked to her Dom's wrist. He tugs it gently and they disappear into the crowd.

"You've *got* to be more careful, *please*," Jas whispers through tight lips.

I nod and hand the tools to the bartender. I don't know anyone's names. Jasmin does, and she hands him a twenty. "You're costing us money tonight."

"I'm sorry," I offer sheepishly, and she sighs. I'm so fucking bad at this and my feet are killing me.

"When shit like this happens, Donovan has the girls wear a red collar, which tells the clients that they're up for grabs. I *don't* want that to be you."

Fuck, I don't either. I'm sure they're compensated, but I wouldn't be good at that. It took me months, up to just recently, to let Noah touch me. And in the past, my one-night stands were rough and quick. My trust wears super thin. "Okay, I'll do better. I promise."

Jas wears a black collar, and I'm curious. I point to it.

"Black means I'm off limits to touching."

I nod and she smiles, then gives me a quick hug before waltzing to her previous spot, where a band of men waits for her. They catch her walking to them, the ground her catwalk, and they hoot. I look to the first floor, eight steps in front of me, and take a new platter down.

Why can't I wear a black collar?

I focus on the area that has a stage in the middle with three poles, each accompanied by nude dancers. I spot small round tables and place three glasses down for three guys with their eyes glued to the stage. I move and notice a man come through the curtain behind the dancers. He's barefoot and sits between two poles and the nude dancers crowd him. They're taking his clothes off and one starts to rub his dick. Another straddles his face.

I look away and walk toward the next set of stairs that lead back to the bar when a man grabs my wrist, whipping me backwards to fall onto his lap. *Don't react, be nice, you need this job; you don't want to wear a red collar.*

"Haven't seen you around here before."

He smells of vodka, and I smile past an urge to gag. I peer over at his table and notice four empty martini glasses.

"I'm new," I purr, eliciting a sultriness Jasmin grilled me with. "I'll fill you up," I say as I lean forward, pushing my ass into his hardening dick, and place the four empty glasses on the platter. Then I get up slowly and smile at him. "I'll be right back," I wink.

Ugh, I want to shake his stench off of me. But I manage to keep it together and bring back a platter with four martinis and a bottle of a bubbly, sweet wine I like. *Closer* by *Nine in Nails* is playing, and the moans coming from the stage grow. I fight the urge to peek when I notice a second man walk onto the stage from my peripheral, and instead produce a skinny flute which I had snuck behind my back. It was tucked under one of the stretchy belts, and the man and his comrades smile big. I open the bottle and fill the glass with bubbly for myself.

"Cheers to meeting the lovely..."

I grin and coquettishly shake my finger at them. I tsk under my breath. "One mustn't ask for what one can't have." I tilt my head back and sip on the wine. "I'll leave you gentlemen the bottle, for when I come back." I wink again.

One of them touches himself, and my admirer licks his lips. "Okay, lovely, deposit eight hundred into your account."

I beam as I strut up the steps, almost rushing to the back, where the staff retreat to take quick but frequent breaks. When a figure steps in front of me. He has a simple black mask over his emerald eyes and has salt and pepper hair.

"You realize those men preferred to look at you rather than the show onstage?"

I startle and press my back against the wall next to the bar, but force myself to recover and produce a practiced smile instead of fleeing to the closed off staff section. "I hadn't noticed."

The man raises his chin, then licks his lips as he covers my body with his stare. Jasmin's words play in my head. *Neck and spine straight, shoulders back, ass perky, tummy tucked. You're a fucking goddess.*

I'm about to issue one of the many lines I memorized when a drunken man walks past us and trips on literally nothing. He lunges forward and spills his tall cocktail all over me. I squeal in response to the ice slapping my bare skin. The silver fox shoves the man and his arm is in front of me, as if to protect me. I stifle a laugh. The drunk guy crawls away and is followed by a naked woman with a paddle in hand.

"I'm sure he'll be punished justly."

The attractive middle-aged man turns and adjusts his tie. "I'd love a private room with you."

"I'll see what I can do," I lie.

"Hopefully this will entice you," he slips a black and silver card into the belt over my left breast with a couple of folded hundreds, and walks away. The metal is cool against my skin, but I don't look at it, instead I move to the quiet space reserved for staff.

The room is dark, with dimmed lamps on tables beside lounge chairs. There's a fridge stocked with water and a snack table. There are two private bathrooms with showers and a section behind a wall that looks like a gym locker room, complete with open co-ed showers.

A nude female covers herself with a robe while chewing on an apple. An oily male server with a black thong and a red collar chugs down a water bottle desperately, and a naked woman is splayed on the couch with her legs crossed. We all keep our masks on.

The room connects to the side that works as a locker room, and I walk past the darkened room and press my back against the cool metal of my locker. *I can do this.*

The emerald eyed, silver fox works for *el cerro*. I'm moving in the right direction. I'm here for the cash flow and to unveil the scumbag. *I got this.*

The rest of my shift goes smoothly, but by the end of the night, I want to yell at someone, *anyone*. I'm sick of smiling; my face fucking hurts. The mask clings to my face as it drips sweat, I stink of booze, my feet are throbbing, and I can feel an ugly blister growing on the back of my ankle. I want to take off the thong that's stuck between my ass cheeks and bathe the fucking night away.

"I have to count the tips for the bartenders. Give me twenty minutes." Jasmin's all business as she lays out the bills on the bar.

"I'll wait outside with security," I tell her as I put my hooded, knee length cardigan on and toss my backpack over my shoulder. I'm tired of naked bodies, and the staff area currently has three naked men and two women going at it—full orgy. I'm good.

"You did amazing tonight," she calls and I smile.

The late night, early morning offers a cool breeze in the otherwise balmy darkness, and I rustle in my cardigan, eager to feel it all over. I want to rip the fucking mask off my face, but I notice the security guard still has his on, even though all of *Nym-Pho's* clients are gone.

He's smoking a cigarette, the cherry bud burns bright, and the smoke travels to me and swirls in my face. He nods, acknowledging me, but keeps his thoughts to himself and I'm grateful. I can't come up with more bullshit to say tonight.

Suddenly, a bright strobe of light beams in our direction, blinding me. A shriek pierces the still night. *Fuck*, cops. I don't know why I freeze. I'm not doing anything wrong, but the corruption brimming their shields stills my heart and suffocates me. Taking me back to the night my parents were killed.

"Remove the masks. Zorro's party is over."

I want to roll my eyes at the stupid comparison, but stop myself. I recognize that voice. It's Detective Lloyd. Fuck, what if Dylan is with him? I don't look at the security guard, and he doesn't look at me, but we both take our masks off.

"Well, well, well. Who do we have here?" He hooks his finger under my chin and lifts my eyes to his. The fucker's face is split in two, a ridiculous smile taking over his splotchy face. "Justice, I'm going to bring you in for underage drinking and employment to an establishment that clearly caters to stuff you have no business being a part of."

There is no better time to come clean. "I'm not underage, Detective Lloyd."

"You can tell me all about it at the station. Come on."

He jerks me around and throws my backpack to his comrade. Not Dylan. Fuck, where is he when you need him? I have a feeling he'd handle all of this differently and wouldn't allow any other to cuff me. Lloyd slaps shackles on my wrists and then pulls me to his squad car.

I cock my head at the security guard. "Can you tell Jasmin I'll be home after this fool figures out his mistake?"

He nods, his face giving nothing away. He's a stoic statue, and I know he'll deliver my message. Lloyd shoves me in the back of the car and I curse under my breath. "If you bruise me, I'll press charges."

His new partner tells me to shut up and I glare at him. I should've waited with the orgy.

"I already fucking told you, I'm not fifteen, you idiot. If you uncuff me and give me back my bag, I'll show you my identification."

I've been here for two hours. Lloyd and his buddies are beaming, ecstatic to have finally arrested Justice. They're threatening to call child protective services, and I swear I want them to so I can rub it in their faces. But then I'm reminded that Jule is only fourteen, and I wasn't given legal custody. *Fuck.*

They don't have to keep the handcuffs on, but I think they like it. It gives them power, and it makes me sick. They believe me to be fifteen. I'm obviously not a threat, wearing nothing but fucking belts and an open cardigan. I want to stab my heel into them, which is the only reason I haven't kicked them off. I'm just waiting for one to get close enough. Seriously, the worst night ever!

"What the fuck is going on here? What is she doing here?" Dylan's thundering voice silences the cackling laughter and gurgles.

Lloyd is the first to speak. "She was outside of *Nym-Pho*, intoxicated. She's naked and underage." He shrugs.

Dylan glares at the men, his eyes darkening as he grabs my arm. His grip is surprisingly gentle, considering he looks like he's about to empty his gun into every man in the room. He turns me around and uncuffs my wrists. I stretch out my arms and then cross them over my body, wrapping my sweater tightly around me.

"I'm not intoxicated. Someone accidentally spilled their drink on me. And I'm *not* underage." I grit my teeth. "I kept telling them to let me show them my ID, but they won't give me my bag."

I don't know why I'm telling him all of this, but he puts an arm around me and leads me to a desk in the back. He smells of smoky leather and rose. Dylan motions for me to sit down, and I dare not argue because he looks like he's going to whip out a fucking machine gun. A vein on his neck pulses dangerously.

"Bring me her bag."

His voice is steady and menacing. It makes the hairs on the back of my neck stand up, but I'm not afraid. The cops are, though, and it makes me smile.

A stocky detective leans back in his chair. "She's probably got a fake ID. That won't work on us, Justice."

"She's twenty-two. And you would know this if you kept your shit together. But simple data collection proves to be too difficult a task for you idiots."

Lloyds places his hands on his belt buckle. He looks at me, and Dylan bristles and moves to stand in front of me, blocking his view.

"Get me her stuff, now," he enunciates slowly.

A cold sweat seizes my body, and my legs turn to jelly. I don't know how long it will take them to connect the dots, but soon enough, someone is going to come around asking questions about Jule. I have a clue as to why the idea of him being my guardian wasn't questioned—a man caring for his little sister sits better with them. But they fucking hate me, I just know they'll try to take Jule from me. Like we'll ever let it happen, but still. *Fuck*.

Someone tosses my backpack to Dylan and he holds it over his shoulder. My bag looks tiny against his massive back. He turns and holds out his hand. I don't hesitate, *I can't*.

We are drawn to one another, joined by a force stronger than either of us has the capacity to explain or understand. At that moment, I'm sure that there is nothing in existence strong enough to wedge our magnetism apart. It's other-worldly, intangible, and it possesses me instantly.

He leads me out, and a quiet stillness wraps around me. He opens the door to his car, and when I slip in, I breathe out, finally feeling the tension ripple out of me. My shoulders slump, and I gently kick my shoes off and wiggle my toes. Dylan gets in and his car rumbles to life. He shifts gears and roars out of the police lot. He's quiet and I lean my head back, way too comfortable in his space.

I breathe his scent in and it intoxicates me and I melt into his leather seat. I feel like I'm falling, losing the semblance of control that I desperately hold on to whenever I'm close to Dylan. The air conditioning cools my feet and the pain ebbs. I pick them up and tuck them underneath me to rub some life back into them. Dylan watches me from under his thick lashes. It's pitch dark out and the road lights toss bursts of light into his car, mixing shadow with light.

The sun will be making its debut for the day in less than two hours.

I look out and notice we're approaching my lot. "You can drop me off at the same place as last time."

Dylan grips the steering wheel and it makes a crackling sound. "Like hell I will."

My head snaps and I glower at him. "You're a cop–"

"I don't give a shit. I'm not letting you walk two steps dressed like that."

"I can take care of myself," I grumble.

"I'm not questioning your self defense skills. I'm driving you all the way home, and then I'm going to wait until you walk inside and close the door."

I don't have the energy to argue. I cannot believe the night I've had. This is definitely a new one for the books. Dylan turns off his headlights and drives into the lot slowly. He parks by my trailer and then steps out to open my door. I'm too slow and tired to argue that I can open my own damn door.

I'm beyond exhausted, and once I'm out, I lean into the closed door for support. "I don't know why you did all of this, but thank you."

Dylan reaches up and cups my chin. The contact ignites me from the inside out. He lifts up my face and then trails his fingers over my cheek. He smooths my hair back behind my ear and grazes his thumb over my jawline. His other hand moves my cardigan open and his breath hitches.

He notices the black metal business card still tucked behind a belt over my breast. It has a gold fox sitting atop a QR code and he peels it off my skin. I freeze at the action, my skin pebbles, and I look at him from under my lashes. He turns it in his hand, separates the money, then slips the card into his pocket.

I gasp. "That's mine."

He shakes his head. "Nope," he says, popping the P. He returns the money to its spot and goosebumps cover me.

His fingers trail down my waist, drawing slow circles over my stomach, and then down to my thigh. The action brands me, claiming me. A low growl escapes his throat, and he leans in. He licks his full lips, and I want to bite them, draw blood and scar his lip. Claiming him the way he unknowingly has me.

Suddenly, Noah's face appears in my thoughts, and a pang of guilt physically knocks me back. I press my hand hard on Dylan's chest and lean away.

"I have a boyfriend, Detective." It comes out all breathy.

Dylan nods and leans back. "And where was he tonight?"

I lift one of my pumps and place the heel of it on his chest and gently push him further away. "*That's* none of your business. Goodnight."

He lifts up his hands as if surrendering and chuckles. He takes another step back and I move away from him quickly.

"Goodnight, Niki."

I take my walk of shame barefoot, and I don't have to look back to know he's waiting for me to go inside and lock my door. He won't leave unless I'm in the damn trailer. I want to turn around and chuck my shoe at him. I hate how he makes me feel. But I stay looking forward, unlock my door, and close it gently behind me.

The following two days are fucking miserable. When I'd gotten home, Jule was thankfully still asleep. Jasmin and I decided it was best if we didn't tell him anything. She'd been pacing when I came in and wanted to dissect the entire thing. But I relented. If I gave Dylan a spotlight, he would complete the invisible race to wholly own me. I wouldn't allow him to occupy my thoughts. Not while I still had a semblance of control. For a reason I still didn't want to understand, I would lose the battle while near him, or in my dreams.

Nights were the worst. My nightmares imagined Noah grappling to keep me in his arms while a sticky blackness coated me, and I would tumble in suffocating waves of tar until landing in Dylan's waiting arms. During the day, if I wasn't staring into space, I was twitching like a fool. I hadn't gone out to scour for information–I worked my hours at the club, munched on scraps, and slept.

"Hey, you're like the walking dead. What the hell is going on, Nik?"

"What?"

Jule takes a seat next to me on the small bed. "You look like shit, you don't sleep, you don't eat. Seriously, I'm beginning to worry here."

Jasmin muffles her laughter and my brother's eyebrows shoot up, suspicious. "Okay, what's going on?"

"Your sister is drowning between two very desirable islands."

I stretch my legs out on the bed and glare at her.

She shrugs, and when Jule turns to inspect me, she mouths, *it's true.* The witch, I'll get her back somehow.

"I don't understand. Are we going on vacation?"

Jasmin bursts into a fit of laughter and snorts. I shoot daggers from my eyes and aim them at her. She lifts up her hands as if surrendering, but doesn't stop laughing.

"Whatever. I'm going to take a shower." Jule stands and tosses a towel over his shoulder.

Once he's in the bathroom, my eyes collide with Jasmin's. I have enough dealing with my very own inner turmoil and self-reproach. I don't need her reminding me of the chaos.

I slip on my old Converse. "I'm going out." I reach for my old and worn leather jacket, my ever equipped bag, and shut the door on my way out.

I shouldn't direct my anger toward her, but she definitely isn't helping. It feels like she's enjoying the view of me writhing between my emotions for two very different men.

It's easy being Noah's girlfriend, and my feelings for Dylan are overwhelming. Noah and I are connected by years of friendship and memories, and I don't know who the fuck Dylan really is. All I know is that my body reacts to him involuntarily.

It's as if he owns me and I'm being lent to someone else. It's a horrible thought, but that's exactly how it feels. The idea of belonging to *anyone* makes my insides turn. But when I picture Dylan's muscular tattooed arms wrapped around me, it feels right.

I'm so fucked.

I want these feelings to go away. Being with Noah feels easy, and it flows in a pleasant way. Even though my body and heart fight it. He's my friend.

I feel horrible about how we left things before his work trip. He'll be gone for three weeks and I never even said goodbye. I was too pissed off at him for being … what? Jealous? He was acting like a boyfriend and I responded by behaving like a fucking harlot. A single one, at that.

Noah is a calm river while Dylan is an ocean, raptured by the fucking storm of the century. I don't know if I want to be in the eye of that storm. And at what cost? Hurting Noah? Never. I could never betray him. I'd fight against my feelings toward Dylan to the death if it meant sparing Noah's heart.

I'm glad that I hadn't heard from Dylan since the night he dropped me off. It was difficult enough to try to understand my feelings for Noah, and I didn't need Dylan around to confuse me any further.

I shake my head and grunt out loud. To hell with both of them. I prefer solitude, anyway. I fling my backpack and dig out my camera. I click through it and adjust the settings. About fucking time I get some *real* work done. *El cerro's* case is sitting on my imaginary desk, weighing it down with each passing minute. I haven't seen him at *Nym-Pho,* but he's bound to show up. It's the perfect place to make dark fantasies a reality. And if I don't spot him, I'll go to his fucking office or house. Whatever it takes.

I'd spent an adequate amount of time blubbering interiorly, and not enough time out scoping the city. After a few hours of walking up and down the city streets, interviewing people, and snapping a few photos of vandalism, or stores that had been recently broken into, I walked into a convenience store and bought myself a bag of potato chips and a bottle of water.

I hated spending money, but I felt like I was going to fucking faint. I finish the bag and toss it in the trash when a long and raspy *tsk* stops me. A discordant voice is saying my name. I think the harsh whisper is coming from the abandoned, three-story building across the street.

I creep toward it as inconspicuously as I can manage, my eyes down, and keep up a casual stride. *I think.* If someone is whispering and trying to keep hidden, it's for a reason.

I'm pretty used to this. Usually, if people had a feed, a clue, or information, they would pass it on discreetly. Jule hates it, Noah even more so. It's dangerous, but it's the way I've always worked. It's an occupational hazard.

Once inside, the stench hits me. It reeks of recently run over skunk, swampy mud, and spoiled apples. The mixture of those three isn't something I want floating inside my nostrils, so I cover them up and hold back a gag, threatening to heave the little food I ate before falling asleep. It's dark and muggy inside, the only sound coming from the loud flapping of the construction plastic poorly stapled over the broken windows. The black graffiti stippled alongside the brick walls calls my attention, and as I'm trying to decipher it, a light-brown haired man in his late twenties appears from behind an aged and molding sheet hanging from a low banister.

He looks behind and around me, untrusting the situation. As if to reassure him, I lower my hands in a gesture of peace. "You called?"

"Anyone else here?" He's a tall and muscled man. Light skin, eyes, and hair. Handsome, but fucking deadly looking. I notice a cigarette burning bright between his fingers. I also notice a rippled scar on his cheek that travels down past his jawline.

"Not from my end. You?"

"Of course not," he snaps.

I have the sudden urge to roll my eyes, but when he lifts the cigarette to his lips and sucks in a lungful of its deadly gas, I shrink back. If looks could kill, I'd be seven feet underground. He doesn't look like a cop, not in the least, but something about him gives off soldierly vibes. I'm immediately uncomfortable, and although I have a feeling that what he's about to say is definitely good, I still want to turn around and run the fuck out.

I swallow back my fear and clear my throat. "You have information or something you'd like to share with me?"

"Not really. This is different."

My face scrunches. *What?* "Okay..." He's going to fucking murder me. I knew it.

The handsome killing machine takes another deep puff and slowly moves toward me, then exhales. He's fidgety, and it's unnerving. His left hand comes up, and he gropes at his bottom lip. "I can't tell you here."

"Then why call me *here*?"

"I didn't know another way. I didn't want to go to your trailer. I've been waiting for fucking *days*."

Days? Here? How many days? And why? I look around, and for the first time, notice a backpack leaning on the wall to my right.

"There isn't time for fucking chit chat. We need you to go to the Ink Tavern on Crevice Corner. Be there at exactly six-thirty."

"Why not six-thirty-five, or six-forty-five?"

He eyes me. "Is that your idea of a joke? Fuck, I knew this was a mistake."

A mistake? He doesn't want to be here–someone sent him. "Who's *we?*"

I think he smiles, but I'm not sure. "You'll see." Mr. No-Humor-and-all-Mysterious turns, tosses the backpack over his shoulder, then disappears into the flapping plastic toward the rear of the building.

"So, where are we headed?"

I normally don't bring Jule along on these missions, but he insisted, since the cryptic and vagueness of the humorless man tugged at his macho need to protect his sister.

"That old bar by Crevice Corner, the one that looks like it's about to crumble on top of whoever's inside."

I'm glad we left Jasmin at home. She pulled a double, and after working with her, I now realize how draining her job is. Not only physically, those fucking pumps she wears are a hazard, but mentally, as well. It truly takes a toll to completely shut down and put on a mask. Both a physical and mental mask, at that.

She has to put her entire personality in a box and pretend for hours to be someone she most definitely is not. I have no idea how she does it, but I have a higher dose of respect for her. And I can't stand her right now. She's the only one who knows I have feelings for two guys and that I don't know what the hell to do about it. It's easier to pretend when she isn't around.

The late afternoon sun bites at our skin, beaming down on us ruthlessly. It feels like I invited the sun to hop into my backpack, and now I'm carrying a ball of fucking fire on my back. I miss the rare bout of rain we had and wish I would've appreciated it.

I have no idea who I'm meeting, and the entire thing has me on edge. I don't want Jule to notice, though. He's so brave and eager, and I don't want to be a little bitch and cause him to feel anything but confidence. We reach the run down tavern and I notice my brother square his shoulders. I keep wondering when the fuck he grew up on me, but I'm glad he's doing a fine job for a fourteen-year-old. He's more responsible and mature than I ever was at his age. In fact, I used to be a fucking snob until I stared the grim reaper in the face.

The metal door creaks open and we rush inside to avoid being spotted. My eyes take time to adjust, and the darkness claws at my scalp. What the fuck did I get us into?

A familiar sing-song voice clears the air. "It's about fucking time."

Piper.

I let out a breath I didn't realize I was holding and unclench my fists. Jule's shoulders relax and he's smiling like a fucking idiot.

"What's with the secrecy?" I retort.

She nods, directing me to sit down on a stool perched up by the bar. "We need to talk about your latest post."

Jule's eyes grow, and he pops his gum loudly before letting out a whistle of air. He leans on the bar behind me as Piper takes a seat next to me.

"What about it?" I shrug.

A couple of days after I caught *el cerro* in his hole of nasty, I posted the video along with a disclaimer that the surveillance was handed to me anonymously. This was only after Jas threatened to take it down herself if I admitted to recording it. It became the newest scandal. The mayor was immediately swarmed with paparazzi, and his lawyers were scrambling to poke holes into my information. I hold back a giggle at recalling an article titled *Little Justice League Wannabe isn't Credible and Here's Why*. The mayor owned the press, and they were desperate.

Once the initial spur of attention died down, he became a regular at *Nym-Pho*, only I had yet to see him attend. A place like *Nym-Pho* promised discretion and anonymity. Of course, he'd end up there.

Piper looks behind her, to the same guy that asked me to present myself, and nods. He rounds the bar and calmly takes a glass, dumps three ice rounds, then pours whisky into it. She gratefully takes it and throws it back. Piper moves it toward him and when he fills it a second time, she chucks it back again. "Another," she heaves.

Jule squeezes my shoulder and I speak his thoughts out loud. "What the fuck is going on, Piper?"

She lets out a strangled breath and stares at me. "I know you're the one who recorded it, but he's convinced it was *me*."

"What the hell are you talking about?"

"Stop the bullshit. I know it was you!" Piper yells and takes the glass and throws it back once more. "Carlton is my father, Justice! Mace and I just barely got away, and now he's hunting me down because he thinks I've caught his sick ass on video."

Oh shit. I wasn't crazy when I saw similarities between the three. Staring at him to figure out who he reminded me of practically burned my eyes off. But why are Piper and Macy in hiding? *What* is she hiding?

"What did he do to you?"

As soon as the question is out, I regret it. Piper deflates before me, the wall she's built crumbles, and her shoulders tremble. I guess it helps that her sister isn't around.

"He raped me." Her words are barely audible, and I'm not sure Jule even heard her, but when he digs his fingers into my shoulder, I know he did.

"And Macy?"

Her eyes snap to mine. "The night we left, I stopped him from..." She chokes on a sob, and I nod to let her know I get what she can't say.

The man approaches her, and he's in visible pain, his shoulders quaking slightly. He places his hands on her shoulders and it's then that she takes a breath and stabilizes herself by wiping tears that haven't yet fallen. It's like she's warning her sockets to sponge up any and all traces of moisture. Behind her, the guy gives me a cautioning glare.

"I figure he wouldn't assume we would pose as sex workers, so that's what we've been doing. Until Vork and his men caught us, and then my plan blew up in our faces."

Jule's voice startles me. "We can help you out of this. Nik, we're going to get them to safety. We can't let him find them."

I resist rolling my eyes because even though we can offer protection, I'm not so sure it's what Piper wants. I've never hidden elite patrons. This would not only be dangerous, but *completely* new territory for us. But the voice my brother uses is authoritative, and he isn't asking me. He's made up his mind, and he's ordering me to offer a *ghost status* to them.

"What are you offering?" Piper's guy finally speaks.

I sigh. "Normally, there's a firm understanding that this is strictly confidential and sensitive information." I steer my attention to Piper.

"Damn it, Nik. We did this and now we're going to fix it. Fuck protocol!" Jule's fist slams on the bar, and I freeze, frustration threatening to spark into anger. But I diffuse it by breathing slowly.

"What do you need from us?" her guy says, and I'm tempted to ask who the fuck he is when Jule answers for me.

"Complete secrecy, *for life.*"

"Money?" he wonders.

Jule shakes his head and the nameless guy looks at Piper and nods. "You have our word."

I scoff, but when Jule glares at me, I raise my hands, surrendering. He's being erratic and stupid. We have no idea who these people truly are. I need answers before I can comfortably offer them hidden shelter and expose what I *truly* do.

Behind my hobby as a freelance journalist and now nightlife waitress, I offer refuge to those desperate for protection, those who need to escape from the terrorism of this corrupt city.

It's where most, if not all, of my money goes. We live in poverty-like conditions because that's exactly how we need things to appear. Jule, Jasmin, and I own a private lot with a main house, guest house, barn, and some farm animals. A trusted couple who we hired to maintain it resides in one of the homes. A few times a year, we offer housing, a sort of witness protection service if you will, free of charge. Once new identities and safe destinations are established, the people move on.

My father came from a prominent family, and when he chose to marry a sex worker, his family disowned him. He still had his own money, though, and he invested it in purchasing a farm fifty miles out of city limits. He left it to me after his death, but instead of moving there, I've used it as a refuge.

We'll move there soon. But not yet.

I glance at Piper; she looks like she hasn't slept in days, and I nod. Fuck, I hope I don't regret this. "Pack light, we leave immediately."

Jule and I have been gone for less than two hours, and by the time we return to the trailer, shit has hit the fan and I'm sure things cannot get any fucking worse. We have a new neighbor. The latest, state-of-the-art trailer is the biggest on the lot and the envy of all. The water tank is enormous, a two-thousand-gallon mammoth.

Why the fuck did he move here? To fucking spite me, that's why. To give me a heart attack. I want to bang on his door and fucking smack him.

Jasmin bites her nails and watches me, all humor gone from her heart-shaped face. Dylan is the owner of a brand-new trailer that looks like a two-story, two-thousand-square-foot, high-ceiling mobile home. He's fucking crazy. I think he even got a fucking landscaper to come and put new grass down.

It's two-hundred feet from us. He's our next-door neighbor, for fuck's sake.

"I'm going to kill him."

"Maybe he likes the neighborhood?" Jasmin offers, dry humor in her tone.

My mouth pops open, and I close my eyes as they roll to the back of my head. "I highly doubt that."

"He's outside, he's going to sit down on an outdoor chair, those that lean back." Jule is giving us a play-by-play.

"He's sunbathing?" Jasmin asks, annoyed.

Soon it will be moon-bathing. I slap the thought away. The last thing I need right now is to fantasize about Dylan bathing in anything. My renewed anger toward him helps.

"Whoa, he's got a dog. Like a *big* one."

Jasmin and I practically run to the window. We hit the shade, and it dances against the glass. *Fuck*, I'm sure he saw that. It's a black Cane Corso, and he's massive. Tall and lean, but muscular, like his owner.

I step away from the window. "I don't have time for this. Piper is waiting just outside the dirt road. I only came by for the truck."

We keep it hidden and the plates are kept under an alias. A different one from the incognito status we use for the property. We don't want anyone tracking it to any one of us. In order to get to it, I'd have to go to the shed directly in front of our neighbors that live two trailers down. The people here would never divulge what's in there. But now we have a fucking cop living next to us. *Shit!* How do I get it out without him seeing it?

"How do we do this?" Jule speaks my thoughts and I'm silent. I have no fucking clue.

"I say Justice goes out there."

My eyes are huge. I'm shaking my head, about to protest, when Jasmin lifts her hand up to silence me. "Hear me out. This will work, *you know it will*. Go out there and talk to him and I'll get the truck out."

"What if he sees you?"

She shakes her head. "He won't be looking at me... *just you*."

Jule squints, finally realizing the reason why Dylan won't notice anything but me. *I don't even know the reason. He's got the hots for me? I don't know. What I am certain of is that he's fucking crazy.*

"What the fuck am I supposed to say to him?"

"I don't know. Make something up. Ask him about his dog," she offers.

Fuck. I have to consider this option because at this point, I don't know what the hell else to do.

"And I'll signal you once it's done. That way, we walk out of here together while Jasmin waits with Piper and Macy."

I run my hand through my face and into my matted hair.

"Maybe you should change and brush your hair. Put on my cherry balm lip oil."

"Jasmin, what the fuck?"

Jule raises his hands. "No, she's right. It will help keep him distracted."

"Okay, okay. Fine."

I turn around to toss my leather jacket on the bed. Jule faces the opposite wall, and I switch my black tee for a white, v-neck tank. I sniff under my arms and shrug. Jasmin tugs my shirt down, forcing my breasts to reveal more skin than I'm used to, and then tosses me a pair of black jean shorts. I gawk at her and she shrugs. I put them on and then finish the look with my worn Converse. Jasmin is combing through my locks as I quickly wash my face and tame my brows, then I apply a thin layer of her lip oil.

"Mascara?" she offers.

"Don't push it. And be quick. As soon as he's distracted enough, pedal to the metal."

I wonder what Noah would say about this plan and instantly shove that thought into the darkness of my mind. Piper is waiting, and she needs this. If her father finds them, I know he'll enslave them and do fucked up things to them. I don't know if anyone will suspect my involvement, but we cannot risk Dylan connecting those plates to us. We've worked too hard for everything we're attempting to hold together. And I won't allow this fucker to mess it all up.

I look into the mirror; it's as good as it's going to get. What am I supposed to do? Put on my *Nym-Pho* attire and give him a private dance? Somewhere in the back of my mind, the inner harlot in me pants. I bite my lip. *Get a fucking grip.*

I look at Jasmin before stepping out and she gives me a thumbs up. *Fuck.*

I hop down the five steps and sashay in his direction. He's in a sitting position, legs up, leaning back slightly, with a book in hand. He's wearing gray joggers, and *that's it*. Holy fuck, I don't know if I can manage going through this plan without my eyeballs combing over his entire body.

His dog sits up and Dylan looks up and moves his sunglasses lower on his nose to peer at me. His lips break into a sinister smile and he says something inaudible to his dog, who relaxes.

He's tattooed *all over*. His muscled chest and rippled abs are covered in swirls of ink. Two ornate guns are criss-crossed over his pecs, there's a rose on his throat and wings that sprout out on either side of it, and they splay around his neck, choking him. Below the rose, between the guns, is what looks like a heart locket with an intricate design etched inside. A siren, with blank eyes and wild hair, is on his ribs, her torso is skeletal, and I can't keep looking—I'll drown in the sea of them.

I clear my throat. "Fancy finding you here."

He lifts his glasses higher up and I catch my reflection in them. I'm standing with my weight on one leg, my arms crossed in front of me. My chest is threatening to spill out. *Good*.

"Really?"

I scowl at him. "No. *Not really*. What the fuck are you doing here?" I hiss.

I realize he's got a direct view of where the large shed is, which really serves as our garage, and I move to the chair next to him on the opposite side. His dog stands, but I ignore him. This needs to work. Worse case scenario, his dog attacks, and then he'll *truly* be distracted. I swallow and focus on the task at hand. I glance at the dog, who is sniffing the air, trying to get a feel for me. He walks slowly toward me.

"Sit down, Max."

Max doesn't listen to his master, but instead, comes to sniff my knee and then licks it. I laugh and sit down, relaxing in the lounge chair with the perfect view of the truck. I spot Jasmin trotting behind him and unlocking the wooden double doors. Dylan faces me, stunned. He rips his sunglasses off his face. His back is completely turned to the truck.

Max sits down directly in front of me, and I pat his head then nuzzle behind his ears. He nestles into my hand and then lays his enormous snout on my thigh. Dylan stares at us, dumbfounded. He's speechless and I smile big. I'm reminded of my father's smile, all toothy and wide. It doesn't make me sad, however.

"You're such a good boy, Max," I praise and then kiss his nose.

Dylan grins and his legs move and he plants his bare feet on his manicured lawn to face me fully. He closes his book and sets it on the round glass table between the chairs. *Fuck, he's hot.* Okay, focus.

"Max has *never* done that before."

"*Please,* you want me to believe you got a killing machine here?" I rub my finger up and down Max's snout and his face eases onto my lap and he closes his eyes. "You're secret's out, rookie."

He laughs and I see Jasmin pulling out the deep blue, old Expedition. Time for my next move. Dylan *cannot* turn around. Slowly, I lean forward, and Dylan looks at my breasts, his eyes sweeping up to mine, and he licks his lips.

"If I didn't know any better, I'd think you're trying to distract me."

Fuck, he's a detective, after all. I shrug and bend down to plant another kiss on Max's nose while keeping my eyes locked on Dylan's–holding him there.

"I came here to tell you that nothing changes. Moving to the neighborhood doesn't make you one of us. You aren't welcome here."

I catch sight of my brother approaching us. He waves at me and I stand. "Except you, Max. You're welcome anytime, aren't you sweet boy?" I pat his head and walk to where Jule waits for me.

"I'm on to you, Niki."

I don't turn around. Instead I wave, wiggling my fingers at him. I know he's looking at my ass, so I make sure to walk as seductively as possible, while at the same time ignoring the look of disgust on Jule's face.

He pretends to gag and hands me my leather jacket. I slip it on and we walk out of the trailer lot. Once we're out of view, we start running, and it takes us a total of ten minutes to make it to where Jasmin, Piper, and Macy wait. Jas scoots over and I take the driver's seat. Once the doors are closed and Jule is buckled in, I drive us out of there. The windows are tinted enough that we're not visible to those on the street. I take the highway to avoid the busy traffic in the city and gun it down.

We make it there in just over an hour, and I jump out to open the metal gate. The estate encompasses twenty-five acres and consists of four buildings, a swimmable lagoon, a stable house, and an avocado field. The main house is for Jasmin, Jule, and myself, though we've never stayed for more than a couple of days. It has six bedrooms and four full bathrooms, an enormous kitchen, two fireplaces, and an outdoor, fenced-in patio with an indoor pool.

Helena, Pedro, and their two kids live in another smaller house with an outdoor pool. I hired them a few years ago to take care of the property, and they're the true reason it thrives. Helena used to be a nurse, and she helps out with any injured newcomers.

The next two houses are kept empty for visitors. They're each similar in size, with five bedrooms and four full bathrooms, a kitchen, living quarters, and enclosed patios. The entire property is heavily gated, and we installed security cameras with motion and sound detectors. Both the main house and Helena's house have a room with monitors to view the surveillance footage. Okay, maybe I took it too far. But a fucking killer was out there, and I didn't want him anywhere near here. My father would be proud of the renovations.

Once we're in, Helena and Pedro meet us at the next gate. This one is electric and requires a passcode to get in. We change it every so often. I park the car and Jasmin rushes to Helena and embraces her. Jule and Pedro shake hands and then hug.

"Junior, you're enormous!" Pedro tells my brother.

"Helena, these two ladies will be our personal guests. They'll stay in our home for now. Do you think you can help me get the two conjoined rooms ready?"

"Of course, *mija*. And supper is ready."

I smile. I love Helena's cooking and she knows it. She also knows we don't ever get home-cooked meals. The makeshift kitchen in the trailer would go up in smoke. Aside from Noah's breakfasts, I've been living off of beef jerky for who knows how fucking long.

While driving to the ranch, Piper asked to stay with us for the night. She didn't want to stay in a new place all alone, especially an entire house, regardless of us being right next door. It would make this the first time someone other than us stays in our home. I would've put my foot down, but Jule is obsessed with being a host.

We're readying the rooms when Helena suddenly stills. "I've missed you."

She embraces me, and it feels a little like home, familiar. Helena was my mother's best friend, the way Jasmin is mine. She's the woman Jasmin threatened to leak my sexcapades to, although I know she wouldn't have the guts to stab my back that way. Helena cares about us, and being here with her feels right.

She stares into my eyes thoughtfully. "You found someone."

My brows shoot up and I clear my throat. "Yeah, I'm dating Noah, remember?"

"Hmm." She grabs my face between her palms and peers into my eyes as though she's searching for something. "No, *not* Noah."

Oh, my fucking she-devil. I'm not getting into this. I shake off her grip and turn around. We make sure the Jack and Jill bedrooms are ready. We'd placed extra bedding and towels in the closet. The bathroom has extra toiletries and there's a canister with water, as well as two glass cups, near the bedside table. Satisfied, I make sure the television works, and when I turn back to Helena, she's gawking at me.

"What's his name?"

"I don't know what you're talking about." I leave the room and step into the hall that connects to the large living room.

The television is on and a freshly bathed Jule is splayed on the loveseat. He's watching an episode of a reality TV show and he's laughing. I grab a stool that's at the bar counter separating the kitchen from the living room, and Jasmin hands me a plate. She too took a shower, and her hair drips onto the back of her shirt. She's barefoot and I smile. My family is home. Soon we'll be able to be here at all times, just like this.

"You'll tell me soon enough," Helena sings as she serves us freshly made hibiscus water.

Jasmin gives her a quizzical look, and I cock an eyebrow at her and shrug. Hopefully nothing else is brought up and I'm desperate for thoughts of any other *someone* to vanish.

Helena looks over our shoulders to my brother. "Come and eat, Junior."

Jule is still laughing and staring at the TV when he sits down. And it's difficult for us to do anything else but enjoy our meals.

10
Redemption

My fox hasn't returned. The new floorboards creek beneath my weight from pacing for the last six hours, a warning from the universe that I'm going to fall through any fucking second now. It's four in the fucking morning, and according to my notations, no one in that trailer works tonight.

So where the fuck is she?

Two fucking times already, I had to stop myself from ravaging her. She was pushing my buttons. She smelled of vodka mixed with her usual citrusy scent. And I wanted to inhale every molecule and bottle it up. I could somewhat see past her working at *Ribbons*, but *Nym-Pho*?

She's allowed to do whatever the fuck she wants, of course, just as long as no one touches her. Getting onto their guest list is at the top of my list; I want to be there every night she is. Especially when her attire consists of a couple of fucking laces over her skin. Her pussy is just out there for anyone to see. It's one thing to know that her delicious curves are being gawked at. The new feeling rushes through me, and I can only categorize it as being possessive. I don't give a shit. They can look, yet touching what is mine is completely unacceptable.

Mine.

It should perturb me that I haven't questioned what's been stirring inside since that first day I laid eyes on her. The only obsession I've ever had is work. But with Niki, I refuse to be an agreeable alternative. I need to be her *only* one. Noah is already on my shit list, but if she's under the delusion that they're an item, I've made it my mission to show her otherwise. I can tell he hasn't had her. Niki isn't in love with him, and he wants her soul before he takes her body. I mean, I'd readily tell him that's impossible. But he'll learn soon enough. My fox will tell him herself.

Noah isn't in town, he's doing whatever the fuck it is he does three counties over. Which reminds me, I have to ask Jason for a file on him. It's a stupid mistake on my behalf.

to have deterred my attention, no matter how slight, from the man who calls himself Niki's boyfriend.

Pathetic. Each time I've caught him with his hands on her, it takes all my training to focus on restraint. To Niki, he's family. No matter how displaced her affections toward him are, I have to acknowledge that he's protected her as much as his pitiful abilities allow him to. I understand why he's obsessed with her. She's fucking perfect.

I'm drawn to the way she looked when she found out I was her new neighbor. The thought of her round and perky tits, that'll just barely fit into my hands, taunts me and my dick jerks in my sweats. Her discomfort was palpable. I can't get her out of my head–the way her little black shorts were hugging her thick thighs and how they slid up when she walked away. *Fuck*.

I knew something was off. I keep trying to pluck the image of her wearing nothing but six fucking belt straps over her creamy skin from my mind. I almost lost it that night. I'm pretty sure *that* was when I decided I had to be near her.

She wasn't going to tell me not to enter this trailer lot again. If I listened that first time, it was because her reasoning actually made sense. Niki's reputation means the world to her; I wasn't going to fuck with that. But then she asked me to let her walk alone, *naked*? No. Not a fucking chance, not happening. *Ever*.

I almost devoured her that night. Her skin, *fuck*, it's my very own entrance to the portal of a never-ending paradise. I wanted to wrap her legs around me and slip her thong to the side and pound into her so hard she screams my name in agony and pleasure laced into one damning assurance that she is mine.

Her touch grounded me and then shot me into the sky. I'd turn away from sin if she were an angel sent to deliver me to heaven. And I'd gladly sell my soul to Hades if it meant I'd get to spend an eternity with her in hell.

I barely heard her reproach, an inaudible and bleak attempt to push me away. She struggled with that. I saw it in her eyes then; she couldn't bear the idea of betraying Noah. He's too important to her. But not in the way he wants. She doesn't love him. But she *will* love me... *someday*.

And this delusional assertion is why I now live here and she can't tell me to leave.

I *belong*. More or less.

My hope is to be able to keep an eye on her. She's too devious for her own good, the trouble that woman gets herself into. You'd think she's searching for it, longing for it. Her tactics are unreputable, but they get the job done, as underhanded as they may be. And her survival skills and will to protect her family are by far unmatched.

I'm still wondering if she truly owns a Tec9. The street camera was down and I couldn't get footage of her from that night. I know it was her; one look into those big brown eyes and I knew. Matter a fact, I hope she *does* own a few guns. And if she doesn't, I'll buy her some. I'd feel a lot more comfortable knowing she's walking around loaded.

Niki's presence created a sort of vortex of cataclysmic proportions. It twisted my reality, took over my fucking thoughts and entire being. The disturbance is so intense that it's entered my system like a plague. Nothing else exists now, just her. Even Max was affected by her. I couldn't even be mad at him, she's a force of fucking nature.

I take my phone from the wooden table near the window in direct view to her place and Jason answers on the third ring.

"Do you know what fucking time it is right now?"

"That's precisely why I called," I growl. "I need a thorough background on Nikoletta Justice Fox."

"What you need is a CT scan, because I emailed you her file two weeks ago."

I had all the basic information. The precinct got her birth year wrong, therefore her age. It's a fucking mess, so naturally, I didn't trust the file they had on her. I'd already looked like a total fucking dumbass for assuming she was fifteen and asking to speak to her guardians. I knew keeping my distance wasn't the correct path to take. If I would've pursued her from the start, I wouldn't have been so clueless. Then again, I thought I was stalking an underage girl, so I guess it can be forgiven.

Jason's particular skills are far better than any police station, and he's allowed me a view no one else had on Niki.

Niki witnessed the murder of her parents at the age of fourteen; her brother was only six at the time. Court proceedings placed both kids in child protective services. But when the paperwork wasn't delivered on time, a letter was sent to the precinct for them to pick up the kids and drive them to a foster home. The dumbasses never picked them up. They did not acknowledge the case or lift a finger for them. They slipped through the cracks, and both Niki and her brother stayed in the trailer—without adult supervision. She dropped out of high school and uprooted her entire life for her brother.

Niki dabbled in trades, from cleaning services, deliveries, manufacturing companies, public works and sanitation, to hauling fucking metal at the junkyard. Her latest, and my least favorite, exotic server. Her friend Jasmin is no different. Same age, she'd been unofficially adopted by Niki's parents when she was eight years old, and after they were killed, she stayed working in the club scene. She'd gotten well known and even moved up to a supervisor position at *Nym-Pho*. Julius Junior was an excellent student and only stepped away to help out with bills. They were tightly knit and unified by one tragedy after another.

Hell, Jason even provided a list of Niki's previous relationships. If you can even call them that. My fox was incapable of settling down. She'd lost her virginity to some idiot at sixteen and then entered a long line of one-night stands. She never took anyone home or slept with anyone more than once. Her last sexual partner was six months prior, and she only started dating Noah three months ago. They'd been a steady item. For now.

"Yes, I know, you fucking idiot, but that was a basic search. I need you to give me *everything*."

Jason sighs, and the background noise tells me he's lifting himself up and out of bed. "You don't need to get all touchy." He drags out the last word and I grind my teeth. "I did that, too. It's on standby, but now that you ask, I'll send it over."

"Why the fuck didn't you send it before?"

"I don't know, maybe be specific next time?" A familiar tapping tells me he's on his laptop.

"I also need everything on Noah Allan, and this time, I do mean *everything*."

Jason chuckles darkly. "What happened? You lost your girl?"

I grind my teeth so hard I think my jaw is going to snap. "Just do what I pay you to do."

He lets out an exasperated sigh. "Noah Allan," he drags out his name slowly and his breathing hitches. "Well, you aren't gonna like this."

Fuck. The precinct doesn't have an existing file on Noah. Just bullshit gossip between grown men about him being a snitch bitch. Which basically means he stands up to them on occasion. And I gather he works alongside Niki in unveiling the precinct's corrupt ways. He was born and raised in this county. He's an only child to Miriam Allan. She works cleaning offices, and she takes a couple of shifts working as a nurse's assistant at the local hospital. Noah's father, Alfredo No Last Name, is a joke. He wracked up an obscene amount of debt and wasted away the family earnings in whatever slap house would allow him entry. But other than what is spoken between the fuckers at the station, there is no official file on Noah Allan.

"Your boy Noah hangs out with the Warlocks."

Your boy. I want to evaporate into practically nothing so I can enter the radio waves as my very own frequency to pass through Jason's ear canal and blow him up from the inside out for his little joke. But I let it slide because what he found *is* interesting.

"Go on," I say through clenched teeth.

"The Warlocks tracked Noah down two years ago and they blackmailed him. He's paying off Alfredo's debt. He's now their little bitch—whatever they want, he delivers."

"Fuck."

"Yea, he's dug up graves, delivered fingers to instill fear in those that owe money, collections–"

Jason goes on, but I'm no longer listening. I'm staring at the tiny screen of my cellphone, reviewing the email he sent me regarding Niki. My little fox owns property and three vehicles. I GPS the location of the lot and it's sixty odd miles out of city limits.

"I want you to send a drone to the farm on Niki's file," I interrupt. I'll deal with Noah later.

"I'll send you a link to view the live feed."

I grab my earbuds and plug them in, then grab my laptop, and it flickers to life. Twenty agonizing minutes later, the video feed comes to life. The sun is rising just in time to catch the perfect image of the stretch of land that's as big as eighteen football fields. I need the drone to keep its distance and it flies over twice, capturing images in its wake. Four structures that appear to be big ass multi-leveled houses, a small body of water that looks more or less like an oversized puddle, a stable and a fucking field of some vegetation. She's even got horses trotting about.

What the fuck?

"What do we know about this land?"

"Just what I sent over. The alias before hers belonged to her father, Julius Senior. It's stayed incognito since the Fox's took ownership, which was when Justice turned two years old. Purchased in cash."

Julius Senior came from a prestigious family who chucked him when he married Flor during his last year in med school. They met when she'd gone to the free clinic to get checked up. He knew what she did for a living, and it didn't matter to him. But his family had some serious opinions and ultimatums. They went as far as getting him exiled at every hospital he attempted to get work. The only place they couldn't touch was a free clinic two counties away where Niki's trailer home was located. Then one day he was offered a job on the wrong side of town. He sewed up some guys for the worst kind of people.

But Julius was a good guy with a conscience, and when he refused to continue to do the work, they came for him. Niki only survived because her mother hid her in a crawlspace; her brother and Jasmin had been at a friend's house.

I paid the motherfuckers a visit last week, surprised them in the same way they had Niki's parents. As much as I wanted to take my time with the pair, I didn't change up the method they bestowed upon the Foxes. I touched their temples to my gun and blew their fucking brains.

They'd been the pawns used to take out a man and his family that had seen too much and was refusing to work for them. I'd gotten enough information from them about who sent them, and that's all they were good for. I'd send my Niki their fingers if I knew it would give her satisfaction to know that their corpses are now rotting away, but I didn't think she'd like that very much.

Jason's voice brings me back. "She got the latest tech in security cameras installed on the outside of the property. It's double gated, and she's got motion sensors."

What are you hiding, fox?

"Damn, your girl has major trust issues."

A text comes through from the police chief at the station and I thumb the screen.

> You've been assigned a new case related to Mayor Carlton. He wants to speak to you directly. Let me know when he comes in today.

I tap back a quick response. Carlton wants to talk about his daughters. According to him, the elder one ran off and took his youngest. They've been missing for some time and he wants someone assigned to hunting them down immediately. He's had the local cops comb the city, but he requested someone with more *experience*. I can find them in five clicks, but I prefer to handle that line of work in the customary way. I'm not here to find runaway brats. Detective work is just a cover.

"Jason, I have to go. Find a way to keep an eye on the farm and send me an update once you do."

11

Justice

"**D**id you sleep well?"

Jule's voice carries a tenderness I've never before heard. He places a bowl of oatmeal in front of Macy, who nods shyly at him. She hasn't said a word. The girl has a permanent darkness that's permeated throughout her entire tiny frame. I'm short, but Macy is at least two inches shorter than my five-foot-nothing, and her frail body forlorns emptiness—it consumes her. Her boney shoulders lean forward and her sunken eyes look to Piper for support.

"We haven't felt this safe in forever." Piper's barely inaudible words are carried to me by a breathy sigh.

I keep my eyes glued to Jule. If I didn't know any better, I swear he's crushing on Macy. He's taken a stool and positioned himself at a safe distance to carry on a one-sided conversation with her while he drinks what I'm sure is coffee. I'm reminded of how young he is, impressionable, yet eager for adventure. He's so grown up and still such a baby in my eyes. Jule loves coming home, and I hate taking him back to the trailer junk box.

But we can't move yet.

Almost. We're so close to our goal, and I've taken up hours at the club to earn five times the amount I normally do.

Just enough for Jule to enroll back into school. He's going to be a lawyer someday. He's got the brains, and I won't let him slip through the cracks.

I can't hear what he's telling Macy, but he's talking with his hands, animatedly, and making her smile. His hair cascades over his eyes, below his ears, and dangerously close to his shoulders. My baby brother needs a haircut, and I'm pulled to a memory from a time where I'd cut his hair for him. Now he just does it himself. He keeps his face shaven, but he's got some stubble now, and he looks like a young man. My heart gets this odd sensation, like a thousand mosquitos have stung it.

Piper looks the way I feel, and I suddenly understand her eagerness to protect her sister. I'm right alongside her on that one.

I breathe out, realizing that I'd been holding my breath. "What are you going to do? What's your plan?"

Macy's back is to us, and for the first time, I see Piper let go. She shoves her hands into her hair and then leans into them, hugging herself. "I have no idea."

I'm sure there is so much to uncover. In truth, I know nothing about the two women I just helped escape. Who is looking for them? What will happen if they're found? How long has the abuse been going on and who knows about it? Will it help if she gets a lawyer or reports him?

"Talk to me," I say suddenly.

She looks at me, stunned by my words, but then stands and cocks her head to the screen door that leads to the back patio. It's a warm fall morning, but the California breeze promises a blistering high by noon. Piper hugs herself and looks to the lush garden blooming with roses, thanks to Helena. I'm no green thumb. Plants hate me.

I approach slowly and stand beside her, enjoying the view. "You can stay for as long as you need."

She nods and I hear her swallow. "I don't know how we can ever repay you."

I shake my head. "This is what I do, Piper."

She turns, and her eyes are full of unshed tears. "And here I thought you were just some tween looking to gain followers and get famous on social media," she chuckles.

"Well, that's good, I guess. I'm sure that's what the entire police force thinks." Up until I got arrested and set them straight.

She nods and dabs at her eyes to clear away any trace of sadness. "Charles, the guy that was with me at the bar, my father thinks he's one of his trusted minions. But he's one of mine. He helped me and Mace get out."

I nod. Charles acted like a bodyguard in love with Piper—I don't question his allegiance. I'm sure of Piper's ability to sniff out a rat. She's been raised by one and is an expert by now at being able to set apart who can be trusted.

Her posture stiffens. "Charles told me that my father requested the force to assign a detective to hunt us down. Like a fucking sport. At first, he just sent his minions, but now, it's more serious. And we *cannot* go back."

I nod. "Have you ever tried exposing him?"

"You saw what good it did when you released the footage of him at the club. It's chalked up to be some conspiracy now. No one cares. He's protected. Too many dirty fuckers backing themselves up, it's disgusting."

I look into my mug. The black coffee swirls slowly and the steam rises, then dances away with the breeze. Oddly enough, the darkness reminds me of Dylan's eyes, and I clench my thighs and grip the mug tighter.

"Charles says the case has been placed on a new detective's lap. He transferred from I don't know where, but apparently he's the best. He's got a reputation for getting the job done, whatever that means."

Shit, *my* rookie is out there looking for Piper and Macy?

Is he telling me the truth? Is he really a *good* cop? Would he help them or expose them? I can't answer that, and I don't want an answer. Cops can't be trusted. "Well, he won't find you here."

Jasmin, Jule, and I are parked under a bridge, waiting for one of Noah's friends. Helena's house has a landline, and we called his cellphone to make sure he'd meet us. We can't drive to the trailer lot and risk Dylan catching us.

If he connects the truck to me, I'm fucked. It has to look like we caught a ride with someone, and for now, Erik will have to do. He walks toward us, and I step out so he can take my place in the driver's seat. He knows the drill and doesn't ask questions. It's better this way, that way if he's ever questioned by police, he truly doesn't know anything.

"Am I supposed to keep this from Noah?" he asks in a rushed whisper.

Jasmin clears her throat and places a gentle hand on my shoulder. I look back with a questionable gaze and she gives me a little squeeze. "For now," she says. "Just let us figure this one out and keep quiet about it."

She's never fully trusted Noah, or anyone but my brother and me, so I don't blame her for wanting to keep Noah in the dark about the truck.

We make it back in twenty minutes, which leaves Jasmin and me exactly one hour to get ready for work. It's dark by the time Erik lets us out of the truck to then store it in the shed. We leave him to it, hoping it convinces the rookie cop that we got a ride from our neighbor, in case he's watching. And then it occurs to me—what if this motherfucker has cameras? *Shit.*

My focus turns to my little family. Whenever we return from our patch of paradise, we're all glum and miserable. And this sets over us as we walk toward our trailer.

Jule is quietly, yet animatedly, explaining an episode of *Stranger Things*, in an attempt to distract us, when a jingling sound rushes toward us.

"Oh, shit," Jasmin squeaks and grips my arm tightly. Jule moves in front of her and begins to wrap his arm around me to do the same when I notice what all the fuss is about. Max is rushing toward us, his tail wagging crazily and his tongue hanging out.

"Hey, boy." I squat down and he shoves me back, then covers me with kisses.

"What the fuck?" Jule gasps. "Your new friend?"

"Yea, he's a cutie." I rub his massive face between my palms and kiss the top of his head.

"Max," Dylan's roaring voice calls. It's not a yell, but it cuts the air and chills you. "I'm sorry, he's deciding to be disobedient. Thankfully, he likes you."

Jule straightens, and I can feel Jasmin's focused stare on me. She knows he affects me but hasn't pressed further.

"Did you move here to unleash the hound on us?"

"Jule," Jasmin snaps.

"No, he's gotta know. Moving here puts us at risk. The last thing we need is a cop sniffing around where he shouldn't. The corruption is uptown, not here."

"I moved here to make sure no one is fucked with," Dylan retorts. His eyes shift from Jule to me and stay there. They darken and he snaps his fingers. Max reacts robotically and moves to sit next to him.

Jule narrows his eyes. "*Right.*"

"Come on, Jule. You have to finish your essay." Jasmin puts her hand on his shoulder and gently moves him to our trailer. "Justice, we'll see you inside."

How my best friend knows that I can't go in just yet, I have no idea. But thankfully, my brother listens. His acceptance to the school depends on him turning that thing in, and he's just about finished. They disappear into the trailer and Max whines suddenly.

"So, who was the ride?"

"What?"

Dylan points behind me toward the shed. "The ride."

I roll my eyes. "What is it with you always interrogating me?"

"Fine, I can find out another way."

Fuck. "A neighbor, okay. We take rides all the time."

"And where were you?"

What in the fucking world? "Listen, rookie, I don't know what makes you think I have to answer your fucking questions."

I turn on my heel and flip my hair for emphasis when his hand reaches out to pull me toward him. His grip is strong yet gentle. Suddenly, Max stands and lets out a low growl. The beastly hound moves to stand next to me and glares at his master.

Dylan looks down and smirks. "Easy, Max. I'm not going to hurt her." His smile doesn't reach his eyes. He looks at me, and I'm suddenly centered in place. My belly flips and tightens and my thighs press together firmly. "I'd never," he murmurs.

He grazes my cheek roughly, and it's as if he's dropped an ice cube down my back. It slides down my spine and sinks between my legs, melting me in its wake. A puddle with his name on it gathers at my center.

"I know exactly where you were, but we can talk about that another time."

He what?

"I just thought you should know that the two men who killed your parents are dead." Dylan lets go of my arm and I instantly feel the void of his hold.

I feel like I'm falling and all the air has left my lungs. But I can't take a breath in. It's as if I've been shoved under water by an unforgiving wave that continues to collide with my body. It smacks me back and forth, pushing me further down into the depths where only shards of rock await me.

I barely recognize that my body is floating and pressed against a solid heat that cradles me. The absence of air consumes me. The vacantness roars in my ears. It blurs my vision and holds me hostage. It's as if the Pacific claimed the land and a wave truly did materialize to fill my lungs with its saltiness.

"Niki?" Dylan coaxes. "Steady. Breathe slowly in and out."

I hold on to the gentle yet stern command in his tone. "They're dead?" I finally manage. It feels like mushy and salty cotton fills my throat.

"They are."

I notice I'm no longer outside but inside Dylan's trailer. Or rather, his mansion. It puts all other trailers to shame. It's enormous and modern. Black and gray furnishings, dark oak tables, and sleek leather. It's unlit except for a dim lamp on an end table. I'm leaning on his loveseat, and he's bent down on one knee, hovering over me.

I was fourteen when three men barged into our home. Vork gave the order and then walked out. One of the men assaulted my father, beating him while the other took advantage of my mom. They tied my father up so he could watch and then they shot my mom. Two bullets, two men. Then one of them shot my father's kneecaps and then they shot him in the head. Four bullets, two men. Their faces were a blur, but I never forgot their voices. The memory of Vork delivering the instructions, in his cold and distant manner, lives in my head rent free. They never saw me, but I saw everything.

"How are you certain it was them? The officer at the time said they didn't leave evidence behind and that there would be no way to find them."

Dylan nods knowingly. "It was them."

I'm not sure why I want to know, but before I can scrounge for an answer, I blurt out, "How?"

Dylan swallows and tucks a strand of hair behind my ear. His touch singes my trembling nerves, taming them. It stabilizes the hurricane in me. "One of the men was shot twice in the head, the other had both kneecaps blown off, as well as two bullets to his head."

The same way my parents were taken. "Do they know who did it?"

He clears his throat. "It's an ongoing investigation."

For years, I dreamed of their deaths, witnessing or delivering them. I wanted to walk about knowing they were no longer breathing, no longer enjoying the same sky that hung above us. And now they were dead. Killed.

I don't pity them. I'm not sure if that makes me as horrible a person as them, but I don't give a fuck. In fact, I hope they suffered, gasped and sputtered for their lives in vain.

Dylan's cell buzzes next to us and I notice the time.

"I have to get ready for work."

"*Nym-Pho* again?"

I bristle at his questioning. "What's it to you?"

He chuckles dryly and shakes his head. "I'm not interrogating you, Niki. Just... be careful."

I stand and move to the door. Ignoring the magnetism between us. "I can take care of myself, rookie."

I leave before he can say anything else. I don't have the energy for him right now. My body's reaction to his is cataclysmic, and it shocks my nerves, vibrating through me. His voice is the symphony that tames my thoughts, his body stabilizes mine into a blissful calm that allows me to feel complete. It's unnerving. I don't know who the fuck he is. And in less than a month, he makes me feel what Noah never could.

But I can't want him. I shouldn't. I ignore my neighbors' skeptical eyes, watching me leave the cop's trailer, and sulk home.

"What did he want?" Jasmin stares out of the moving car. We caught a ride with one of the bouncers. He doesn't mind giving us a lift for fifty bucks a night. It's more than he should get for taking us in literally the same direction and destination he's headed toward, but beggars can't be choosers.

"Mom and Dad's shooters were killed."

She gasps loudly and faces me. "When?"

"About a week ago. I don't want Jule to know. He needs to focus on getting back on track with school."

She nods slowly. "Of course."

Something tells me there was more that Dylan refused to say. I don't know, something about the way he said *ongoing investigation.* An inkling beyond my brain's ability to understand or perhaps accept. Also, I'm wary about the manner of death, eerily exact to the way they took my parents. If I didn't know any better, it gave off *revenge kill* vibes.

"Did he really move there to keep us safe?"

I sigh. "I don't know. I didn't get to ask him anything about that." Nor did I get to ask him what he meant about knowing where I was. *That* would be catastrophic.

Our ride slows down and we both pin our eyes to the exterior of *Nym-Pho's* massive structure. I don't have the strength to put on my fake smile. Fuck, what if *el cerro* shows up tonight? I have *got* to get it together.

As if sensing my thoughts, Jasmin reaches for my hand and squeezes. "I'll put you in a cage for your shift."

I nod and lean into her. *Don't cry, don't cry, don't cry.*

"No one will bother you. Just sway about and we'll make sure to collect your tips."

The music vibrates off the metal bars of the birdcage structure that holds my body elevated twenty feet off the ground. It's an elegant gilded mini fortress, immovable and secure. There are two others with semi-nude dancers inside. I could get used to this.

But I keep replaying the deaths of my parents in my head.

I'm sitting in a makeshift closet, a crawlspace in the wall. A sliver of light gleams in and I press my face to it. The broken wood of the doorframe splinters my face, my eyes burn, but I refuse to close them. My parents died that day, but they took my soul with them. A part of me died right alongside them that night, but I forced myself to continue for my baby brother. He didn't have anyone. I needed to step up and grow the fuck up.

Whatever problems I thought I had in my hormonal teenage rebellious stage were stripped from me, like acid filling my veins and cleansing away the purity of being a child. I forced myself to suffer right along with them so that I would never forget.

And now the bringer of their deaths was gone, too. Did they suffer? I fucking hope so. Did they cry and beg for their lives? I don't know, but I pretend to hear their voices screaming for someone to pity them. I only wish I would've been there to replace my parents' screams with theirs, so that their shrieks would fill the remnants of the tattered memory that's stuck on replay. I don't want my mom and dad to suffer anymore.

The music is upbeat tonight, the aesthetic stays the same, but the beat coming from the speakers alters from night to night. Today's theme is sexy pop. I think it's one of Ariana Grande's songs, but I can't be sure.

My hearing is fucked tonight. I gyrate my hips and flip my hair to the thrumming of my parents' heartbeats. I'm covered in sweat and my hair clings to my back and neck. The full face mask is surprisingly comfortable, but still hot as hell. I know I'll be red as a tomato when it comes off. It's a black fox mask with gold piping along the pointy ears, eyes and nose.

I have a sheer lace bra on with a faux gold chain attached to a black choker around my neck. The gold chain drips down my front and connects to the garter wrapped around my belly. The chain dangles near my thighs, and it looks like frozen dew drops over the flesh. My pussy is covered by a lace thong. I get to be barefoot in the cage, thank the she-devil that commands the existence of this kingdom of sex and booze, because I wouldn't be able to make it if I had to dance the night away in six-inch heels.

Suddenly, I feel someone's gaze on me.

I'm dancing basically naked in a dungeon of sex, so of course, people watch me, but this feeling is different. It's a palpable grip on me, a tug toward the one person whose gaze alone peppers my skin with goosebumps. I can literally feel someone's touch, their thoughts mingle with my own. It forces my attention to a man sitting alone, feasting on me. His penetrating gaze influences a reaction in me. Without ever even touching me, his eyes alone have provoked a physical interaction as my body leans into the bars, a gravitational pull that forces me toward him.

He's in an all-black suit, black tie, black shirt, and a black mask over the top half of his face. The man licks his lips then lifts a short glass with a dark brew up, as if to salute me, then drinks it slowly, his eyes caressing my moving curves. I blow him a kiss, then flip my hair and turn around.

I don't have the headspace for meaningless flirting to gain some more cash. The table below me holds a five-gallon glass jar and there are only hundreds inside, all mine. And although something about the man stands out, I shove it away. The pain in me is too great to care to investigate.

I bend down, and Billy, the bartender whose name I learned right before I entered the cage, hands me a double shot of tequila. I knock it back, relishing in the burn it leaves in its wake down my throat. I prefer this feeling over the continual stab that repeatedly pierces the hole where my heart is supposed to be.

I hand him back the glass and signal him to give me another. After shooting it back, I lean on my haunches and tilt my head back until it touches the floor of the cage. I lift my arms and caress the air, then slowly lift back up, my hips moving in circles, then up and down. I stand up slowly, my hips dip low, and I expand my arms to hold both ends of my prison.

I close my eyes and give in, the roar in my ears building, and I finally allow myself to let go. I'm in the sky, but not quite in heaven. I'm floating on a black rain cloud. It's the darkest part of eternal paradise. It isn't hell, where we'd be subjected to the perpetual flames of torture. I'm in a place of bliss, of quiet content and peace.

Here, in this cage, I let go, baring it all except for what lives deep inside me, tormenting me. No one ever sees that. I can't expose that side no matter how much I try, so I feed off of the energy of everyone's hunger, their thirst for excitement and their approval of me.

I don't know what I thought would happen once my parents' killers were found, imprisoned or executed. But somehow, I thought it would make me feel *better*. Yet I still feel empty.

12
Redemption

My little fox dances in the birdhouse tonight and she looks fucking riveting. I almost laughed out loud when I saw her mask, as if hot-wired to my thoughts and drawn to it as it sat among all other options. She believes her identity is safe, and that might be so, but not from me. I can single her out while blindfolded in a crowded room. In fact, every woman here is blurred, drawn out from my vision like a filter, dimming away all flesh that isn't hers.

She looks sad tonight, and I can't help feeling responsible.

The death of her parents weighs heavily on her this evening, and although knowing that their killers have been extinguished brings her peace, she's upset at the fact that she wasn't solely responsible for bringing them pain. If only I could tell her she was. I reminded them of their victims, making them scream out their names while they begged for their miserable fucking lives.

Niki comes alive in this element of toxicity. She desires nothing more than to be consumed by her darkness, to be saved from the nothingness she feels inside. She wants something to bring her to life, and she clings to the addicting sensation of desire and sin because it makes her feel *something*. The adrenaline pulses through her and me both, and I know exactly what she's going through.

I want to set her free, to open the door of her cage and seep into the crevices of her lonely soul and steal her pain. She doesn't know how strong she is, but I'll remind her. My little fox carries the world on her shoulders, and it's got her all knotted and torn. I can see her leaning into the shadows that soothe her, begging for me to guide her through it so that she may come out on the other side complete, the hole in her heart filled and patched up. Filled with my heart, sewn up by my hands.

She has the power to bring me to my knees, and she doesn't even fucking know it. But she will. Out of all the eyes pinned on her, she senses *me*. She's looked at no one else but me tonight, and she doesn't even realize who I am just yet.

I lean back and call a server over. She's dressed in nothing but a black thong and nipple clamps that connect in the center by one word—*slave*. I hand her my empty glass and another materializes. I scan the room; all eyes are on my Niki. Many have added their silver cards into her glass bowl, requesting a private show.

Over my dead body.

I don't give a fuck if they watch her. Let their eyes feast on what they will never have. She's mine. But I'm certain they'll try to get their hands on her.

The people employed by *Nym-Pho* abide by strict rules. Most servers are up for grabs, and unless they are distinguished by color-coded collars that dictate their status, they're basically there for the taking.

Niki doesn't wear a collar, just some necklace that blends with her uniform for the night. Her beautiful long neck is bare of claim. I'll have to remedy that.

My phone vibrates in my chest pocket, and I ignore it. Cell phones are prohibited in this establishment.

The invisible earpiece in my left ear reads the message for me. It's from Jason.

> Your boy, Noah, was arrested three counties over. He's being held on charges of racketeering, possession of an unregistered firearm, and they're trying to pin arson on him, too.

Shit. What the hell is he getting himself into? I stand and make my way to the back. Niki's shift will be over soon, and I'd rather she have a ride home than be bumming one from any of these fuckers. After watching her get out of the old beat up truck, I connected the plates to one of her aliases. She uses it sparingly. I'm not sure for what exactly just yet, and as far as everyone else is concerned, she hitches rides or walks. She's good at remaining undercover, my clever fox.

I don't even try to build a backstory or create an excuse as I wait out front for Niki and Jasmin. I've taken my jacket and tie off, threw them in the trunk, and rolled up the sleeves of my shirt. I unbuttoned the top, just to appear more casual. I'm leaning on the passenger door, and as soon as they walk out, I open it. My little fox glares at me and her friend fails to mask the stupor on her face.

"We have a ride," Niki snaps.

My lips quirk up at the edge and I furrow my brows. "I don't give a fuck. Get in the car, Niki."

She glares up at me, her thick lashes alluring in the dim light. Her face is flushed and sweaty, and she crosses her hands over her chest. She's changed and wears a simple white t-shirt and loose black shorts and sneakers. Her hair is gathered in a bun atop her head. I approach her and take the backpack from her. "Get in."

Jasmin reaches out and grips Niki's arm. "You too," I tell her.

Niki rolls her eyes, and just when I think she's readying herself for a heated argument, she glowers, but languidly makes her way into the car, a tired Jasmin not far behind. Once they've both climbed in, I close the door and make my way to my seat and we're on the highway in less than two minutes.

"You can't make this a routine, rookie."

I watch her reflection in the rear-view mirror. She's angled herself to lean against the window and her forehead is pressed up against the glass dismissively, her lids heavy and threatening to give out. Jasmin leans on my girl's shoulder, and she yawns and then cuddles into her. Anyone else unaware of their history would think they're blood-related. They look nothing alike, but their bond is strong. I've met fraternal twins that look nothing alike. That can easily be applied to them.

My little fox is exhausted, but she refuses to let her guard down. She adjusts herself so that her friend can get comfortable.

"Why not? I was in the area, and we're headed in the same direction. It's not like you have *your own wheels,* so you can commute in a safe manner to and fro." I raise my brows at her.

She turns to peer at me and purses her soft, pouty lips. I want to hold them between my fingers and then nibble on the skin. She looks spent, and I almost regret throwing that comment out there to wrack her brain about it. I want her to know that I have discovered absolutely everything she hides from everyone outside her brother and adoptive sister. Including Noah.

"It's not really your concern how I get around, Detective. And our neighbors are already questioning why you're there," she says sleepily.

I scowl at her. I think I prefer it when she calls me *rookie,* though that's far from what I am.

At twenty-eight years old, I have more experience than your typical veteran who's been on the job for twenty-odd years. I was adopted into a long family line of CIA agents. I joined the Marines as soon as I graduated high school, ranked at the top of my class, and joined the FBI right after serving my term. Now I work for a ghost agency that sends agents out as an undercover Internal Affairs officer with intent to uncover corruption within the force.

But the pet name has grown on me, and the way Niki delivers it makes it seem as though she has uncovered something new in me. Something only *she* owns. But when she calls me Detective, she's annoyed and wants me far away. It unnerves me. That's something I *can't* do.

"Well, let's agree to disagree, then," *my little fox.*

She sighs tiredly and leans her head back. Her friend is already snoring lightly and Niki wraps her arm around her and tips her head further back until it rests comfortably on the seat. Her neck is exposed, and I almost steer off the lane from the sight of it.

I want to curl my hand around it and control the amount of air she takes in. I want her to understand that breathing her next puff of oxygen is in my hands. That's the control she's seized upon me, and I need her to feel the same exact way. Once I allow her to take her next breath, I want to trail the length of her neck with my mouth from the tip of her chin until my tongue slides between her legs and I taste her. My dick stiffens and I move in my seat to adjust it. I look back and her lips part.

She's asleep.

I try to keep my gaze on the road, but the look on Niki's face while she sleeps is like an open gated archway to heaven. She looks beautiful and at peace. She whispers something and I lean back like a madman, desperate to hear the words that will divulge some secret she won't even dare admit to herself.

"Dylan."

I hold my next breath. She's dreaming of me and calling my name. I smile like a fucking idiot and my dick jerks again. Her subconscious knows she's mine, and it's delivering that message to her in a dream. If only she'd accept and roll with it.

Instead, she fights it and stays with a man she's been with for only a couple of months. Whatever she thinks she owes him, she's wrong. Noah is a liar, and he'll drag her down the same way his father did to his family.

I won't allow it.

Twenty minutes later and I'm driving up the dirt road that leads to the lot. I turn off my headlights and park my car between our trailers. The sun hasn't risen, and the early morning is quiet, lest the crickets and cicadas singing their tunes. Jasmin pops up and looks around, then rubs her eyes.

"Don't wake her," I say.

I open her door and hand her Niki's bag, then reach in the car and scoop up my little fox in my arms. She looks so fragile while asleep, though I know she's anything but. She's snoring softly, and it reminds me of a kitten purring. She smells of tequila and oranges. I want to crush her against my chest and drag her to my bed, where she belongs. But instead, I take in a deep breath—that will come soon enough—and I carry her to her trailer. Jasmin fishes the keys out and holds the door open for me.

"She hasn't slept in three days," Jasmin whispers and points in the direction where she wants me to place her.

I haven't had a good night's rest since the first time I saw her. I can't sleep knowing she isn't in my arms where she belongs. I wonder what's kept her from allowing herself to succumb to her exhaustion.

I have to keep my body low; the inside of the trailer is tiny. It's literally a rectangular box. There are no rooms. I move to the left where two toddler-sized cots lay on the floor and gently bend down to lay Niki on the mattress Jasmin signaled. I'm sure she'd want a shower, but I also know she's a feral, wild fox when woken up. So I set her down as gently as I can and move her hair off her face. I untie her sneakers and slip them off, then I lift her puffy duvet covers over her.

I move to stand and crouch so that I don't hit my head on the ridiculously low ceiling. Jule is tall for his age; I wonder how the fuck he lives here, forced to permanently hunch in his own residence.

Jasmin follows me, and I take a quick scan of their living quarters. Jule sleeps on the opposite end of the trailer. It's dark, but the small window in front of him allows the moonlight to shine over his sleeping frame. His legs are entirely off the cot and he snores loudly.

"You didn't have to do that," Jasmin whispers.

Of course I did. "Goodnight." I step out and she nods and then closes the door.

Why are they choosing to live in these conditions when they have a massive house sitting empty at a plantation they own? Then it occurs to me—*is it* empty?

I pull my cell phone out and send a quick text to Jason.

> **I want to know exactly who occupies Niki's property.**

He responds immediately.

> On it.

I hear the locks click behind me, and I rush over to let Max out. He's coming with me on this next assignment.

The drive out to the police station holding Noah was a two-hour drive south. I had Jason email the release papers and called ahead to make sure it would be set by the time I made it there.

The drive out to the police station holding Noah was a two-hour drive south. I had Jason email the release papers and called ahead to make sure it would be set by the time I made it there.

Max waits in the front seat with the air-conditioning on, and I almost want to leave Noah here for a couple more days, but the torture wouldn't sink in.

He's not that easy to crack.

"Detective Montreal?"

I roll my eyes at him and hold back a snarl. "The one and only."

Noah's bloodied face stares at me stupidly from behind the metal bars of his cell. One of his eyes is swollen shut and purple, his lip is busted, knuckles raw. His eyes search behind me worriedly. "Did Justice send you?"

I laugh humorlessly and shake my head. "*Please*, you think Niki would even speak on your behalf if she knew who you work for?"

His nostrils flare, and I think a growl escapes him. He looks beat, and I almost feel sorry for him. The empty hell he's going to encounter once my girl learns the truth is almost enough fuel to laugh in his face, but my patience is exhausted. I have better things to do than bail his ass out, but it's the only assurance I have to make him talk.

"I see, so you just jumped at the opportunity to ruin me."

I snap my fingers at the guard with the keys so he can let the dumbass out, and then I lean against the wall. "You did that yourself."

Noah laughs and then nods. "You gonna tell her?"

I shake my head and point toward the exit so he knows where to go. "*You're* going to do that."

"She's going to hate me."

I focus on the road instead of Noah's stupid face. Max sits in the back, his eyes focused on my passenger. He lets out a snarl each time he speaks. This time Max just chews the air, as if agreeing with him.

I, however, disagree. "She'll be disappointed, but she can never hate you."

Noah looks out the window. "Yea, but she can never love me, either," he says this quietly, more to himself.

It looks like he's smarter than I give him credit for. "You're going to tell her the truth and fix this, and then you're going to leave her alone."

"I'll tell her the truth, but Justice can decide if she wants me to back off. *She'll* tell me."

"Right, so that the criminals you work for can come and collect her once they realize your fuck up?"

In an attempt to screw his boss over, Noah set fire to one of their smaller storage spaces. A rental spot where they kept their merchandise right before it was shipped. He was trying to get out, hoping that the discovery of their whereabouts would set him free. He was wrong. They knew exactly what he'd planned and waited to confirm.

"They're *not* going to find out."

I roll my eyes. "You're a fucking idiot. They're the ones that gave the green light for your arrest. Those cops beat your ass because your boss gave them strict instructions to."

"They won't hurt her. My Justice is–"

A snarl rips through me; Niki is *mine*. "It's about damn time you stop playing yourself into thinking she *ever* belonged to you."

Noah laughs, and I almost give Max the word to chew his fucking head off. "*Please,* let's be real. Justice doesn't *belong* to anyone."

And then I'm the one that's laughing. "At least not you."

Niki can't belong to anyone because her very soul is spliced, and I'm the other half. From my peripheral, I see him give me a look that says he thinks I'm insane. I stop the car and climb out, and Max snarls at him to do the same. Once out, he gawks at me, and then at my trailer. He's about to retort something stupid, I'm sure, but Jasmin's frantic voice halts my next breath and catapults me to another life, one of pure torture and violence.

I want to shake her. "What the fuck did you just say?"

"They took her." She runs to Noah, and he believes she's going to embrace him, but she claws at his face instead. Jule suddenly appears and rushes to her, then gathers her in a tight hug.

Jasmin points at Noah accusingly. "You son of a bitch. What the fuck were you thinking?"

Noah looks at me, his mouth hangs open, but nothing comes out.

I don't have time for this shit. They can figure out their family drama. Jasmin can tear his eyes out for all I care. I whistle and Max jumps into the car through the open window. I take my phone out and roar away from them. The gravel wafts up and spits back angrily. I glance in the rearview mirror in time to catch Jule land a punch to Noah's face before I turn the corner.

Jason picks up before the first ring can finish. "Get me Niki's location. You have thirty seconds."

"Fuck, who do you think I am? God himself needs a bit of—"

"I'm not fucking around, Jason. I swear to—"

"I got her. She's being held in a warehouse thirty minutes from your location. I've sent you the coordinates."

I hang up and tap on the link, then follow the green line on the map. I roar the engine past its usual mode and the wheel trembles in my hand as I switch gears with the other.

Of course, I placed a tracker on her. I attached a little onyx fox charm on her bracelet when I laid her in her tiny bed, and thank the fucking heavens I did. If they so much as touch a hair on her head, I'll rip them apart with my bare hands.

13

Justice

"**D**id you tie her up?"

"Yea, boss."

"You sure? Because I don't feel like getting kicked in the fucking balls again."

I spit out the collection of blood that's pooled inside my mouth. "Aww, are you scared? Why don't you untie me and we can find out if you have balls at all?"

The ball-less prick slaps me with the back of his hand and my face throbs in response. But I only laugh out loud, relishing in the pain. I wriggle in the chair, my restraints digging into my ankles and wrists, and two of the men jump back.

I never got the chance to shower or even change after my shift a few hours ago. I was still wearing my shorts and t-shirt, but I was barefoot now. I don't remember walking into the trailer; last I recall, I was in Dylan's car. Then somewhere between sleeping soundly in my bed and now, three men barged in and beat my ass into their pedophile-looking van. They held Jasmin back, and I yelled at her to keep my brother safe.

"Shut her ass up," he growls.

I look up and shake the strands of hair off my face. I want to look into the face of the man who would *shut me up* so I can fuck him up later. My wrists are almost free. The burn settles into me and I focus on the sting.

It'd taken three men to finally tie me down to the old wooden chair. I knew one of them had a broken wrist, two had been kicked in the groin, one had my bite marks on their thigh, and another on their forearm. I'd bitten someone's ear and had all of their skin under my fingernails.

A tall, thinly built, but handsome man walks up to me and caresses my face. "Behave, little one," he coos in Spanish, and I gather from his accent that he's Puerto Rican. "I don't want to hurt you. It's your boyfriend we want."

My boyfriend? What the actual fuck?

I think my confused expression gives it away because, after lighting a cigarette and puffing the air into my face, he smiles. His forearm is bleeding, and I figure he's the one I took a chunk of flesh out of. "Noah fucked up, baby girl. And we're going to hold on to you until he pays us back."

A large penguin-looking man laughs behind him. "Either that or we'll keep you as payment."

I bite back the urge to call him by every obscene name in my book. "Fucked up how? Who are you?"

"Ay, baby girl. You should really do your research on someone before allowing them into your bed."

I scowl. What the fuck is he talking about?

A short and twitchy one snorts something up his nose and shakes his head. "Shut up. You think Vork wants us discussing business with this cheap pussy?"

I bristle at the mention of Vork but compose my expression. "Hey, come here, I'll show you how good it is," I purr.

His eyes brighten and he licks his lips, but the Puerto Rican stops him. "She's only taunting you, *pendejo*."

I smile through the pain. I can feel my lip is busted, the left side of my face burns, my body aches, and I'm all sweaty and probably still smell of tequila. But I take my chances and blow him a kiss.

He pushes past and leans down. "What you gonna do for me?"

I tilt my head and look at his crotch while lifting one brow and I lick my lips, insinuating a blowjob.

"Don't do it, man, she'll bite your dick off," the handsome Puerto Rican warns.

But the cokehead raises his hand to shut him up, and I gently suck on my bottom lip. "Come here. I want to tell you what I'll do."

He moves closer and leans to press his ear to my lips. I tilt my head back and forcefully thrust forward. My forehead hits his nose, and he cries out in pain. His hands shoot up to hold back the bleeding and he stumbles.

"You fucking bitch!" he yells.

I let out an energetic burst of laughter and spit out the blood that keeps accumulating.

"I warned you to stay back," his comrade laughs.

The large penguin that stayed back against the wall storms toward us, then punches me in the gut. The air leaves my lungs, a shooting pain gathers in the pit of my stomach and travels up to my neck, twisting my insides. I cough, sputtering and spitting violently, desperate to catch my breath.

"Cover her mouth, and her eyes, too."

My eyes sting from the tears threatening to spill, but I refuse to give them permission. Be it tears of physical or emotional pain, they won't see me cry. The only thing they can take from me is safe in my trailer. Jasmin and Jule–as long as they're okay, I would survive this.

Fuck these pricks.

Rough hands hold my face still as I snarl and bite like a rabid animal, and then duct tape is forced over my open mouth. Next, they toss a black cloth over my head.

"Pussies," I muffle the insult. They understand.

Someone's fist connects with my temple and a million white specs invade my vision, even behind closed lids. I catch the sound of ringing, and at first, I think it's just me. But I quickly realize it's a phone, and it's on speaker. I force my breathing to quiet down, but it's difficult. I'm riled up, and my muscles beg for me to jump and toss the chair over to writhe on the floor crazily in an attempt to break free from my restraints. I can feel the cover over my face move back and forth from my forceful breaths.

"Well, hello, Noah boy. We have your girl."

I freeze.

"Let her go. She's got nothing to do with this."

The penguin laughs. "That's not how this works. We gave you a chance to work for us. It was an opportunity, and you fucked up. So this is how it's going to go–bring us what you owe, or we'll take the pretty lady as payment."

Noah responds, but I can't hear what he says. I'm yelling at myself; my mind pounds with the sound of my screams. How fucking dare he! Noah works for Vork?

No wonder he never agreed whenever I wanted to pursue the crook. If ever I received a good lead, he would make up some shit to keep me from turning up. Had he gotten with me for the sole purpose of keeping me from gathering enough information on his boss?

No. It can't be. Noah and I have been friends since we were children. And he's been obsessed with me for years. There had to be another explanation. But at this moment, I don't give a shit. He fucked up by putting my family in danger. He worked for the very man that authorized my parents' murder—fuck up number two.

Someone's hand travels down the center of my breasts and begins to lift my shirt, and I brace myself. My tummy crashes against my ribs in an involuntary move to keep away from whoever is touching me. A whimper escapes me. As much as I want to be strong and not have these fuckers witness my fear, I can't manage the idea of their filthy hands on me and remain a statue. Grain-like hands move over my stomach to the fabric of my bra and then they tug it down roughly. Fingers squeeze and aggressively tug at my nipple, and I squirm in my chair, sickened by their touch.

A voice cackles and I recognize it. The cokehead I head-butted is seeking his revenge. I flail and he laughs again. "Not so tough now, are you?"

I thrash in my restraints. The fire of their bite a distant caress when compared to the man's hands feeling me up. My mind races with scenes of my retribution and my blood boils. I jerk my thighs up, but they barely move; they're held down by the tight rope at my ankles.

A deafening crash abruptly drags me from my wallowing, and I move my head trying to soak in the noise. Someone yells a warning, but then they slump to the ground near me. My toes feel a warm liquid accumulating beneath them and I wriggle them. It's thick, and I instantly know what it is.

Blood.

The yelling continues, and it's followed by grunts, punching, and bodies falling. A snarling animal growls and gnashes on flesh. I'm triggered to bolt up and ready myself for a fight, but I'm stuck, blind, and can't speak.

Through the tape, I try to yell, "help me," but it's muffled and garbled.

Minutes later, it's quiet, and a piercing ringing replaces my thoughts. Someone walks slowly and deliberately toward me and I freeze, my hands straighten, and I move my wrists, desperately rubbing them together to free them. I bounce in my chair and move my thighs up and down in an attempt to break away from the rope binding them to the chair legs.

The chair shifts suddenly and I brace myself for the impact of a fall, but I waver in the air instead. It hovers midair and then straightens again. I can feel someone's presence; the heat of their body forces my muscles to relax and my thoughts ease to one single realization.

The black pillowcase is slowly lifted up and off my face, and I blink up at him.

I want to scream, but his black eyes cradle me, soothing me, and I slump in the chair. He reaches to my mouth and gently strips the tape off my lips. He looks me over, his eyes trailing over my face and body, searching. He moves behind me and cuts the remainder of the rope from my wrists and then my ankles.

I stand, and he's in front of me again. I'm barely aware of the men on the ground, some bleeding from their bullet wounds. I just see *him*.

"Dylan," I finally breathe, and I collide into him.

My body reacts on instinct, drawn to him the way a starving animal is to nourishment after weeks of foraging for scraps.

He wraps me in his arms, his hands crush me, and it pieces my soul back together. I trail my hands up his chest and wrap my arms around his neck. My brain is still trying to decide if I'm hallucinating.

I don't understand the need, and I don't want to take the time to question. I pull him down and he picks me up off the floor and I wrap my legs around his waist. He feels like home. I stare into the depths of his eyes and find myself in them.

I can't let him go. I just want to swim in the dark pools that drag me deeper into a heavenly oblivion of peace. I keep my eyes open and hungrily crush my lips to his. His tongue is in my mouth and our lips move hastily, tasting one another. I press my lips into his, feeling his teeth graze my swollen and bloody cut, and I moan. Our eyes stay open, as if we're afraid the other will disappear, or like we'll wake up to realize this was just a fucking nightmare.

"How badly hurt are you?"

I hear a whine, and I'm instantly aware of what the beast-like sounds were. Max waits patiently behind Dylan.

I close my eyes. Our lips are still touching and I shake my head. "I'm fine."

His jaw clenches, and he moves to walk out, still holding me against him.

I wrap my hands tighter around his neck. "What, no backup, rookie?"

A voice croaks suddenly, and Max barks in the direction of a man on his back. "Justice."

While still holding me, Dylan reaches to the small of his back and retrieves a revolver with a silencer, and points it at the man's head. "Don't you fucking dare speak her name."

His eyes roll back and he coughs. "Vork knows who you are, and he's coming for you."

Vork.

I touch Dylan's arm and he looks at me, wondering why I'm stopping him.

I unwrap my other hand from around his neck and gently push off, and he places me on the ground. My bloody toes leave blotchy imprints as I walk toward the dying man. He looks at me, and Max growls while he snakes closer to him, eager to protect me. I know Dylan still has his gun pointed at his skull, and I smile while I crouch down beside him.

It's the penguin, and I squish his face between my hand while the other flicks him on his yellowing forehead. "Here's hoping."

I look down at his bleeding gut; he's got two bullet holes. I free his face and press my palm into his stomach and use him as leverage to stand.

Dylan offers his hand, and I twine my fingers with his, my hand tiny in comparison to his. He pulls me into a hug, and I bury my face in the hardness of his chest, and he shoots. "Let's take you home, little fox."

14

Redemption

My phone buzzes and I take it out of my pocket and place it on the mount that sits in the middle of the console. Jason is calling me, and I reach for my earbud and pop it in.

"You out?"

I clear my throat. "Yeah, burn it down."

"Got it." I can tell he's smiling; Jason loves blowing shit up. "Done."

I hang up and tuck the earbud away. I can sense Niki watching me, and after switching gears, I dare a glance. I can't tell if she wants to punch me or kiss me again. "Something on your mind?"

"How is it you're always there?"

"There, where?"

She sighs, exasperated. "*Everywhere.*"

She tucks her legs underneath her and backs away from me. Her white shirt is stained red with blood. I'm amazed there are no broken bones. Just some bad bruising. Her right brow and the corner of her lip got the worst of it—the areas are swollen and bloody. She got in a good fight before being tied down. The men only shackled her out of fear.

I breathe in a calming breath, but I know it appears rabid and unhinged. My grip tightens and I control the images flashing before me. If I allow them to take over, I'll fucking crash. What would've happened if I'd gotten there just three minutes after?

I swallow and move my head sharply, cracking the bones in my neck and grip the steering wheel. "You don't have to be afraid of me."

She grimaces. "I'm not scared of you, rookie."

"Then what's the problem?"

She shuffles and I glance at her, desperate to read her expression. "I don't trust you."

But Noah she trusts? I scoff. "What have I done to make you doubt me?"

"You're a cop. That alone is enough."

The leather underneath my palm crinkles and snaps, and I shift the car off the road suddenly and slam on the brakes. I can't lie to her. She's incapable of forgiving the betrayal of something being kept from her. Once the truth is out and she finally has a real reason to hate me, at least I can hold on to one tangible emotion instead of the mess she doesn't understand.

"I'm not a cop."

She's quiet, and I watch her eyes scan the area around her, as if she's contemplating an escape. Her eyes settle on Max and her lips falter. A smile tugs at the sides, and she breathes in shakily before settling her big brown eyes on mine. "Explain."

Fuck. "I work for a separate organization as an undercover Internal Affairs agent. I came here to uncover the corruption within the law enforcement force."

Her lips pop open, but nothing comes out. She blinks a few times, then squints as if she's trying to clear her vision. A long silent moment passes, and when I think I should start driving again, she clears her throat. "You're undercover?" she asks slowly.

"I'm not a cop," I repeat. "This city is broken. I was sent here to uncover who exactly is responsible. It's been rumored to go all the way up to the mayor."

She nods and then swallows. "I understand." I breathe a sigh of relief and shift the gear when her voice stops me. "You're still a cop, though."

I roll my eyes and she laughs softly. The sound pulls me in, and I turn to take a mental image of her like this. Her lips part back, her cheekbones rise, and her perfectly white teeth are on display. Her smile is breathtaking, and I reach out and smooth my thumb over a single dimple on her left cheek. "I'm a lone agent hired by an agency who wishes to remain anonymous."

"Ooohhh, like an assassin on a secret mission," she mocks.

I chuckle and drop my hand to the gear shifter. "Time to take you home. I'm sure your family wants to make sure you're safe."

Her eyes widen, as if she forgot how she was taken and who she left behind. "Did Jasmin send you?"

I clear my throat. I don't want to lie, but this isn't the time to reveal how far my stalker tendencies have brought me. "I have my ways, little fox."

She blows a tiny raspberry at the mention of my calling her a fox. "So what's going to happen back there? Should I expect a *real* cop at my door soon?"

I shake my head. "It's taken care of."

She nods. "Right. A secret assassin always has someone in the background cleaning up their work." She wiggles her fingers, pretending to be mysterious.

Silence falls and I'm suddenly irked by the fact that I have no way of communicating with her when she isn't next to me. "Why don't you own a phone?"

She grimaces. "It's a way to track people." She shakes her head. "No, thanks."

"You don't strike me as someone who wants to hide." She owns a fucking farm and stays in this shit hole, in plain sight, taunting the police force and posting shit on her little blog. She's purposely allowing herself to be tracked.

Niki narrows her eyes. "You'd be surprised, rookie."

15

Justice

I don't want to hide. I want to completely start over. I want a new life where my brother can go to school and my best friend can do whatever it is she wants with whoever she decides. I want to be free of the plague that encircles my family and keeps finding us generation after generation, fucking us over. I planted the seed, and I'm waiting patiently for its fruit. All I want is to enjoy it in peace.

Dylan's car stops beside his trailer, opposite to where mine is, and turns the engine off. "You should know—when I left, Julius had just knocked Noah out."

How the fuck did this get out of hand? I gape at him, and I'm about to open the door when Dylan takes my hand. "Wait."

He exits the car and shuts the door after Max jumps out. The dog suddenly growls and pounces over to my door and bites out a snarl. I turn to see why he responded so aggressively and catch Noah jogging toward us from across the lot. I open the door and wince as I step on the gravel.

Dylan raises his hand up and Max barks. "That's close enough, Noah."

"Justice, you okay?"

I cross my arms over my chest, ignoring the small crowd of our nosy neighbors that's already formed. "No thanks to you, *Noie*."

Noah's shoulders slouch forward as if the weight of the world has been set on them, and he sweeps his hand through his hair nervously. I was beginning to like the way his hair felt between my fingers. But now, I can't stand to look at him without feeling repulsed. His face is beat and I don't even care enough to ask what happened. He wasted too many opportunities to be up front.

"I thought I told you to stay the fuck off our property!" Jule's voice shouts.

I look toward our trailer and see him jumping off the steps with Jasmin not far behind.

I wave him off. "It's okay, Jule. I got this."

Noah's eyes scan our surroundings, and he locks eyes with Dylan. A history of their own crackles in the blistering heat surrounding our shadeless standoff. From the corner of my eye, I notice Dylan giving him a solemn nod, and Noah gulps.

"I'm the one who called the cops the day you had the gun. I needed to warn Vork, but... I couldn't come up with another way."

"*You?*" But... "Why, Noah?"

"They knew about... my connection... to you. And your blog. I was in charge of keeping you away."

My bottom lip falls and the corner throbs. I wince, but it's not due to the physical pain of my minor injuries. This hurt gathers somewhere in the hollow of my chest and pulses. It jabs at me from the inside out.

"How many times, Noah?"

"Justice, I'm sorry. I had no choice. They threatened to take my mom." Max snarls and moves to stand in front of me, between Noah and me. "Can you tell your hound to back the fuck off?" He glares at Dylan, who raises his hands up.

"Hey, he's doing this of his own accord."

The rookie isn't lying. I've seen Max stand up for me, even to his own master. I'm not sure why he's decided to defend me against anyone he thinks is a threat, but I want to get close. So I walk up to stand next to Max and place my hand between his ears to stroke his fur. He looks up and lets out a soft whine. "It's okay," I whisper, and he sits.

Behind us, Jasmin reaches out to grab Jule's arm. She talks to him gently, and he crosses his arms and stands still.

"Did you delete the footage?"

Noah looks to the ground and stuffs his swollen knuckles into his pockets. His guilt-ridden eyes snap up to mine.

I walk slowly up to him and look up. His light brown eyes are glossed over and pain stricken, but I don't care. "Somewhere deep inside, I knew I shouldn't have trusted you."

"Justice, please—"

I stab a bloodied finger into his chest. "I let you in, and you fucking lied to me."

"I didn't have a choice—"

"There's *always* a choice!" I yell, spit flying out. "You work for *him*, Noah. What did you think was going to happen?"

Behind me, Max growls, sensing my growing anger and desire to rip Noah apart. It was all a lie.

"I never met with him directly, I swear."

"Oh, well, that makes it better." I nod and smile sarcastically.

Noah glares at Dylan when he lets out a soft chuckle. "You think you can give me and my girl some privacy, Detective?"

Max growls, and Dylan's entire frame straightens, his jaw clenches, and it looks like it's about to break from the pressure. A vein in his neck pulses, making the inked flesh rise up. I lift my hand up to him and turn to glare at Noah.

"I'm *not* your girl."

Noah winces and lowers his head. "I didn't mean for you to get hurt."

"Hurt? You think I'm *hurt*?" I seal the distance between us, a strangled laugh erupting from my dry throat. "You broke the friendship we've had since we were fucking toddlers. We're done, Noah."

I look up and down his frame, disgusted, and move to turn when he reaches for my wrist. It happens in an instant. Max rushes to my side and growls as he jumps to snap his mouth shut around Noah's arm, who wails out in pain and falls back.

Dylan calmly delivers a command for Max to release him, and he moves to stand beside me, his master standing on my other side. "You should get that checked out." He points to Noah's bloody gash.

"Fuck, Justice. You know me! You're going to trust this psycho over me?"

Max and Dylan both growl beside me, and I have half a mind to tell them all to back off, my brother and best friend included. The fucking mob of onlookers be damned. I don't need a whole army for this. I can handle Noah. I step toward him.

"I don't know you. The Noah I know would never plot alongside criminals. And he would never lie to me about something he *had to do*."

He stands up, an angry rage building behind his eyes, and he points at me and then Dylan. "This isn't over."

Dylan snorts. "Oh, it's over. You should find yourself an attorney. I'm sure the paperwork I produced was only good for a release without bail. But they'll want to find someone to blame. And it won't be Niki."

I look up at Dylan. What paperwork? He pretends not to notice, and I turn to my brother. He reaches us and pulls me into a hug. Jasmin follows suit and the three of us hold each other tightly. I turn and witness Noah's heart breaking even further. He looks at me once more before turning around.

I don't hate him, I can't.

I don't know what I would have done if someone threatened the lives of Jasmin and Jule, but I would never agree to work for Vork. I'd rather slit my wrist open and watch the blood drain from my body than place myself in his hands.

Noah could never break my heart, since he never had it to begin with. But I gave him my time, allowed him to connive his way into my little family. I agreed for there to be a title for what he wanted us to have. I let myself believe that I could fall in love with him and rejoiced in the absurdity of his future plans. I sanctioned the entire thing, paved the way for his lies to snake into my fucking brain and convince me he was someone else.

Noah's silhouette disappears in the distance, and Jule clears his throat. "Thanks for bringing her back," his voice breaks, and I hug him tighter.

Jasmin sniffles and wipes her face aggressively. "I thought I'd never see you again."

"Don't mention it." Dylan's thunderous voice vibrates through my frame and I pull away from my brother to glance at him.

"Not bad, rookie. But this doesn't mean you belong. You're still unwanted here."

He chuckles and whistles for Max to follow him. "You should get some rest, Niki."

I frown. Why do I want to follow him inside his mansion-like trailer and strip him naked? My mouth goes dry—*fuck*—I should have never kissed him. Because now that I've tasted him, I want more.

I wake up and it's dark, but I'm not sure of the time. It's quiet outside, lest the soothing melody of the hundreds of crickets right outside the trailer.

I'm sandwiched between the giant heat pad that is my brother and Jasmin, whose heavy breaths tell me she's still deep in slumber. After retreating to our little shit box, I showered and swallowed back eight beef jerky links, along with four cups of water. Jasmin refused to be apart, so she put our toddler-sized mattresses together and we huddled close until we dozed off.

My body felt sore, my limbs ached, my head was flattened to nothingness, and I wanted to disappear into a dreamless sleep. Jasmin made me ice my face, and she tended to my wrists and ankles by slathering a salve. Jule burned my clothes, and I would've argued if his eyes hadn't blazed brighter than the small bonfire he'd started in our crappy yard.

They didn't push me to talk, they never did, but Jule watched me eat, never taking his eyes off me. And then he let me comb his hair the way I would when he was little. Each night before bed, I would make him brush his teeth, and then I'd comb through his locks. The routine had stopped right around his tenth birthday. But he would allow me to bring back all the things that made me feel a slice of normalcy and the nostalgia of our broken youth.

And now, hours later, the gravity of the early afternoon events weigh heavy on me. I arch my neck back in order to peer out of the tiny window; it's pitch black out. Jasmin and I missed work tonight, and she promised our time for the next four days at *Nym-Pho*.

I lift my legs up slowly in an attempt to gain momentum and roll to sit up. Jule lets out a loud snort and chewing sounds; he's still asleep. And I glance at them before quietly retreating to the tiny bathroom.

After relieving myself, I tiptoe into our living quarters and open up the locker-sized closet carefully, so it doesn't creak. I dig at the bottom, lift up a tile, and pull out a small velvet pouch. I dig inside and grip one of the devices and cautiously head outside.

I climb down the steps and walk around the trailer, making sure I'm alone, before turning the burner phone on. The crickets near me scatter and chirp loudly once nestled in the comfort of the grass just outside the trailer's gravel.

The phone buzzes to life, and I take a deep breath and dial the house. It's almost midnight and I should probably wait until morning, but I can't keep this in any longer.

Piper picks up on the fifth ring. Her voice is a croaky whisper, deep and throaty. "Hey, tell me you're okay."

I breathe out. Am I? "Yes, we're all okay," I lie. "I saw *him*."

Her gasp is almost inaudible. She knows who I'm talking about, and I'm glad I don't have to say his name out loud. "He came into the club. I didn't get the *opportunity* to serve him personally, but I'll make it my mission the next time he comes in, which will be in the next two days."

It's so silent that I hear her swallow. "Then what's next?"

"The son of a bitch is throwing a party. Some ball that initiates a sort of camaraderie for those interested in sex slaves. I'm going to get myself ginvited."

"Fuck, Justice. You're fucking crazy."

I ignore her. We don't have time for opinions. "It's being held at The Mansion, Piper. This is our chance. Didn't you say you had footage—evidence? You can tell me how to get my hands on it, then you can use that as leverage, or blackmail, and finally get this motherfucker."

"You're seriously demented," she pauses, and I hear her breathe out a shaky breath. "But this could work."

I smile. "I'll call you once I get that invite and you can draw out a map, or whatever it is you need me to get. We're going to bury him."

"Promise me you'll be careful, *loca*."

"Yes, yes, I promise," I say in Spanish.

And then the call ends. I smile and press the phone to my chest. *This has to work.* If we manage to uncover *el cerro*, then all his stooges follow, no? They'll all be exposed and I'll be that much closer to Vork. My smile grows and I know I look like a lunatic, as Piper loves to call me, when I turn around.

But my smile dissipates, sucked right out of my face as if I walked into a black hole. Only it's Dylan's eyes glaring at me from a short distance.

16
Redemption

"What are you doing out here?"

Niki goes from staring at me with a hopeful vulnerability, which is truly unlike her, to glaring at me. *That's more like it.*

"You know, just because you're our neighbor doesn't mean you get to question us every time you see us," she pauses. "Even if you *did* save me."

I take a step toward her. "I asked you a question, little fox."

She snorts. "None of your business," she enunciates slowly. Like I'm an idiot who's hard of hearing.

She crosses her hands, forcing her full perky breasts to stand at attention, even under a much too large shirt, and I salivate. She did this the last time she wanted to distract me. I smile; two can play that game. I was awake when I heard rushed whispers and peered out the window to find her outside. I only caught a glimpse of her before she disappeared behind her trailer. Then I saw her shadow dancing against the automatic light that turned on from the trailer on the opposite side. I threw on my sneakers and crept out. By then, she was staring at the bleak night in sweatpants and an oversized t-shirt that I hoped belonged to her brother and not Noah.

If I ever saw her wearing his clothes again, I'd strip her on the spot.

I, however, only wear my sweatpants, and they sit low on my hips. I walk toward her slowly. Like a predator stalking its kill. Her tits bob up and down quickly and the pulse in her neck sputters rapidly. I leave no space between us, her arms grazing the skin of my abdomen, and I tuck two fingers under her chin and lift her eyes to mine.

"What were you doing out here?" My voice is calm and soft, but commanding, and she gulps nervously.

I know it's my proximity that unsteadies her. She's forcing herself to be still, hanging on to the edge of her strength, as if hanging off a cliff. If she dares let go, she fears she will fall to her death. If only I can tell her to look back, a ledge awaits to hold her steady.

But instead, I stay still and hold her eyes. I know she'll mimic them. And so I look down at her plump mounds and lick my lips. I crave to rub my dick between them, and the bulge in my sweats jerks suddenly.

Just as I presumed, she too looks down and trails her eyes over my chest. As if governed by something beyond her control, she reaches out with an unsteady hand and trails one, and then two, then finally all five fingertips, slowly over the swirls tattooed on my skin.

I hiss through my teeth. Her touch brands my skin in a delicious fire of desire, setting me ablaze with an aching urge to plunge my cock deep inside her, finally sealing the call to unite us. I almost don't catch the glimmer of a black metal box pressed against the underside of her right breast, peeking just above her forearm.

"*Contéstame.*"

She looks up, stunned, and I chuckle.

I have no idea where I come from. Since the age of six, I bounced from one foster home to the next. I remember my mother didn't speak English, but I don't recall where exactly she came from, much less the scum that left her after finding out I'd been conceived. Spanish is my first language, and I experienced different cultures while in foster care. My adoptive mom is Dominican and made sure I never lost my Spanish. But my *roots*? Who fucking knows.

Niki's thick lashes fan down in a seductive sweep, and she clears her throat. Her nail scrapes gently over my skin before she retreats and tucks her hand away, hugging herself.

"I needed some air."

"Hmm," I muse. I tuck a loose strand of her hair behind her ear and she follows the movement, transfixed by the ink, I think. But I can't be sure. "*Y con quién hablabas?*"

She gapes, her eyes give her away, and she swallows nervously and looks around, as if grasping for an answer from the air or the critters nearby. And I laugh softly.

"Hand it over, Niki." I stick out my palm knowingly.

She clicks her tongue like a chastised teenager, and I laugh again.

"Why do you gotta be such a fucking cop?" She slaps the phone on my palm and crosses her arms once again.

"I thought you didn't own phones because it's *a way to track you.*"

She rolls her eyes, and I stiffen. I want to throw her over my shoulder and drag her into my trailer. Then I want to bend her over my leg and spank her ass until her flesh turns a perfect shade of pink. I'd run my tongue over her milky pink skin and soothe it until she writhes and begs for me to eat her pussy.

"It's a burner," she whispers almost inaudibly.

I nod. "Okay, I'll dispose of it." It slides into my pocket, its weight slightly tugging one side of my sweats, and I hold out my hand to her.

She breathes in an unsteady breath. "What did you mean earlier by knowing where I was?"

She puts her hand in mine, warm in comparison to my heated and calloused grip, and I pull her gently. "Who's questioning who now?"

I nudge her toward the front of her trailer and wrap my arm over her shoulder. I feel her shudder and her knees buckle ever so slightly, and I fight the urge to claim her. Instead, I fill the short distance with a question I hope she gives an answer to. "How are you?"

Her face isn't as swollen as I thought it would be, but the delicate skin is a shade darker than pink, murkier than red, with hints of teal peaking around the edges. My jaw tenses and I look at her wrists, smeared shiny and slick with some balm.

She gives me a solemn nod. "Good."

Our pace is slow but deliberate, and I get the feeling she doesn't want to be apart. She starts to twiddle her fingers and then stretches the shirt in her hands, twirling it into a knot and then letting go. I know she isn't a shy or nervous type of person, that much I've deduced. She's comfortable in her own skin, unabashed and confident.

"*Qué es lo que sabes de mí? Y que con todos los secretos?*" Her Spanish is clear and comes with a barely noticeable accent resembling two cultures meshed into one.

"*Todo a su tiempo.*"

"What happens when Vork's guys come around looking to avenge whatever happened back there? Noah can't possibly cause so much damage. What happens when that fucker realizes that it wasn't Noah who came for me and killed all of his men?"

I stop walking and turn her to face me. I put both my hands on her shoulders, then glide them down and wrap my fingers gently around her arms. "No one is coming for you. I'll make sure of it."

She swallows and her throat moves with the forced motion. "*Y mi familia?*"

"*Todos a salvo.*"

She doesn't ask about Noah and the savage caveman inside me beams. We're by the steps of her trailer, and I take my hands off her, prompting her to enter.

She exhales loudly, annoyed suddenly, and when she turns, I wrap my arm around her waist and collide her back against my front. She gasps and I push my face into the back of her head, breathing her in. She wants me to answer all of her questions and not just the ones I choose to respond to. And so I move close to her ear and whisper. "I know *everything* about you, cunning little fox."

And now we both have what feels like incriminating information about the other. She knows who I am, more or less, and I know exactly who she is. It feels like something's shifted in the cosmos, as though we're both finally at the same center, holding hands and journeying the next terrain side by side.

I graze my lips on her ear and take the lobe between my teeth. She trembles and grips my arm and hugs me tightly against her. She pulls in a deep breath and I let go, she almost stumbles back, if not for my hand at the small of her back gently pushing her forward. She takes two steps, and when she turns, I'm already walking back to my trailer.

"Swear you won't say anything," she hisses in a harsh whisper.

I turn and touch a hand to my heart, feigning a deep hurt. "Niki, I'm appalled you'd even have to ask."

"Swear it, rookie!"

She points a finger at me accusingly, waiting. Her face scrunches up and her brows furrow, glaring at me from the distance, and I chuckle at her threatening glare. She's fucking perfect.

"I swear I won't tell a soul, fox."

She puffs up and crosses her hands and I motion for her to get her ass inside. She relents, her lips move saying *okay, okay,* while her hands flare at her sides. And once she's indoors, I, too, retreat to my trailer.

17

Justice

I replay Dylan's question over and over in my head—*how are you*—and try to find an answer to it. After learning that the men who killed my parents were murdered in pretty much the same way they were taken, being abducted by Vork's men, and the cherry on top: Noah's betrayal, I'm fucking peachy.

But then again, nothing compares to witnessing the two people you look up to, who keep you safe and love you beyond words, your favorite people in the entire world, brutally murdered in front of you. I shrug and settle in between Jasmin and Jule, whose body is sprawled almost entirely off the mattress and onto the floor.

I'm actually pretty good. I have a new item on the agenda that I'm sure will steal my focus. Somehow get myself invited to *el cerro's fiesta*.

Noah can take his bullshit work dealings and shove them up his ass and dissipate from my life. It's of no consequence. Thankfully, I never told him about the ranch, the truck, *or* burner phones. As far as he's concerned, I'm an obsessed blogger who borrows the kid neighbor's laptop and Wi-Fi to upload my photos, videos, and written reports.

He has no idea that since I was fifteen, my best friend and I worked our asses off to save every penny in hopes of bringing the farm back to life. The idea of using it as a sanctuary came later, and it was mostly Jasmin's doing. She refused to back down from working at the club, which offered her the most cash.

The nerve of Noah, sneaking his way into the empty hole where my heart once was, attempting to claim what is incapable of belonging. And shame on me for thinking it could work or that he deserved a part of me that no one ever had. I think I came close to ceding, bringing each brick of the wall I'd built, years and years prior, down for a man who patiently waited ages for a speck of attention.

I guess if there were a lesson to learn here, it would be to listen to my fucking gut and my best friend. Jasmin saw through his perfect boyfriend demeanor, the *I will wait for you* and *will always love you* routine. I'm guilty of putting him above my own common sense and instincts. After all, we were friends for what seemed like forever, I told myself.

Gah, I'm so angry with myself for letting him in that all I want is to throw myself into my work. I smile wickedly and tuck the blanket under my chin. I can't wait to see the *cerro* man, I'll work all the magic I can to get an invite.

Jasmin and I will be heading out of the city to a store she prefers for purchasing outfits for work, and I have my mind set on skimpy outfits; how the tables have turned. Piper divulged what he most likes and I'm set on enticing him.

For some reason, thinking of Piper reminds me of our phone conversation outside and the fact that Dylan was snooping about like the damn detective he is, *or isn't*.

I shake my head. My smile and tiredness are gone, evaporated like the privacy I once had before he lived next door. He claims to know *everything* about me. Does everything include the truck? Possibly. The ranch. *Fuck*, I hope not.

Dylan.

I trap my lower lip between my teeth and press my thighs together. This man has wreaked havoc in my life, and somewhere inside me. *Everywhere* inside. My mind, my center, and the hollow cavity in my chest. Something within me vibrates.

"Fuck," I hiss through clenched teeth and adjust my neck further into the pillow.

Don't tell me my stupidity is going to take me from one fool to another. I wouldn't be able to survive succumbing to someone like Dylan or the betrayal that would surely unfold.

Somewhere deep in my mind, a vixen dressed head to toe in sheer, see-through lace smiles wide. Her eyes are dark with lust, her center dripping for a man who she believes we are connected to. She dangles chains that propel her to a higher existence where she is whole. And who holds the other end to the metal ropes, but Dylan himself. Black smoke wafts between us until we are nose to chest and his fingers bring my face to look up, up, up to his dark pools.

My breath catches, and he gives me a smug smile. Fuck, he's so hot. His tattoos shimmer in the dark, rimmed with the brightest silver, and they're everywhere, illuminating him in the night.

I sit up suddenly, a light sweat covers me, and Jule is heating up the food Helena made us to come back with in the small microwave. He turns to me and gives me a quizzical look.

"Dreaming?" he asks.

Jasmin is in the shower, and I throw my arm over my eyes. "Yea, I guess I was dreaming."

Somewhere between trying to soothe my thoughts about the mess my life is and the encounter I had with Dylan outside, I fell asleep.

My mother's bracelet stabs my forehead, and I adjust it lower toward my wrist and spy a new black charm. I sit up suddenly and pinch it between two fingers, bringing my wrist up close to my eyes and squinting. It's a black fox head with two tiny silver round stones for eyes.

"Son of a bitch," I hiss.

"What happened?" Jasmin questions. Her hair is dripping, a large towel is wrapped around her body, and she has another one draped over her shoulders.

I glance at Jule, who's gathering his notebooks into his backpack; his ride is already outside waiting for him. I clear my throat and mouth, *I'll tell you later,* before he turns and waves goodbye.

I stand hurriedly, tossing the mess of blankets over me to the side, and rushing to him before he steps out. "We have a present for you, a 'back to school and we're proud of you' gift."

He rolls his eyes, but gives me a sheepish grin. Jasmin tosses me a small box and starts towel drying her hair.

Jule opens it and gasps. "I thought owning phones was too much of a risk?"

"Not this time. The risk is not being able to communicate with you or losing you out there. It's already set up and ready to go."

He rolls his eyes again but laughs. "Wow, Nik, what a way to act like a sister and *not* a mom."

Behind us, Jasmin laughs, and I punch him lightly on the arm. "I would wish you luck, but you don't need it." I tell him in our Native tongue. I ruffle his hair and push him toward the door. "*Andale,* before they leave you."

He takes one look at my busted lip, and his jaw tightens. His eyes crinkle at the corners and he breathes in slowly. "*Cuidate,* Nik."

I nod and shove him toward the door.

Once the door closes and he's gone, Jasmin sighs. "Wow, I can't believe he's in high school already."

My eyes are burning, unshed tears threatening to roll over my cheeks, and I bring up the collar of my t-shirt and dab it on my waterline. I sniffle and give one sad nod. "Best high school in the fucking state."

My parents would be so proud of him. *I'm* proud of him.

Jasmin comes to give me a hug, and I use the towel that's now draped over her shoulders to dry my tears. She clears her throat and holds me by my shoulders, then takes a step back. "Now that we're alone—"

Shit. "I think Dylan put a tracking device on me."

She gasps. "A what? Like a fucking bug?"

I nod and lift up my arm and point to the fox charm. "This one wasn't here before and I don't know where it came from."

She chuckles and my brows knit together in response. I don't think having a stalker, who's some special ops, undercover agent for a non-existent organization, is a laughing matter, but I read my best friend's mind.

"What else, right?" I shrug and slap my hands to my thighs. What else is the universe going to throw at me?

"And what are you going to do?" she asks in Spanish.

I bite my lower lip. "Leave it on so he doesn't know that I know. But when we visit the ranch, I'm taking it off."

She gives a quick nod. "Good plan."

We both laugh, but then a serious and dark expression drapes over her usually chipper face. "What's going to happen now?"

I know she's referring to me getting beaten and dragged to a warehouse and the very real possibility that the repercussions of getting rescued by a fucking cop come back to bite us in the ass.

"Dylan said he would take care of it and that we would be safe."

I expect Jasmin to scoff and question his promise, like she always does whenever it comes to believing in anyone's words. But instead, she nods quietly and continues to towel dry her hair.

"That's it? We're believing him?"

She turns and shrugs. "He's trustworthy."

I click my tongue against my teeth, making a snapping sound, and put my hands on my hips.

"He brought you back, didn't he? And the other night, he carried you inside and asked me not to wake you and—" She halts and looks up, as if searching for the perfect way to describe what she sensed. "He's got this weird, otherworldly connection to you. It's like he exhales, you inhale."

I gawk at her, and her shoulders lift up, abandoning the notion of trying to explain herself. Then she points to my drawer, prompting me to get ready for our day of shopping.

"Hurry up. Sara will be here in fifteen minutes."

"Okay, okay." I wiggle my eyebrows at her and her cheeks flush.

18
Redemption

The surveillance on the trailer lot is finally up and running, and I swipe my finger over the screen of my phone at the different angles and points of view around the property. The job required a couple of men because I wanted a view of the roads before the entrance, the perimeter, the trailers, as well as Noah's side of the lot. I didn't want anymore fucking surprises.

Then I check on Niki. She's accompanied by her adoptive sister and Sara, Jasmin's girlfriend, and they're safe, shopping in the city. I assigned a bodyguard to my little fox and made sure he understood that a safe distance was key. She'd soon catch on that she was being followed, my clever girl.

"Alright, the device that pinged inside Justice's trailer was a cell phone that she purchased for her brother. It's got a block on it, so we don't have access to its contents, but we can track it. I dropped a pin on his location and sent it to you."

Jason can't see me nod. "High school."

Jason lets out a breath that turns into one long whistle. "Your girl knows someone. This block isn't one that just anyone can install."

"You think you can figure out who coded it?"

I can't see him, but I know he's smiling. "Already on it."

I guess I'm lucky Jason thrives on a good challenge. "I have to go. Let me know when you figure something out."

"Busy again tonight?" There's still typing in the background, and I catch an amused tone to his voice.

I place the phone on top of my dresser and strip the t-shirt off my back, then toss it into a black clothes hamper in the corner of my bedroom.

"The mayor is a guest at *Nym-Pho* tonight. No way am I *not* going."

"Come on, D. We both know who your eyes will be on the entire night. And it won't be Carlton."

"That's why Olivia will be there."

His typing stops and now it's me who's smiling.

Jason's words struggle through a tense jaw and tight lips. "*My* Olivia at *Nym-Pho*? Doing what exactly?"

"What do you think?"

The noise in the background tells me he's moved away from his computer and he's rummaging through stuff. "Absolutely fucking not, Dylan. No. She'll stay and work on uncovering the block and I'll go to *Nym-Pho*."

My lips tighten so as not to leak my laughter out loud. "And what sort of help can *you* offer? Olivia can at least gather intel by offering a private dance and—"

"I said no. I'll see you there."

Jason hangs up, and I burst into laughter. I wouldn't ask Olivia to go in as an undercover at *Nym-Pho*. She's one of the best cyber scientists I know. If anyone can find out who placed that block for Niki, it would be Olivia, with her hands tied behind her back. And I needed another set of eyes in the club tonight. Jason was my first choice, but seeing that he enjoys giving me shit about my developing obsession, I thought I'd pay the favor back.

Jason and Olivia have been together since they met in college; they're inseparable. And he is as tormented as me, if not more. The reciprocated infatuation makes their relationship sizzle, ignited by a twin flame and captivated by their appeal to one another. Neither of them fight it. Not for a long time, at least. I remember a time when Olivia would scurry away from Jason. Not anymore.

My situation differs, in that Niki is a force of nature all on her own. I don't want to capture or contain her. Soon she will understand that, and then she will accept us.

Not before.

Since my fox released explicit information on one of the most beloved political leaders around and would no doubt continue to chase her lead, I won't allow the risk of that son of a bitch touching or grazing a single hair of hers. Knowing she will throw herself at another opportunity to catch him in activities that will further tarnish his reputation? *Fuck*.

I can't promise her safety if she keeps throwing herself into the pit of hell. Stopping her will only inhibit an integral part of who she is. It'd be crushing her. But if I allow her to do what she does best, *and* keep her safe—the best of two worlds, if you ask me.

"Damn, Prada over here clocking in to work the night shift?"

The detectives' laughter makes its way to my ears and the hairs on my arm stand at attention.

I stifle a growl and lift up a black binder. "Just dropping these off." I toss it on the Lieutenant's desk. "Noah had nothing to do with the burnt down warehouse. It was an electrical fire, and the forensic analyses notations state that there was a shootout among the men pronounced dead at the scene."

"You sure? What about the witness that states they saw Noah leaving the scene?"

"From where, thirty miles away with super binoculars?" I shake my head. "Look over the file yourself. I went over it with a lice comb and checked each piece of evidence myself."

The idiot who referred to me as Prada, which, by the way, is not what I'm wearing, snatches the binder up and roams through the pages. I made sure to include fresh photos and thorough records. "Noah is a petty crime incubator. He couldn't possibly have orchestrated an electrical fire, disarmed men, beat their asses, *and* shot them. All five? No. He isn't capable."

"Huh," another chimes in. "Well, where was he during all of this?"

I cross my arms and lean on the desk opposite of the small group hovering over my notes. "Page thirty-two. Photos of Noah licking his wounds outside of his neighbor's house."

"How the fuck did you manage all of this?"

I check my fingernails and open my palm. The ink on my wrist has faded, and I realize I'll need to retouch my hand tattoos soon. I turn my hand over to examine the spiral better. "Don't worry, I'll make sure to hold a workshop that will instruct on proper methods and techniques when conducting an investigation. Use a recording app so you don't miss anything."

The fucker stands tall and actually begins to approach me. He's all blotchy in the face and I stifle a laugh.

"What about his little girlfriend?"

I stand and get ready to punch him in the face when Lieutenant Bauer reacts and rushes to put a hand on his chest.

I shake the feeling of wanting to smash his face in. "The file on Mayor Carlton's daughters is with the Captain. He asked for it to be directly handed to him."

Every detective freezes, and Bauer takes a guarded step toward me. "You found them?"

I shrug. "You'll have to ask the Captain."

A few of the cops nearby snort or make frustrated grunts, the nosy detectives crowding my space make similar reactions. But Bauer just stares at me and smiles. "Have a good night, Detective Montreal."

I nod and make my way out of there. I'm eager to catch up with Jason before either of us enters the club tonight. He's bound to stand out, the fucker always does. Aside from his fancy wheelchair, he's always the fucking life of a party. People are drawn to him like moths to a light. If anything, his chair further highlights his lively and amusing personality. He always has one good story after another.

He's the yang to my yin.

I park my car in its usual spot and head over to his massive truck and he unlocks the door. He's looking over the file I emailed him.

"Keep your attention on those elite guests. Don't be fooled by Dominica, she's a fucking wolf decadently dressed in fleece."

Jason nods and then peers at me from under his lashes. His gray eyes wary.

He sighs and I instantly know there's a problem. "What?"

"Liv knows who installed the block."

"Well, then? Who is it?"

He shakes his head. "She won't say."

"Why the fuck not?" I growl and the truck moves with my outburst.

Jason raises his hands. "Best she can do is keep tabs on the phone's location. She won't touch the code guarding it."

I breathe out through my teeth. "Will she at least tell me *why*?"

"Yea, she says to come over for lunch tomorrow and she'll tell you all about it."

Seriously? If Olivia knows who created the block and decided to protect them, that means she knows who they are. *Fuck.* "I'll be there."

"Great! We're making *la bandera*. It's white rice, beans—"

"I know what it is," I snap.

"Right." He nods and then opens his laptop. "There's something you should take a look at before heading in."

Great, what the fuck else can happen?

He clicks a few keys, and an image pops up. It's Niki's ranch. He zooms in and the image grows hazy. It's of three women riding horses through a pasture. Jason clicks a few more times, and the picture clears up.

"Thought you should know that your Justice is harboring two very prestigious and sought out fugitives."

Why the fuck is my little fox hiding the two women? It has to be more than Niki just trying to get back at the mayor by keeping him away from what he currently wants most. For some reason, which I know is definitely not a *good* one, his daughters ran off and want nothing to do with him. For weeks they were rumored to have lived in the streets posing as street workers. Why would they want that life instead of their supposed prime upbringing?

What does Niki know?

Carlton is a conniving political mastermind with hidden agendas. I know he's involved with Vork and his crew. Jason and I were able to look over the surveillance of one of his warehouses before it was deleted. Carlton made a rare appearance and personally handed a case to Vork before they shook hands. We're so close.

The scum chose an enclosed section on the second level, and Jason somehow already infiltrated his way into their numbers. He rolls away after almost an hour of being in their company and heads toward a table on the opposite side of the second floor that lowers into the first. Dominica is there, along with two others from the file I shared with him.

It's funny how all these idiots think a simple mask over a part of their face will suffice in keeping their identities secret.

I keep my eyes away from their area and watch cautiously through my peripheral. The music tonight is dark, violent, but still emotional and captivating. The red and white strobe lights move slowly over the furniture and it gives the appearance that we're all barely here. Ghosts in the otherwise black existence.

The lights break suddenly, a stark semblance of tar dripping over the walls, and the white chandelier in the center illuminates the club in soft red lights.

Niki steps out of the cage she was dancing in and hops onto the bar. She's ignoring my presence, but I know she's finally made the connection that it's me.

Her skin is covered in a sheen of sweat, making her appear wet and sultry. The desire to run my tongue over her skin and taste her, to push her tossled hair back and stare into her expressive walnut-colored eyes is holding me fucking hostage. I can't look away from her; the need to wrap her with my body is fiercer than ever. I grip the armrest of my chair to stop myself from walking over to her.

I want her to tell me everything I've failed to gather and understand about her. I need her lies to be mine. I want to unveil the secrets she keeps from everyone else and be the safe she needs to hold them.

After knocking back a shot of what I'm sure is tequila, she saunters to the backroom.

Jasmin is busy patrolling each floor, giving orders to every single bartender, and she stops in front of three security guards next and points to two sections, one being Carlton's. Her face is tight, and a guarded frustration ripples through her tall frame.

I request a drink refill from the server nearest me and when she returns, she hands me a bottle of Jameson, a rare vintage liquor worth over five-hundred fucking dollars.

"From our guest dressed in red," she explains.

I let her pour me a drink from the bottle and she places it on the glass table next to me. I look up and spot Dominica. She's the only guest wearing a red dress, it matches her copper colored hair. She blows me a kiss and I elevate my glass, thanking her.

She smiles, her cherry red painted lips growing wide, and begins to make her way toward me slowly. The lights make it seem as if she's moving in slow motion while everything else behind her whizzes past.

"Hello, handsome." She extends an empty glass to me and I reach down for the bottle she delivered and fill her cup two fingers high. "Do you have a name?"

"The great thing about places such as these is complete anonymity." I smile casually and hand her the bottle.

"It's yours, a gift."

"Normally, when someone makes a gesture as grand as this one, it's for a reason." I lower the bottle onto the table and we both take a sip from our glasses. The redhead reaches for my forearm and squeezes gently, then she smooths her hand up and toward my face.

I stay still, removing a mask, whether your own or someone else's, would breach the contract that *Nym-Pho* is built upon. Movement far behind her pulls my undivided attention to a shadow lurking, piercing me with a forbidding glare. Niki's mahogany eyes grow large, a threatening glow from across the room, while her entire body tenses.

She's changed from her two-piece leather ensemble that, for the first time, covered more than most outfits she's worn, and now has a black lace corset, a ruffle skirt that just barely covers her pussy, complete with garter and black stockings. She stands tall in stiletto heels, a goddess statue killing me with her eyes alone.

She knows it's me. Her eyes move slowly, tracing everywhere the redhead touches me.

"I do wish I could see your face." Dominica clicks her tongue and then places her hand on my chest and bites her lower lip before retrieving her hand and dipping her fingers into her left breast. "Perhaps we can make it official and go some place a bit more private."

She pulls out a blue metal card with a red heart shaped into a QR code and then hands it to me. Niki's body trembles and her jaw goes rigid, but she flips her hair and moves slowly toward Carlton's table.

"Perhaps," I offer, and I put the card away in the inside pocket of my jacket.

The redhead smiles and takes a few backward steps before walking back to her table on the second floor. But I'm glued to Niki's moves, seductive and languid. She approaches a metal pole directly in front of Carlton's table and joins the naked woman already dancing against it. She's incredible, and the men all watch her instead of the nude flesh before them.

She doesn't even realize how fucking sexy she is. I sit down so I don't look like a fucking idiot and keep my eyes on her, but she pretends I'm not here. On the same floor some tables away, I can feel Jason studying me, but I ignore him. He can handle himself.

It isn't until he's rolling his way toward Niki and positions himself among Carlton and his men that I sense something is off. He's chatting them up and then orders a bottle. Carlton's eyes stay on my little fox and he licks his lips.

I grip the glass in my hand, and it makes a noise in my grip, reminding me of its fragility.

The bastard moves as if he's going to stand when the fucker next to him, a lean built, tall motherfucker with gray hair, beats him to it. He walks away from the conversion and approaches Niki. He hands her a metal card, and she smiles seductively at him, then calls a big security guard standing nearby.

It's a red card—she's accepted a private dance. Son of a bitch.

I struggle but force my glare to Jason, who's staring at me. His masked face gives nothing away, but his eyes give me a warning. What does Jason know that I don't?

19
Justice

"He's here."

Jasmin smooths my next outfit on the bathroom vanity countertop. The white plastic resembles marble, but only in appearance. There's a standup shower, and in order to wake the fuck up and start fresh, I needed to wash away the first half of the night. My goal was to get in with Carlton, and I couldn't approach him stinking of sweat, tequila, and whatever else this place consisted of.

"*Who's* here?"

The lace is soft and comfortable, and I splash on my favorite citrus-scented body spray and loosen my waves. I flip my hair and adjust my breasts, then reach for a black leather fox mask and adjust it over the top half of my face. "The rookie," I whisper.

"*What*? How can you be sure?"

We exit the bathroom and walk toward the far wall that's covered with a ceiling to floor length curtain. I move the velvet, burgundy-colored drape to expose the one-way glass window and point.

"I'm sure."

"Fuck!" Jasmin bites her nail, and I reach out to tug her hand away from her mouth.

"He's here to keep tabs on *me*, Jas. He's not working tonight."

She eyes me suspiciously. "Are you two..."

"No." I shake my head. "I don't know."

"Well, go out there and pretend it's any other night."

I peer out again and he's serving whiskey to a woman. *Expensive* whiskey. "Who the fuck is that?"

Jasmin looks over my shoulder and whispers. "Elite client named Dominica. She wears a mask, but that's just because of the rules. Everyone knows who she is."

Lava fills my veins, searing away any and all clear thoughts in their path. A red film drops over my irises and then my fire-filled vessels turn to stone. A long and fluid ring fills my head, and I don't even notice that I'm moving out of the staff lounge and back onto the club's floor.

The base pulsates over my skin, but I can't hear it. I make my way toward the incline to the second floor and freeze when the red bimbo's hands sweep up Dylan's arms and toward his chiseled, masked face.

His jaw tenses, and his nostrils flare slightly. And it's the only thing that holds me back. He doesn't want her touching him. *Then why the fuck is he letting her?*

I can't stop watching. She hands him a cobalt blue card, which basically means she wants them to fuck.

He takes it, and my heart sinks to my stomach. *I think I'm gonna fucking throw up.* Maybe those three tequila shots were a mistake. I look away.

I can't fucking handle the pain that seizes me, holding me prisoner in my own body. I imagine his eyes undressing her, his dick growing hard for her, and I snap. For a reason beyond me, I fight the urge to claw her fucking eyes out and smash her to the floor like a WWE wrestler, and instead, take my sulking self to the nearest dance pole. I don't want to keep watching.

I knew it was him, the same mystery guest who couldn't take his eyes off me for the past three shifts. But perhaps I was wrong, and he wasn't here for me. *Fuck!*

Noah's betrayal might have left me more vulnerable than I care to admit.

This ... *this* is *exactly* why I never allow feelings into the mix. I find a man, flirt, fuck, and then I'm done. I don't want to let them in. For what? So they can stab me in the back like Noah? So they can flirt, fuck, and leave like I have for years since I lost my v-card? The route Dylan apparently wants to take things. *Shit.*

I lean against the pole, and the naked dancer reaches for my hand. I let her guide me in a dance where our hands roam one another's bodies in a carefree yet gentle manner, almost romantic. The idiots in front of us are eating it up, but I'm not even paying attention to them *or* anything else. I'm using all of my strength to not look back.

I can't. If I do and he isn't there, I'm going to fucking blow. I can feel it.

A frantic lunatic searching for him *as if* I have any sort of fucking claim.

What the fuck *is wrong with me? Fuck, snap out of it!*

He's in my head and I need to get him out. Now.

As if the universe heard my idiotic and desperate plea, a man who was sitting next to *el cerro* approaches me. I recognize him. He's the silver fox with green eyes that handed me his card on my first night, requesting a private dance.

He's as handsome as I remember, tall and lean. Muscular, but not too buff, and with salt and pepper hair. I don't care if he's twice my age. My heart is pumping in my ears and I can't hear shit, but he hands me a card and I smile and signal to the nearest security guard and hand it to him.

He gestures to the man to follow, and I force my legs to move toward the bar.

"Give me a double," I say, but hold up two fingers just in case. I chug it back and it tastes like fucking water. *Shit.* "*Otro.*" I don't even know if the bartender speaks Spanish, but he does as I ask.

I need this. I can't even look back to where Dylan was. Fucking ridiculous. Stressing about this rookie is no fun at all. A fling is exactly what I need. If the silver fox wants more after this private dance, I'm in. I haven't had sex in over six months. Maybe that is why I'm acting crazy.

I slam the shot glass onto the bar and take two deep breaths before walking to the opposite end of the club. If you stand in the center on the first floor and look up, you can see all the way to the very top floor. I can't look up right now, I'll bust my shit. Instead, I focus on my steps, and I keep my spine straight, my head over my shoulders.

I don't walk across; I don't want to cross the path Dylan and the red-haired bimbo just stood at. So I take the long way, which ropes around the center of the club like a maze. I turn left and then right to a long and dark corridor with flickering lights hanging near each door like a candle would during ancient times.

The wallpaper is a luxurious black and gold with blue specs that shimmer in the dim lighting. Each room has a magnet that the card attaches to, notifying guests which room is occupied by whom. I stop in front of the room with a black and gray card with a small white fox on the front and adjust my own fox mask.

My insides twist, and I stare at the tiny onyx animal Dylan attached to my mother's charm bracelet. Out of all the charms she added, this one stands out. Hers are a collection of sorts, a memorabilia of her life. Her horoscope: libra, a piano: her favorite instrument, a pink gem: her favorite color, a volleyball: her favorite sport. Dylan's charm stands out like a bright light in an otherwise pitch dark room.

I pinch it between my fingers, *my little fox.*

My eyes blur, tears pool and threaten to leak past my lids, and I squeeze them shut.

These rooms are for private dances. The rooms for blue cards are on the opposite side, and they're for exclusive clients that pay a ridiculous amount of money for discretion and a fucking bed. Literally.

All sorts of kinks are included.

Stop. I shut those thoughts out, forcing a wall between Dylan's soft lips on mine, his nightshade stare, his overpowering presence, and calloused hands touching *my* skin. *Fuck. I can't do this.*

I can *feel* him. That same feeling that first made me realize he wasn't just any other client. The magnetic force stitching our souls together with the thread of life, and it pulls at me now. I take one step back and stumble into a hard wall.

Suddenly, strong hands shove me back against whatever barrier I stepped into and hands grip my waist and twist me around.

"Where the fuck do you think you're going, little fox?"

His voice melts me the way a solid stick of butter on a sizzling skillet would. "Dylan?"

I'm too relieved to see him, but when I remember Dominica trailing her hands all over him and how he hadn't even tried to stop her, I recover by shoving a finger at his masked face. "What the fuck are *you* doing here, Detective? Canvassing for clues?"

He grins and gently pushes me until my back touches the wall next to the door I'm supposed to enter. It's cold against my shoulder blades, but Dylan's heat warms me to my core.

"You go ahead and give him his little dance, but if he touches you," he cups my chin and forces me to look at him, and his pupils disappear, "I'll fucking kill him."

I press against his chest, but he doesn't move. I try a smidge harder. Nothing. I sigh in frustration. "*Oh,* so it's okay for little Miss Jessica Rabbit to put her hands all over you and invite you to a fuck fest, but I'm not allowed to be touched?"

Dylan reaches into his custom-made Tom Ford suit jacket, and I swallow back a lump in my dry ass throat. I think a noise escapes me, something similar to a croak. He produces the vibrant blue card and a red heart glimmers and threatens to slice my cornea in three parts.

"I'm only yours, Niki."

He folds the card in half, bends it back, and it cracks easily in his hands. He folds it until there are six metal pieces on his palm and then he sprinkles them over the plush carpet at our feet. His hand seizes the back of my neck and his lips collide with mine.

I open his jacket and fling the sides open and hungrily glide my hands over his torso and around him. I press my palms onto his back and crush him closer. Our masks collide and slide over our faces. It's a desperate and hungry kiss. As if our lips will feed our starving souls and bring them back to life.

He slows and kisses my lips gently before taking my bottom lip between his teeth. He pulls at it softly and then licks the tiny indentations before sucking them. "*Y tu eres mia.*" And you are mine. "I'll be watching, fox."

He lets go and disappears down the hall. He isn't heading back to the club, and I watch his silhouette disappear. Just one fucking kiss and I'm smiling like a damn idiot alone in a dark hallway.

Did that even just happen? I look down to the scattered metal pieces of Miss Rabbit's blue fuck-me card and smile big. Yes, it happened.

Is he really going to be watching? I snort out loud. *Whatever.*

I adjust my mask and turn the gold knob to let myself in. I helped Jasmin stock the mini fridges in all the rooms, so I know my way around. It's a fair-sized circular room, definitely bigger than the inside of my trailer, with two exits. Leather couches circle around the center where there's a stage and a silver pole. The walls are lined with a deep blue velvet and red, elegant strip lights line the floorboards.

The stocked mini fridge is to the left, and a bluetooth stereo sits on a black table. The silver fox chose his music, and it plays over the room's built-in, unseen speakers. He sits directly across from me in a gray leather lounge chair with a bottle of scotch in hand. The second door is directly behind him.

He points to a small bar to my right where there's a sealed bottle of Patron x Guillermo Del Toro, a copper-colored brew, and an empty shot glass waiting for me. I step toward it, pop off the ornate topper, and serve myself a shot and slowly toss it back.

Fuck, that's some good tequila.

"You're fucking exquisite."

I go down two steps and walk to the pole. I'm surprised by his playlist. A track by *Lady Gaga—Love Game—*is playing.

Interesting choice, I guess.

Whatever, this private dance will put three grand in my pocket. He's spending a pretty penny for a mere strip. He could've watched me dancing in a cage with barely any clothes on.

Behind him, dark irises are brooding from across the room, and I struggle not to roll my eyes. As promised, Dylan stands motionless, leaning against the wall, his arms crossed over his broad chest.

I focus on the song's lyrics and stare straight into the darkness, right into Dylan's eyes, and I allow them to drag me into their depths. I unzip the corset. Underneath is a matching lace bra; the elegant pattern covers my nipples but reveals the creamy skin of my large breasts. Dylan smiles and I toss the girdle to the ground, then grip the pole and twirl, pushing off my feet and circling twice before landing on my toes. My hips gyrate to the beat, and I flip my head so that my hair falls to one side. I circle my waist and lean my ass on the pole, then drop to my knees.

My eyes stay on Dylan, and I dedicate each move to him.

The beat changes and I realize it's a mix curated by the club and not a selection made by the man I'm not even looking at. It's one by *Rihanna—Where Have You Been*—and I smile at the man standing in the dark, watching me.

I use the pole and balance my body on it and twirl. Then I lower myself to my shins and arch my spine like a cat. I whip my hair and lean back. The song changes again, and I shimmy the skirt off my hips and kick it to the ground. I turn and touch my toes, only the thin string of my thong between my ass cheeks separating my goods from the two men eating me alive.

I straighten my spine slowly and twirl on the pole again.

I unclasp my bra, and with one hand, I hang on to the pole and lean my body out as if I'm going to fall, then I toss the bra at my guests' feet. I hold my breasts with one arm and turn.

Dylan's smile falls when the man stands and approaches me. I freeze as he climbs the steps up to stand before me on the small stage. He pushes my hair back gently, the movement allowing two of his fingers to graze my collarbone, and my skin turns to ice.

Dylan's shadow moves on us and he whacks the silver fox on the side of the head with his gun. How the fuck did he manage to get that in here? The man collapses to the ground and Dylan points it at his limp body.

"Wait," I shout and run to move his arm away. "Don't fucking shoot him."

One of his eyebrows arches. "I warned you, fox. He touched you."

I breathe in deep and exhale hard. "He *barely* touched me! You *can't* kill him."

He sighs, exasperated, but relents and puts his pistol wherever the fuck he was hiding it, somewhere behind him. Then he lowers himself and easily carries the man up and sits him on the lounge chair like a rag doll. He grabs the bottle of scotch and places it between the man's legs.

He turns slowly and sweeps his gaze hungrily over me. I'm suddenly very conscious of the fact that I'm naked except for a thin lace thong and my heels. *Love on the Brain* starts playing and Dylan smirks as he stalks toward me.

He takes his mask off and then pushes mine back until it falls at our feet. He lifts me up and I wrap my legs around his torso.

He bites my lip then, prying them open with his tongue. Dylan walks until my back is pressed against the wall from the side I came in from. He sucks on my lower lip and then kisses his way down my jawline, then my neck, sucking softly until his mouth finally closes around my nipple.

He moans appreciatively, and I let out a soft wheeze, relishing in his touch. I'm held in place, existing from one touch to another. My body awaits expectantly, leaning into his perfect body, begging for more. He kisses up the center of my throat until our lips are at it again. Teeth colliding. He suddenly lowers me to the ground and drops to his knees, then lifts up one of my legs and places it over his shoulder.

Dylan licks up my inner thigh, my breath hitches, and then he presses his nose into my covered pussy and breathes me in.

"Fuck," he murmurs to himself. Then he moves the thong over and slowly draws his thumb over my wet slit. "Is this all for me?"

I nod, incapable of putting words together. His finger moves delicately over my clit, outlining it in a slow, circular motion. It's like adding lighter fluid to a flame.

My back arches, and his mouth is on me. He licks, then nibbles my clit gently. Dylan wraps my other leg around and presses me further into the wall, his palms digging into my thighs. He devours me, as if he's famished and desperate. I'm highly aware of how he holds me up *so easily*, as if I'm a fucking feather.

I rub my hand over the stubble of his scalp and press his face into my center. I almost squeeze my thighs shut when I feel my body trembling, my breaths turning shallow and quick. I look up and yell his name at the same time the telltale buzz finally reaches my core.

He continues to lick me, lapping up every drop, before placing me back on the ground. Dylan touches his lips and uses his fingers to clean up the moisture from his chin and then he licks me off his fingers.

My shoulders tremble, then my legs begin to quiver and he unzips his pants.

My lids droop, and I'm sure I appear lust driven at the sight of him. His erect cock springs upward and reaches his midsection, hidden by his black button-down shirt. He moves his shirt and grips his shaft tightly and my mouth waters at the sight. The room is poorly lit, but I spot drops of precum, and I lick my lips, suddenly thirsty for him.

Dylan scoops me up, and I wrap my legs around his waist. He pumps his length, dragging his hand up and down before pressing the hard tip against me, and I'm dripping wet for him.

He stares into my eyes while he forces past the tight threshold, almost closing them when my muscles relax to allow him inside.

I keep them open and gasp at the intrusion. I think his shoulders shudder. He's enormous, and he pulls out before he's even in all the way and then plunges into me.

I scream out and Dylan grunts approvingly. I press my fingertips into his shoulders and wish he were naked as well. My fingers fumble to the top buttons of his shirt and clumsily work through the top few and tear the rest open, ignoring the sound of his expensive shirt ripping in the process. His taut skin heats my palms, and I dig my nails into him and rake them across his shoulders.

He pounds into me, never looking away, and my world pieces itself back together. Like tectonic plates shifting, but in reverse, a shattered glass on rewind to when it was pristine once more, winter melting to summer, skipping right over spring. A dead flower coming back to life, plumping to its original, healthy form.

One of his hands moves up behind my neck and he presses his forehead against mine. I'm close.

I can feel my core flexing around him, pumping him, and the tingling rush starts up at the pit of my spine again. I bite his lip and then suck on it and breathe his name. "Dylan."

I moan and he grunts with me, and together, we come undone. He thrusts into me, five pumps before we're both spent and breathing heavy. Our bodies tremble and take in air erratically.

"*Eres mía.*"

I nod while he kisses my lips. "Yes."

I can't be sure when, but the background music changed and *Muse-Undisclosed Desires* blasts on the speakers. Somewhere in the more solid and level-headed parts of my mind, I wonder if Dylan himself chose these songs. He's definitely capable and insane enough to get it done.

"Say it, Niki."

He grunts when I squeeze my muscles tightly around his semi hard shaft still buried deep inside me. "*Soy tuya.*"

Dylan's dark eyes gleam and a possessive air blazes through him. He nods and a soft smile tugs at his lips. He exits me, and I suddenly feel empty as he bends and takes my thong off and then stuffs it in his pocket. Then he takes my heels off and rubs each foot in his strong hands. The ache subsides in his heated grip.

I watch as Dylan walks to the bar, his towering stance full of confidence and power, seeping of masculinity and sensuality. He reaches around and brings me a black satin robe and a water bottle, then kisses my forehead while he covers my shoulders and guides my arms into the robe. I gulp down the entire contents while he retrieves our masks. I toss the now empty water bottle behind me into a small trash can.

"I knew he was going to touch you." Dylan gently puts my mask back on.

I chuckle. "Now what?" I look behind him to the knocked out man snoring loudly on the leather chair.

Dylan shrugs. "Nothing. He'll wake up and assume he passed out while you danced for him."

I shake my head. "My shift is over in a couple of hours."

"I'll be waiting."

I roll my eyes. "You don't have to do that, rookie. Jas and I can find—"

"I'll be waiting." He lifts my chin up and bends down to kiss me, then nudges me toward the exit. Before closing the door behind me, I watch as he leaves from the same door he stood by just minutes ago.

I close the robe and clutch my heels to my chest. The door clicks shut, and I practically sprint to the employee's only section. It's buzzing inside. Dancers are heading to the back showers while others are stuffing their night bags with leather thongs, lingerie, props, and fishnet outfits. I make my way to my locker and hunt for another outfit before freshening up and shuffling into it.

It's a simple black one piece with a slit across my stomach and another right above my breasts. I match it up with thigh-length boots. I pull my hair up into a sophisticated-looking bun and attach a pair of long faux silver earrings to my lobes.

I hurtle through the motions of getting ready, placing a matte fox mask on, and head back out to the main floor, still alive with patrons.

I smile stupidly and brush my fingers over my lips. My skin tingles, and the soreness between my legs prompts a delicious throb, reminding me of Dylan's impossibly large and hard cock pounding into me. He said he was mine, and that I was his. What the fuck does that mean?

"There you are."

I jump back, startled. It's a tall, fair-skinned, light-brown haired man with piercing blue-green eyes, a simple gray mask over the top half of his face. I recognize him instantly. Charles, Piper's man. He looks uncomfortable and out of place. He shifts his weight from one leg to another. Pretending that I don't know him is easy, I mean, it's basically true. My chin rises to meet his tall stance.

"We've been looking for you. You're cordially invited to attend a ball. The rules are within this envelope. If you'd like to attend, follow the instructions, and an address will be provided to you one hour before the party begins."

He hands me a shimmering black envelope and disappears.

It's four in the morning as Jasmin and I exit the club. It's two hours til closing, but we came in a couple of hours before opening and get to leave early. I'm still dressed in my one piece with my thigh-length boots, but I throw on a black trench coat and practically run out. Jasmin managed to throw her sweats and a shirt over her outfit and seems overly excited when Dylan takes our bags and opens the door for us.

"I can get used to this." Jasmin smiles big.

I roll my eyes at her. "Don't."

We climb into the back, and the cool air conditioning tames the fire threatening to melt the clothes off my body and turn me into a hissing puddle.

Three minutes later, Dylan makes it onto the highway and I breathe in deep. His car embodies his scent. Leather, patchouli, and rose. I want to reach out and contain it, then lather my body in it.

"I got an invitation to Mayor *cerro's* little ball."

Jasmin's sleepy eyes pop open, and she sits up. "Really?"

I nod and peek at Dylan, my expression guarded. "A henchman delivered it."

Jas's eyes blanch, but she keeps her cool and takes the envelope from me. "There aren't very many details. Doesn't say when, where, or even a time. Just rules and shit."

"Yea, secrecy is key. Plenty of high rollers are sure to attend, political henchmen among them. Obviously, they know one another. I'll have to sign a non-disclosure agreement."

"It says here you can take guests, who'll have to sign that shit too, of course."

"You and Sara up for crashing a party?"

Jasmin smiles wickedly. "You know it."

"I'm attending with you." Dylan's voice startles us and we both gape at him.

"You can't go as my *date*. I'm supposed to attend as a possible treat."

His jaw tenses, and he turns the soft playing music off. Jasmin's face contorts and mouths, *oh shit,* but I ignore her.

"Then I'll go as your bodyguard or your fucking pet if I have to. But I'm not letting you step foot into their hell without me."

I nod, and my face elongates while I stroke my chin. I point my finger at him. "I like the pet idea."

His lips break into a wide toothy grin and the air leaves my lungs. I squeeze Jasmin's hand and struggle to breathe in. *Fuck.*

She squeezes back, and when I look at her, she's beaming. She closes her eyes and nods approvingly. *I like him*, she mouths.

Me too. Too much.

Dylan's phone buzzes and he thumbs through it, then places it near the gear shifter. The dark pools of his eyes meet mine in the rearview mirror, and just as quickly, his gaze shifts back onto the road. His expression is guarded and stealthy, fixed on something dire.

Who the fuck is messaging him?

He pulls up into the lot and Jasmin and I both pop up and lazily snake out of his car. Max barks and Dylan shushes him.

"I cannot believe you left him outside." I bend and Max rushes to me and lets me lean into him for a hug.

What if he ran off? What if he got hungry or thirsty? What if the bugs crowded his space? I look up and shoot Dylan an angry glare.

"He's fine. He loves it. He's got his own shed out back and it's stocked with water."

I scratch behind Max's ears, and he leans into my hands. "Yea, what about snacks?"

Dylan crosses his arms, and Jasmin clears her throat.

"Right, well, I'm gonna head on inside, and I'll leave you two to discuss pet care arrangements."

I stand, and Dylan takes my hand. "She's staying with me tonight," he says to my best friend, who's retreating to our trailer, her eyes drooping and body ready to collapse.

I look up at him quizzically. *Am I now?*

Jasmin waves at me and winks. "Goodnight, Justice."

Dylan brings my knuckles to his lips and nibbles them gently. "Come on, I'll let you in. Make yourself at home. I'm going to feed Max."

Dazed, I follow him to the door and watch as he unlocks it and guides me inside. The screen door closes behind me and I'm alone in his tiny mansion.

The inside is temperature controlled and impeccably clean. Nothing is out of place. Everything is sleek, new, and sturdy. The last time I was here, I was in a complete funk. Denial guided me and tore me open from the inside out.

Today is different.

I look out the window; the night sky is reaching its end, and a dull orange is creeping up the horizon. In less than forty minutes, the brightness will take over. I lean away from the shutters and search for a bathroom.

20
Redemption

Max's dog house is a climate controlled shed that looks more like a one-room studio for a person. He's trained with me since he was a newborn pup and loyal to a fault—until he met Niki. He's sitting at the front door now, whining for her to let him in while I fill his food bowl, refill his water canister, and adjust the temperature. I whistle for him to come and eat, and he struggles to follow the command. I roll my eyes and stroll outside.

"Your food is there, Maximus. Choose wisely."

Jason couldn't have warned me about the invitation. He wasn't able to get one, even if he'd upped the ante of his charms. But he knew more than one man was consumed with Niki and would make a move on her. It's why he grew tense, watching me and praying I wouldn't snap. I actually think I reacted quite well, considering the situation.

I pat Max's head and stroll into the trailer, then lock the door behind me.

It's silent inside, and for a second, I worry my little fox has retreated to her own trailer, but then Max wouldn't have been glued to the spot he was still probably in. I take my shoes off and set them near the door, then peel my suit jacket off and toss it on the couch. I take my shirt off and smile when the missing buttons remind me of Niki's eagerness and writhing body.

My dick begins to harden at the mere thought of her wet cunt taking me, her whimpers and lust-filled eyes.

I look around at the open space and frown. There are two bedrooms hidden from view, and I make my way to the master suite. I find her staring at my open closet, her fingers entwined in one of my shirts, her back to me.

She's barefoot and wearing a black oversized t-shirt. It's slightly tucked in by her hip, which shows off tiny blue shorts. Her hair is pulled back into a neat yet loose braid. I lick my lips at the sight of her. I've seen her dressed in seductive lingerie and naked, but this is her temptress outfit. When she's relaxed, comfortable, and genuinely herself. I want to drop to my knees and do her bidding, kiss her ankles and pleasure her until she screams my name.

A woman like Niki doesn't just give herself to anyone. Not *really*. And I want to be the first and last man who gets the true her. Aimlessly, I throw my shirt into the hamper, and it alerts her to my presence. She turns and languidly trails her big brown eyes over me.

"Are you hungry?" I'll present a buffet of whatever the fuck she wants if she requests.

Niki shakes her head and moves her eyes from the floor to my face. "When someone texted you during the drive, you changed. What was that?"

I take in a deep breath and unbuckle my belt and take it off slowly. Niki needs *truth* more than she wants *me,* and I'm sure she'll split if faced with deceit. And if I want to strip all the lies she tells others, she should have mine.

"Jason. He works for me and had some information on Carlton's group."

Niki grins. "So he's the sidekick that cleans up the mess you leave behind?"

"Something like that." I walk to the closet and hang my belt, then unbuckle my pants and slide them off.

"What is this?" Her hand moves in the space between us.

"*This* is exclusive." I throw my pants toward the hamper, and Niki leans on one leg, then crosses her hands in front of her. She shoots me an incredulous glare.

"Why?"

I scan her features, looking for hints of her wanting to make a run for it. "Why what?"

"Why me? And why should I trust you? Why should I agree?"

Slowly, I make my way toward her and move a few strands of her hair and tuck them behind her ear. Then I graze my thumb over her healing lip. "I don't know why. All I know is that I won't fight it."

"How long will this... *feeling*... last?"

I understand now that what she needs is beyond the truth. Niki wants confirmation, a look into the future through a nonexistent glass ball that I won't turn around and betray her. She's at the edge of her fight against the unmistakable grip that my presence has over her. I don't want her forced into it, because once she relents, I'm never letting her go. Instead, I need her to accept it. But what can I say that will open her eyes to what simply is?

"I broke my celibacy—" My fox pauses as if debating how much to share with me. After a few beats and steady breaths, she continues. "Apparently, my *promiscuity* scared Jas, and she forced me to see a shrink. To my surprise, my therapist suggested I stop... er... sleeping around. I thought they were crazy. It wasn't until I began to feel empty that I realized how far I'd gone, chasing for something to numb the pain. Giving Noah a shot made me feel normal. But I'd forget we were an item and would often use my celibacy as an excuse. I knew we'd always be just friends. But then you came along and—"

Niki shakes her head, and her hands instinctively move to her chest. She clutches the area above her left breast, like each thump strangles her. "I didn't think I was capable of... *this*. I'm afraid... what I feel when I'm with you... It's addicting and *healing*, in a way."

I know what she means, and I reach for one hand and place it on my chest. "How many times do you think we come back... if reincarnation were real, I mean." Niki shrugs and her brows shoot up in question. "The details don't matter, not when we meet our definite end. We," I point to us both, "will be *infinite*. When death comes, my very soul will search for yours—I am forever yours either way, fox."

The last of her hold crumbles, and she reaches up and wraps her hands around my neck. I feel her weight shift when she stands on her toes, and I crush my lips to hers eagerly. The hem of her shirt threatens to rip in my grip, and I tear it off her in one fluid move then lift her up in my arms and playfully toss her on my bed. Her laughter reaches my ears and I smile while I take off my boxers.

Niki looks at me, and her hungry glare is enough to set my skin on fire. I climb on top of her and kiss her stomach and bite down on the waistband of her shorts. I lift her ass up and glide them off her. The skin between her bellybutton and her pussy call to me, and I inhale the scent of my soap on her.

"Fuck."

It slips out, the innate command to ravage her until she succumbs to the possibility of *us*. A blind desire ripples through me, and I part her thighs and caress her wet pussy with my thumb. I draw lazy circles over her swollen clit, and she trembles when I lick up her slit. I taste her, moving my tongue slowly up and down and just bury my face between her legs. It's ridiculous to assume I'd ever get enough and be satisfied; she's fucking perfect. Her thighs move, and she lets out a soft pant-like, husky whisper. She breathes my name out in a sigh and I think I'll combust right here and now.

I pull back and suck on the soft skin of her inner thigh. I'm desperate to have her, and so I kiss, lick, and nibble my way up her stomach until I finally reach her tits. I can't take my eyes off them. She's so fucking beautiful. I cup them in both my hands, knead them gently, and push them up, then pinch both of her nipples. I take one in my mouth and suck.

I'm hovering over her and slide my dick between them while squeezing them around my shaft. I spit at the base and then glide it up and down. She feels so fucking good. "I've wanted to fuck your tits since I first saw you."

Niki bites down on her plump lower lip. "*Not* my smart mouth?"

She *oozes* seductiveness. I'm a fucking goner. A growl escapes my heaving chest while she dips her chin into her neck and opens her lips, then sticks out her tongue to lick the precum off the tip of my dick. My thighs tremble. Yep, I'm a goner. I release her breasts and wrap one hand around the bun atop her head and hold her. My other hand guides my cock into her mouth. I can't take it slow, I can't go easy. I'm fucking *desperate* for her.

My hips buckle and shake when her lips wrap around my hard dick. She reaches behind, grips my ass, then pushes me deeper into her mouth. She moans, and the vibrations reach my balls. I pump into her, erratic and eager thrusts and the sloppy sounds of my fucking her mouth are almost too much. My balls slap her chin and I look down to her lustful eyes, watering at the intrusion but telling me to keep going.

I pull out right before falling apart and she pouts. She's so fucking sexy, and I reach for her lips to clean the spit around her mouth with my thumb. "I want to feel your pussy clench around me when I come."

I lean back, and she sits up, then walks on her knees toward me. She sits on my lap and wraps her legs around my waist. I lift her ass up and sit her on my dick, and she slides down slowly. Niki whimpers and struggles at my size.

"You take my cock so good, fox."

I reach up to let her hair fall, and I smooth it out. Her lash line tickles my lips and I kiss her eyes and then her lips. I can feel as she snuggles my dick, adjusting to my size. She lifts her hips up and down, grinding and shimming on my length. I wrap one arm around her waist and press her close to me while I lift up on my knees and lay her down, my dick still buried inside her.

I'm suspended over her outstretched body and lift up one of her legs to wrap it around my waist. Niki's eyes go wide when I press into her, driving deeper than I have been and making her squirm her exhale in the process.

I'm hitting a sweet spot that makes my balls quiver with a need to burst, and she claws her nails on my back. If she says my name, I'm fucking done.

"Come on, rookie. Ruin me."

Her breathy voice is a calling, and I comply. Pummeling into her, bruising her insides, and I'm balls deep when her pussy tightens around my dick, pumping me dry. I'll leave her body desolate, zero need for anyone else but me, *she's mine.*

Just before I come, I press into her and bite down on her shoulder and let go. I grunt my release just when she yells out hers.

"Dylan!"

We fucked through the sunrise until she dozed. I stare at her naked body and draw ginger circles and swirls over her milky back and kiss down her spine.

Her soft snores continue, and I cover her slowly until the duvet reaches her shoulders, then place a note and a small box on the pillow next to where her head rests.

I want to wake her with my dick buried between her thick ass cheeks, but I can't bring myself to rouse her. I adjust my aching yet hardening dick and walk away slowly. I'm running late for lunch with Jason and Olivia. I exit into the blinding light and lower the sunglasses to shield me from the fireball.

I whistle and Max trots happily to me. While I used the bathroom, Niki had let him in, and I found him snuggled on the sheets at her feet. Before showering, I forced him off and back to his shed, where he finally ate his food. He jumps in the car and I smile like an ardent teenage fool.

Niki is mine. She finally accepts it.

21

Justice

I'm oddly comfortable, too cozy. Nothing hurts. Usually when I stir awake, my back and neck sore from sleeping on a flat wannabe mattress on the floor. I stretch, and a delicious soreness gathers between my legs.

I breathe in and a leathery rose and patchouli scent startles my eyes open. Adrenaline claws through me and prompts me to stand. I toss the thick, black sheets off and squeal. I'm naked! I gather them and throw them on top of me instead and crawl off the large bed.

Dylan's bed.

I press my hand over my racing heart, forcing it to calm down. "Dylan."

Silence responds to my call. I yell his name a bit louder and wait. Nothing. I circle his spotless room and notice a white box and a folded paper on the pillow. It's about to fall. I roll my eyes when I realize that I'd pushed it when I jumped up, thinking I'd been kidnapped again.

I don't know if I want to laugh or roll my eyes as I take tentative steps to the note, but a smile tugs my lips apart when I spot Dylan's too neat handwriting. He writes in small, boxed in, all capital letters.

> GOOD MORNING FOX,
> MAKE YOURSELF AT HOME. INVITE YOUR SIBLINGS
> OVER, RAID MY KITCHEN, TAKE A SHOWER.
> CONSIDER THIS SLIP OF PAPER YOUR SEARCH
> WARRANT. YOU MAY PRETTY MUCH DO AS YOU
> PLEASE.
>
> I'VE LEFT YOU A KEY AND A PHONE. I'VE MADE
> SURE TO SECURE IT, NO ONE WILL TRACK YOU ON
> IT, NOT EVEN ME. I HAVE OTHER MEANS OF
> KEEPING TABS, AS I'M SURE YOU KNOW. I HAD TO
> GO TO WORK, I'LL SEE YOU LATER.
>
> —D

I stare at it and reread it almost over ten times. The phone I'm not too bothered with. The latest iPhone model sits in a little box waiting for me. It's the key that burns a hole in my palm.

A fucking key.

He's psychotic. There's no other explanation. Why else would he invite me to have open access to his personal space?

I rub my thumb over his ending signature, a single letter D, and a smile tugs at my lips. I tap on the screen of my new phone and slide up. There's one unread text waiting for me. And what do you know, it's from Dylan.

> **Good morning, little 🐾. Hope you slept well.**

I smile. He sent it at noon. It's now almost three in the afternoon. I blanch. I completely missed Jule heading to school and he'll be home in a couple of hours. *Shit.*

I scramble to put my clothes on, then stash the note, key, and phone into my pockets. Grab my backpack and scramble into the heavy heat. Fuck, Dylan's mini mansion was so cozy I forgot about the desert sun eager to incinerate everything below it.

The quick sprint to my trailer forces the gravel to shoot up, and it crunches below my untied sneakers. I take in one deep, steadying breath and push past the door.

"*Vaya*, she lives."

Jasmin sits on the floor painting her toenails. A fan is plugged in nearby and she has it facing her. She's wearing her long coils in a tight bun and she whistles at me.

I roll my eyes and drop my bag near the door, then go to my drawers and tuck Dylan's note under my intimates. My too short nails struggle to part the keyring as I maneuver his key next to my house keys. Once they clink together, I slide them into my pocket and sit down next to Jasmin while I move the fan, so it hits us both.

"Someone had fun," she pokes my neck.

I almost fall flat on my face when I rush over to the long mirror behind her, crawling. My face falls; there's a fucking hickey on my neck and another on my jawline! My lips are swollen, but I still break into a big, goofy grin.

"I had fun." I nod and my cheeks burn as the memories of Dylan drilling into me invade my thoughts.

Forget Greek gods and Vikings. Dylan is built like an Aztec god. He's all muscle and wrath with a hefty dose of sin. He took me passionately as lightning exerted from his hands and lust from his midnight eyes. Even his fucking calves are sexy. Thoughts of his naked body fill my mind, and I ache to sink my teeth into each one of his steely muscles, beginning with those calves. If I had him in front of me right now, I'd climb my lips all the way up toward his massive tattooed shoulders and rigid arms and—

"Good!" Jas interrupts and I blink.

Out of all the guys I've fucked, no one has possessed me the way Dylan has. My stomach suddenly growls, and Jas and I both laugh. I'm not sure if it's hunger for food, Dylan, or both.

"I ate the last of the leftovers we had from Helena."

Dylan's key stabs me as I sit back on my calves, and I tap at it. "Let's go raid Dylan's kitchen."

"I cannot *believe* he gave you a key *and a phone*!"

Jasmin is thumbing through the device, adding applications as she sees fit. She added Jule's number and texted him. He responded, explaining that he would be home no later than six.

I did as Dylan advised and rummaged through his kitchen. Finding the ingredients I needed to make rice, breaded chicken breast, and a salad. I place a plate in front of Jasmin, who's sitting on a stool at the long marble island. I flip the tortillas, and once they're ready, I toss them on a plate and place them between us. I hand her a can of Coke and turn to cut open an avocado.

Once I take my seat, she and I dig in.

"I know, too soon, right?" I leave out 'he's fucking crazy,' because I'm afraid she'll agree. But her next words surprise me.

"He's good for you."

It isn't the first time she's told me this. "So... it's *not* too soon?"

"I'm not saying you should move in with the guy, get married, and have babies. All I mean is that he's your match." She shrugs and stuffs her mouth, humming in appreciation.

My new phone buzzes and we both hover over it.

"It's a text from *your man*," Jasmin teases. "Answer him!"

My man. Somewhere inside, a thrilled diva jumps up and down. I just hold my stomach in place. I feel like something is going to claw its way out of me. Butterflies?

Trembling fingers unlock the thing.

What are you up to?

I'm at your place. I made food. Jas and I are eating and when we finish, we're going to put that search warrant to good use.

Have at it!

I'm glad you're making yourselves at home.

I blush, and Jasmin chuckles. "What's he saying?"

I clear my throat and lock the device. "That he's glad we're here."

"Uh huh. *Right.*" She drags out the last word, and I avoid looking at her.

We finish our meals and clean up. I save a plate for Dylan and put it in the oven, and then wrap up the rest for Jule.

"Listen to my gut, Justice. *This one* is your guy."

We exit Dylan's trailer, and I'm about to tell her all about how I feel when we spot Noah at the foot of our door glaring at us. He climbs down the steps and stuffs his hands in his pockets.

"You think he saw us leaving your rookie's trailer?"

"I don't give a shit if he heard me screaming Dylan's name this morning."

Jasmin coughs back her laughter and shakes her head at me. She takes the food from my hands and nudges me with her elbow. "If you need me, just holler."

I nod at her and cross my arms over my chest. She gives me one last look to make sure I'm okay before disappearing into our home.

"You gave me *nothing,* and I've been here since we were brats. Then he shows up and you give him all of you."

I shake my head. "You have no right—"

"You gave him *everything*!" he shouts. "For years I lived on your sweet nothing. Because that's what you gave me. But *him*?"

"Noah, you're drunk. You should go home and—"

"What, like you give a shit?" He shuffles his weight from one leg to the next and his shoulders shake.

"I do care—"

"Bullshit," Noah spits. Then he tosses his hands in the air and almost shouts. "I fucked up, okay? But I'm *here*. Please, Justice."

"You work for the man who killed my parents!" I roar. And Jasmin opens the screen door to our trailer. A few neighbors who were already out stare at us, but I don't give a shit. "Might as well pull the trigger yourself by allowing him to get away with it. And not just that, you kept *me* from finding him. You played me."

Noah shakes his head. His eyes are blotchy and red, swollen. One eye is still black, and he looks pale. His white shirt is dirty, and somewhere deep inside I want him to go home, shower, eat, and sleep. I want him to go back to the Noah I thought I knew. The friend that would never in a million years betray me or put my family in harm's way.

Jasmin steps out. "They used her as leverage because of your fucking jobs, Noah. They would've raped and then killed her."

Noah slaps both his hands over his face and he yells out a sob. "That wasn't supposed to happen. I was trying to get out, I was trying to out them. But they own the cops. I wouldn't be surprised if *he's* in on it!" He points behind me to Dylan's trailer.

I turn on instinct and when I look back, Noah's eyes almost pop out of their sockets. He points to my neck. "You *fucked* him?" His fingers dig into his chest, holding the spot where his heart is.

"If you would've told me the *second* Vork and his men came to you, my respect would still be yours. You betrayed me in the worst way possible. And if it weren't for Dylan, I'd be dead right now."

The realization of this truth washes through me. Ice fills my veins and I tremble. But Noah glares behind me, fixated, *obsessed*.

"So you *fucked* him?"

I can hear Jasmin throw a *wow* at him, and my fingernails dig into my palms. "That's none of your business."

Noah nods and inhales heavily through his nose. He wipes at his snot and dabs his eyes roughly. "This isn't over, Justice. It *can't* be."

In my peripheral, I see Jasmin shake her head softly.

"You should go." I walk toward my best friend and don't look back. I turn her around and we both retreat into our tiny rectangular box. I hear Noah shout incoherently, and we both peer out the window to watch him kick the ground paving his walk of shame back to his trailer.

"What do you think he means by *'this isn't over'*?"

I look away from the window and touch my mother's bracelet. I stroke and count each charm and almost smile when I get to the black fox. "I don't give a shit."

"What if he does something stupid?"

"What's stupider than joining Vork's crew and doing his bidding?"

"It was horrible watching him," Jasmin whispers almost just to herself.

I nod. I've never seen Noah so torn. Not when his father left them. Not when he broke his arm four years ago. And not even when his mother fell ill and had to stay in the hospital for two weeks recovering. Tonight, he looked like a writhing man struck down by flames and bullets all at once. I swallow the lump forming in my throat and squeeze my eyes shut. Warm tears fall over my cheeks.

"Hey, you didn't do anything wrong, Justice. I watched you push Dylan away for weeks. You didn't lie or cheat on Noah. But *he* did."

I know what she means. I'm sure Noah never cheated on me with another woman. But he cheated me out of the truth. He didn't allow me the benefit of knowing what issues plagued him. We would have joined forces and come up with a way to catch Vork in a net of a mutually plotted deceit. Instead, he chose the man who took everything from me and kept everything from me. He underestimated me, betrayed me, mocked me, and conspired against me.

The door creaks open and a cheerful Jule sinks as soon as he sees me. "What happened?" he demands.

I sniffle and dry my treacherous tears. "Nothing."

"Noah came by," Jasmin offers and lifts her shoulders up at me when I glare at her.

"I thought I told him to keep off our property." He drops his stuff near the door and is about to pounce out when Jasmin and I both reach for him. We pull at his arms and tug him back.

I plant a firm hand on his chest. "I'm okay. I said what I needed to say, and he left."

"Sure?"

"Yes," I tell him. "It's just a lot. We've known Noah for a long time. All of this feels—" I pause and grope for the right word, "wrong."

"He played us. I almost killed him the other day."

I nod. As Jasmin tells it, if she hadn't begged Jule to stop, he would've beaten the life out of Noah. I'm surprised he even came back at all. But then again, Noah has never been a coward. No, apparently he was just stupid.

I heave a shaky breath and swat away at my grief. "How was school?"

22

Redemption

I pull up Jason's gated driveway and park in the roundabout directly in front of his door. To my right are two massive pickup trucks, two rovers, and three motorcycles. I roll my eyes. He has a six-car garage, which I'm sure is stocked with more.

Of course, Jason wouldn't give up his dreams just because an accident had paralyzed him, but did he have to be such a fucking show off?

I reach for the bottle of wine that Olivia asked me to bring as a token of apology since I canceled lunch and invited myself to dinner. Max rushes out. He knows where we are, and he's eager to be let out in their yard. I barely graze my knuckles on the door when Olivia opens it and smiles wide.

Olivia is a dirt bike riding, rock climbing, beer drinking, vulgar tongued sort of woman. I'm sure she was a viking in another life. A sleeve of tattoos cover her left arm. She's tall, slender, and has delicately charming features. The left half of her head is shaved, and the tattoos from her arm continue to collect on her neck, behind her ear, and up to her scalp. She's wearing a black t-shirt and white shorts, the gray material of the prosthetic liner inches above her right knee shimmers slightly. Her straight brown hair falls over the right side of her face and she pushes her glasses up her slim nose and smiles.

"The king of Rome has arrived," she shouts in Spanish over her shoulder. She winks at me and takes the bottle from my hands. "His favorite, you remembered!"

"Hi, Liv." I step through the massive entryway.

"My aunt wants to know when you'll visit."

I roll my eyes and close the door behind me. "Tell my mother to stop sending messages through you."

"I can't help that I'm her favorite niece."

Max saunters in as if he's home and wags his tail-less ass at Jason, who halts his mechanical chair in its tracks to greet him properly. "Hey, Maximus. How's the boss treating you?"

"I imagine he's treating him better than most," Olivia chimes in. "Come on, Max, the boys are outside."

Olivia hands Jason the bottle and he pulls her gently down and kisses her. She and Max disappear to the back where their three dogs wait. I follow Jason into their kitchen, and while he opens the bottle of red, I wash my hands.

"*Someone* paid Justice a visit today," he says.

I grind my teeth. I had to make an appearance at the police station, submit some hours of labor and paperwork. I also had to write up a report for Mike, the middleman for the agency that hired me to get the job done. No one had spoken about a deadline, but the completion of a job is always a debatable, tentative, and delicate topic that they always want executed as quickly and cleanly as possible.

But of course, I had to check up on Niki. I was honest when I told her that I wouldn't track the cell phone I'd given her. I wanted her to have the privacy she deserved while being able to communicate with her whenever I wanted. But I checked the cameras honed in on the trailer lot and almost climbed out of my skin when I saw a jittery and pain stricken Noah losing his shit like a crackhead going through withdrawals, while he yelled at my woman. I don't know what he said, or what she responded, but from the looks of it, she took care of it.

"I noticed."

I grab two wine glasses and Jason fills them up. Then he spins and grabs a Guinness for Olivia and hands it to her as soon as she reappears.

"Dinner is set. Let's head to the table before it goes cold."

I nod and give Jason his glass of red and we make our way to their dining room. A rectangular, handmade mahogany table is set, complete with bread, pastries, and the main dishes in the center. Like a buffet.

I take my seat. Olivia smiles warmly at Jason while they fill their plates, and I push back the need to text Niki. *Fuck*, I miss her.

"So, who's this great, *mysterious* coder that helped Niki with the block?"

Jason glares at me, and Olivia chuckles. "Wow, you can't even wait for dessert, can you?"

I breathe out heavily through my nose. "Would *you* wait if Jason had unlikely ties to someone who helped secure his phone and possibly his *secret* property?"

She takes one long and hard look at him and then shakes her head. "Good point."

Yea, I thought so.

"Liv cooked, the least you can do—"

"Alright, alright," I interrupt him. I reach forward and plop a generous serving from each pot, take two loaves of bread, lean into my chair, and put a spoonful of everything into my mouth. "Happy?" I garble.

Jason fakes disgust at my eagerness, but smiles. "Yea, actually. I am."

I motion for Olivia to begin talking. She watches me carefully under a guarded gaze and clears her throat. She takes one long swig of her cold beer and gently pushes a manila folder toward me.

"Sara Martinez, one of the best in the field. We met in college, when I was in my last year. She was a freshman and *already* had jobs lined up, top organizations chasing her. Last I knew, she worked for one that focused on finding and apprehending human traffickers."

I've heard of her but hadn't made the fucking connection. Sara, Jasmin's girlfriend. Fuck!

I stop chewing and swallow the lump down and gulp the entire contents of the dry wine. I should've opted for water. I set the empty glass down and Jason dodges to the kitchen.

"I won't touch the block. It's the least I can do, the work she puts in..." Olivia shakes her head like she's filled with inspired awe. "Out of respect."

Jason returns and takes my glass, then fills it to the brim with more wine. I thank him with a nod. I don't even care to spy on Jule's phone at this point. What I can't get past is the incredible twist of fate. I don't believe in coincidences.

"And you trust her? *Completely?*"

Olivia puts down her beer. "With my life." She points to the file and I open it.

A three-page document summarizes Sara's work from when she was twelve years old to today, at her twenty-six years. She was a freshman in college at the age of sixteen and managed to graduate in three years. As Olivia pointed out, she works for a private organization that single-handedly brought down seven child predator sex rings, three politically affiliated human trafficking associations, two in the states and one abroad, all in one year. The coalition is rumored to consist of eight armed bodies and two tech workers, which includes Sara.

"Do we know how Jasmin met Sara?"

Jason dabs a napkin over his mouth. "As far as we know, looks like at *Nym-Pho*. Sara was there on a job."

My next question is an obvious one, and Liv puts her hand up and arches a brow at me. "I can't be sure if Jasmin or even Justice are fully aware of Sara's background. And you *cannot* interfere."

My mouth falls open, and I cough back the palpable threat of her scrutinizing glare. "Niki and Jasmin are taking her to the mayor's party. I *need* to know if—"

"The best I can do is set up a meeting... *here*. Some common ground."

The warning look in Jason's eyes tells me I've reached a wall and that I'm treading on thin ice. I don't give a fuck. I've seen him crawl toward his beloved, *literally*. Nothing they do will stop me from protecting mine.

"Fuck, Liv. You act like I'm going to carve the woman's eyes out." I just want to make sure Niki is safe.

Olivia rolls her eyes. "*Please*, I've seen you do worse for less."

My face involuntarily scrunches up, and I rub my fingers hastily between my brows, smoothing out the tension. I let out a sharp breath through my tight jaw, agitated with the pair. "I invited myself to chaperone, and I'd like all of us to coordinate. I don't want any surprises."

Jason raises his brows at the same time Olivia leans back in her chair. "*Chaperone?*" she interrupts and raises her hands and then slaps them down on the table. "You *invited* yourself to chaperone three *grown ass women*?" She laughs and shakes her head. "Of course you did."

"I don't understand what the fucking issue is."

"Nevermind the issue." Olivia dismisses me with a shake of her hand. "I think this is the perfect place to stop and reconvene. Have us *all* look over the plans."

Impressive. "You have The Mansion's blueprints?"

She turns to Jason. "*Este pendejo que se cree—*"

Olivia puts me through the shredder, spewing the entirety of insults in her book, all directed at me, and Jason smiles at her and then laughs. Great, what am I, muse to her fucking comedy show?

"Alright, alright. I'm sorry for doubting your skills, *oh great one*."

She lets out an exasperated breath. "I have more than just *blueprints*."

Olivia smiles wickedly and then turns to blow a kiss to Jason. I roll my eyes in response.

23

Justice

I don't want to be here. Well, I never want to be here, but tonight, a burning ripple bubbles in my stomach and an invisible weight sits on my windpipe. Like a bad feeling, a warning or premonition of sorts. My body is trying to tell me something, but there's a connection failure. As per usual.

Typical me. I never listen to my gut.

My shoulders roll with a need to ease the tension, but it's no use. Instead of figuring out a way to relax, I adjust the chain dangling over my ribs. I have on a cute pleather brasier with six rings dangling down the center, and six chains connecting the rings to both sides under my armpits. My black lace undies are covered by a ruffled skirt that looks like a tutu. I flip my hair so that the confetti from earlier falls to the floor, and adjust my black and silver fox mask.

I hate birthday celebrations at *Nym-Pho*.

Greedy motherfuckers with slippery hands—there aren't nearly enough bills being thrown at us for the extensive and prolonged ass shaking we do.

This is my second outfit for the night, and now I'm off to a private dance reserved by someone unknown to me. I want to go home.

And not the trailer. Nope. The shit box hasn't felt like home for a while now. Maybe it was when Noah fucked me over, or perhaps when his posse beat my ass in my own home. Or when Dylan moved in next door.

I'm not sure. When the fuck did my life take a sharp left at FML Lane?

I close my eyes before leaving the breakroom and the ranch appears before my closed lids. It's the first time I feel this overwhelming need to jump into my old truck and race to the lot my parents left us. To one of Helena's home-cooked meals and the warm duvet covers of my bed. I want to crawl underneath their secure embrace and turn my back on the life I created for myself here.

An annoyed voice clears their throat behind me. "Can you move?"

Shit. "Yea, sorry." I open the door, shake the sadness away, and head out to the dark and cool hallway that leads to the main floor.

The veiled goddess that stood behind me struts ahead and flips her hair. I swallow, hoping that the act soothes a dry tickle threatening to cower my body back into the *safe* confines of the staff room.

The flashing lights dance across my face and hit my eyes, stinging them. The music tonight is a seductive and promiscuous staccato of hip-hop and the crowd is eating it up. The club is packed tonight. The birthday of some hot and filthy rich broker brought in a crowd of hooting men ready to smack asses and toss singles on the floor like raindrops.

I was supposed to be headed to a cage above the stage, but some mystery man reserved the last hours of my shift for himself in a private room. I fucking hate private dances.

I wonder what Dylan would say.

He's a no-show tonight. I hadn't heard from him since he last texted me while I was with Jas in his kitchen. Something about our fuck sessions made me think he'd reach out by now and I don't know why. He's got tabs on me, and there's no need to message me to find out where I'm at. He can figure that out himself. I don't feel foolish so much as somewhat empty.

I'm comfortable with 'fuck and forget', but not with Dylan. I can't forget him and I don't want to. Especially not after I confided in him.

He says I'm his, and he is mine. Whatever the fuck that means.

I was intoxicated by his entire persona and the words that left his sexy lips were like a siren song pulling me to the deep. This has never happened to me. It feels like I'm both drunk and high and roaming about, starving for a man covered in tattoos, with calloused hands tainted by unknown sins. Searching for him blindly, desperate to be consumed and ruined by him in whatever fucking way he wants.

I need him.

"Hey. Shake it off, Justice."

Jasmin collides with me at the circle where all the halls connect. *How long have I been standing here?*

"The client is waiting. Here."

She hands me a matte black card with a shiny, embossed black wolf on the surface. I nod and tuck the card in my bralette, then saunter toward the right corridor.

Spine straight, shoulders back, tummy tucked, tits perky, ass-bone up. I go over the mental checklist detailing what I have to present myself as and swallow back my sudden cowardice and sulking thoughts. Once I reach the door with the same card now stored in my bosom, hanging on the magnet just above eye level, I turn the copper doorknob.

The room is cooler than the heated hall and the music is unrecognizable but sultry. Like something you'd hear on a tantra, erotic album.

I skim the bar surface and frown. Normally, clients purchase a bottle of something and leave it for dancers to sip from. Instead, there's a glass canister of water and a matching cup next to it. I clear my throat and avoid looking at the man covered in shadows below the steps, sitting comfortably on a single leather couch. His hands rest on the armchairs and he waits motionless.

The room is darker than I expected; the only lights come from the soft red glow of the decorative staircase lighting. Most of the light shines on the small stage where two black metal poles stand. I walk slowly behind the bar and open the fridge and pull out a bottle of Patron. I pop it open and fill the glass cup next to the water canister and smile into the darkness.

No one tells me what to drink. I'll sip whatever the fuck I want, and at the moment, I don't want water. I set the glass down and walk around the top until it leads me to a decline in the carpeted ground and onto the round podium-like stage.

A glimmer catches my eye, and I sneak a glance at the mystery man. He wears a silver wolf mask, complete with fangs and carved to look realistic and intimidating. It has a smoke colored finish with blackened markings so it appears textured and *so fucking real*. Darkness stares back at me through the carved out eyeholes, turned down in a glaring stare. It only covers half of his face, but I can't see anything else. Only the lights that reflects off the metal wolf mask.

A shiver runs up my spine and sputters my body into a short quake. *Contrólate.*

I start my movements slow and try to pace them to the music. I use one of the poles for support and bend and shimmy seductively. The chains over my ribs glide and roll, tickling my sensitive flesh.

Jasmin convinced me to keep on the black pumps—she'd said the added length they gave me was hot and that my ass would thank me. But all I want to do is chuck them across the fucking room. My hips feel the burn as I sway them slowly, enticing the stranger.

Ten minutes later, and I need another drink. With this in mind, I walk as best I can, attempting to look sensual, and hop onto the bar. I take off the shoes and drop them to the floor. My poor feet ache, but I ignore the need to rub them and reach for the bottle and take one long swig. The stinging meets my throat in a soothing burn that melts away the nausea creeping below my nerves. I tuck it away and lower my back and arch my spine. Wolf man wants a show, and he's going to get one.

I sit up and tuck my legs under my ass. Water seems like a good idea, so I reach for the canister and drench my face with it. The liquid cascades down my breasts, past my thighs, and collects near my shins. I perch onto my knees and set the glass canister down, then take a look at the man who's shifted in his seat. He's leaning back with one hand tucked under his chin.

I think he's smiling, and the contents in my stomach threaten to climb up and out. His smile turns the water on my skin to ice, and I sit on my heels and cover my mouth. Why the fuck did I spill the entire contents on me? Now I have nothing but tequila to drink. *Shit!*

The shape of his mouth turning upwards causes a delicious wetness to gather at my center. A frightening gnaw eats at the edges of the hole that lives where my heart used to beat. An electrifying buzz bangs there instead and fuels me to hop off the bar and saunter back to the pole.

The man's eyes don't leave me, and his masked face follows my every move. I grip the pole and give him my best moves, swaying in perfect unison to the music. Something weaves between us, a thick thread spinning to the beat of our hearts. Warping the air and spinning out, tangling itself and uniting us somehow. I can't explain it, I can only *feel* it. And like a fucking lightbulb being flipped on, I know exactly who the mystery wolf man is.

As if he's guessed this, he reaches up and pulls back his mask.

Dylan.

I grin my big toothy smile and toss my head back, a laugh escaping me.

I don't stop dancing and swivel slowly down to bob my hips. My chest moves like it would underwater. I hang on to the black metal pole and use it as leverage to keep me steady while I continue to move up and down. I flip my hair and almost laugh again when I catch Dylan's jaw tightening. His perfectly chiseled face reveals nothing, but I can sense his hunger for me burning through his coal-colored eyes.

He pats his leg for me to approach, and when I stand to climb down the first step, he raises his hand, halting me.

Dylan shakes a finger at me. "Crawl to me, little fox."

The command in his voice melts my bones and brings me to my knees. I never even decided to follow the order in his words, but my body is compliant to him in ways I still don't know or understand.

He pats his leg again, and I slither toward him slowly, the plush carpet soft against my knees and palms. I stop before him on all fours, my core buzzing with anticipation. I swallow, the need to throw myself at him has my limbs trembling. When I look up to his perfect face, the blackness of his eyes consumes me, and I rise up and sit on my heels, waiting for his instructions.

He unzips his pants, and I lick my lips when he suddenly stands up and his hard cock springs out. It's like seeing it for the first time, the sheer size of it, covered in veins and already wet at the tip, and I bite my lip in response to it all.

I open my mouth and move toward his hips when he lifts a finger to stop me. He makes a low tsk sound and my lower lip sticks out in a pout. He chuckles and reaches for it, pinching my lips between his fingers.

He parts my lips with his thumb and grazes my bottom teeth. "This isn't going to be soft and slow, Niki. I'm going to fuck your pretty mouth until I spill the contents of my balls into your throat. And you'll swallow every drop."

I'm salivating, and I close my lips around his thumb and bite down. "You promise?"

There is no warning. Like a rabid animal, Dylan squeezes my jaw and lets out a low growl while he thrusts his cock into my mouth.

My eyes water at the sudden intrusion and I stretch my mouth wider. While I concentrate on breathing through my nose, the forceful thrusts of his hips push me back, and I spread my knees and angle them for better support. I grip his thighs for leverage and blink back the tears that have collected in the corner of my eyes. The plush rug burns my knees, and I want to smile, but my lips are already pushed back taut. Dylan groans deeply while he pounds my face, pushing deeper and deeper. He isn't holding back; instead, he shoves himself into my mouth and swivels his hips, thrusting like a mad man.

Saliva gathers on the corners of my lips and leaks out, coating him and causing delicious sounds that have both him and me trembling. I think he's expecting me to gag, which I'll gladly do if that's what he wants. But I don't and it seems to fuel him. The mask is slick on my cheeks and uncomfortable over my nose, but I ignore it.

Dylan grips the back of my neck and looks down, his eyes ablaze with desire. His free hand smooths my hair back and then he twines his fingers and yanks my head back, tugging at the strands and gripping tightly to hold my face steady.

"Good girl," he purrs.

His words force my chest to puff up with pride, and I attempt to lick up his shaft while he's fucking my throat. Sloppy wet sounds fill the space and Dylan grunts and picks up speed. I imagine his dick multiplied and fucking me in every hole at the same time, and I moan at the idea of how exquisite that would be.

He suddenly trembles and pumps my throat more deliberately until he momentarily freezes.

"Fuck, Niki."

He thrusts into me, his balls slap my chin, and a tremor shivers through us. I feel the warmth of his cum filling me, and I try to smile, but greedily swallow back each drop until he pulls out slowly.

Before he can retreat, I grab the corner of his shirt and dab it over my mouth, and he chuckles. Dylan grabs my wrists and pulls me up, then lifts me, forcing me to wrap my legs around his waist.

He takes my mask off and tosses it somewhere near his feet. "I missed you, little fox."

Then he buries his face in my neck, breathes me in, and bites down at the hollow of my neck. He sucks and then licks at the indents his teeth most likely left behind.

"Did you now?"

I rub my hands over his scalp, loving the way the buzzed cut scrapes along my palms. My thumbs smooth out the wild hairs of his brows and then glide down his chiseled face to trace over his bottom lip.

"Thank you for the food. It was delicious." He kisses my thumb, and the air escapes my lungs.

So he went back to his trailer and found the plate I left for him. It must have been after Jas and I left. I'd been watching his property like an obsessed hawk. I wonder at what time he got back and what he's been up to all day.

Fuck, I'm tormented by his absence. But he's here now, and the need to leave with this man besets me. Where? It doesn't matter. I just want to be in his arms, on top of him, underneath him. Just smelted into one body, one complete being. But doubt eats away at the hollow cavity in me, and I sigh as my thoughts take over. I press my forehead against his and throw my arms around his neck.

"You don't think this is moving too fast?" *Says she who just got her mouth shamefully fucked at her place of work without a single protest.*

I want to rewind and take my words back. I can read his eyes. *Here we go again*, he's thinking. Dylan clears his throat. "No."

I could laugh, but I don't want him to take this as a fucking joke. Of course he would give me a one word, flat response. I suddenly want to choke him, but instead, I squeeze my thighs around his waist like an anaconda would its prey.

"How long have you been looking for this?"

I look at him questionably, and he gently sets me on my feet and pushes my hair back behind my ears.

"*Home*." The word makes my head snap up to meet his eyes. "Trust this... trust *me*. I don't want to hold back when it feels like I've finally found my home. *Do you*?"

I shake my head. "No." Of course I don't. "But," I look around sheepishly, "I don't know who you are. Where you come from, the truth about how much you know about me. About *everything*."

"Okay, that's fair."

My palms press against his hard chest, and I lean into him. I definitely hadn't expected his response. His hand searches the inside pocket of his jacket and he produces a black leather choker with a wolf embalmed at the very center. Dylan wraps it around my neck and easily secures the clasp at my nape. It fits comfortably snug, and my fingers graze the glossy figure at the center. I look up, and I'm sure I wear a big ass question mark on my forehead while he wears a smug grin.

"Now everyone will know. Dances are allowed, touching what's mine is not."

I punch a closed fist playfully at his right pec and roll my eyes. I can't with this man, and I opt to change the subject. Either way, a black collar is better than a red one. Patrons won't fuck with the rules and hands will stay off. I can live with that.

"So, what do you know?"

Dylan's lips spread into a wide grin. "*Everything*."

24
Redemption

I laugh at Niki's bewildered look. Her eyes are wild while she scans my face. I can't help the ease that washes through me at seeing her wearing the black band around her neck.

"What is *everything*?"

I paid for the remainder of her shift. At least three men had requested a private room with her. No way was I going to allow some drunk, affluent-wannabe fucker to paw his hard-on while drooling over my woman. Not tonight. I couldn't explain why, but I *needed* her in my arms.

They wouldn't be able to contain themselves, and I would've had to rip them apart for thinking they could touch her. I almost didn't make it and I was close to asking Jason to shut the place down. The black collar will help chill me the fuck out a bit. I hope.

It had been a long and difficult night, and I craved her closeness more than ever. I loop a finger through one of the rings dangling down the middle of her top and tug her toward me as I walk backward to the couch.

I sit her on my lap and draw circles below her breasts. "I know your father left you a plot of land which you converted into a farm. Your mother's best friend, her husband, and two kids reside there."

She stops breathing, and I stare into her big, expressive brown eyes. I slowly trail my hand down her ribcage, past the ruffles of her skirt, and underneath the layers.

"I know that you own three trucks, each under a different alias. *And*," I move my thumb between her legs and push past the elastic of her underwear, "I know you're currently housing two very sought after fugitives."

I lean in and suck on her top lip, then nibble on it. She tastes of citrus, tequila and *me*. I rub up and down between the lips below her waist and her thighs spread slightly, allowing me better entrance.

Niki licks her lips. "And what do you plan to do with this information, rookie?"

I shrug. "Nothing." I shove two fingers into her tight, wet cunt. "For now."

"Well, you've come a long way, for someone who knew absolutely nothing."

I rub the tips of my fingers against the wall of her insides. She's perfectly warm, soft, and wet. Her head tips back and a moan, raw and pure, escapes her. I shove my fingers deeper and gently flick her clit with my thumb. I bring my free hand to her neck and squeeze. Her pupils ripple out and threaten to paint the entirety of her mahogany irises.

"That won't *ever* happen again, little fox. From now on, I'll know *every* fucking thing."

Niki's expression darkens, and her lips pull back to a mischievous grin. "Squeeze harder, rookie."

Fuck. I comply, and my dick is rock hard the moment she gasps. Her eyes glaze over and her lips part–not to take more air in, but as a seductive invitation to do with her what I please. But I want her to take control, to do as she wants with me–to give her what she needs–full fucking reign.

I move her up and lower my pants, then position her over my now throbbing dick. Without caution, I drop her, and she yells out her pleasure.

"A warning would've been nice," she complains.

I clutch her neck, careful to only apply pressure on the sides, allowing her windpipe to suck in just enough air to remain alert. When she tips her head back, I know she's there. Niki enters that place in her mind where darkness resides and her fantasies beg to be freed.

"*Cállate*, and fucking take it."

My fox smiles wickedly, and her insides grip me before she begins to move up and down. Her spine bends back, tempting me to focus on her breasts, and I do. I take one nipple between my teeth and nibble. When her breath hitches, I suck hard and knead the other in my palm. I fucking love her tits–they're perfect. *She's* perfect.

Niki draws her hips up and doesn't come back down, but instead, she moves her waist in a circle. I groan; she's fucking toying with me. I want to pound into her, but I let her play. She needs this, and I enjoy watching her bring herself higher.

She lowers herself but then comes back up, and when I groan my complaint, she fucking laughs.

"Watch it, fox, or I'll overpower you and fuck you until everyone hears you scream my name."

She sucks in a breath, then finally pumps my dick with purpose, grinding whenever the tip hits the deepest parts of her. I'm fucking weakened by her movements, her scent, and the sounds she makes. I'm too close and I lose the last of my control when she whispers my name against my lips.

I grip her waist forcefully and ram my hips up, lodging myself deeper until her muscles contract around me and she's trembling in my arms. I come seconds after, grunting my release, and I sink my teeth into her shoulder to stop me from yelling three words I'm sure would frighten her.

"I still don't know who you are."

My semi hard dick is still buried deep inside her and I squeeze her ass, lift her up, and then adjust her hips and slip out. I smirk when a shiver wracks her body and again when she melts once I sit her on my lap sideways. Once I tuck myself away, I press her closer to me, digging my fingers possessively into her hip, and I clear my throat.

"What do you want to know?" I ask in Spanish.

Her shoulders rise. "Who are you? And I don't mean your *job*. Where do you come from, your parents, do you have siblings? Your age... normal stuff."

"*Normal* stuff. Okay." I scan the room as if it's going to provide quick responses for the mundane yet complicated nature of my past. A past I've never really openly discussed with anyone, even my parents. "I was adopted around the time I turned ten. My parents are great and—" I frown, feeling ridiculous and uncomfortable. "They're great people."

Niki searches my face with furrowed brows, and her expressive chocolate eyes shoot beams of quizzical speculation at me. "What about before you were ten?"

I shift uncomfortably and hold her closer so that she doesn't think I'm trying to pry her off of me. If anything, I want to end this conversation and bury myself balls deep inside her. Better yet, I want to fuck that pretty mouth of hers again, so she'll shut up already.

"I was in foster care from about age six."

She stares at me. "And before that?"

I let out a breath and swallow, then move my neck so that it cracks. I hope it relieves some of the tension already building. "I don't remember much."

Niki's eyes glaze over and she tucks her bottom lip in and bites down. I've never seen her like this, so vulnerable and twisted up by unknown sadness and grief. I sigh and tuck a few wild strands of her hair behind her ear, then push my thumb gently down on her chin to free her lip.

"My parents are really great people and I don't have any siblings. I grew up near D.C. and I'm twenty-eight years old, little fox."

"Foster care—"

"Was a nightmare," I interrupt. "As you can imagine."

She gives one solemn nod. "Yea, I avoided it at all costs."

"I know. You *still* do." I arch a brow. I've remedied that, but now isn't the time. "Anything else?"

"*El cerro*, my guests, what do you know?"

My brows shoot up, and I breathe back a chuckle. "*El cerro* is deep in my net, fox. I know enough. Regarding your guests–*not enough*."

I'll have to secure her airspace, at least for drones belonging to prying eyes that aren't mine. Niki touches my chin and grazes her fingertips up my jawline, past my ear, and cups the back of my head.

Her glare is hostile but not aimed at me. "You'll help me ruin him?"

I grin. "Done."

A knock at the door startles her, and she jumps off me. I stand and smooth my shirt.

"Justice?" Jasmin's worried voice calls, and Niki relaxes.

She rushes over to the door, unlocks it, and Jasmin slithers in. Her eyes scan the room nervously until her gaze locks with mine. Niki closes the door behind her.

"Detective! I... I had no idea you were the one who booked the rest of the night with Justice." She sounds relieved.

"Just Dylan, please."

"I wish I would've known it was you. Here, I thought I'd have to come up with an alibi for her."

So she too figured that no man would be able to keep their hands off my woman. I smile at the thought of the chaos that would've surged, the beating she'd instill upon being touched by another. Niki clears her throat, and I walk up to her, put my jacket over her shoulders, and wrap her in my arms. Her back is pressed against my front and I drop my chin to the top of her head. I have to hunch a bit; she's tiny in my arms.

"They were like vultures tonight. I couldn't hang back," I say.

Jasmin smiles and I get the feeling it's a rare sight. She's the most serious and guarded of the trio. Constantly wary and skeptical. She'd tear a human's eyes out in order to protect her adopted siblings, and I want to thank her for all the silent times she put her very own skin on the line for them.

She nods and reaches to grab Niki's hand. She squeezes it a few times and I watch an unspoken exchange between the pair.

Jasmin points to Niki's collar and waggles her brows. "Nice."

I don't need to look to know that my little fox rolls her eyes and I give her a squeeze.

"Thanks in advance, Detective."

"For?"

Jasmin's hand is on the doorknob, and she turns, an amused grin on her face. "The ride."

She leaves, but I'm sure she heard Niki groan at the same time I let out a booming laugh.

25

Justice

I'm in Dylan's sexy ride while he maneuvers through traffic easily; he reminds me of a snake swiveling across the ground dangerously undetected with a mission of malicious intent. It's been five days since he popped up as the mysterious, wolf themed-masked-patron and stapled a black collar around my neck.

I hate to admit that it's worked to keep clients' hands off me, and intriguing enough, it's made them want me more. The requests for private dances are unmanageable, but no one dares to put so much as a finger on me. They just watch with intense jitters and blinkless eyes.

I received a message with details about tonight's party at The Mansion, and Dylan wants us to *prepare.* Whatever that means.

"*Now* can you tell us where we're going?"

"Yea, I mean, even Sara knows. Not sure how you managed that, but she just texted that she's there already."

"There, *where*?" I look behind my shoulder to Jas, who's in the backseat with Max. She pivots the phone, which we've been sharing, so I can view the text.

Dylan takes in a breath and rolls his shoulder. "You'll see."

What's with all the secrecy? I cross my arms and lean my head back. At first, I thought he was taking us shopping. I don't have shit to wear to a ball with strict attire guidelines. We're also not allowed any electronic devices. The thought of going through the massive structure, in hunt of a fucking USB, makes my stomach turn. I mean, hadn't Piper heard of the Cloud? She freaked out when I called to tell her the party was today.

Max lifts his head up and lets out one loud bark that startles me into looking outside. I hadn't realized Dylan had exited the highway and was nearing a secluded bend off a private road. I sit up, intrigued, and spot a massive house with an impressive stone paved driveway. A gigantic waterfall sits in the center of the curved road. He parks his car behind a monstrously sized pickup truck, and I notice two dirt bikes and one motorcycle parked on the other side of a tiny red sports car.

"Who lives here?"

Max pants excitedly when the large double wooden doors of the house open and Sara waves. She's holding a beer in one hand and her phone in the other. Dylan opens the door for Jasmin, and both she and Max climb out. Sara gives me a wave and rushes over to Jas and embraces her. The giant Cane Corso disappears into the house.

Sara wears loose black joggers, a white cropped top, and sneakers. Her platinum blonde dyed hair gleams in the sunlight, and her pale skin blushes easily in the suffocating heat. She's tall and thin, like Jasmin, but they're complete opposites. It's even more evident when they stand next to one another. Jasmin's dark complexion appears like smooth onyx, while Sara's tone is similar to a soft pink pearl.

I follow behind Dylan when a gorgeous woman in blue skin-tight jeans and a v-neck black t-shirt greets us. My breath halts, and I feel my cheeks burn. She embraces Dylan and acid sears the delicate tissue behind my eyeballs. My hands quake softly.

"Niki, this is Olivia—"

Olivia doesn't let him finish. She shoves him playfully with one hand to make room for me and collapses her body into mine in a hug. She smells of roses and leather. Similar to Dylan, but hers is a much more delicate scent mixed with lilies; she smells of springtime. Half of her head is shaved, and I glance at the intricate vines that wrap their way up her neck and behind her ear. They keep climbing and vanish into her hair.

"Finally!" she exclaims. "It's a pleasure to finally meet you."

My mouth opens, but nothing comes out, and Dylan chuckles.

"Olivia is my cousin, and this," he points behind her, "is Jason, her—" he pauses. "What are we calling him?"

Olivia rolls her eyes and stands back. She moves to stand next to me and tosses her arm over my shoulder. "My *marinovio*."

We all laugh except Jason, who glares at Dylan. His expression changes to a more playful glower when he looks at Olivia. Was I not supposed to laugh? I'm a stranger, after all. But no one seems to mind.

He pushes a button on his wheelchair, and it brings him forward. "Hi, Justice. It's great to put a face to the woman who's finally given this man something to obsess over that isn't work."

I smile sheepishly and take his hand, but before I can say anything, Sara and Jasmin thankfully join us. Dylan faces them and extends the proper introductions, then we all walk into the house.

I peer up at Dylan and give his hand a squeeze. "Your cousin?" I mouth, and he gives me a crooked smile.

I have to admit that the introduction was like a bucket of water being tossed over glowing embers.

The inside of the house is beautiful. The floors are made of glossy marble tile, and the creamy walls are decorated with angelic art from painters I cannot name. Everything is immaculate, tidy, and warm. The wood furniture looks carved with intricate patterns, and a massive crystal chandelier hangs from every room. We enter a room larger than both my and Dylan's trailers put together, and we take our seats on the cream-colored couches.

Jason secures his wheelchair with a press of a button, and Olivia sits on his lap. He kisses her arm and wraps one hand protectively around her waist and another grips her thigh. The seat next to mine sinks as Dylan collapses next to me. His long legs spread out in front of us and he pulls me closer to him. I allow myself to lean into him.

Jasmin sits on the couch next to us, and Sara joins her. They hold hands, and I notice Jasmin's tightly knit brows. She looks angry and I flash a questioning look at her. She blinks, letting me know she'll tell me later, and my stomach turns.

It all clicks suddenly. Sara already knew both Olivia and Jason; she's much too comfortable in their space. Had Dylan introduced them? And if so, when did he approach Sara? I watch as Olivia chats with her and they smile pleasantly at one another. My heart rate spikes, and I instinctively move away from Dylan.

He looks at me and frowns, but I ignore him. I don't like secrets. Maybe Sara explained herself to Jas while outside, but my best friend is still upset about something. I can tell.

"How do you," I point to Dylan, Olivia and Jason, "know Sara?"

Sara's eyes grow, but Olivia grins wickedly. Her full lips move into a tight line, and she hugs herself smugly. She looks at Sara and sweeps her hand to emphasize the room we're in. "The floor is yours."

I notice she squeezes Jasmin's hand, as if to keep it in hers, and my best friend/sister's nostrils flare. *What the fuck is going on?*

Dylan clears his throat. "We don't have time for this shit. I don't believe in coincidences, but apparently these two met in college. They're *old friends*," he says, and it sounds like a challenge.

"We all want the same thing," Sara suddenly says. "To put that fucking scumbag away."

Jasmin finally tears her hand free and crosses her arms, as if guarding herself. She looks to her right, where the front door is, and then at me.

Something in her icy look makes me stand. "We need a minute." I turn to look at Dylan, who's already towering beside me. "Alone."

Olivia pops up and approaches me. "Of course. I'll show you the kitchen. It's this way."

She leads Jasmin and me out of the fancy sitting room and into one of the cleanest, brightest, and most exquisite kitchens I've ever seen in my entire life. Including a television. An enormous-sized island sits between the walls lined with white cabinets. A stainless steel fridge is to the left, directly across is the stove. She opens the fridge, grabs two beers, and pops them open, then hands them to us.

"My house is your home now. Make yourselves comfortable."

Once Olivia walks away, Jasmin and I both place our beers on the island and she grabs my hands.

"Sara doesn't work at Best Buy." Jasmin rolls her eyes and her arms tremble. "Apparently, she works as a tech specialist for some private, unknown company that tracks and apprehends predators of all sorts."

Fuck. Well, that sounds familiar. I close my eyes and let out a slow breath.

"You know something." She lets go of my hands and when I open my eyes, she's backing away from me.

"Of course not!" I hiss. She relaxes but searches my face. "But…" I look around and throw my hands in the air. Fuck it. "It's basically what Dylan does, too. Jason works for him."

"*What?*"

"I'm sorry I didn't tell you. I didn't know how to take it all in. He's…" I search for the right word.

"*Psychotic?*" Jas offers and we laugh. "Are we going to trust them?"

I sigh. "I don't think we have much of a choice."

"Yea, well. I'm still fucking angry that she lied to me. I mean, *Dylan* fessed up."

Dylan *did* tell me. *Everything*.

He understood I wouldn't forgive a lie or an attempt to cover something up. Regardless of its importance. He risked me turning him away and bared his truth. I'm not sure why Sara kept things from Jasmin, but we have a fucking party to go to and standing around in this exquisite kitchen isn't going to help us get ready for the sick and scary night that awaits us.

We take our beers when Dylan appears in the archway. He steps into my space and tentatively places his hands on my waist.

"I just recently found out about Sara and looked into her once Olivia told me. She pans out." He glances at Jasmin, who's frozen beside me. "But I have no way of tracking it back to when you two met."

Jasmin nods and looks down at her beer. The dark glass sweats in her hands. "Not very good detective work, huh?"

Dylan chuckles, but it doesn't reach his eyes. He doesn't trust Sara, and immediately I'm suspicious. "Maybe we should call this whole thing off. Or at the very least, you two should stay put. Jason and I can attend and—"

"Absolutely not. I was *personally* invited... I'm *not* sitting this one out, rookie."

Olivia suddenly pops her head in. "I agree with Justice. We can handle this, D."

"*We*?" Both Dylan and Jason ask in unison and we all turn to face Jason.

Our gazes bounce from one person to the other.

Olivia is the first to speak, and she leans on the wall, exuding confidence. "Yes, *we*. I think it's time you gentlemen allow us to have some fun. Besides, it gives us the opportunity to show you how a job is *really* meant to be done."

I like her already.

"Absolutely not," Jason announces through a clenched jaw.

Olivia approaches him and moves to touch his face. He reaches for her hand and brings her knuckles to his lips. "I'm going to be just fine, *Professor*. And if anything happens to me, you can take it out with Dylan here."

She winks at Dylan, who puts his hands up as if surrendering. "I have nothing to do with this."

"If anything happens to her, I swear I will—"

"Yeah, yeah. You'll skin me alive and detach muscle from bone, all while keeping me alert to feel every second of it."

I blanch. Looks like this isn't their first time exchanging such threats.

"What about *me*?" Sara walks in and we all turn to her.

Her emerald-colored eyes appear pained as she stares at Jasmin, who takes a sip from her beer and then crosses her arms. "You and I have a conversation pending. But for now, this takes precedence."

Sara swallows and stuffs her hands deep into her pockets. "I can stay with Jason and monitor the situation from here. I brought some tech that you all can wear; it's undetectable. They won't find it on their scanners. I'll make sure you have the best fucking connection for us to be able to communicate. You can also add another person, someone not here... *nor there*."

She looks at Olivia and then to Dylan. *How the fuck does she know about Piper?*

"Olivia communicated some privy information," Dylan explains, and he glares at his cousin.

"Hey, I've known Sara for years and I vouch for her. I don't agree with some of her... methods. But she's good people."

"It's up to Niki and Jasmin," Dylan crosses his arms. "I'll back up what they decide."

It's like a standoff between the two family members. They stare at one another, neither one backing down.

Jasmin clears her throat. "It's alright, she can stay."

"Great." Olivia's hands clasp together near her chest. "I have outfits for us." She weaves her arms through mine and Jasmin's and leads us out.

I turn, and Dylan offers me an encouraging smile, then waves at me. Behind us, I hear Jason grilling Dylan about Olivia accompanying us, but we reach a turn and their voices become too muffled for me to eavesdrop.

"I went a little crazy and bought us a variety of outfits for the night." Olivia takes us into a master suite and then we walk into the biggest closet that I'm sure absolutely no one needs.

The room is the size of an entire apartment, with bright lights and a lush, ivory-colored carpet. Three walls hold hundreds of color coded outfits, and directly to my right is an open room and I get a glimpse of shoes lining the walls from floor to ceiling. She directs us to a spot with an ornate screen cornered against a wall. To my right, a rolling cart, like one you would see behind the scenes at a modeling show, holds at least twenty outfits.

"The blue hangers hold your outfits, Justice. And the yellow ones are for Jasmin."

I freeze, temporarily blinded by the bright lights, and I lean against a cushioned bench and sit.

"You got these for *us*?" Jasmin manages.

Although my little family owns a ranch with all the elements of a cozy living, we've never truly taken advantage of it all. We embody the living standards of the trailer park, and we always felt it kept our situation more believable. I couldn't walk around with the latest and most fashionable boots, Jule couldn't own the best gadgets, and Jasmin could never have a single item from this expensive array of dresses I'm sure she'd love to own. We had to fit it, regardless of what we owned miles from our trailer shit box, and we grew to appreciate and value what we earned. It made everything we had at the ranch extra special.

Olivia smiles at us. "Let's get ready."

I stare in the mirror. "I can't walk out with this."

"You can and you will," Jas says while she practically flirts with her reflection.

I have to admit, her outfit is *much* more revealing. She wears a red, silk cut-out dress haltered over her right shoulder. The slit extends throughout the entire thing, revealing the skin between her breasts down an open wave sweeping her entire frame. A gold brooch connects the fabric at her hip. She wears her tight curls down, and her lips are a shade darker than the dress. Her sky high black heels have a red bottom and she bends her leg and smooths a finger over the shiny material.

She's in her element, while I'm still barefoot and sitting on the bench. I bury my face in my hands.

"Hey!" Olivia chastises. "You'll fuck up your make-up. Stop that."

Her dress is revealing in a whole different way. Olivia wears an all black, jersey-like material, backless and skintight dress. It looks like a second skin, as if it were painted on. And dainty, silver strappy heels. The beautiful chrome prosthetic cover catches the light, and I try not to stare. I wonder what happened to her, but I silence my question and press my lips tightly together.

"Here," she offers, and hands me a pair of pearl white pumps. "It's time to gear up with our tech."

Jasmin laughs quietly. She knows I despise high-heeled shoes. Although at least now I'm better at wearing them—I no longer wobble.

I slide my feet in and stand to look at myself again.

I have a long, high-waisted skirt that stops two inches below my breasts with a slit that opens up the bottom and stops at my waist. This part of the outfit I'm okay with. The material is stretchy and comfortable. It moves with me and doesn't strain me. The top... is a whole different story. I'm reminded of my *Nym-Pho* attire. This is what I get for allowing Olivia and Jasmin to select my clothing. My top is made of hundreds of pearls sewn together into sectioned, necklace-like partitions. A white material cut identical to a daisy serves as a nipple covering. The beaded straps over my shoulders connect in the back the same way a bra would. I wiggle in it and adjust my breasts.

"You'll be fine. That's what the tape is for." Olivia pats my back.

She provided me with clear sticky tape to hold my breasts up as if I were wearing a push-up bra. They're in place and don't budge, and it gives me comfort. My hair is straightened and tamed, it's longer somehow, and falls to the small of my back.

Except for my mother's charm bracelet, we don't wear jewelry. That's where the tech comes in. It's fashioned to look like earrings, a necklace, a watch, and even a garter. I smile when I think of the special piece I have for Dylan. I mentioned it to Olivia, and she passed it over to Sara, who promised to add an undetectable camera, complete with a built in sound absorber.

My skin tingles and I finally feel ready. I can fucking do this.

26

Redemption

Jason's all about decorum and respect until it comes to the safety and wellbeing of Liv. A flip is switched and he no longer acts like a man, but a fucking maniac. But I get it now, so I just listen to him. Or at least I let him think I'm listening. He's been blabbing for the past forty-five minutes—offering threats and vivid imagery of what he'll do to me if so much as a hair is touched on Olivia's head.

I put on my jacket and glance in the mirror. I'm not meant to look like Niki's date, or her Dom, so I dressed in a classic yet modern all black weave suit trouser. No button-down shirt or collar. I'm meant to appear simple and meek next to her. My reflection stares back at me, I'm making sure I shaved correctly and smooth my hand over my scalp, searching for imperfections. I didn't bother shaving the five o'clock shadow on my face.

"Are you fucking listening to me?"

"Jason, you really think I'd let something happen to my own family?"

He moves his chair inches from my thigh, a warning. "What about Madrid, or Cabo? And how about Cuernavaca?"

He says the last part slowly, drawing it out, and I roll my eyes. "That's hardly my fault. Liv is adventurous, and if anything, *she* dragged *me* into all those disasters."

He bumps his chair closer. "No adventures tonight. I need her back."

I look at him, and there's no humor in his eyes. "Done."

Sara pops her head in. "They're ready."

I give her a single nod and put my hand on Jason's shoulder. "There's no controlling Liv, you know this. But I won't leave without her. She will be safe."

He turns and we exit to meet the girls in the dining room. It's been converted into our tech room. Three computers and five laptops cover most of the table, along with various tiny lens tech that Sara brought for us to wear. I pull a chair back and sit at the far end. In front of me are a few sets of, made to look invisible, earbuds. They're really something. I grab one and inspect it between my fingers. It's a flexible see-through plastic, malleable to the touch. *How the fuck will this serve as a communication device, and why don't we already own this shit?*

Sara takes a seat at the far end of the table in front of a laptop and clicks a few buttons. Jason joins her. He presses a button on his chair and it reverses toward the wall, where he flips a switch. Above us, the chandelier begins to retreat back into the ceiling and in its place, a projector whirs out. It flickers and lights up, emitting an image on the wall to my left.

"You made a presentation?"

He shoots me a deadly glare. "My woman will be there; we can't leave room for errors."

I roll my eyes and they dance in their sockets while I bob my head. I let out a breath. "Whatever makes you feel better."

"You don't fucking get it," he yells suddenly. "You'll be there, watching everyone, making sure no one touches Justice. And if they do, you'll be right there waiting to cut their fucking hands off. And I'll be here, glued to this fucking chair, while my woman is out there with those fucking sick bastards who make a living out of selling people as if they were objects."

The room is silent except for the loud purr of the projector.

I raise my hands in surrender. "You're right."

Jason stares, unblinking, with a clenched jaw. I know there's no convincing him and he won't settle down until we're back.

Sara clears her throat. "If I may, no one will be out of our sight, gentlemen. Because we have these."

She presses a key on her laptop, and an image appears on the wall the projector faces.

"Starting the show without us?" Olivia questions.

She and Jasmin walk in first, temporarily blocking my view from Niki. I know Liv takes a seat, and that Jasmin is next to join her, but my mind can't register the conversation that begins to unfold. I can't peel my eyes away from my little fox. She looks absolutely ravishing, her milky skin glows against the pearls that make up her top. Instead of her usual look, tonight she appears regal; nothing is out of place.

Niki always looks drop dead gorgeous—she's got a natural sexiness that allures any and every person. Her look demands attention. But it's also very casual and effortless. Tonight, however, she is anything *but* a breeze. She can easily knock the wind out of anyone with that outfit.

"If looks could render a man speechless, I'd say we have a winner," Niki teases and smiles while she takes a seat next to Jasmin.

I frown; she's too far. And so I stand, gently push her chair back, and take her hand in mine. I ignore her confused gaze and lead her to sit on my lap instead. Beside us, Jasmin chuckles.

She smells of fresh citrus and honey. I move her silky, smooth hair over her shoulder and press my nose to her neck. I lick up from her collarbone to her earlobe and her skin is immediately covered in goosebumps. I smile into her ear and keep quiet, letting her know that she indeed has rendered me speechless.

All thoughts of invading Carlton's party leave my head. Instead, I imagine I'm with Niki somewhere warm. She'd love Rapa Nui. Her soft skin would glow and I would tire her out by teaching her to surf during the day and fucking her all night under the moonlight. We can explore the national park and fish and—

"What do you think, Dylan?"

Niki chuckles, and I groan into her neck. I don't know what the fuck they've been saying. "About what?"

Jason sounds exasperated. "The quality of the picture and clarity of sound."

My face is still deep in Niki's neck, and I lift my eyes to the wall where a detailed image of the room appears. I nod absentmindedly. I'm still in Rapa Nui with my fox.

"The lens is hidden behind a stone that works like tiny mirrors, allowing for a more authentic—"

I nibble on Niki's earlobe. "How is it being captured?"

Sara points to a dainty gold chain with a teardrop shaped ruby around her neck. She reaches back and unclasps it and rises out of her seat. She makes her way to Jasmin and the image on the screen moves with her. She settles it around Jasmin's neck, and we get a clear view of what is directly in front of her in crisp quality.

Someday soon, I'll take Niki, and all of this shit will be a blur in our past. But today, she needs my focus *here*. My face dips into the hollow of her neck. "What else is there?"

Sara proceeds to equip us with jewelry containing built in surveillance. A diamond bracelet and drop diamond earrings for Olivia. A matching ruby-encrusted hair brooch for Jasmin, along with ruby studs. A silver bangle and hoop earrings for Niki. None of it is *real,* but they look genuine and exquisite, nonetheless.

She gives Niki an expectant look and slides a black jewelry box to her. It's big enough to house a watch. Niki moves to stand, and I push the chair back slightly.

She turns to me. "Jacket off."

I frown, but I'm intrigued enough that I slide it off and toss it onto the chair next to me. She skims her eyes over me and gives me a mischievous grin. Niki pops the box open and takes out a chrome chain-mail collar with a long leash. She approaches me and reaches up and collocates it around my neck.

"Perfect," she purrs. She connects the long dangling leash to her free wrist and tugs.

The chain around my neck squeezes gently, and I'm forced to comply. My body is shoved forward slightly and my shoulders buck. Liquid lava fills my veins and steam hisses in my ears.

"What the fuck is this?" I tug on the leash.

"You're my pet," Niki offers sheepishly, but I see right through her facade of innocence.

I clear my throat and put two fingers through the collar and push up to release the grip. "Absolutely not."

"If you insist on joining us, *this* is the only way. Unless you want to finagle your own invite, which I hear is a pretty complicated server to hack into." She turns to Sara, who avoids looking my way.

"I think you look dashing."

"You shut up, Olivia." I point and she lifts her hands up in surrender.

"She's right—"

I interrupt Jason with a glare.

"About the difficult server," he finishes.

"Niki, you can't possibly be serious." I sit down and wrap the long leash in my palm and pull until it forces her to sit on my lap.

"Oh, I'm dead serious, rookie."

Sara continues her presentation, and a different image appears on the wall. "I installed a chip to the collar–it contains its own unique, built-in router which will enable all our devices. I'm sure they'll have something to block anyone sneaking in a phone. This will protect our tech and keep it up and running. It's also undetectable and shields us in case their system does catch on to the proximity of our devices."

I rest my chin on my hand and pull Niki closer. "So it won't allow their server to knock the power out of our devices and it will serve as our own personal Wi-Fi system?"

She nods. "Exactly."

I grip all of Niki's hair in my hand and tug slowly until her ear connects with my lips. "You'll owe me for this one, little fox."

She swallows, and I laugh before releasing her.

"Now for the mics," Sara continues. She walks around the table and provides each of us one earbud. "They're virtually invisible. These will allow the entire team to communicate back and forth."

"Seriously?" Niki questions while she twirls the plastic bud in her hands.

"On my life." Sara smiles proudly.

Jason points a finger in her direction. "I'll take you up on that."

There's a particular hostility in the room and it's aimed at her. It mixes with the anger Jasmin emits in her direction—it's fucking palpable. The only person who offers an unquestionable and authentic conviction in her abilities and intentions is Olivia. Even Jason is filled with doubt, and he normally agrees with everything Olivia delivers.

"When it comes to a third party, someone not here nor there, that's another matter." Sara looks at Niki and then Jasmin. "We'll need them on a conference call when the time comes. I can patch them through."

Niki stiffens in my hold. "Meaning…"

"Meaning they will need to contact Jason on a specific line, then I can combine the calls to one server."

Jasmin releases a breath and looks at Niki. They exchange a look no one but they can decipher, and my woman reaches in front of her for her phone.

27

Justice

The ringer buzzes six times before Helena answers. She's worried and speaks to me in our first language.

"*Mija, todo bien?*"

"Everything is okay. I need a favor."

"Okay," she answers slowly, and I hear the chickens in the background.

"Our guests, are they around?"

"*Sí*, both. Which one do you need?"

I look up and find all eyes on me. "The eldest."

I free my wrist from the leash and gently toss it to Dylan. Then I take my earrings and matching bangle off, then place them on the table. I can't have this conversation with everyone listening.

I turn and leave the room. The hall that connects this space to the kitchen also leads to the rear of the house, and I weave past everyone, make my way, and finally push past the glass door. Max looks up from his spot where he lounges in the sun and happily trots toward me. I close the door behind me and take in a deep breath to calm myself. It feels like I'm breaking a promise, and a stab-like pain in my gut makes each breath a struggle.

"Block the door, Max."

I don't know why I gave the order, but he obeys and sits directly in front of the glass door. I walk further into the expanse of the yard until I'm near the edge lined with tall and bushy privacy pines.

"Hey, what's up?"

I release the breath I was holding. "Do you trust me?"

"What's going on, Justice?"

"Just answer the question."

Piper sighs, agitated. "So far, you've proven to be one of the most loyal people I know." She pauses. "Yes, I trust you."

"The party is tonight and…" How do I tell her that it won't just be Jas and I? "It's a delicate situation. They're going to have signal jammers and a bunch of really bad people in attendance."

"Yeah, that's the way it normally goes. It's an auction… *people* are the prize."

I swallow, and I'm sure she can hear my heart beating in my throat. "I have help tonight—"

"What do you mean, *help*?"

I hear a low growl and turn to see Max facing the glass door. No one is on the other side but the massive dog bristles, nonetheless. He lets out a warning bark and then relaxes after a few beats.

"I can't explain it all right now, but you *have* to trust me. I would never divulge your story, or any specifics, around our situation. But I need to be able to have them patch through your call when I'm inside."

"*Them?*"

I take in a deep breath. How can I explain that Dylan is *not really* a cop? That Sara works for a government organization, but that she, too, isn't a cop. And both Jason and Olivia… I don't even know what they do or how they all fit in.

I also never really requested their involvement. I extended the invite to Dylan, but was thrown into accepting his crew. Truthfully, I like the outcome. Aside from trusting Dylan, the others come off as a legitimate team that knows what the fuck they're doing. But we haven't had time to talk about what we will all do when and if I get my hands on the file Piper hid.

The seconds trickle by and the only solid explanation I can come up with, one that is definitely set in stone, spills from my lips.

"I trust them and I will *not* give them the file. It goes directly from my hands to yours. No one will open it."

"You need their help?"

I take in a lungful of air. "I do," I admit.

Piper sighs. "Okay, Justice. But promise me that as soon as you come into possession of the USB, you'll bring it directly to me."

"I promise."

"So, how is this going to go?"

"When I'm in position, a man named Jason, the tech guy, will phone the house. He'll patch your call to me."

I imagine her nodding. "Be careful, kid."

Kid. I wonder if her little nickname for me will ever go away. I smile my annoyance away.

"I'll see you soon, Pi."

28
Redemption

We're in the backseat of an *UberXL*, set to drop us off at a location predetermined by our host. From there, a car service will pick us up and take us to The Mansion. I don't fucking like it, but it's within the fine print of the invite.

It's a way to control the guests' arrival and departure; the host isn't willing to house vehicles and further proof of attendance.

I had Jason add a tracking device to each of us. It's a state-of-the-art chip the size of a fingernail and it sticks to any part of our skin like a bandaid. It's undetectable and reliable. We use them on all our missions. This one is no exception.

We arrive at our first location and quickly put our masks on before stepping out. Three men in black suits escort us into a tent. I'm incapable of acquiring the behavior necessary to pass off as Niki's submissive, and I show this by wrapping my arm protectively around her.

Olivia's brows knit in my direction, then looks pointedly at the men that led us in.

"Put any and all electronics in this lockbox."

Their security is a band of ten idiots. We've definitely got brains over brawn, and I scan the interior to find it empty of anything that can be used as a weapon.

Four rectangular folding tables occupy the space, along with heavy duty rolling bins. Each is marked with a number that corresponds to the batch of lockboxes placed inside. Ours is number eight.

"We don't have anything," Olivia says.

The man looks her up and down, scanning her with his eyes, and I suppress the urge to punch him.

"The instructions specifically stated the rules," Niki offers, and I squeeze her waist.

She doesn't show an ounce of fear or nerves, and I'm so fucking proud of her.

"Well, we can easily figure out if they have any hidden electronics on them," a bulky one says.

Three men approach us, and I bristle at the action. My shoulders tense, and suddenly Jason's voice tames the animalistic-like rage building in me. "Deep breaths, everyone. They're not going to find anything. Just let them use their scanners."

I do as he says and watch as one of them waves a wand over Olivia.

Jason keeps talking to us. "Good job, Libby. You're next, Justice."

I bristle at the mere realization that this fucker is waving a metal detector less than an inch from my woman's skin, his eyes drinking her in. A snarl rips through me and a laugh resembling a snort leaves him.

"You're next, tough guy."

Jason's voice directs his attention to me. "Deep breath, D. Kick his ass later."

Kick his ass... Another chance and I'm going to fucking pummel his face in. He moves to Jasmin, who seems lost in her thoughts. She barely acknowledges the scanner.

The soon to be dead man turns and faces his comrades. "They're clean."

Olivia smiles a haughty grin, and Niki's shoulders drop in relief. She isn't used to this, and I get the sudden urge to throw her over my shoulder and get her the fuck out of here. But she would never forgive me. She *needs* to do this. And for someone who's crept within the shadows, gathering intel on a device to then share it on a media platform, she's doing phenomenal.

I step away and lower to whisper in her ear. "I never did confirm whether the Tec9 was a myth or not."

Niki faces me and smooths her thumb over my lower lip, as if cleaning her lipstick off me. "Guess you'll never really know, rookie."

Oh, I'll find out. I wonder if Jason can read my mind after he clears his throat in my ear. That fucker seems to know what I'm thinking even before it crosses *my* mind. I realize now it may be due to his undeniable obsession and undying commitment to my cousin. He lost her once and is on a fucking mission to never let it happen again. I want to say he's pathetic, but one look at Niki and I know I'd do worse. I don't want to exist without her.

I hear the engine of a car and one of the men raises the tarp, guiding us outside where an SUV waits.

"Here the fuck we go," Niki whispers.

The Mansion is enormous inside and out. The premises are guarded by a forest for a fence. It sits in the middle of a ten-thousand acre stretch of nothing but trees. The connectivity sizzles in my ear and I pretend to scratch at my lobe.

I clear my throat. "The music is nice."

Niki faces me and glares. Her elbow bends and she pulls at the leash. The collar around my neck hugs my skin and my Adam's apple bobs uncomfortably. "You will only speak when spoken to," she hisses.

My eyes are about to roll and my fingers stretch to smack her ass when Olivia pulls her slightly away from me and shoots me a look that would have any other man eight feet underground.

Liv curls her fingers around Niki's arm and leans in. "The static is part of the song, but I hope it doesn't continue. It ruins the music."

"Our connection is clear. I'm sending a drone to check out the perimeter," Jason explains, and the women nod a sigh of relief at one another.

Niki moves her wrist and tugs at my collar gently. I smother the snarl that wants to slip out. She'll pay for this.

We move deeper into the enormous dance hall. I scan the room and spot at least four security guards at every exit. Male servers offer the guests hors d'oeuvres on silver platters and female servers provide guests with champagne glasses. A glittering glass chandelier hangs above us; it clashes with the entire premise of what this night entails.

I keep quiet while Niki, Olivia, and Jasmin keep a steady conversation about shit I don't care about. Instead of a meek mouse for a pet, I think I look like a massive watch dog. It's as if Niki brought Max instead of me. Olivia keeps shooting me looks that tell me to ease the fuck up. I roll my shoulders and crack my neck. *Fuck.* When thinking one of us was going to fuck the plan up, it *never* dawned on us that it would be *me.*

"You made it."

I've never proven myself more true until this very moment. A growl rips through my throat as the fucker I knocked out at *Nym-Pho* waltzes toward us. I should've killed him when I had the chance. My hands instinctively ball into fists at my sides.

Niki's jaw drops, but she recovers quickly and smiles at her admirer. I want to reach out, grab him by the collar, and crack his skull open.

"I was hoping you'd be part of the auction tonight." He kisses Niki's hand and then wiggles it in his grip, making the long chain swivel side to side. "What's this?"

"My pet." Niki waves a dismissive hand my way and smiles. She doesn't look at me—I think her facade would crumble—but he does.

"Quite the pet."

She hums in agreement. "I'd be careful. He's *protective*."

He drops her hand, and it's in this moment I realize I was practically standing in an attack stance. My shoulders are tense and leaning forward, my lip is quivering up in a snarl, and my hands are balled still.

"Bummer. Maybe I can offer you special seating for the auction. Right up front?"

"For me and my friends?"

The idiot looks at our group and nods in appreciation. "Of course."

If everything works out according to plan, there will be no auction.

29

Justice

My palms are all sweaty, and if I didn't have Dylan practically attached to my left hip, I'd pass out the moment we sat in the Escalade. The metal bracelet connected to the chain that links Dylan and me is my constant reminder, and it works like a fucking pill to my anxiety.

The lights dim and the music pulses. It's a precursor to the fucking nightmare that will begin in less than a couple of hours. Jasmin and Olivia stick to one another like glue, and they join a few others to dance. Jason mumbles details about a few prestigious members that have arrived and I tune him out.

I wiggle my wrist, twisting it in a circular motion, and then I reach for my mother's charm bracelet. I count the charms, then twirl each one between my fingers.

Dylan suddenly moves away, and the motion pulls at my wrist. Confused, I turn to him and tug on it, forcing him closer to me. But he continues to pull me and walks toward a hall that leads to a corridor with private unisex bathrooms. I follow and adjust my face. I don't want it to be obvious that I lack the ability to control my *pet*.

"Where the fuck are we going?" I whisper.

I don't understand his barely audible words. "Keep your ears open, but turn your eyes away from us. Give me three minutes."

Jason's voice speaks next. "Your three minutes start now."

Dylan guides us into an empty bathroom, and once he locks the door behind us, he presses me against the wall. I'm about to protest, but he silences me with his thumb over my lips and then replaces it with his lips. He moves his hand down my neck, and I know he feels the instant my pulse quickens. It spirals against his touch and I swallow back a whimper. His eyes darken, and the fucker moves a finger over his lips and then he points to his ear. He's reminding me that Jason is listening and his words suddenly make sense. Dylan asked Jason to turn our cameras off but to keep the sound on.

His hand resumes its glide over my skin, causing a shiver to run down my back, and then it wraps all around me, shooting a sensation of desire between my legs. My treacherous body leans into his touch as liquid lava is released from the ventricles of my heart. His touch heats every cell in my body and I swear, steam hisses out of every pore.

He moves my hair off my shoulder, removes my mask, and presses his lips to my collarbone. I'm practically panting and he hasn't even touched me below my neckline. Dylan pinches a few pearls on his way down to my waist, and then he sinks his hand to cup between my legs.

I suck in a breath, shocked, and he mouths, "*two minutes*". No way is he promising to make me come in only one-hundred and twenty seconds. I blink away my surprise as he moves my thong to the side and slips one finger in and then out. He smiles at me and licks his lips.

Fuck. I'm supposed to keep quiet during all of this? I press my lips together as Dylan nibbles on my shoulder and slowly slides his finger back and forth, smoothing my wetness in a way that makes my cheeks redden with mortification. My body loves what he's doing and I'm frozen, unable to stop him.

What is it with Dylan taking me wherever the fuck he pleases, and why do I let him? Oh right, because I'm a shameless slut. What would my therapist say? Somewhere in the back of my mind, the harlot in me writhes and smiles wickedly; *his slut*, she purrs.

Damn if she isn't right. I couldn't care less where I'm at as long as I'm in Dylan's arms.

He glides his thumb over my clit suddenly and begins to gently rub the area in small circles. He slips his finger inside me, and then another. So now two fingers pump in and out; at the same time, he keeps a steady rhythm over my clit. A cool and numbing sensation begins to coil inside me, and I know soon it will let loose and take over.

It can't fucking be. I haven't been counting, but I'm sure not even a minute has passed.

"*So wet*," he mouths. "Open your eyes, little fox."

I don't want to comply, but I belong to him in a way my subconscious has adamantly accepted. My lids flutter open, and I find him staring into my fucking soul, guiding me to complete bliss. My lips feel dry and when I part them, an unabashed moan slips out.

"That's it," he croons. "Come for me."

I bite my lip, forgetting why I was supposed to stay quiet to begin with, and focus on the intense feeling at my center as all the blood in my body goes to where Dylan's fingers work me. I'm practically writhing. My hips move on their own accord, a frenzy taking over as my insides explode with sheer pleasure.

"*Yes*, good girl."

His voice sounds strained, raspy, and I realize in my euphoric state that I've wrapped the long chain around my fist and I've been tugging on it. I'm *choking* him.

I'm done. I yell out his name. *Yell*, and then melt against his hard chest. My pussy pulsates around his fingers, and I think my body is ticking to its rhythm. A hazy, blissful, and lazy feeling encompasses me, and it registers that I'm fucking smiling into the folds of Dylan's shirt.

He slips his fingers out and licks them clean, a satisfied grin splayed on his perfect face. Dylan looks down at his watch and nods approvingly. He unclasps the chain attached to the collar and drapes it over my shoulder. "I'll wait outside."

I glance at my own watch, thirty seconds to spare. *Fuck*.

Dylan steps out, and I know he's standing on the other side of the door I just locked. I freshen up, a stupid grin on my flushed face, and I stare into the oval mirror above the sink. My makeup is somehow still as it was when Olivia expertly applied it. I smooth my hands over my hair, adjust the faux, pearl-made top, and make sure the skirt slit is where it was meant to be.

The ear canal housing Sara's device beeps softly. "Welcome back, Justice."

Jason. *Oh shit*. I clear my throat nervously.

"Don't worry, I turned both of your devices off. Dylan would fill my ears with acid if I would've kept connectivity—literally."

I laugh. "Good to know."

Once my mask is on, I open the door and find Dylan guarding the entryway. I know we have to keep up with appearances and that he is here as my *pet*, but a sensation, similar to a buzz or a high, builds as I gather the chain and clasp it back to his collar.

Jason sighs. "You look like a fucking bodyguard, D. Ease up."

Dylan ignores him. He reaches for my hair and gathers a few strands to place them over my shoulder. "Feeling better?"

My cheeks burn, but I nod. I tug on the chain roughly and the action forces him to bend down slightly. His nostrils flare, and I bite the inside of my cheek to stop myself from laughing. "My pet knows best. Perhaps I'll reward you like the good boy you are."

Dylan's lip furls and he opens his mouth to retort, I'm sure, when Jason interrupts. "You two got company coming your way."

I turn, and behind me, Dylan straightens. My eyes widen when I realize who it is. *El cerro*, accompanied by Charles, Piper's man.

30

Redemption

I follow close behind Niki and keep my eyes on her back. If I look at Carlton, I'll rip his fucking throat open. He's never seen my face in person, though we've had plenty of on-screen meetings. Thankfully, they've all been while I'm in a darkened room, with my best attire that kept all of my tattoos hidden. He won't recognize the man standing behind the beautiful woman he's talking to. My woman.

The guy standing next to him not only notices me, but he takes me in as well. He's a lean but tall motherfucker, and he watches every move closely, examining and memorizing every minute fucking detail. I recognize the sort. He's ex-military. My eyes scan behind them to the left of the ballroom, where I spot Olivia and Jasmin peering at us.

My cousin gives me one solemn nod, and I glance at the man standing next to Carlton, who's scanning the area behind me, and then I look back to Liv.

I hear Jason through the earbud. "Olivia asked me to gather intel on the man who's with Carlton."

I know he blocked Niki's earbud, as to not overwhelm her with unnecessary chatter that may scatter her thoughts. She's concentrating on keeping her voice steady.

I knew my suspicion would get across to Olivia. Jason is constantly failing at his attempts to keep her busy with in-house work. His fixation with keeping her out of the field goes beyond words. But Olivia and I grew up side by side since I was adopted. She was the first person in the family that I spoke to, and quickly, we were communicating without words.

"I'm disappointed to find you won't take part in the auction," Carlton tells Niki.

"Oh, I will."

Carlton's eyes brighten, and the man beside him remains unfazed, bored even. *Interesting.*

"As a potential buyer," Niki explains.

"Ah, well, Charles, make sure our guest receives a menu."

Charles looks at Niki as if acknowledging her for the first time. "You'll have to go through a mandatory screening. Once that's complete, you'll have access to the menu." He produces a device. "Your fingerprint."

Niki reaches forward with the hand that's connected to my leash, and it forces me to press my front against her back and lean forward slightly. Gingerly, she places her index finger on the screen and it scans her digit.

Jason's voice speaks into my ear. "Sara created profiles for each of you. You'll be fine, Justice."

The device beeps, and Charles examines it. His eyes connect with Niki's and his semblance slips. Just for one second, but I notice it. He knows who she is.

I tense, ready to pull her behind me and strike, when his voice interrupts my plan. "What's the saying? Flying colors?" He slips his hand into an inside pocket of his jacket and hands her a small tablet. "Your code." He shows her the device that scanned her finger, where a QR code waits. He looks bored again.

Niki slides her finger up, and the tablet comes to life. Her hands tremble slightly, but she stays in control and opens up the camera app to scan the code.

Carlton steps and leans forward to take a peek at her screen. "Perfect! Scan through the images and make your offers. Good luck." He smiles and then they're gone.

Niki turns to face me. "I don't understand." She flips through the images roughly. "They don't look like," she looks around and lowers her voice, "*victims*."

I try to appear inferior and amenable. "It's advertising clothing and jewelry; each model is different. It's a cover, little fox."

She nods in understanding. We move toward Olivia and Jasmin when she stops. I look to see what's made her almost drop the device and see a child on the screen. She's no more than five years old and wears a soft green dress with ruffles for a collar. She stares at her hands, delicately folded over her lap. She has a diamond encrusted crown.

Niki's hands tremble, and I press my front to her back and put my hands on her shoulders and squeeze. I want to tell her that we're here to avoid this shit from happening. No one's *buying* anyone tonight.

"Let's join the girls." My voice is soft but stern. If anyone sees her reaction, her cover might be blown. I'll kill every fucker that even tries to touch her, but I need us to make it out in one piece. *All of us*. The little girl included.

She moves forward, an empty shell, unable to pretend to smile anymore. I don't blame her. No one at this party is phased by what appears on their screens. They're clicking ecstatically, comparing and goading. My blood boils, and I practically hear it as it travels through my fucking veins.

"What's wrong?" Olivia speaks first, her words hushed, giving nothing away. She scans the room, a tense smile splattered across her features.

Jasmin moves in close and she can't take her eyes off the screen.

"Shit," I hear Olivia say. "We need to move fast. Find a clear path for us, Jase. The auction begins in less than an hour."

31

Justice

The calm I felt less than fifteen minutes ago has vanished. The tension has returned with a vengeance and my shoulders are grazing my earlobes. My brows are furrowed, practically knitting a fucking sweater with my eyebrow hairs. I can't, for the life of me, remain positive. How can I? The little girl being sold can't even look at the camera. Her fear is palpable, and I feel it in my fucking bones. She's probably wondering where her mommy is—alone, hungry, frightened.

My eyes sting and tears threaten to pool out. I bite the inside of my lip until I taste copper and I hear the tablet crinkle in my hands.

Jason's voice rings loudly in my ears. "Okay, Justice. Your *third party* will be on the line in five, four, three—"

"I can't do this... why is getting a file important anymore? Fuck Carlton. Fuck all of this! What's going to happen to this little girl?"

I don't know who I'm talking to. Dylan? Olivia? Jason? Piper, who I can hear breathing into my ear? But it's Dylan who approaches me in the empty corridor. He presses me against the wall and grabs my shoulders in his strong hands. His hold is secure but gentle, and it forces me to look up into his night-sky eyes.

He reaches up and unclasps the chain from my wrist and removes his collar. His hands are back on me and they hold me tight. "We're going to get the file because we need all the evidence we can get our hands on to make sure Carlton doesn't get away with this. It's happened before, too many times. If we don't do this, he'll be out in less than twenty-four hours. He's got the best fucking lawyers money can buy."

"But what about the little gir—"

"I will get her out. I swear to you, Niki. And any others they have."

Olivia comes into view then, and Dylan moves when she gently pushes her way in front of me. He stands next to me and pulls me into his chest. Olivia grabs both my hands and squeezes them, and I realize they're freezing. "Jasmin and I will locate their prisoners. We aren't sure if they're kept on the premises just yet. But the remote location and all the bells and whistles tell me they're here. You focus on the file."

"Olivia—"

"Jase, *don't*." Olivia's voice is clipped and stern. "You stay with Justice, and Sara will monitor our part."

Miles away, Jason punches something. We all hear it and Olivia's shoulders jerk painfully, but she straightens and takes three steps back, giving Jas the space to embrace me.

"*Todo va a salir bien*," she tells me in Spanish.

"*Cómo puedes estar segura?*"

Jas shakes her head. "I don't know. I'm not sure of anything, but... what I am certain of is that I can't stand back and do nothing."

I nod in agreement, and we hug like when we were little girls. "Be safe," we say in unison and almost laugh. If the moment weren't filled with such dark tension, one of us would've called *jinx* and erupted in a mischievous giggle.

I think Jason is talking Olivia's ear off because she hugs herself and whispers hastily until I hear her demand he patch Sara through. Her hands drop to her side and she looks at Dylan and they nod at one another. "I'll see you on the other side, *carnalito*."

Dylan chuckles dryly at Olivia. "In one piece, Liv."

Jasmin leaves my arms and joins her, and they walk in the opposite direction. Olivia is already conversing with Sara, who is guiding them to a cellar hidden from current floor plans, but was in the original blueprints of The Mansion. I watch them turn the corner and lean against the wall.

Jason's anger reverberates through the earpiece, and I get the urge to pull it further away from me. His voice chills the air around me. "Your third party remains on the line."

For a second, I forgot she was there. "You heard all that?"

"It's fine. Even I question the sanity of this ridiculous mission. But your man is right: Carlton will get away without the file."

I sigh and pinch the bridge of my nose. "It better be one helluva file."

"I promise you it is."

I twirl my mother's charms up and down the metal rope bracelet. "Did Jason share our location?"

"Yep. I even have a live feed of where you're currently standing. Your friends have very fancy equipment. You should utilize their help for your blog, kid."

Next to me, Dylan's brows shoot up in question. But I roll my eyes and scoff. "Right. Well, tell us where to go."

I wish I would've worn my sneakers. Fuck these heels.

"How much longer?" We've been dodging staff and ducking cameras for a good fifteen minutes, and we still need to get to another floor.

"There's a service elevator at the end of the hall."

Dylan and I jog down the long corridor and stop in front of the metal door. There's a keyhole and an electric keypad. Piper gives us the code and a loud ding echoes down the hall as the doors swoosh open. My stomach drops and presses against my lower organs, making me queasy. I reach out and squeeze Dylan's forearm, digging my nails into his flesh. Crescent moons appear below my fingertips and I rub against the dips before the doors open.

Dylan's arm shoots out in front of me like a fucking seatbelt and he exits first, slowly. He crouches and steps out, examining the area, and I follow closely behind.

It's a kitchen.

"It should be empty. I made sure to give you a five-minute window."

The small kitchen looks out of place. It's outdated, plain, and too neat. Quiet and alone, as if shunned by the rest of the house.

Piper's voice leads us past the kitchen and into a bedroom. It looks like a motel room. It's tidy, empty of personal artifacts. Generic and bland. It even smells of cleaning products and a faint scent of vanilla mixed with coffee beans. I don't know how, but immediately I know who this space belongs to.

A white desk with a lamp and simple office supplies sits directly in front of the bed. Piper directs me to it, and I flip the switch on the lamp to illuminate the space.

"The stapler."

What? Dylan and I share a look. He lifts up the metal, heavy duty stapler and turns it in his hands before opening it.

He removes the staples and shrugs. I'm not sure what I was expecting, but it's a regular stapler. Piper chimes in and responds to my unspoken questions.

"Carefully pop off the top."

Dylan does what she says, and I lean forward to peek inside. Nestled against the cool metal, a tiny USB sits secured by a strip of transparent tape.

"Once you take out the USB, replace the top, and try to put it back exactly as it was. Leave *everything* the way it was."

I turn off the desk lamp and scan the room once more. I'd bet my right hand and left eyeball that this space belongs to Charles. Dylan hands me the USB and puts the stapler back in its place. The tiny cuboid feels heavy in my palm, and I tuck it into the sticky adhesive supporting my large breasts. Dylan licks his lips and stalks toward me, but I lift up a finger and shake it slowly.

He's crazy if he thinks this is an ideal spot to get lucky. As much as I love losing myself in his arms and expert touch, I've never wanted to get the hell out of place more than I do this instant.

"Guide us out, P."

In the same moment Piper begins to give us directions toward a different exit, Jason's manic voice fills our ears.

"Olivia and Jasmin were ambushed, D. Four men got to them as they entered the level Sara believes the prisoners are being held in. They tried to sweet talk their way out of it, saying they were lost, but the guys didn't buy it."

Dylan swears under his breath and shoves me toward the elevator entrance we just came through. Piper's voice doesn't return. Jason probably cut her call, finding her guidance meaningless now that my best friend and his girlfriend have been apprehended.

"I can't just sit here, Dylan. I'm headed your way."

"No!" Dylan barks. "We got what we came for. Send Mike my approval to enter the premises. Give them the coordinates of the victims' location."

I can practically feel Jason bristle with anger. "What about Olivia?"

We're in the elevator and time slows. It cannot be moving any fucking slower. Dylan sighs heavily and holds me close. "Jason, I won't leave without her. You have my word."

The doors slide open and we step out and rush down the hall.

"Mike and the team are approaching on foot. They have the premises surrounded. The chopper should be there in three minutes. When the lights go out, that's the signal that our team is in."

Jason's robotic tone clouds my vision, and I twirl around and smack into Dylan. "*Team?*"

"I have orders to shut this place down, little fox. That's what I do."

I take a step back. This was nothing but a job to him, and he used me to get in. "You *lied* to me!"

Dylan reaches for my arm quicker than I can register his movements and pulls me to continue down the hall. "I never lied to you. I understood the danger. Did you expect to waltz in and out of here without any issues?"

I can't answer his ridiculous question. He's being an asshole. Of course I didn't, but I would appreciate him being entirely open about what he plans to do. He completely took over and drew advantage from the situation. He used my ticket, involved his whole fucking team, and in two minutes, the entire place will be surrounded by fucking cops.

He didn't trust me enough to clue me in. As if I'm some idiot incapable of understanding and agreeing to a decision based on better judgment and the best route when going undercover. I pull my arm from his grip and lean my hand against the wall to slip my heels off.

Dylan moves to grab me, and I lift up my shoe. "Touch me and I'll fucking stab you with this heel."

Dylan suffocates me with his looming presence, and in less than one second, he presses his entire frame against me. "I don't give a fuck if you bury *both* your heels in me. I won't risk your safety. Pull away again and I'll throw you over my shoulder."

I glare at him. "You wouldn't dare."

My arm is encased in his iron grip. "Don't tempt me, little fox."

I shake my head and let him pull me away. His strides are long and hurried, and I struggle to keep up. I'm practically jogging. One of his steps is five of mine. If Jasmin wasn't possibly in trouble, I'd throw my shoe at his head. I knew I couldn't fully trust a fucking cop.

"Forty-five seconds." Jason's voice is all business.

I suck in a breath. I can't believe this fucking mess.

"Niki, listen to me. We leave the way we came—together. I don't care if you're angry at me, but now isn't the time to misjudge the situation. I would never let anything happen to y—"

"Watch out!" My warning comes two seconds too late.

Dylan's body crashes to the ground in a deafening thud and it takes my soul with him. I'm screaming, but I can't hear a sound. A man built like a fucking mountain kicks Dylan in the stomach and I lunge forward, but strong arms hold me in place. I throw my shoes at Dylan's attacker, and he turns.

"Get this crazy bitch out of here," he yells.

I flail like a fish out of water, and I claw at the arms pulling me backwards. I yell Dylan's name. Not for him to rescue me, but because I need to see him move, I need confirmation that he's still conscious. His shoulders elevate slightly, and I smile just in time to see his sharp cheekbones lift up. His coal eyes meet mine when a sharp stab collides with the back of my head, and then everything goes black.

I wish it were because I was swallowed by the twin black holes that I'm sure live behind Dylan's eyes, but I'm afraid it's something closer to death than the life he offers.

32
Redemption

I rage forward like a fucking tsunami. The earth shakes beneath my feet and the room goes dark.

"What the fuck is going on over there?"

Jason. I want to rip the earbud out and stomp on it. I ignore him and use the absence of light to my advantage. I know exactly why the lights went out, but the motherfucker in front of me doesn't and he wanders aimlessly like a headless cockroach.

I can hear him; his breathing and his heavy steps. I launch myself in his direction and knee him in the gut. I wrap my hands around the back of his fat head and thrust it down into my knee three times until he passes out before me.

I kick him for good measure and bend down and search him. "I'm blind, and someone took Niki."

"Fuck. I knew it. We should've never let them go—"

"I don't need you to fucking scold me, Jason. Check on her. Tell me where she is."

Jason swears under his breath. "It's pitch black. I can't get a hold of her."

"Fuck!" I punch a hole in the nearest wall. "Direct me to where the prisoners are kept."

My head is pounding and a warm liquid oozes down my forehead and I slide the back of my hand over it before it reaches my eye. I take the gun from the dumbass on the ground and move through the darkness.

The Mansion is in an uproar. Mike's made it in and no one is getting out. That is, except for the tunnels Sara suspects lead out to a road fifteen miles south of the property. Just in case, we sent a group to position themselves in the area. But what they may or may not do to the girls in the meantime is why I'm sure Jason is growling directions into my ear.

I can't think that far; my imagination runs through a dark filter, and if I allow myself to even peek behind the curtain of what they could be subjected to? I'm not sure where those thoughts will take me. So I push forward instead. I'll find them.

I press my back against a thick wall when I spot a light flashing in the distance. It isn't my men. I take in a deep breath and focus on the sound of steps. "I count three," I whisper.

Jason gives me directions, and I ignore him. I know what the fuck to do. He grumbles about this not being the time or place to be hardheaded, but I'm not listening. Someone steps into a table and a vase shatters on the ground and I step out, my gun in hand.

Their light fills the floor and covers them in shadows. The person holding the flashlight feels my presence and points it at me. They've got a gun in hand and I simultaneously aim my weapon at his forehead.

"Dylan!" Olivia crashes into me.

Jason breathes into my ear. "Is that my Liv?"

She's still holding me, and I look back to Jasmin and watch as the man holsters his gun. I clear my throat. "Your tech?"

"They stripped us of all our jewelry, including the earbuds."

I nod and give her mine. While she puts it in her ear and attempts to reassure a beyond furious Jason, I focus on the man. Charles.

Jasmin circles us. "Where's Justice?"

My eyes dart from hers to Charles. "Someone took her."

"And you let them?" Jasmin yells.

Charles's arms flail up in frustration. "Fucking hell. First, I have to save these two and now *her*? I thought you were *a professional*?"

I step forward. "I didn't just fucking *let them take her*. And who the fuck are you?"

"How about we interrogate me later, *Detective*."

Charles turns to leave, and I call out to him. "I'm coming with."

He nods, irritated. "Of course you are."

Liv catches my arm and gives it a gentle squeeze. "Jason arranged transportation for us. He's going to lead Jasmin and me to it. I won't leave without you, Dylan. Your mother will kill me if she finds out I left you behind."

I want to laugh but can't; not while my Niki is who the fuck knows where. I think Olivia understands, and she lunges toward me and hugs me quickly, then tugs a frantic Jasmin with her.

"If you don't find Justice, I'll kill you myself!" Jasmin yells.

I'm sure Jason reminded Olivia that, although she may be in her element, Jasmin is not. That realization, along with the dreaded responsibility of keeping Jasmin alive, was what most likely convinced my cousin to follow Jason's pleas to exit the premises. And I'm grateful. Selfishly, all of my attention is on Niki's safety, and that's how I need it to stay.

I stay close behind Charles. He's just a couple of inches shorter than me, thinly built, and possibly my age as well. Why the fuck is he helping us? Right before she was taken, Niki was furious with me for keeping my plans from her. But she's got secrets of her own. I'll have to rectify that.

My chest tightens at the mere thought of never seeing her again, of never again tasting her sweet lips or becoming energized by her brash attitude.

"We're close. Follow my lead. It's the only way we won't get slaughtered."

I watch his posture change as his shoulders drop, and I check my gun. I take out the magazine and then shove it back in. "My men have the premises surrounded. They're already in the building."

Charles turns and rolls his eyes at me. "I know. But *your men* won't find the cellar. It's not on any blueprints. It's a new construction."

Was Sara wrong? "Did the girls find the prisoners?"

He snorts. "They weren't even close."

"And the tunnels?"

"Filled with cement."

Fuck.

The lights flicker on and off and then stay on, which tells me Mike's got the guests all lined up. He's probably wondering where the maggot mayor is, along with the rest of his crew. We're in front of a service elevator similar to the one that took Niki and me to get the file. Charles punches a code in, then slides in a key and turns it. Once inside, he does the same thing.

"I'll go first," he says and I nod.

I understand his need to bestow an element of surprise. I don't trust him, but all I need is for him to lead me to Niki. They may not attack him if they don't know he's playing for both sides. If that's what he's doing. It fucking irritates me that I don't know how he ties in with Niki. I stare at his posture, athletic, and definite military-like movements. Could he be one of her previous lovers? I bristle at the thought and a red film clouds my vision. No, they were all one-night stands. Hookups that never went further because she couldn't stand the thought of anyone lingering long enough to enter her personal space.

I shake my head. Since when did I allow such thoughts to cloud my mind, especially when actively on the hunt? Fuck.

The doors slide open and gray cement walls loom before us like the gates of fucking hell. My thoughts evaporate, forcefully set aside so that I can concentrate. Niki is here somewhere.

The cellar is a fucking maze, with short ceilings and narrow halls. The ground is a mixture of dirt and sand and wireless construction lights are placed three to four and a half meters apart. Charles stops and presses his back against the wall. I mirror his movements and he turns and begins communicating with hand signals.

Up ahead, nine, maybe ten meters. He mouths the next words and my entire body tenses–*Carlton and Justice.*

I lean forward and notice that in four paces, the floor changes from dirt to cement. I nod at Charles and we move forward. He signals directions to stay low and to allow him to enter first. I nod in agreement. The closer we get, the louder the voices become. At first they were muffled, the sound waves guarded by the stone walls. Charles signals for me to stop and he moves to enter the room.

I roll my shoulders and keep my breathing steady. I've been on hundreds of missions, but none felt like this. The danger of losing Niki feels worse than death itself. I walk further, ignoring Charles's command, and hear Carlton's voice.

"Did you actually think I didn't know it was *you*?"

"If you knew it was me, then why go through all this invite shit? Why give it any more attention or thought?"

Carlton laughs and then coughs dramatically. He's got a sickly knot of phlegm stuck in his throat. "*Justice Blog*," he guffaws and almost chokes again. "That little blog of yours has been a thorn in the sole of my foot for some time now. But then I was told exactly who you were, and well... I had to have you."

The fucking nerve of this son of a bitch. I want to see her, make sure she's okay. I hold my breath and slowly peel away from the dark. The need to have her in my line of sight is too much. My eyes dart quickly to scan the area and then they settle on her. I have a side view of a large room that resembles a garage.

Carlton takes a step forward, forcing Niki to take one back. "I do love a good chase," he says between garbled grunts.

There's silence, and Niki's face contorts to express disgust. I hear a click of a gun and my muscles coil. I want to barge between them, but the control in her voice halts me.

"Don't fucking move. You think I won't shoot?"

Three men lie motionless on the ground. Two are breathing erratically, one complaining still. Another is in agony and practically whining. His leg is broken, and he lies on the ground face down, blood pooling near his misshapen leg.

Niki's got a gun in hand. Her target—Carlton's head. Her arms are steady, posture firm—unceasing. For a tiny person, she looks like she's ten feet tall. Confidence oozes off her and my dick jerks. I shake my head. Only Niki could manage to elicit such feelings during the most inopportune moment.

Charles moves into view and Carlton gasps. "Finally! Where the hell have you been? This bitch knocked your men out."

Niki practically growls at Carlton. "Your first mistake was to underestimate me."

He ignores her and points a commanding finger at Charles and then at Niki. "Finish her!"

"Your second mistake," Niki smiles, "was to assume I worked alone."

Carlton's eyes bulge, realization settling in. He swallows and tugs uncomfortably at his tie. He loosens the first button and glares at Charles. Niki takes a step forward. She doesn't even look at Charles or bother with scanning the room. She trusts him implicitly. Who the fuck is this guy?

"Restrain him." Her voice is ice and laced with venom as she barks her command at Charles.

Without a word, Charles holsters his gun and glances at the men on the ground. His foot taps each one and then digs in his jacket pocket and produces zip ties. His men glare at him in question. The one with a broken leg is quiet, probably passed out, succumbed by the pain.

Carlton reaches for him in disbelief but Charles swats his arm, a low tsk sound escapes his lips. "Don't move or she'll shoot."

"I didn't think you were the type of man who'd give up their career over some pussy!"

Charles snaps. He grabs Carlton's shoulders and shoves him to the ground. Then he comes around and delivers a punch to his face. Charles grips him by the shirt and pulls him up. Then he tugs his arms forcefully behind his back to collocate the zip ties securely around his wrists. Three minutes passed as I stood frozen, enthralled by Niki's command of the room. She managed to single-handedly disarm and knock out two men, mangle one, as well as hold her own against Carlton. I step into view then and Niki taps at her ear, stunned. She doesn't see me just yet.

Her voice is low and cautious. "Jason, is that you? I'm okay, in a basement somewhere. I've got Carlton. We'll find the victims next."

Niki catches movement in her peripheral and whips her head in my direction. Her brown eyes grow wide at the sight of me, her lips breaking into my favorite smile. "Dylan is here, he's safe," she breathes. "*For now.*"

I frown. It's obvious from her first statement that she was worried about me, but her second remark is laced with anger. I want to wrap her in my arms.

Carlton groans painfully. "*You?*"

I shake my head. "Nah, this was all *her.*"

Niki smiles wickedly as she faces Carlton. "I had help," she shrugs.

Charles moves to restrain the men on the ground. He ties up their wrists and ankles and then positions them against the wall. He drags the man with a broken leg and does the same. I want to tell him that's pointless since the man's bone is jutting out, but I look at Niki instead.

I point to the injured men questionably, lingering over the one with a broken shin bone and she shrugs. "It was either that or shoot him with his own gun."

I move closer and she retreats. Just one step, but it feels like she's miles away. The desire to run my hands over her entire frame, to examine that she's physically alright, twists my insides, but her sudden withdrawal cuts me deeper. It's evident that she's angry and I need that shit to stop.

"Come out with it."

"You used me."

A heavy sigh escapes me. *Fuck.* "Never."

Her nostrils flare, and she allows one bare foot to take a tentative step toward me. "Then why didn't you tell me? Why keep it from me?"

From the corner of my eye, I notice Charles manhandling Carlton, ignoring his questions and instead demanding he take us toward the innocents who are held somewhere in the maze-like cellar. "I couldn't walk in here empty-handed. Men like him always play ugly, and I needed to make sure we came ready for anything. Would you honestly have allowed me to tag along if I'd told you?"

She's thinking, and I watch as scenarios play before her lids, images of disaster after disaster, and her tense jaw gives a tiny flex. I reach out and gently stroke the back of my hand over her jawline and her wall crumbles. "I couldn't risk it, fox. You can't expect me to dangle your safety in a den full of fucking vipers."

The edge of her lips curve up and I relax. Her grin is addicting and the anger she was holding melts away. For now.

Charles's agitated voice brings us back. He whips Carlton's wrists, jostling him, and pulls him backward in a forceful thrust. "The prisoners."

"What, like I'll lead you straight to them?" Carlton scoffs.

Charles shakes him roughly and whips his gun out. He cocks it and touches the tip to Carlton's temple. "You will, unless you want your brains scattered all over these walls."

Carlton can't turn fully, but his eyes search for me desperately. "You gonna approve this sort of infraction? You're an officer of the law, for fuck's sake!"

Charles and I laugh. His is a cynical one, as if he lacks trust in me or any law enforcement agency. My laugh is one of true humor. I approach Carlton, my smile gone. I tap his chest with the gun I stole from one of his men. "If it were me, I would've shot you on sight."

Niki keeps the gun she's holding aimed at Carlton's head. "Do we need him to get to those who are captured?"

Charles sighs loudly and taps his gun lightly against Carlton's temple. "Unfortunately, we do. I don't have the codes for the next two doors."

I roll my shoulders and try to move my neck from side to side until I hear the bones crack. "Can we blow it up?"

Charles clicks his tongue against his cheek. "Not unless you want the cellar to collapse."

"Dylan, take my earpiece. Jason wants our location."

I walk to her and circle behind. Her skirt is intact, she's still shoeless, and her top is missing so many pearls I want to strangle someone. I growl under my breath and move her hair back behind her shoulders and take the earbud.

"Did the girls make it out?"

Jason breathes into my ear. "They did. Looks like when you entered Justice's space, I was able to reestablish connectivity. I suppose you're still wearing the collar?"

I ignore the slight humor in his tone. It's on my person still, but I don't want to explain myself. "You'll need to guide the team to an elevator with black doors directly behind the east wing lavatories on the third floor. There's a double code access."

Charles clears his throat. "Eight, seven, two, nine, Bravo, Echo, Quebec, four, eight, Uniform. The code will lead them to this specific tunnel entry. Any others are programmed to open on a different level. Which is why breaking into the server is nearly impossible."

"Oh, so we're dealing with smart criminals. Wonderful," Jason says. "I can't track you. I only have access to the earbud as long as that pretty choker of yours stays close. The cameras and locator are all offline."

His mood has shifted, must be due to his woman being at a safe location away from all of this shit. I huff a sigh of frustration. I want to be out of this fucking tunnel that suffocates the air all around us. I want to be with Niki, lying in bed naked, with her big brown eyes breathing life into me.

I breathe out an exhausted sigh etched with a grim purpose. "Guide the team down and I'll direct you the rest of the way. We're going to move."

I nod to Charles, who shoves Carlton forward. "Let's go, we don't have all fucking night."

33

Justice

The grainy stone floor is icy-cold, and it seeps up the pores from the soles of my feet, practically coagulating my blood from my toes up. A shiver runs up my leg and it's as if ants are rushing up my body. But I don't want to say shit. I should've stolen a jacket from one of the fuckers who dragged me to the cave-like cellar. I can't believe how easy it'd been to take their asses down.

To be fair, it isn't so much the cold and my lack of attire that's got me frazzled. It's the mere situation I find myself in. If you would've asked me just three months ago what I thought I'd be doing on a Saturday evening, walking barefoot through a maze-like, underground lair that belongs to *el cerro*, wouldn't have even made it to my list.

I can practically feel Dylan's eyes scanning my frame from behind. His looming presence is enough to warm me from the inside out. It reminds me of one of my dad's famous cookouts. My mom had placed the lid over our coal burning grill and it snuffed the fire out. She'd suffocated it. My dad explained how, in order for the fire to thrive, it needed oxygen. He demonstrated, and we all watched, amazed as if he were a scientist and we were his pupils, enthralled by his experiment. My dad used a thick cardboard to ignite the fire, feeding it puffs of air. The flames grew so high my mom thought the leaves on the massive trees would catch fire! Dylan is like a gentle yet powerful breeze, igniting my soul back to life. Who knew he'd quickly become indelible. It's as if he alone supplies the oxygen my lungs required in order to expand. *What the fuck has this rookie done to me?*

I don't dare sneak a glance back. Instead, I focus on Charles, who's shoving Carlton forward down the narrow passageway. We've been walking for seven minutes, but it feels like a fucking eternity. My stomach growls and I clear my throat. I hope nobody heard that, but just as I send my silent prayer out, Dylan presses his front to my back. We keep a steady walk, his feet moving in unison with mine so we don't collide and collapse. Dylan snakes his hand around my torso and lowers his head so his lips brush the side of my face. He lingers near my temple.

"Cuándo fue la última vez que comiste?" he whispers.

I want to answer him, but I have no fucking idea when the last time I ate was, so I shrug. Dylan responds by taking in a ragged breath, and with a smack of his lips, he *tsks* three times.

"Coming into battle famished isn't a good idea, little fox."

I smack my own lips in retort, but he's right. I'm fucking starving. "Noted."

He chuckles softly and all too suddenly, his body stiffens against mine. Dylan takes a small step back, alarming me. Has our path changed? Is someone coming up behind us? Is Carlton trying to escape?

Nothing's happened. We're still languidly making our way through the dimly lit corridor, the cement block tunnel looming as ever. But what made him pull back? I sneak a peek at him and watch as he stares into space. His head is cocked to the side and his lips are in a tight, firm line. He gives a curt nod with a single word response, and I know it's Jason who's just spoken about something that's altered his mood.

I'm about to ask what's gone wrong when Carlton clears his throat.

"They're past that safe."

"*Vales pura mierda*, a fucking *safe*?"

Charles speaking Spanish is almost enough to distract me from the mammoth safe before us. *Almost.* He shoves Carlton forward and *el cerro* falls to his knees, then yells obscenities at us.

Dylan walks up to him and forcefully yanks him up. "Fucking open it. No games. Do it *now*."

Dylan is like the fucking elements mixing into one colossal force, ready to destroy anything in its path, like a goddamn apocalypse. He may have the unnerving power to heat me to my core, but just as equally, he can bring grown men to a bowing position. *El cerro* wants to protest, but I watch as his body literally folds inward. Utter fear cripples him in place; he gapes at Dylan and his fingers twitch. He's terrified and doesn't know what the fuck else to do other than give in to Dylan's barked orders. *El cerro* fumbles forward, he looks like a toddler taking their first wobbly steps to then collapse into loving arms. Only *el cerro* trips on air and his conjoined wrists buckle against the pressure of the zip ties. They're on tight and they cut into his skin as he tumbles forward and hits the safe face first.

Carlton grunts and tries to stand straight, but the fear wracks his body. Charles sighs tiredly, but he lifts him up and positions him to stand in front of the keypad.

After punching a sequence of digits, he stands slightly back. "Pull the lever." *El cerro's* voice squeaks like a boy going through puberty.

Charles reaches for the handle and turns it. A loud, skull cracking sound breaks the air, splintering shards of its aftermath into our brains. It echoes down the cellar and is followed by a long ring.

"Fuck!" Dylan barks.

Charles points his gun at Carlton. "Turn it off or I'll fucking shoot. Don't play with me."

El cerro teeters past the large metal door and punches buttons onto a small keypad hidden on the inner portion of the doorframe. Three loud beeps silence the blaring alarm and I finally lower my hands. I hadn't even noticed my palms flew in an attempt to shield my ears from the attack.

Piper's man shuffles his shoulders and wiggles his gun, tapping the *cerro's* shoulder. "If you haven't noticed, saving your prisoners isn't my priority. Any more surprises and I blow your head off."

"If you don't care about being a hero, then why are you helping them?"

Charles's eyes meet mine, and he hesitates. It isn't wise to let Carlton know that we wouldn't be here if his daughter hadn't helped us. *El cerro* is fucking blind anyhow, it's obvious to anyone who sees Charles and Piper side by side, he would burn the world to the ground if she asked him to. I sweep in so that he doesn't have to respond. Not like he would. Charles looks like the type of man who does what he wants when he wants. Unless it's his redheaded goddess divine asking shit of him, of course.

"What the fuck do you think this is, tea time? Shut up and walk."

"*You,*" Carlton muses in his garbled voice and glares at me. "Your little blog isn't enough, you had to drag in the *reputable* Dylan Montreal?"

I didn't drag Dylan into anything. In fact, he forced his way into my life so thoroughly I was shocked he hadn't shown up at my daytime jobs. Though I doubt he wasn't watching. But the *cerro's* voice strikes a chord in me and not a soft lullaby-like tone you'd hear from a violin.

It happens in a flash—I elevate the gun in my hands and drop it, making it slash across his cheek. "I told you to shut the fuck up."

Every sinister occurrence delivered by his hand beams before my lids, like lightning dancing across a dark skyline. The photograph of the frightened little girl, Piper's sunken eyes, Macy's battered body, the fifteen-year-old girl he fondled at the club, and just my inner thoughts of the most fucked up shit imaginable.

Charles avoids meeting my eyes, and he forces Carlton to stand so that he can continue to guide us through this shit hole in the ground. *El cerro's* cheek is torn and his blood trickles down to his white collar. He winces, but moves past the new opening.

The safe revealed a long corridor with a direct turn into a prison. Metal bars stand between us and about a dozen people.

"Fuck."

My voice is meek, depleted, and fucking agonized by what I see. My bottom lip wobbles and I tuck it between my teeth. I can't break down now, not here. Dylan walks past me and holsters his gun. He's giving clear directions to Jason so that his team can find us in the labyrinth we're buried under. But I'm not listening. His words are muffled between my breaths, heart pounding in my throat, and my blood boiling in my fucking ears.

As far as we can tell, not one person is over any age that would qualify them to be a consenting adult. *Children.* They all gather in one corner of their cell, crouched closely together in a sign of collective fear. From the corner of my eye, I watch as Charles instructs Carlton to turn around and sit on the ground, with his back facing the victims. He wants them to see we're here to help and that we've apprehended their captor. In all the chaos, I've managed to remain in control. Not once did I feel as though Carlton would get away tonight. Specifically, after his men brought me into the cellar. They assumed I was a hurt dove or something, a fractured girl longing for a savior. I won't deny I was terrified, but I learned years ago how to channel the adrenaline and train myself from freezing during a time of chaos. But *this.* No mental or physical training could've prepared me for this.

I bend down until my knees hold my weight, and I grip the cold bars in my hands. It's my only anchor—they keep me in place before I deteriorate into vapor and suffocate Carlton from the inside like a noxious gas. Obviously, that's not possible—this isn't a fantasy. But here's hoping. A little girl's breath hitches, and it reminds me that I'm on the free side of the bars. *Pull yourself together.*

"You're safe now," I whisper.

During my little moment of weakness, Charles had pulled Carlton off to the side, delivering fist after fist that was supposed to convince him to cooperate and open the fucking prison cell. I don't know how long I've been on my knees, but the kids on the other side of the bars have moved closer. I realize they're within reach when someone's fingers softly lace over mine, and I stare past the iron ingot to meet several skeptical eyes.

Carlton suddenly starts to laugh, and it startles the few kids who've gotten near me, and they crawl back to their corner of safety.

"Get them out."

I know it's my voice, but I don't recognize it. It's harsh, tormented, and hoarse–as if my screams were real and not just in my head.

Dylan's hands wrap around my shoulders and he pulls me up to crush me against his iron grip. He twists me around, and I get a glimpse of the room. It's surrounded by what looks like a fucking SWAT team.

El cerro isn't laughing anymore, instead he's pleading for his life and swearing that this is all some terrible mistake. Everyone ignores him.

I roll my eyes. "You're so fucking pathetic." He stiffens but manages to glare at me.

"Open the cell immediately," Dylan orders. "And get this piece of shit out of here."

A full tactical team surrounds us, and two men huddle near the bars and produce an electric saw. Another gives the victims instructions, and he slips them a tarp and tells them to get underneath so their eyes are shielded from the metal shards that will fly toward them.

Dylan holds me close, but everything is a blur. Three men force *el cerro* to stand and they haul him out. Charles leans on the wall, staring at the ground blankly. Dylan is barking directions. But I'm frozen in place. I vaguely feel when Dylan wraps me in a wool blanket and squeezes my shoulders. I feel the instant he leaves my side. Dylan approaches the men working on getting the bars open, and I move to stand next to Charles, who brings a cigarette to his lips and inhales deeply.

"Some Saturday night, huh?"

"Way to break up a party, kid."

I roll my eyes. "Not you too?" *Kid.* What makes both Piper and Charles think that the five- to-seven-year gap between us is enough to consider me a child?

It's my first time witnessing a smile ghost Charles's face, but it disappears before its completion. "I assume you kept your promise."

I round my shoulders and wiggle. The tiny rectangular piece of metal digs at the skin under my breast and I smile at him. "I'm offended you even feel the need to ask."

Charles's jaw tenses and his lips go taut. "I want to be there when you deliver it."

I give him a lazy nod. Of course he would. Anyone else would think he isn't a man, but a fucking robot. He's so serious—a look of stoic resignation and sheer embodiment of a soldier at a kill zone—it's unnerving. But whenever he talks about Piper, or if she's in his presence, he comes to life. His devotion is unmistakable.

Two officers approach us, and I think they're going to give us a couple of water bottles like they did the prisoners, but they flip us around and crush us against the wall. My chin scrapes against the grainy cement.

"You have three seconds to back the fuck up!" Charles manages. His face is pressed up against the cement wall, eyes glued to mine.

Someone, who I'm sure is Dylan, forcefully yanks my aggressor off. The wool blanket drops from my shoulders and just as I'm about to turn, I witness Dylan transform from man to beast. His upper lip furls back, his fingers wrap around the guy's neck, and he tosses him aside like a fucking gum wrapper. The armed one who'd tackled Charles apparently heard the commotion and stepped away, his expression apologetic and terrified.

"Who the fuck told you they were to be touched?"

"I did."

A guy in a gray suit waltzes in. He smooths his hand over his tie and adjusts it, even though it's perfect, then he slips his hands into his pockets. Charles leans on the wall and lights up another cigarette, and I bend down to retrieve the blanket. I don't want to be practically naked anymore. I would kill for some joggers, a t-shirt... *and my sneakers.*

I move to press my back against the wall and stand next to Charles. I feel like he wouldn't risk his neck for me and he'd abandon me in a second. But I also know he would never be able to face Piper if he didn't retrieve the USB before fleeing. His eyes dart between the man in the suit and Dylan, as if taking mental notes. I watch them and do just that.

Dylan stands at least five inches taller and he's packed with lean muscle. The man, however shorter, is built like a fucking rock. I imagine he's in charge because he doesn't wear tactical gear and looks completely out of place. His hair is perfectly coiffed, suit expensive and tailored to fit like a glove. An almost bored yet commanding expression on his chiseled face. He's an older man, maybe ten years Dylan's senior.

Dylan moves to stand in front of us, and I'm forced to move slightly to my left to still have the man in the suit in my vision.

"They're the reason we got this far."

"And they are... *who,* exactly?"

Dylan shakes his head. "None of your business, Mike."

The man, Mike, nods, and lets out a soft, nonchalant chuckle. "Okay, Dylan. Get them out of here before the feds arrive."

Dylan faces me and I can't read his blank expression. It fills me with worry and a million uncertainties bubble within.

"What about them?" I point behind me to the prisoners, who are finally being escorted out of their cell.

"They'll be safe now," Mike interrupts whatever Dylan was about to say. "I can't wait to thank you in a more appropriate setting for your dedication to bringing this case to an end."

"It isn't over," Charles mumbles, but I don't think Mike hears.

"That's unnecessary," I say. I don't really want to officially make his acquaintance and I get the feeling Dylan doesn't either.

"Nevertheless, we'll meet again *soon*, I hope."

"I hope not," I admit, and he laughs once more. That single calm and collected chuckle of his.

Dylan covers my body with his and presses his lips to my temple. "Come on, little fox. Time to go."

"Oh, and Dylan?" We all turn to Mike as if his call was for *us*–a united front, a team. "Any other material collected during the assignment, something of note?"

Dylan holds me closer. "No, nothing."

Although his tone and delivery is confident, secure, and everything else Dylan is, the USB weighs heavy against my skin, practically burning a hole and searing itself to my rib. But I'm not saying shit. This USB belongs to Piper, and I'm not breaking my promise to her.

34
Redemption

"So, when are you going to tell Justice?"

I clear my throat and tug on my earlobe. Jason's voice echoes in my head and bounces off a few scenarios that lie in wait. Which one will win? What will be my little fox's reaction? *Fuck*, I gotta tell her. I don't want to, not after everything she's been through. I can tell she's exhausted and that all she wants to do is reunite with her family and bask in the comfort of knowing they're all safe. But if I don't tell her, she'll slice my balls off for assuming I have the right to keep shit from her. Even if the unknown will keep her safe.

I clear my throat. "There's a situation you need to know about before we get you home."

Niki turns to me as if the word *home* refers to a place that is unknown to me, and I wonder if she was hoping to head out to her ranch instead of the trailer. Her curiosity quickly absolves any and all her thoughts. She's changed into baggy gray sweats, a t-shirt, and Chucks. Apparently Olivia had thought about a wardrobe change, and she made sure to stock the getaway van with bags for a change of clothes for everyone but myself. A getaway van that no one bothered to tell me about, by the fucking way.

Niki sits next to me. Her best friend directly across, while my cousin argues with the driver about which route is the best one to take to avoid the late night traffic. Charles sits quietly, staring out of the window. He looks dazed and bored, but I know he has an ear on every little thing in his surroundings.

"Just tell her already." Jason's voice rings again and I rip the earpiece out, then stuff it in my pocket.

A strangled look crosses Niki's features. "Jule?"

"No! Jule is fine. He's great, actually. Jason had him picked up, and he's at Liv's house now."

Her brows knit together. "Why was he... what's going on?"

"Noah was, uh…" I swallow. Had I anticipated Noah being an even bigger idiot than he already was, perhaps this wouldn't have happened. "Apprehended."

In front of us, Jasmin snorts. A 'who gives a fuck' sort of gesticulation. But Niki's eyes grow wide with fear. "By who?"

I wish I could tell her he's behind bars again. Getting him out of jail is easy. This, well… this is different. "Vork's men. He forced his way into one of their well-known establishments. Made a scene, shot his gun a few times."

Threw some names that he assumed would get him out of the situation he'd buried himself in—my name, to be exact. But I'm not going to tell her that. If Noah thought blaming me would get him off of Vork's radar, he quickly found out how wrong he was. Vork can give two shits when it comes to weeping, finger-pointing men.

"How? When? And where is he *now*?"

The panic in her voice strikes at a part hidden deep inside my chest cavity and a pang of… I don't know what holds the ventricles of my heart in a vise grip. I remind myself of Niki's feelings toward Noah. I always knew she cared. I focus on the platonic aspect of that love, and remind myself that my fucking ego isn't important. She's worried about the dumbass, and if she wants to run to his rescue, we'll do just fucking that.

The car is silent.

"He's going to need reinforcements. Noah was drunk and yelling about all sorts of shit. I didn't know if it would implicate you somehow, so I had Jason send someone to pick Jule up, just in case. Noah's… being held." To put it lightly.

"You're not *seriously* considering going to rescue him?" Jasmin leans toward Niki.

I already know the answer, but it seems everyone in the car, even the fucking nosy ass driver, perk their ears up.

"I can't just leave him. What about his mom? He's all she's got. Noah is my friend, Jas. I have to go."

"I take it that Noah is the ex." Olivia turns completely and elevates one crisp brow at me.

I grind my teeth, and the bones in my neck pop loudly when I pivot my head. It was a mistake to turn away from Liv. My eyes meet Charles' and the look of awe coupled with his stupid grin is enough to send me to my fucking grave.

"You guys don't have to come with me—"

Jasmin rolls her eyes. "Right, like we'd leave you to resolve that fucker's problem."

Niki buries her face into her hands, and I wrap an arm around her shoulders. Her breaths are sharp yet hollow–as if she's finally about to let go and break down in front of everyone. But she doesn't. My heat envelops her and her body relaxes into mine.

"How bad is it?"

Her big brown eyes stare into mine and the need to travel back in time to beat sense into Noah twists my insides to knots. Son of a bitch. "Last his tail informed, pretty bad. Vork knows he burned down a small warehouse of supplies. He doesn't respond lightly to betrayal."

Niki snorts. "Neither do I but... shit. What do we do?"

"Vork isn't there. He never lingers after delivering a death sentence."

I want to put a dent in Charles's face. Why the fuck does he think uttering the words *death sentence* is a good way to go? Seriously, who the fuck is this guy and why is he still here?

"*Death* sentence?" Niki searches my face. "We have to get him out of there."

I choose to ignore the worry in her tone and instead pull out my phone. Jason was smart enough to deliver our devices along with the getaway van. I tap on the link he provided and hand my phone to the driver. I knew this was exactly how shit would play out once she was told, but it's not something I can keep.

"Do I get a voice in this? I'm not really in the mood for another search and rescue."

Jasmin nods, agreeing with Charles, but Niki glares at him. "We'll gladly drop you off on the side of the road. But that just means you'll miss out on the ride to *paradise*."

What? What fucking *paradise*?

Charles seems to know exactly what Niki eludes to, and he responds by leaning back and lighting another cigarette. His silence is filled with more vexation than if he would've spoken his retort. Not like I would ever tell Niki, but I agree with the fucker–I don't feel like going off to rescue Noah's dumb ass after the shit we just went through. I don't know if I want to mentally fist bump Charles or kick his ass out of the van.

"I can practically hear your thoughts, but you won't get rid of me that easily, *officer*. Justice and I have unfinished business," Charles says, but he doesn't even turn to face me. He's still staring out the window, the cigarette smoke covers the space around him like a gray clouded aura.

"Who the fuck are you?"

Olivia giggles to herself, amused by my jealous bout. But Niki grabs my hand and squeezes it, and I turn to face her serious glare. "Not here... not now," she says, and it sounds like she's fucking lecturing me.

I breathe in sharply and clear my throat. If everything would've gone smoothly, I would be reviewing Jason's report on Charles and learning exactly who the fuck he is and how he connects to Niki. Instead, I'm riding in a fucking van with him to rescue another idiot from my woman's life. Shit just gets better and better. I glance at my phone sitting atop the van's dashboard and regret not asking Jason if he managed to dig anything up. The uncertainty is practically gnawing at me, an out of control and painful spasm tearing at my fucking tendons, and I wriggle both my wrists and shoulders in an attempt to rid myself of the sickening feeling.

Charles chuckles, and when I look up, he's still staring out of the window. Yet, somehow, I know he's fucking *laughing* at me. Son of a bitch. I open my mouth to spit some obscenity at him when Jason's trusty driver interrupts.

"We're almost there. Want me to park out back?"

"It's late. The bar will be mostly empty, with only their usuals present. I think it should be a simple recovery," Charles offers. He inhales a puff of smoke and it seeps out of his nose in one long drag before he flicks his cigarette out the window.

"Out front," I offer, but it comes out harsh and full of fire.

Niki turns to read my expression, and I lean my head back to hide my misplaced frustration. I don't want to think about the men in her life and what they mean to her. I know what she feels for me, even if she doesn't understand or fully accept it. My green-eyed monster has no place here. I force him to take a backseat and sneer from that angle–the possessive and overprotective discontent pours over me like a suffocating blanket of flames. Fuck.

It isn't until Niki leans into me and lowers my shoulder to her lips, so that she may whisper in my ear, that I realize I was squeezing my eyes shut so tight, my eyeballs were beginning to hurt.

"What do we do once we're there?"

Her eyes are full of fear, and she stares into mine in hopeful prayer. Their doleful look tug a desire in me to gather her in my arms and repair her dejected heart. I understand she loves Noah, he's like family. But I'm also aware of the fact that she chose me and that she could never want him in the same way she needs me. I also knew his relentless betrayal wouldn't win her hatred but only alert her to the inevitable truth–she couldn't love Noah the way he wanted. Regardless of Noah and whoever the fuck Charles is, her worry supersedes all of my misplaced emotions. I'll do whatever the fuck she needs.

"We get him out," I tell her.

The determination in my voice lights her eyes up and she breathes out a sigh of relief and smiles. It doesn't reach her eyes, but I know I've offered enough comfort to ease some tension. Niki presses her cheek to my shoulder, and when I straighten to look forward, Charles is watching us. His brows knit together, and something about his look tells me he's a man who both understands pain and love, yet it's a vacant glance. It isn't directed toward Niki, I realize. *Interesting*.

Charles was right. The bar's interior is mostly vacant, aside from three patrons and a barman. Music from an old jukebox playing alternative rock from the nineties mixes with the noise from one of the two televisions playing a kickboxing match. Two men and the bartender debate on the match, enthralled by it, while another is passed out at a nearby table. Charles points toward a beaded curtain and we walk through it. The curtain separates the small and dark lounge area from another poorly lit backroom.

No one notices our entrance, which I wasn't expecting. I'm not complaining, though, since I was unable to stop Jasmin and Olivia from joining us, and I don't want to think about the hell I'm going to get from Jason. I motion for my cousin to stand guard near the doorway so that she may let us know of anyone entering the area, and I'm grateful she complies without a fight. Charles continues to lead us through until we hear another television playing the same boxing match.

A man with his back to us sits on a couch, eyes glued to the fight while Noah's beaten body is strapped to a chair, slumped forward. He isn't moving. Charles quietly walks up to the dumbass who's supposed to be on watch and swiftly twists his neck in one silent motion. The guy immediately slumps down to his death.

Charles turns around and shrugs. "Seemed quicker."

Niki rushes over to Noah, her hands hover over him, like she doesn't know where to place them. His clothes are in shreds, he's covered in blood, and in desperate need of stitches, and perhaps reconstructive surgery. He looks like he's been through seven hells.

He's been stabbed in multiple places and beaten beyond recognition. Jasmin covers her mouth and stays frozen in place.

I've never seen Niki cry. Not when I took her home after she spent the night in handcuffs being ridiculed by cops, or when I found her in the warehouse, when she put Noah's heart through a shredder, or even when I told her about her parents' killers. But silent tears fall down her pale cheeks now.

"Noah," she whispers, and the beaten fool groans, as if awakened by her voice.

Niki falls to her knees before him, and I walk over and take the blade Charles hands me. There's a rope tugging his arms back and connecting them by the wrists, and when I cut them off, Noah slumps forward into Niki's arms.

She falls back into a sitting position and holds him in a hug. The cry released from her throat shatters me into a million fucking pieces.

"Justice?"

Noah's voice is weak and barely audible, but he unmistakably spoke. Niki sets him down gently and brushes his hair off his forehead.

"Yea, Noie, it's me."

Noah tries to look around, but he's only got one working eye and it's drowning in his own blood. *Fuck*, he isn't going to make it. I don't think Niki gets that yet. I pull out my phone and dial it in.

"Hey, Mike, send a bus to Time Out on Aberdeen Street."

I hang up before he floods me with his curiosity, and when I look back down, Noah's eyes find me. I think he rolls his one working eye, but he closes it instead and gasps before coughing and spewing up blood.

"I'm sorry," he manages.

Niki shushes him and presses the back of her hand against his cheek. "Save your energy. Dylan called for help and they'll be here soon. You're going to be fine."

"I'm not, but it's okay. I'm as good as dead without you, anyway."

"Noah, don't say that—"

Noah nods in my direction. "He knows what I mean."

I absolutely do. Niki gulps back a sob, and I hold my fucking breath when she brings her face down and leans her forehead against his. She stays there, sobbing and clutching onto the tattered threads of his shirt.

"Kee... keep an–" Noah gasps and shudders in her grip. "Eye on my... mom for me–"

There's a gurgling sound in his throat, followed by a hissing sound.

"His lung is punctured and can't expand. He's dying–"

"Shut the fuck up," I snarl at Charles. The man has no fucking filter. Niki sobs while she looks for a place to put her hands, but his entire body is mutilated. There's nothing we can do.

Noah lets out one last struggling breath before his body gives in and succumbs to his injuries. I take one step toward Niki when Jasmin stops me.

"Let me," she says with a soft shake of her head.

Her eyes are brimmed with tears, and I nod my okay. Jasmin bends down and wraps my little wounded fox into her arms, and they both slump down near Noah's lifeless body.

"It's my fault. I should've listened to him. He told me they threatened him."

Jasmin smooths Niki's hair off her face and then holds her. "Justice, don't say that. You know it's not your fault. Noah made mistakes and unfortunately chose to work for a criminal. Vork did this–not you."

The sound of a siren shrieks in the near distance and Charles lights his fiftieth cigarette. "I'll wait in the van. I'm sorry, Justice. Truly."

He bobs his head, acknowledging me on the way out, and I stand there, like a fucking useless statue, until the paramedics rush in.

35
Justice

I'm covered in Noah's blood and feel completely numb. Dylan's weirdly handsome and wildly over-professional boss is back, and they're discussing something off in the distance. I don't care enough to try to eavesdrop. I'm still wrapped in Jasmin's embrace, but we're sitting on a bench just outside the bar instead of the bloodbath where Noah's body is being tucked into a black body bag.

I break out into another sob and hiccup into Jasmin's shoulder that's already covered in my tears. I can't believe he's gone. And suddenly I'm filled with rage. That motherfucker, Vork, took another person from me. When will it stop?

The red and blue lights flash and blind me when I stare in the direction of the EMTs. They're pushing the stretcher that is carrying Noah's body, and instinctively, I rush to them.

I crash into Olivia, and she holds me. "Don't do it, babe. Think of him when he was at his strongest and hold on to *that* memory. *Not* this one."

I try to tell her that I just need to look at him one last time, but words don't come out. Instead, a loud wail escapes my throat, and I scream out the pain that's been gripping my heart like a barbed wire. Jasmin comes up behind me and they both hold me until the ambulance drives away and Noah is gone.

"I can't wait to have a bunch of kids," Noah says.

Well, that came out of nowhere. I stare at him in shock, my mouth agape, and he laughs. I don't know if he's joking, but I don't think he is. The way he stares at toddlers playing at the park and how he volunteers to round up all the kids at the trailer lot to play basketball? Most would assume he's some weird pedophile. But I know better. He's too sweet. After what his father did, he can't wait to have kids of his own and show himself what a real dad is supposed to be like. I don't deserve him.

"I want to adopt," I blurt out.

"Sure, Justice. We'll adopt."

I laugh. "What makes you think we'll adopt?"

Noah leans toward me, his caramel eyes burn against the rays of the sun setting behind me. It reflects back to me in a wave of honey glaze. "If you end up being somebody else's, I'll die of grief."

My hand pushes against his chest. "Stop being dramatic."

I don't want to tell him that I agreed to be his girlfriend just two days ago because I felt bad saying no for the eighty-fifth time. He's my best friend. I don't want to be his in that way. I think he'll see that, too, and in a few days, everything will be back to normal.

Nothing went back to *normal*.

"Two gates, huh?"

"Can't be too safe."

"I guess not."

Jasmin and Charles exchange words, but I'm not listening. My best friend glances at me from the rearview mirror, her tired eyes searching my features, and I know she's worried. But I don't have the energy to reassure her that I'm going to be fine once the nightmares and flashbacks stop.

I didn't even bother to insist on driving like I always did whenever we made our way to my parents' ranch. I've stopped crying, but I don't have the energy required to drive some fifty miles through the blazing California desert. Jasmin and I had been staying with Olivia and Jason. Regardless of their multiple vehicles, I insisted we bring my truck. What was the point in keeping up with pretenses? Dylan already knew everything about me.

Dylan.

He's the only reason I'm even slightly okay. After everything I've been through—watching my parents brutal killings, raising my baby brother, and constantly worrying he'd be taken, to finally having one of my best friends die in my arms—Dylan's presence is unmatched. He's filled the seemingly irreparable hairline fractures to my soul with the liquid gold of his healing companionship. I'm a real life Kintsugi. He's repaired my damaged fragments in a way I never thought was capable. And I'm better for it.

It'd been eight days since Noah's death. Eight agonizing days, and Dylan never left my side. He was there when I delivered the news to Noah's mom and she clung to me, yelling his name into the abyss. He held me through nights of cold sweats and nightmares and made sure I ate and drank water instead of kicking back a bottle of my favorite tequila. He kept me on my feet when Noah was buried. And he sits next to me now, holding me, while Jasmin drives us to the ranch.

I know it isn't easy for him to watch me grieve for an ex boyfriend. But Noah was more than that. He was like family. No matter what, even after his betrayal. I knew I'd eventually speak to him again and demand a thorough explanation.

My face feels sticky, and I'm sure the folds of Dylan's shirt left lines on my cheek when I manage to peel myself away from his chest and dare a look out to where Helena and Pedro wait. Jule is between them, and my heart aches to hold him. Once the van stops and Charles opens the door, I do just that. I rush out and crush my brother. I half expected him to be tiny, but he's a giant, of course. I still can't shake off how much he's fucking grown.

"I'm sorry, Nik."

I nod and squeeze his face between my hands. "I'm just happy you're safe."

As it turns out, Dylan was right. Vork ordered his men to raid my trailer, and I don't even want to imagine what would've happened to Jule if Dylan hadn't sent for him.

"I'm happy you're *all* safe," Pedro says, and Helena nods in agreement.

I breathe my sniffles away and clear my throat. I guess introductions are in order.

"This is Dylan and Charles. They... helped."

I don't know how else to explain their presence. Anything else seems small in comparison. If it weren't for them, I don't think any of us would still be alive.

After a few thank you's and some awkward hugs, we all head inside.

It smells like home.

Orchids and calla lilies decorate the space, and the urge to collapse on the couch is staggering. Charles is about to light a cigarette and I glare at him. Helena would fucking kill him. He gets the hint and slumps his long body onto the couch nearest him. His back is to us, and I ignore his dejected scorn and focus on Helena as she showers Dylan with questions.

I glance around and, as if guessing what my thoughts are, Jule nudges my arm. "The girls should be back in just a few minutes. They went riding and—"

"I can't believe you brought a fucking cop! I trusted you." Piper's angry voice echoes in my head.

"Piper, wait. He hel–"

I don't get the chance to explain. Charles gets up, and as soon as Piper sees him, she rushes into his arms.

"Helped," I finish. But she isn't listening.

They're practically making out, and a semblance of understanding covers Dylan's perfect face.

"I get it now," he mouths.

I shrug. *Get what?*

Dylan gives me a smug smile, and my knees wiggle weakly, warning me to snap the fuck out of it before I swoon into his arms. We don't need two couples making out in the living room when there are five bedrooms in *this* house alone. *Couples?* Is that what we are?

Macy walks in and sits next to Jule at the kitchen island. She clears her throat loudly and Piper finally breaks away for air.

"You *can* trust me," I say before she goes nuts on me. I walk to her and grab her hand and deposit the USB onto her palm and close her fingers over it. "Always."

"He's alright," Charles says as he nods toward Dylan and the son of a bitch smiles. I mean, he *really* smiles. He pulls Piper into his chest and stuffs his face into the bend of her neck.

My mouth pops open. "Wow, so you *aren't* a heartless tinman."

"*Oh,* I have a heart," Charles retorts, but he isn't looking at me. He's staring at Piper and I roll my eyes.

"Okay. Go... have your moments in privacy. We'll talk later, Pi."

Helena cautiously approaches them. "If Justice brought Dylan, he's to be trusted. She would rather die than jeopardize the safety of those she's promised to help."

Piper glances at Charles, who gives her a reassuring nod. "Okay," she whispers.

They disappear, and I sag onto the couch. Jasmin drops next to me, and I smile at her. It's a genuine one this time, I can finally feel a twinge of happiness without the remorse.

"I'm preparing your favorite, *mija.*"

"Do you need any help in the kitchen?" Dylan offers.

I can literally feel Helena's eyes digging at the back of my head. She loves a man that can cook or one that signs himself up for tasks. In this case, *both*. I know she's trying to send me messages via some weird, non-existent telepathic communication, and I wave my hand at her without even turning around.

"No, *mijo*. I want Justice to show you around. Ask her to introduce you to Prince Charming."

I slap both my hands against my flushed face, and Jasmin practically shakes from the laughter she's struggling to keep in. When I turn, Dylan is staring at me.

Who? he mouths with raised brows.

I'm up and pulling him by the arm before Helena can divulge any more embarrassing details of my life.

"Have fun," Jasmin calls.

"Dylan, meet Prince Charming."

My horse neighs in response to my voice. He's a giant beast, black from head to hoof.

"May I call you Prince for short?"

"No, he prefers Charming."

"Of course he does."

Dylan steps forward with an outstretched hand, and I instantly tense up. "Be careful, Charming doesn't like strang–"

I don't finish my sentence because, although I'd spoken up to warn Dylan about Charming's very uncharming traits, my horse responds exceptionally well. My horse snorts softly and pushes his muzzle flat against Dylan's palm, and then he lowers his head.

"I'm not a stranger." Dylan clicks his tongue and moves to stroke Charming's massive chest and then slowly works his way to his withers. "Tell me, little fox, how long have you been riding?"

"Why do you call me that?" I ignore his question and ask one of my own instead.

"Well, besides it being your last name, it's a fierce animal. The first to use the earth's magnetic field to hunt its prey. Beyond cunning, beautiful, loyal, passionate, perfect–"

"Okay," I interrupt. "I get it, rookie."

"I don't think you do."

Dylan walks up to me and gathers my hair in his fist, and then he tugs it back so that I'm forced to look up at him. His midnight eyes light a fucking fire in me; my cheeks feel warm and I think I'm going to combust. He bends down and runs his nose along my jaw, and then he nibbles on my earlobe and pulls gently at my earring.

"*Te necesito conmigo,*" he rasps in my ear.

My heart drums to an erratic beat, a song just for him. "I'm here."

Dylan sighs and presses his forehead to mine. "I'm not letting you go. You know that, right?"

I swallow, and I know that if I dare speak, my voice will crack, so I nod against the pressure of his upper body leaning into me.

I realize that it doesn't matter where I'm at, as long as I'm with him. Dylan is my anchor, he's what holds me level and sane. He's my drive, the current that propels me forward, the flame to my campfire. I never believed in 'meant to be' bullshit, but he's my other half. I'm not ever letting him go. I can't. It'd be like trying to never blink, or holding my breath forever. Impossible. The human body does these things naturally. And suddenly, it hits me, like two trains heading in the opposite direction and finally colliding–I love this fucking man.

Is it too soon to be feeling this way? It's only been a couple of months, but for some reason, it feels like he's connected to me on a level beyond my understanding. Maybe my emotions are due to all the shit I've been through. My stress scale has been put through the shredder, yet Dylan's presence stabilizes me.

Dylan begins to pull away, and I grip his arms and hold him close. We haven't had sex in over a week. My mind wasn't in it, although my body responds to him on instinct. We'd slept side by side, the heat of his body kept me sound, and his heartbeat became my very own lullaby. I refused to sleep without him, but we hadn't been naked or touched one another sexually.

I breathe him in now and a heady swirl spins my senses into a tumultuous desire deep inside me. My lips lightly rub over his, and then I pepper his bottom lip with kisses. Three words sting the tip of my tongue and I have to clamp my teeth down to keep me from spilling them. *It's too soon, it's too soon, it's too soon.* What was it my mother had told me years ago before I ever gave a shit about boys?

When you know, you know. And don't ever let it go, she'd said.

I suck on his full top lip, but he slowly eases me away suddenly.

"Come on, fox. Dinner will be ready soon and I hear it's your favorite."

I frown. Since when is Dylan prudent and respectful? A wounded and slightly sad girl in my mind rolls her eyes at me–*since he watched you bawl your eyes out for losing your ex.*

"I wasn't in love with Noah," I blurt. "I mean, I *did* love him. But not like that."

Dylan nods. "I know."

I don't know where to look, but I refuse to meet his onyx eyes. And right when I'm about to release the words I've been biting back, my phone rings.

"Hello?"

"Good afternoon, Ms. Escamilla. I'm calling regarding the application Julius submitted, but then retracted."

I'd given Jule's school administration my number. It was about time they had one. Jule had missed a few days from school, and I wanted to make sure the excuse I made up stuck and that he wouldn't get in trouble. Days before the mess we found ourselves in, Jule was forced to stop the process of applying for early college programs that his teachers recommended. He needed parental consent and proof of parental status since he's only fourteen.

"I'm wondering if he'd like us to resubmit now that the paperwork is all in order."

"In order? What do you mean?"

The woman seems confused by my question. "The er... paperwork. Everything is complete. We received a copy of the certificate of adoption and your signature for parental consent. Would you like me to resubmit Julius's application?"

I'm fucking stunned and speechless.

"Ms. Escamilla?"

I meet Dylan's watchful gaze, and he smiles knowingly. My heart quickens and immediately I know–he made this happen.

"Yes, resubmit it. Thank you."

I slide the phone into my back pocket. "You... *how?*"

Dylan cocks his head to the side and palms the five o'clock shadow dusting his cheeks and chin. "I couldn't let a piece of paper get in the way of Jule getting into a good college. He's too fucking smart. And you? You've worked too hard."

Fuck. Tears rim and threaten to spill over my bottom lid, and when I blink, they stream over my cheeks. "Dylan, I don't... thank you. Seriously, just... thank you."

I collide with him, smothering my face with the front of his black cotton shirt and bawling for the ninety-eighth time this week. But this time, they're happy tears.

36

Redemption

"So, I heard you're planning a vacation."

Niki drops her fork and glares at Jule, but I just chuckle. Everyone at the table stops eating and stares at us. Except Macy. She can care less.

"Where are you planning on going?" Helena asks.

I take a sip of my *agua de horchata* and squeeze Niki's hand. "It's a surprise."

Jule glares at me skeptically, deciding if he trusts the secrecy of my plans.

"Well, I think that's excellent news. You *need* a vacation," Jasmin says before she continues eating.

It's our last night at the ranch. We've been here for a week and after convincing Niki that Jule would be perfectly safe, with a round-the-clock body guard, she finally agreed to take her first out of the country trip with me. Charles and Piper left two days ago. They needed to meet with a lawyer who'd had his eyes on the mayor for years now. She wanted him to rot in prison without any help from his many connections.

Niki had been on high alert since both Jason and Olivia announced they lost Vork's trail. Apparently, he fled once the mayor lost access to his bank accounts, thanks to Piper, and failed to post bail. They hadn't returned to the trailer lot, so when I made sure to have the entire moveable home that once belonged to her parents brought directly to her at the ranch, she was over the fucking moon. She'd kept a box of her parents' belongings, photographs, clothes, and I couldn't stand the thought of them being lost to her. I understood the meaningful attachment we grew for items that once belonged to a lost loved one.

"Well, you'll make sure to let *me* know where you're taking her, right?"

I meet Jule's worried stare from across the table. "I wouldn't dare keep that from you."

He nods, convinced I'm okay, for now, and resumes eating. Niki releases a frustrated breath and nudges me softly. *Sorry,* she mouths, and I give her a reassuring nod. I understand the protective bond he has with his sister. She raised him, and it's his way of showing his gratitude and love. He doesn't know any other way and I respect him for it.

***

The rest of the evening is spent readying for our trip the next day. Niki is a meticulous packer and only reserves space for the most essential needs. She doesn't over pack, but instead, over thinks every small detail like a neurotic and compulsive maniac. I stay out of her way and focus on making sure our trip is in order. Mike let me borrow his private jet, and I can't wait to fuck Niki thirty-five-thousand feet in the air.

After watching her obsess over folding both our clothes into perfect little cylinders and organizing toiletries for two hours, I finally give in and stand between her and the luggage.

"I think we're good, fox. I'm beginning to feel neglected over here."

She combs both her hands through her still damp strands and then plants them on her hips. "I'm just going to add the shoes and—"

I lift her up and toss her over my shoulder. "*No mas.*" My palm swats her ass and when she squeals, I pinch her. "You can't just parade in nothing but panties and my t-shirt, then expect me to just watch."

She bounces on the bed when I toss her, and she crawls backwards, a sly smile spreading across her face. She smiles big, my favorite of all her grins. "But you love watching."

"That I do." I sit on my haunches, grip her ankles, and slowly move her legs apart. "*Tócate.*"

Her smirk changes to a dangerous and almost sinister gaze, as if she's threatening me. Like she knows I'll regret asking her to touch herself. Her eyes stay on mine when she slowly takes off her panties. And when her hand glides down and a moan escapes her, I do. Her fingers part her lips, giving me the perfect view as she dips her fingers lower and glides them up and down. She gathers her wetness and draws it toward her clit, where she tortures the delicate skin with expert movements.

Niki uses her other hand to torment me even further. She lifts up her shirt and rubs her nipple, pinching the pink pebble and sending a direct jolt to my throbbing dick. She starts panting, and her tits sway with each breath. I can't take it—I *have* to touch her. But I don't dare interrupt, not when she's so close. She doesn't even notice me anymore; she's too wrapped up in the climax she's chasing. Her fingers begin to move quicker, rubbing at her clit with crazed movements. Her mouth falls open and her shoulders go rigid, and right when she freezes, I plunge into her without warning.

I don't slow down. She's still dazed from coming and *so* wet. I pound into her, balls slapping her ass, thighs clapping, and I know I'm bruising the fuck out of her ass with my grip. But I hold her in place, driving even deeper until she's screaming my name. She feels so fucking good, and the electrifying buzz slowly builds to its peak like a fucking techno remix beat at a club. There's a sudden change in our rhythm; we're both moving against one another in a daze, chasing the break at the end when stars fucking burst before us.

"I thought you only wanted to watch, rookie."

I grit my teeth. The sound of her voice will be my undoing. I press my finger against her clit and rub, forcing her release. She groans and her eyes roll back. "Come for me, little fox."

When her pussy clenches around my cock, I groan her name through clenched teeth and collapse on top of her. I let her pump me dry, the raw markings of the scratches on my back beginning to sting, and I relish the burning sensation.

37

Justice

One Month Later

"Jule, we had no reception. It was a fucking volcano, for fuck's sake. You have *got* to chill."

"I couldn't get a hold of you for five hours. I panicked, Nik."

I sigh into the phone. Dylan and I had been traveling from one glorious place to another nonstop, but I missed my little brother. "We'll be back next week, and I can't wait to show you all the charms I added to Mom's bracelet."

"Jas wants to know what you got for *us*." He laughs and my chest tightens.

"Lots of surprises." I swallow back my sappiness. "I love you guys, but I have to go. We're arriving."

"Arriving where?"

"Bye!"

I tuck the phone away into my pocket and frown. Dylan pulls up to the rear entrance of an apartment building on a slope. The property is guarded by civilians with rifles strapped to their chests and immediately I turn to him in question.

"I have a surprise for you."

"*Here?*"

Dylan steps out and motions to one of the men nearby. As if instructed, he moves to my door and opens it.

"*Buenas tardes, señorita. Estamos a sus órdenes.*"

What the... I exit the car and join Dylan, who's waiting with an extended hand. Once I take it, he pulls me into him and drapes a possessive arm over me.

"What the hell is all this?" I whisper.

I know better than to ask, but I thought we were going to a local bar to grab drinks and some fucking appetizers. Not a makeshift prison. Surprise or not, I need a shot if I'm going to be entering a space that needs eight armed men right outside the rear entrance of a destitute and illicit establishment.

We walk up a flight of stairs and the man at the top hands Dylan a duffel bag and a handgun.

"*Todo lo que pedí está adentro?*"

"*Si, señor.*"

Shit, make that a double shot.

"Dylan–"

"We'll go for drinks *after*, fox. This takes precedence."

The wooden door creaks when we push past into the dark room, and the first thing that hits me is the stench. It smells of sewage and waste mixed with sweat. I don't gag, but I take small breaths between holding my respirations. Someone turns on the light and I gasp.

"You found him." My voice is barely audible, but the man in the chair stirs, nonetheless.

"It took us some time, but we finally got him. He's been holed up here for weeks."

Vork lifts his head and his bloodshot eyes grow wide. Dylan drops the bag to the floor, and it makes a loud thump, startling our prisoner. He's fucking huge, but somehow seems tiny and broken.

"I'm not sure why you thought you were finally free," Dylan says.

He produces a long-bladed knife from the bag and slowly stalks toward Vork, who wriggles like a worm on a hook. He lines the tip of the blade with Vork's wrist, then slowly drags it up his arm and finally stops when the knife is directly under his chin.

"You're a wanted man. What do you say, Niki? Should we extradite or execute?"

Vork's sunken cheeks tremble and his dry, crusted lips part. "Kill me. Just fucking end it already."

"I have a better idea."

Dylan's black eyes glance at me questionably.

"Keep him here, just like this. Feed him a small meal once a day, give him water, but nothing else. Let him continue to rot until his last day."

"Whatever you say." Dylan retracts the knife, and he drops it into the bag. He bends down, forcing Vork to look at him. "*Aquí te vas a podrir.*"

We turn to leave, but I whip around and approach him slowly. Words from our first real face to face encounter flood my brain and I stifle a laugh. "Guess our business is finally settled."

I leave him there yelling for us to go back–crying for *anyone* to finish him. *Begging* for a swift end that won't come. And a burden lifts off my shoulders. His cries replace my parents', melting away the ancient weight of grief and brokenness. Dylan gives instructions to the men and then we walk to a nearby bar.

The warm air breezes past us and causes the flowers to sway playfully, sending a delicious aroma about the air. We opted to sit outside when the inside of the bar grew too noisy and hectic. Thankfully, I'd already stuffed myself, and the outside was empty and peaceful. The sun set glows behind Dylan, illuminating his silhouette and highlighting his features. He reaches for my arm and turns my palm up, then draws slow, lazy circles on my wrist.

I smile, encased by his presence in a sheer bliss I haven't felt in years.

"I love you, Niki."

My breath catches and I stare at him blankly for a couple of unhurried seconds. I want to say something witty, but I can't think past the beating drum in my chest.

"'Til death?" Ohmigod. I did *not* just ask that!

Dylan snorts. "You think something like dying will stop me from loving you?" He moves a few loose strands off my face and tucks them behind my ear. "Infinity."

I try to swallow past the dryness, and I regret shooing the waitress away before asking for a double shot of tequila. But the next words leave my lips easily, and I know I won't regret saying them. I don't even know how I held back this long.

"And I love you... infinity."

∞

Epilogue
Justice

Seven Months Later

"You grew up *here*?"

Dylan chuckles at my bewildered expression. It's freezing, and the ground is covered in white, fluffy snow. His enormous childhood home is at the edge of a cul-de-sac, in a town fifteen minutes outside of D.C. The front has elegant, gray brick, white window trims, two giant, wintergreen doors, and when he rings the bell, it sing-songs a chipper tune and my knees clatter together.

Max can't possibly be more excited and barks until the door finally opens, and he bursts in. An older gentleman with auburn burnt hair streaked with gray chuckles before he faces me. "You must be Justice."

"Niki, this is my dad, Daniel Jacobs."

I take his hand and he gives me a warm smile. "It's my pleasure," I say, and I hope he doesn't notice the slight nervous tremble in my voice.

"No, the pleasure is definitely mine. Welcome home. Here, let me take your coat."

"Where's Mom?"

"I'm right here—Oh, Quin, she's absolutely beautiful."

Quin?

A woman maybe in her late fifties, with dark, mid-back waves and bright hazel eyes, meets up with us at the entrance, and she smiles a big contagious grin. I barely hand off my coat to Dylan's dad when she pulls me into a hug. She smells like a cinna-bun and freshly brewed coffee. I like her.

"And this is my mom, Isadora."

"*Ay*, Quin, *tu siempre tan serio*. Call me Isa. It's so great to finally put a face to our text threads."

"It's great to meet you, Isa. Both of you."

"Come, let's sit down and chat. I made snacks."

Dylan takes my hand and we follow his parents into the large kitchen, open to a connected dining area. The space is elegant but homey and warm. The ice in my lungs begins to melt. I'm not fond of the cold. I'd never left California until Dylan took me all over the world to his favorite places and then we explored new places together. We'd been ice fishing in Alaska, sun bathing in Malaga, and cave diving in Quintana Roo.

We sit at the large, oval mahogany dining table, and Isa gives each of us a plate. Dylan packs his with fried plantains, bollitos de yuca, arepitas, and chicharrones de pollo. I grab two of each and thank Daniel when he serves me sangria. Isa suddenly reaches over the table and yanks Dylan's wrist to examine it. She smooths her thumb over his newest addition–a small, black, majestic-looking fox.

"Another tattoo, Joaquin?"

Daniel laughs. "I'm surprised you can spot any new ones. He's completely covered, love."

I finally break my silence. "I'm sorry, *Joaquin*?"

Dylan's parents stare at him, and he grins, his mouth full. Once he swallows and takes one long swig of his drink, he clears his throat. "My given name. We changed it once I was adopted. My choice."

I blink, maybe one hundred times in three seconds, and raise my shoulders. I thought I had learned everything there was to know about Dylan, whose non-undercover last name is Jacobs. I'd been texting with his mom for over a month now, planning to bring Dylan over for his birthday in February. Turns out, he's a Valentine's Day baby. He hadn't been home in over a year, and Isa was grateful that I agreed for us to visit.

"Mom's the only one who still calls me that."

No one touches the topic again, not until we're cleaning up and Dylan joins his dad in the garage to check out the new snowblower. I tried not to laugh at the mention of it. From what I hear, it barely snows here. But we all deserve to dream. I'm helping Isa clean up the dishes when she clears her throat.

"Quin's birth mother chose that name. It's special. I couldn't let it go."

"Why did he change it? I mean, why did he choose another name?"

"I think he wanted a fresh start. He was so little when he lost her. The system wasn't good to him; foster homes were hell. I think that instead of being reminded of his mom, it connected him to all that he wanted to leave behind. He wanted to start over, completely."

I watch Isa carefully fill the dishwasher and then follow her to the kitchen island and gladly accept the cup of coffee she offers.

"I couldn't conceive and I was spiraling. I wanted a child so badly, and then we met Joaquin. He had the most beautiful and expressive eyes. He never said a word, but he didn't have to. I made up my mind the minute I saw him. His process was to turn the page and never look back."

I smile at her. "And *your* process was to allow him to heal, in whichever way he chose to do that."

She nods. "He was incredibly introverted. His only friend was always his cousin, Olivia, my sister's daughter. Never brought friends home. He kept to himself, studied hard, worked even harder."

Isa shrugs and takes a sip from her coffee. I get the feeling she doesn't want Dylan to hear her telling me all of this, because once we hear them conversing in the hall, she wipes a tear forming in the corner of her eye and stands to serve them.

"So, when do you two get back to work?"

Dylan and his father joined forces and together they founded the corporation I now find myself a part of, Untamed Fox. Olivia, Jason, and Sara work with us to apprehend human traffickers and sexual predators. Mike lost it and blew up Dylan's phone for weeks, trying to change his mind. He finally let him go–I think he understood Dylan's need to move on to something bigger.

"Next week," Dylan grins.

He's eager to get back to work. More like desperate. Especially since we work together now.

"I like your mom."

Dylan pulls me close and then lifts me to set me on the counter. He opens my legs and positions himself between them. It's late, and after spending the afternoon touring his childhood hometown, I was too eager to take a hot shower and rummage through his parents' fridge for a late-night snack.

"Yeah, she's cool," he says lazily while he snakes his hand up my calf and palms my thigh roughly.

My hand moves up to push him away. "We *cannot* get frisky in your mom's kitchen, rookie."

He shrugs. "It's their fault. They're the ones who decided to go out and leave us alone. Now, shut up and lean back."

"Dylan, no."

"Don't make me ask twice, fox."

I open my mouth to protest and he flips me over in one swift move and pulls down my shorts. He presses my back down and separates my legs with his free hand. I squeal in disapproval but freeze when his lips graze my ass, and then he bites. I squirm beneath him, but my hips rise on their own, searching for more.

"What happens if they walk in?"

"Relax, they're not going to catch us. Besides, we came down for a *snack*."

My body responds to his touch and I'm already dripping, trembling, as he trails his fingers up my inner thigh. He parts my legs, spreading me wider, and groans.

"You look good enough to eat, little fox."

I push my hips up, and when he loosens his grip, just for a second, I roll off the island and land awkwardly on the balls of my feet in a very unsexy humph. "You're going to have to hunt down your snack, rookie."

I make a break for it and sprint off. I leave the shocked-looking face, mouth agape, perfectly sculpted man alone. Last I notice, he's scooping up my shorts and smirking devilishly before he stalks after me. His steps are calm, but purposeful, while mine are loud and clumsy. I want to make it so that he's chasing me all over the massive home, but I barely make it six steps up the stairs when he snatches my ankle in a tight grip. Instinctively, I reach for the wooden banister, my shoulders burning when I try to tug myself forward, but his strength overpowers me.

"Now, if they walk in, the first thing they'll see is me fucking you on their steps."

I lean sideways and look behind his looming torso. The staircase sits directly in front of the double doors.

"Dylan, you *wouldn't*."

His eyes darken; the nightshade black threatens to swallow me. He turns me so I'm facing him and I lift my foot and press it against his bare chest. "I'll shove you back," I warn.

Dylan grabs my ankle and easily peels my foot off, then he rubs the sole and massages up toward my calves. He slowly spreads me open and kisses my knee, then trails tiny kisses up my thigh.

"Tell me to stop."

I don't... *can't.* I stare at his movements, watch him drop to his knees just a few steps below, and then he dips his head down until I can only see the top half of his face, his nose buried between my legs. He inhales deeply and moans.

"I didn't think so, fox."

Dylan peels the last of my clothing off at the slowest pace possible. He palms my breast, my nipples hard underneath his calloused hands, and my head lulls back. The cold wooden steps cause my skin to pebble, but his body heat warms me, sending a shiver up my spine. He works his way down, tasting until he's just where I want him. I can't take my eyes off of him—it's addicting. His hunger, his *obsession*, it's contagious, and it forces me to drop my knees back, allowing him access–baring me completely.

Dylan's torturous tongue finally lands on my pussy, moving slowly at first, as if savoring his favorite snack. His pace quickens and my hips buck. He moves suddenly, and I think he's going to stop, so I grip the back of his head and shove his face closer. If he was enjoying me before, this is something else entirely. Dylan desperately feasts, licking up my slit and drawing circles over my clit until it's the only sensation I manage to feel. I don't notice the cold, hard steps beneath me, the echo of my yelling his name, his fingers digging into the insides of my thighs, or his stubble rubbing against the sensitive skin at my center.

I come undone, thrashing against his face, riding the wave of my release until I think I just might drown him. When I finally remove my hands, he stays in place and rests his cheek against my inner thigh.

"*Eres mía*, Niki."

Before I can respond, Dylan flips me and lifts my ass up, then spreads my knees apart. A sass-filled complaint stings the tip of my tongue, and I'm about to try to get away again when the head of his rock hard dick slides between my legs and slowly circles the sensitive skin of my clit.

"Going somewhere?" Dylan smirks.

I lick my lips and I want to nod, then slip away, but my seditious body responds to his touch like a ravenous tramp. I shake my head and bend down to look at where he tempts me.

"That's what I thought," he chuckles, and then he sinks until his balls touch my clit. "Fuck, Niki. You're so tight."

I tighten my muscles and revel in what it does to him. His shoulders tremble, and the bruising grip on my inner thighs holds me in place. My hips elevate and grind against his, desperate for movement. I almost regret my actions when Dylan pulls out to then ram into me over and over until I'm a panting mess.

I'm fully aware of my predicament. I'm splayed naked on all fours, on the steps of Dylan's parents' house, which happen to be directly in line with the front door. Our sex languidly runs down my thighs, mixing with my sweat covered skin to coat the step I'm on. But I don't give a fuck. All I want is for Dylan to keep hitting that sweet spot deep inside that brings me closer to my peak.

My kneecaps hold the pressure of our bodies colliding into one another, but the sloppy sounds of Dylan's cock slipping in and out numbs the pain, holding me prisoner in our little slice of heaven. He wraps his hand around my waist and dips low to rub his thumb over my clit, then he brings it to my lips. His thumb glides over my tongue and I suck.

"Good girl," he purrs. "Now, come for me, fox."

And I do. My body responds to his command the second he speaks. The pressure building inside rushes through all my limbs and lands at my center. My pussy pumps him until he too finds his release. His hips lose the steady rhythm of his control and he snaps, grunting my name, professing his love for me, until we're both spent and naked on the steps.

"They were never going to walk in, they're at a benefit. I just love fucking you when your pulse is racing."

I roll my eyes. We didn't continue on the steps and we never did get our snack. Well, at least not from the kitchen. We fucked in the hall, the shower, and finally made it to his bedroom. Dylan drapes his arm over me and tucks me closer to his ribs. I trace the intricately etched ink marks on his skin and he shivers.

"I was going to give you your birthday gift tomorrow, when everyone was here. But I'd rather do it now, when it's just you and me."

I feel him watching me, curiosity stewing in his onyx eyes. We are expecting Jule, Jas, Olivia, and Jason to join us for his birthday party. We even managed to convince Piper to drag Charles out of his cave and into the bitter cold. It was a rather pleasant surprise to learn that Dylan didn't hate birthdays as much as I did. He wasn't thrilled to celebrate himself so much as he was to be gathering with our loved ones. As meticulous as he presented himself, Dylan loves letting loose almost as much as he loves his work.

I scurry away and squeak when he playfully swats my ass. After digging to the very bottom of our suitcase, hidden behind a pile of journals I refuse to travel without, I produce a manilla folder. His eyes don't leave me, slightly annoyed that he has zero clue as to what I'm up to. It's incredibly difficult to keep shit from my obsessively compulsive man. Nothing happens without him first knowing about it. But I was super careful about this.

"I know why you never looked up details about your past," I say, and Dylan perches up to lean on his elbows, a cautious look cloaking over his sharp features. He's nervous.

I move to smooth my fingers over his brows, an attempt to soothe the tension. Dylan has a single, very vivid memory of his birth mother. She was young, a teen, and full of life. She adored him, and he refused to look up details that would tarnish the little he had of her. He owned one photograph of the two and that's it. He didn't want the reality to wash away the memory he had stored away–her look, scent, voice, their history. But I was absolutely sure that what I found would only reinforce it.

I open the folder and slowly drop its contents between us. A couple of documents, a photo, and a link. "I found a video that a shelter released in an attempt to advertise their programs. Your mom was in the art room when they recorded and—" I grab my phone from the bedside table and type in the link. "It's a short clip of a '*Mommy and Me*' painting class."

I hand him the phone and freeze when he presses *play*. The singsong voice I'd been replaying since I found the video feels familiar now, but I watch Dylan's eyes gloss over when it finally collides with the voice he stored in his head. The video is simple, a young woman paints with her toddler-aged son. She's singing a lullaby to him, eager to keep him steady, perched on her lap. He dips his fingers in green paint and turns to smudge her face with it and she laughs. The video ends, but Dylan replays it over fifteen times before he finally looks up.

"Thanks, little fox. You have no idea what this means to me."

For months, I wondered what I could give him for his birthday. Both a gift and a way to thank Dylan for everything he's done for me. I was shattered beyond understanding, and he became my tonic, a healing remedy and my ultimate peace.

I lean forward and take his face in my hands. "But I do. I love you, Dylan. Infinity."

$\mathbf{T}$ hank you for reading H E R! I'd love it if you'd consider leaving a review on the platform of your choice. To keep in touch with me, you can find me on the following social media platforms:

Instagram: instagram.com/xochitlgarciaguillen_author
TikTok: tiktok.com/@xggbooks
In the case that any of the info above changes, hit up my Linktree:
linktr.ee/xggbooks

ACKNOWLEDGMENTS

First, completing this book would not have been possible without the extensive support of my husband, my muse, Carlos. Thank you, my love, for always lending an ear during our walks, when in the car, breakfasts, and dinners, and for staying up late listening to me ramble on about fictional characters as if they are real people. You're the real MVP. You also inspired so much -wink- Te amo.

To my family, thank you for thinking I am brilliant to write a novel. I'm not, but thanks anyway. I know you're proud of me and even if you don't read any of my books (yes, there will be many more) I feel the love. Karla, Lourdes, and Marilyn, I know I whined constantly, can't promise I'll stop my bitching, 'ya'll don't read my stuff', that's just me being me, Girl Scout's honor. I am forever grateful for your undoubting love and support in my storytelling obsessions.

Marilyn, my boss bitch bff, your help in regards to the business aspect of what I do was monumental. There were so many things I did not understand and you never failed to help me every step of the way.

My baby sister, Karla, seems like you and I will keep sharing book titles we must read and as a result, our love for reading expands to genres we would otherwise not know. You pushed me to keep going even when I wanted to give up, nunca olvidare eso. You also served as my assistant when it comes to the important details of running a successful business. I'm clueless when it comes to all that. Thank you, te quiero, hermanita.

To my kids, Gera and Nati, who think their mom is so cool for being an author (even though I never want them to read the books I write... seriously, if you're reading this, STOP RIGHT NOW) thank you so much for blindly believing in me and boosting my ego. You are my shining stars during dark times in the imposter syndrome world.

Mom and Jax, I didn't write your names above because I wanted you here, in this specific spot, so that I may thank you for what's above but also something else. You may not know this but you are the two people who fueled my love for writing. Mom, your love for the little novelas and Isabel Allende's books served as my reading role model. I wanted to be a reader just like you, so I became one. Jax, where do I even start? My love for dark poetry and horror began with late nights of you reading Poe out loud to me when we were kids. I wouldn't be half the writer and obsessive reader I am today if it weren't for you two. Los amo para siempre.

To my editor, Sarah, well you are just fucking amazing. You elevated this novel to what it is today and I'm sorry you had to read it before you made it better. Don't tell anyone I suck lol (please) because I'm sure while you edited you thought "what in the ...". Thank you for your insight, guidance, expertise, and above all thank you for loving H E R and genuinely looking forward to its journey. I'm so glad I found you!

My first novel without a thank you to my book girlies, would be fucked up, to say the least. So, to my Spice Cabinet girls... where do I start? You've been supportive beyond words, some of you are far far away yet you manage to extend your hand and feel closer than most. You cheered me on and made me feel like some grand smut poet, encouraging me to keep going. You made me laugh when all I wanted to do was curl up and hide under the covers. Thank you.

To my readers: alpha, beta, ARCs, and beyond, thank you so much for reading this book. You have no idea what it means to me. It's truly a dream come true. Thank you for sharing and loving it and reaching out to me to express your love for it. It's made me beyond happy.

Most importantly, I want to give thanks to my Creator, who without I'd be a pile of rubble. You are my constant reminder that life is precious. No matter what dark hole I find myself in, You are there to help me. I cannot express, in my basic human words, how important You are to me.

ABOUT THE AUTHOR

Xochitl Garcia Guillen lives in Chicago with her husband, two kids, and their lab-mix Daisy. She loves spending time with her family when not ignoring the world to write. Xochitl enjoys exploring new restaurants (send any suggestions her way!), being outdoors, and freezing in hockey rinks.

Keep reading for a Sneak Peek of Book 2.

Book 2 begins approximately 3 years before Dylan and Justice from Book 1.

1

Drakaina

Leave it to me to arrive late to a Shibari Instructional Presentation–I bought these tickets months ago, for fuck's sake. The young lady taking tickets warned me about sneaking in while a set was in motion, but I didn't want to wait. I'd be forced to stand outside in the January frostbite of New York. So what if I can't see where I'm going and cell phones aren't allowed? Which means I wouldn't be able to use my flashlight to guide me down the steps. Instead, I feel my way around, touching the backs of chairs, peoples' hair, and coats while occasionally tripping over my own damn feet. My cane saves me multiple times in what I'm sure is a graceless entrance.

Someone shushes me and my cheeks burn. It's bad enough I'm late, but now my ingress of shame is highlighted by who knows who. Fuck me.

Mortified, I can't look up to the stage. Instead, I make my way to an empty seat in the very first row somewhere in the middle. I find myself crouching, and my embarrassment spikes to yet another level. In hushed mumbles, I apologize for getting in the way and stepping on a few toes, but I notice all eyes are glued to the front where a deep and seductive voice carries on his rope-tying methods for all of us to watch and perhaps learn.

I plant my ass down on the soft plush and take my yellow notepad and mechanical pencil out of my backpack. My trusty walking stick looks like sapphire quartz, sparkly with inset bubbles, and I lay it gently near my thigh. The inside of my mouth instantly waters when I finally look up to the instructor of the hour. I couldn't grab a pamphlet, therefore have no idea what the presenters' names are–the one tying and the one being tied. A blonde woman wearing a nude-colored, skin-tight romper sits on her haunches and a man is slowly, yet efficiently, binding her arms behind her back, creating art with rope.

I can't peel my eyes off the man. He's exquisite. Everything about him, from the sound of his voice–deep and seductive, dripping over my skin like velvet, caressing me–to the elegance of his body. He's barefoot and has gray joggers and a black tank. His rippled biceps move effortlessly as he hoists up his model, pulling on the rope and touching her skin where the material sits on her forearms. His presence alone is soothing and commanding. He could be standing or sitting on a fucking chair, literally doing nothing, but he's a god, nonetheless. Perfection. It's like a dance, an opera special, or a one-of-a-kind, classical concerto.

A masterpiece.

I find myself scribbling a free hand of his body instead of his work. It's beautiful, but I can't seem to take my eyes off of *him*–Shibari forgotten. My glasses begin to droop down my thin nose and the bright blue of my hair now drapes dangerously close to my peripheral. In a frustrating move, I push my glasses up and scrunch my nose, as if the wrinkles will keep them up. And I shake my locks away like a madwoman, eager to return to my drawing. I can't let him disappear without committing every detail to paper.

Truth be told, I should be back at my dorm studying for my last final tomorrow morning, but I couldn't miss this show. Originally, I bought two tickets, hoping Rose would tag along with me. But she prioritizes her studies, whereas I *obviously* don't. I couldn't get a refund, and it's not like a line of people were outside dying to get in and looking to buy tickets from a complete stranger. At least now, I only lost one entrance fee, not two.

I keep my eyes busy, watching the nawashi, his expertise beyond masterful. The rope overlaps perfectly on the model's upper thighs and arms, which are now secured behind her back. His movements are slow and deliberate–a caress. Two pieces of overlapping rope slice between her legs like a thong and it pushes against her most sensitive parts. She hangs with her breasts facing the ceiling, her hair cascading back, and when the rope artist wraps a fist around her locks and tugs, I'm instantly wet between my legs. I squeeze my thighs closely together and attempt to swallow back the dry lump in my throat. My heart drums in my chest, and sweat begins to accumulate in tiny drops between my breasts and lower back.

He's no more than five years older than me, I think. His skin is slightly tanned, and I wonder if he just landed from a warm place. You can't possibly maintain such a beautiful tone during New York's bitter winter. He keeps his brown hair short but long enough on top that it drapes over his eyes if he bends down. His bright grayish eyes remind me of the gloomiest day, right before the storm hits and lighting flashes across a cloudy sky. And his lips... oh fuck, *his lips*.

Sitting in the front row doesn't seem so bad now.

I take in every rippling detail, down to his perfect man-piece, barely hidden behind the soft material of his sweats. The outline of his dick forces my heart to palpitate and spike beyond normal range, and I focus on it a little too much while I dedicate a whole page in my notebook to drawing that specific part of him.

As if my fixation alone alerts him, he suddenly turns and our eyes meet. I don't shrink back into my seat like I want–nope. Instead, it's as if his eyes are a magnet and I'm a piece of fucking metal. I lean forward slightly and push my glasses up again. I don't want my poor eyesight to miss one single beat.

The rope expert looks at my notebook and the sides of his lips quirk up, and then he winks at me.

He winks.

I'm a fucking puddle. But I keep my composure somehow. Or at the very least, I try. A girl's gotta have some pride, damn it. It's not every day a handsome man catches you both gawking *and* drawing his dick.

He goes back to his model like our moment never happened. I'm feeling somewhere between sad and relieved, but I have no other choice than to be a spectator. It's the reason I came–to learn about something I'm drawn to. I just never thought I'd be more interested in the artist than in the art itself.

"How do you think we did?"

I push my glasses up almost absentmindedly. "I don't know about you, but I did alright."

Rose twirls her fingers around the long, beaded chain attached to her cell phone. She studied more than me *and* she's a genius. How is it that *she's* nervous? I didn't even study.

One more semester and I'm done. I can hardly wait.

So far, I've existed as one fuck up after another, striving for I don't even know what–something that will make me feel alive. I know what many see–a daughter to a wealthy, successful family with zero need to work. Spoiled, indecisive, and rebellious.

They aren't entirely wrong. But what isn't understood is my desperation to live life to the fullest. I know firsthand what it's like to have your life goals ripped from under you.

In a blink of an eye, everything can change, twisting up your reality and morphing it into a real-life nightmare. And I, for one, am not going to waste a single second of my life.

I keep chasing the inevitable, every possible thing that others run from, and I plummet towards it. Desperate for what courses through my veins when the rush grips me in its visceral hold. I want to *live*.

My parents don't get it. I know they just want what's best for me, and, in their minds, that means completing my education. It's easy to accomplish their expectations of me and finalize that aspect of my life. I can't bear to disappoint them. Whether they accept all of my other choices, well, that's a definite hell to the no.

"So you'll come with me to this lecture, right?"

Rose's voice brings me back to the now and I roll my eyes. "You don't need extra credit. What we *need* is to go out and celebrate with a few drinks!"

She shakes her head. "We need all the points we can get. What if this lecture is the difference between a strong A or a low A?"

I gawk at her. *What?* I want to tell her that she failed to tag along with me last night and that I had to sit all alone while watching people get all roped up. The money that went towards her ticket is gone, but her big brown eyes bore into mine in a puppy-like plead and it melts me on the spot. I don't want to be petty.

"Fine," I breathe. "Whatever."

She squeaks in my ear, and I clasp both my hands down to muffle the deafening sound. Who the fuck gets this excited over extra credit? Rose and I have three classes together, but our Algorithms course kicked both our asses. I don't know if I'll ever recover. To rectify the stream of panic from the majority of the student population that took the class, our professor offered a one-time extra credit opportunity. Assignment: to attend a two-hour lecture on discreet math and algorithms given by some hot shot genius-level spyware geek who invented software used by special ops military.

I'd rather be at the bar down the street, but I guess I'm a sucker for brown eyes. Rose leads us through the auditorium and selects two seats in the middle front row. I'm scrolling through motorbike reels and the occasional baking clips while the space around us fills with students and professors alike.

The soft chatter surrounding us stills when a second-year computer science student clears his throat. Rose prepares herself and takes out her iPad. Something about the tech makes me cringe, and I wiggle my yellow notepad in my hand, making her scrunch her face at me.

My cell phone disappears into my bag as the speaker is introduced, and everyone claps when a tall figure emerges from the thick curtains to the right of the stage.

My hands freeze mid-clap.

The six-foot, tanned skin, brown hair, and silvery-eyed lecturer is the master nawashi from the Shibari Instructional Presentation. My skin prickles. He's wearing a gray suit with a button-down, crisp white shirt underneath. His hair is combed back, and it waves to one side perfectly. He looks like the Henry Cavill version of Clark Kent, minus the glasses. I suck in a breath and steady my trembling fingers, but when he finds me in the crowd and winks, my limbs turn to jelly.

Son of a bitch.

The school auditorium is jam-packed, yet he manages to lock eyes with *me*.

He looks at my notebook and smiles. "Thank you for that lovely introduction. My name is Jason Hodgins, and I'm confident you'll be an expert on the subject once the lecture is over."

Jason takes out an oblong-looking pen from his coat pocket and clicks it twice. Images appear behind him and the discourse begins. He holds me in place, speaking to everyone, but maintaining eye contact with *me*.

Rose elbows me. "Do you two know each other or something?"

Or something. I shake my head in response. I mean, it's the truth. I don't know him. But he looks at me as if he knows every dark secret, each alluring thought and perverse desire. His eyes hold me as if he understands each path life has taken me, as though he was present for each of my steps.

It takes every ounce of willpower to stay in my seat, practically squirming at the way Jason's jaw moves while he speaks, the way he holds the fucking laser between his fingers, and each time his eyes caress every part of me—I can't help feeling exposed. Who the fuck is this guy?

Rose squeezes my arms. "Wow, that was fascinating!"

I blink away the sting caused by forcing my eyes to stay open during the entire two-hour lecture. I couldn't look away from him. Not unless it was to sketch his hands in precise detail. Or his jawline, those full lips. And his quizzically charming, burnt charcoal eyes. I snap my notebook shut and shove it in my bag before she notices.

"Ladies, did you enjoy the lecture?"

My heart beats in erratic thumps that threaten to throw me into cardiac arrest. Jason stands in front of the exit, blocking the doorway with his massive height. I'm not a short person, at least I don't think I am. I'm what I would consider average height–five-six. But in Jason's presence, I feel tiny. I get the feeling he makes everyone around him feel proportionately small.

"It was excellent, Professor Hodgins!"

I stare at my best friend, begging her to shut up so that we can get the hell out of here. But she continues. My grip on my cane is softened by the plush cover over the handle, but I know my knuckles are white as bone.

"I can't wait to take your class next semester. How do you like New York so far? It's got to be different from the West Coast."

Rose is the shy yet talkative type, eager to make you feel warm and fuzzy all over by remembering your name. She's a smidge shorter than me, beautiful, with elegant features. I, on the other hand, appear grimy and unkempt. My bright blue hair sits atop my head in a messy bun, with last night's black eyeliner smudged under my lash line that I'm sure my gold-rimmed glasses are highlighting. My nose ring reminds the usual stoic folk in my field that I am most definitely not taking anything seriously. And if it wasn't for the winter season forcing us to layer clothing, my tattoos would be on display.

Wait, *his class next semester?* Oh no. I take a small step back and lean on the wall for support.

"Very different indeed, but I'm adjusting. How about you? Will you be taking my class as well?"

Me. *He's talking to me.* "No." It comes out like a weak whimper and I clear my throat.

Jason smiles, and my hand instantly trembles with the desire to run my thumb over his laugh lines. I imagine his teeth scraping the delicate skin of my neck and I hold my breath.

"Good, I'd prefer to see you attend my *other*, more eclectic course."

I give him an awkward nod and pull Rose, dragging her, and practically sprinting away, ignoring her confused glare and excited farewell. It's a miracle that I don't trip. I'm wearing an older and ungently used prosthetic after placing an order from my favorite company. It'd be one more week before the shipment arrived. I wasn't trying to put my best foot forward, hence the constant use of my cane. After losing my right leg thirteen years ago, I was more than used to the artificial limb. I curse myself for being irresponsible and failing to always wear what I know carries me best.

"Okay," she breathes in a skeptical huff once we're far away from the drop-dead gorgeous speaker... er... *professor*. "You *definitely* know him."

I ignore my friend. It was one thing to assume that the Shibari expert is part of the brainiac squad, invited to present a topic he's an expert on, yet he's a *professor* working at the university I'm attending. If I did happen to enroll in one of his classes, I'd drop it like the hottest beat in a popular song. I am *not* taking Jason Hodgins' class. Not after he caught me fixated on every inch of his body, committing him to paper and visibly turned on by his every move.

In fact, it'd be best if I didn't see him again. Ever.

2

Apollo

Blue hair, almond-shaped, caramel-colored eyes, thick lips that look as soft as a rose petal. Even their naturally shaded sangria tint is seductive enough to make me want to bite into them. I can't get her out of my head. Is it a coincidence that she showed up at my show and lecture? I doubt she's stalking me. She looked completely shocked to have seen me today. She pushed her glasses up her perfectly symmetrical nose so many times I thought I'd see her delicate skin go raw.

Somehow, that makes me think of her round ass, raw from a good spanking. Great, now I'm getting flashes of her naked flesh covered in my rope. Her delicate skin shielded to then glorify the imprints of my doings. My dick twitches and I clear my throat.

I could get Irene to look up the names of attendees. I shake my head. No. That's ludicrous.

She's a student. Not *my* student, but still. I can't risk losing my position and reputation. Although I've been trying to step away from academia and instead focus all of my attention on my company, teaching a class opens up a different horizon for the business. The support of the school board is substantial, and it will help the execution of the next transition, allowing it to roll as smoothly as possible. The clause to teach at least one course was a no-brainer.

One year, one class, is all I needed to give them.

Working in education is just one stepping stone, but an important one. The program I created allows the user to both create and erase data from the system. Wiping away entire profiles or generating them from nothing. Maintaining secrecy and believability with the government itself is no easy feat. It's a key element specifically designed to find, manipulate, and destroy terrorists in their tracks. As the sole creator and owner of the software, blending in as a professor works in my favor.

If I lost the support of the university for becoming involved with one of their students, it would equal losing their funds. Not to mention the scandal that the press would have a feast with.

No. It isn't worth it. As intriguing as she is, it'd be the one mistake I wouldn't be able to erase.

Viktor sits directly in front of me with his wool trenchcoat pulled together at the top.

"Relax, we're staying."

"If we leave now, we can still make it to the spot down the street."

I suppress a smile. "You made reservations?"

"Of course I did. I knew you'd pick whatever hole in the wall first popped up on your Google search."

"Don't be a snob, I like it here," I shrug. "We're staying."

The place isn't as bad as his body language suggests. It's a small, quaint establishment with simple menu options. All brick walls in its interior, concrete flooring, dimly lit candle fixtures with faux flames flickering throughout. A bar with a black granite counter lines the far wall with more booze options than any restaurant Viktor would select.

A strum of an electric guitar's chords booms from a nearby amplifier and my comrade's eyes bulge. I force my lips together, stifling my laughter. Light tapping on a cymbal begins, and Viktor shakes his head.

"You're kidding me."

Word on the street is that one of the finest local indie bands is playing at this location tonight, and I love the opportunity to listen to live music. Especially when their collection entails both English and Spanish alternative rock that dominated the nineties. I wasn't going to miss the opportunity of witnessing my old college roommate's ears bleed in public because he's subjected to listening to some of my favorite tunes.

I signal our waitress, and she rushes toward us.

"Your strongest whiskey for my friend here and your cheapest wine for me."

She walks away, and my booming laugh competes with the band's notes. "Come on, humor me. I need this."

Viktor shakes his coat open and smooths it over his chair. "Their fries better be good."

After six songs and halfway through his second drink, my old friend finally eased up. At least as much as can be expected from an uptight, pompous socialite. As self-righteous and overbearing as he may be, hanging out with Viktor brings back old and familiar memories that ease the tension of uprooting your life across the country.

It's not his fault he was bred with the need to bottle fame and glory. He chases it, and therefore cringes at the mere thought of stepping into anything he deems unworthy of his presence.

"So, tell me the real reason you fled your Golden State."

I exhale in exasperation. "Business opportunity."

"Right." Viktor nods, his eyes drawn to slits.

"Well, that and I missed you."

We both laugh and he lifts his glass to salute me. "Of course you did."

I don't know if he's serious or if he understood my sarcasm, but his next words are muffled behind the sound of a woman's voice. It's the band's drummer, and while all of their songs were sung by their lead guitarist, I never once looked at the stage until now.

Fuck me, *it's her*. This has got to be more than just a mere coincidence.

Her azure blue hair gleams in the dim light, forcing rays of sapphire to collide with brighter hues of my new favorite color, striking me each time she moves. It's one of *Evanescence's* songs, *Everybody's Fool*.

Her voice grips me in a trance. I know I look crazy and it's all *her* doing. I leave Viktor behind mid-sentence and allow the current of her vocal cords to propel me forward. I watch, mesmerized, as she strikes the drums and keeps the melody, dare I say, even better than the original.

So she's a computer science major, draws expertly well, plays the drums, *and* sings. What the fuck *can't* she do?

How the hell am I going to walk away now?

9 798989 621071